D1536746

Autumn Bends the Rebel Tree

Carolyn Guy

FRANKLIN COUNTY LIBRARY
906 NORTH MAIN STREET
LOUISBURG, NC 27549
BRANCHES IN BUNN.
FRANKLINTON, & YOUNGSVILLE

Canterbury House Publishing

www. canterburyhousepublishing. com
Vilas, North Carolina

Canterbury House Publishing

225 Ira Harmon Road
Vilas, NC 28692
www. canterburyhousepublishing. com

First Printing May 2011

Copyright © 2011 Carolyn Guy
All rights reserved under International and Pan-American Copyright Conventions.

Book Design by Tracy Arendt

AUTHOR NOTE: This novel is based on the life story of an Appalachian woman. Certain chapters are intermingled with a combination of fact—and fiction derived from stories told around the big chestnut-wood table that Papa built. Clarinda, Rufus, and eight of their seventeen children are at rest in the family cemetery. It is my wish the story of their lives may inspire and keep you turning the pages of *Autumn Bends the Rebel Tree.*

Library of Congress Cataloging-in-Publication Data

Guy, Carolyn.
 Autumn bends the rebel tree : a novel / by Carolyn Guy.
  p. cm.
 ISBN 978-0-9825396-9-9
 1. Widows--Fiction. 2. Motherhood--Fiction. I. Title.

 PS3607. U89A94 2011
 813'. 6--dc22

 2010051687

The scanning, uploading, and distribution of this book via the Internet or via any other means without permission of the publisher is illegal and punishable by law. Please purchase only authorized electronic editions, and do not participate in or encourage electronic piracy of copyrighted materials. Your support of the author's rights is appreciated

For information about permission to reproduce selections from this book, write to Permissions, Canterbury House Publishing, Ltd. , 225 Ira Harmon Rd, Vilas, NC 28692-9369

Autumn Bends

the Rebel Tree

Dedicated to the memory
of
my beloved mother, Mary Victoria

Two of a Kind

They share a stony ridge,
Mountain woman and rebel tree.
Their roots go deep
In olden time—
They stand on ancient foundation.
The weathered two,
Though lashed and tossed by icy winds
And stroked with fingers of fire,
Look heavenward,
Their rugged limbs outstretched,
Soaking up sunshine—
They bloom,
And bear fruit in due season.
With shield of faith and fortitude
And God-given wisdom,
She shall conquer every trial.

Prologue

Chestnut Grove

On a blustery March day in 1898 a midwife called granny woman by local people, held a newborn up by the heels and slapped her behind smartly. The wee babe let loose a loud squall of protest. The granny woman grinned."Hit's shore got a pairful set a-lungs." After finishing her birthing chores the granny woman wrapped the infant in flannel and placed her in the outstretched arms of her mother.

Mary Darningbush stroked her baby's head and cooed, "I'll swanee, jest look at all this black hair... 'tis black as a crow's feather. I'm gonna give ye my name... Mary Clarinda. What do ye think 'o that little girl?"

Little Clarinda squirmed and opened her mouth wide. She bent the granny woman's ear with another blast."That baby's a-hawngry. She ain't gonna hesh till she gits her supper."

Mary put her baby to her breast and the crying ceased. Little Clarinda needed all the nourishment and strength she could muster. Appalachian life was hard. Many women died giving birth, and the community casket-maker fashioned more baby caskets than he cared to remember.

The baby grew and thrived. Mary kept Clarinda's cradle near her as she worked. The hum of the spinning wheel was comforting as a lullaby. By the age of two, Clarinda noticed the silence that fell over the household when her father, Enoch, darkened the door. Her older siblings were afraid of him because he ruled his house with fist and club. A young, redheaded logging camp cook solved their problem when she took up with their father. Enoch abandoned his family. Weeks later, they heard he killed a lumberjack with a cant hook for making passes at his mistress. Dodging the noose, he hitched a ride on a westbound train. Little Clarinda never saw him again.

Mary, a devout Christian woman, struggled to feed her family. The two oldest of her three boys, headed west to find work on the railroads. Alexander stayed behind to help his mother and sisters. From their mother's example, Clarinda and her sisters learned to manage their homestead. They sheared sheep, milked cows, took turns at the spinning wheel and kept house. Their skills came in handy when their mother fell ill. When her condition became life-threatening, she traveled to a village in Carter County, Tennessee and stayed in the home of a well-known country doctor who treated her malady. Necessity made her leave the children at home.

Living alone on the edge of the wilderness for months at a time the children adapted to their responsibilities. Although barely fifteen, Mina took charge of cooking, laundry and general household supervision. She assigned tasks to her siblings according to their abilities. Beautiful, eighteen-year-old Malinda Rose did only light sewing. Born with a respiratory ailment, her mother knew she was not long for this world. Cassie tended five-year-old, Etta, and kept the water buckets filled. Alexander, chief woodcutter and herder of sheep, considered himself the man of the house. Nine-year-old Clarinda twirled the paddle of a hickory churn and turned out crocks of Guernsey butter as yellow as a harvest moon. Come milking time, she'd climb the winding mountain path to the high pasture and bring the cows down.

Late one afternoon, she reached the mountain field at sunset. The cows were nowhere to be seen. They're lollygaggin in the woods agin, she thought. Transfixed, she stood on a mountaintop in North Carolina and gazed at mountains stretching away into infinity. The sun looked like a pulsing, flame-colored ball, glowing on a dark ridge in Tennessee. While she watched, birdsong ceased — all was quiet — too quiet. Clarinda thought of her mother so far away in Tennessee and her heart filled with longing. A lump rose in her throat but she swallowed it down. "Mother, when are ye comin home? What will become of us if ye die?" She blinked back tears and watched the sun sink lower and lower. Its fiery rays fanned out across the west and lit up the mountaintop in gold. Sudden movement in the northeast corner of the field caught her eye. Ol' Bren and Bossie burst from the undergrowth with their tails lifted high — as stiff as a fire poker. They crossed the field in a hard run. The comical scene wiped the sadness from Clarinda's face. A bot fly is put 'em on the move, she thought with a giggle. A high-pitched scream shattered the stillness. Clarinda saw a large tawny cat leap from a chestnut snag at the edge of the woods. Cows and child raced down the mountain, slipping and sliding into the milk gap. Heart pounding, Clarinda dashed into the cabin and slammed the door.

Startled, Mina dropped the milk bucket."What in the world's the matter?"

"Don't... don't go out there, Mina. A mountain lion is after the cows!"

"Alexander! Git the gun!" Mina rushed outside and ran toward the milk gap with Alexander at her heels. The big cat squalled again, but she couldn't see it in the timber. The snorting cows — scared popeyed, tried to jump the bars. She reached for the hickory switch kept at hand and laid on the lash."Stand back—dad-gummed ye!" They fell back until she could lay the bars down safely. Alexander kept watch with his loaded musket whilst Mina and Clarinda drove the skittish bovines into the log barn. They fastened the stable doors tight."Ain't no use of even tryin to milk 'em. They're so skeerd they won't give their milk down." Mina picked up the milk bucket and headed for the cabin.

The children didn't sleep well that night. Just before daybreak they heard the mountain lion squalling on Horse Ridge."He's headed fer the river bluff," Alexander called from his bed in the loft. Thereafter, he and his musket went along with Clarinda to fetch the cows.

Weeks went by when the children didn't see another living soul. The girls were taking turns on the washboard when a woman named Betty Jane poked her black face around the door jamb."How's you chil'ren a-farin?"

Clarinda darted behind Mina.

Mina pushed wisps of damp hair from her forehead with a limp wrist."We're gitten along tol'able, I reckon."

Betty Jane shuffled inside."Yore mammy axt me to see 'bouts ye whilst she's gone."

Clarinda peeped around Mina's skirt.

Betty Jane made a face at her and chuckled."What's ye hidin fuh, chile? Do I look lak de booger man?"

Twelve-year-old Alexander came indoors carrying his musket.

"What you doin wif dat gun, boy?"

"Bear huntin. We heerd 'em a-growlin 'round the hog pen last night."

"What did you'uns do 'bout dat?"

Alexander grinned and pulled himself to full height."We lit the lantern an' went outdoors. I shot to'ards the hog pen. I didn't hit 'em, but I will tonight."

"Don't do dat, boy — yer too young to be metsin wif guns."

Alexander put the gun across two pegs on the wall."Aw... I've been shootin since I 'as a youngun. Them bears ain't gitten our hogs."

"Lawdy mussy, you be keerful. Where's de oldest of ye... de one dat's ailin?"

Mina nodded toward the window."Come an' see. Malinda Rose is restin on a quilt by the redheart cherry tree. She gits tard real easy an' hasta lay down. She likes to watch the birds eat cherries. She declares a white dove flies in ever day."

Betty Jane looked out the window and shook her head sadly."Um-um-ummmph, dat white dove be's a sign frum hebem fuh sho. I'lls tawk wif her. Yore mammy tole me to make sho she 'as all right." Betty Jane's eyes traveled around the room taking notice of the clean puncheon floor and sparkling window panes."Well, I'll go tawk wif de ailin now. If ye git in trubble, come a-runnin. I's got to be goin, but I'lls be back fo de moon gits ripe."

Clarinda tugged at Mina's skirt and whispered, "Tell 'er we won't need 'er."

Mina hushed her with a pinch.

Gradually, the doctor's treatments returned Mary to health, but her absence from home had matured her children beyond their years. Clarinda, with hair black as a crow's feather, put her corn shuck dolls away before she reached the age of ten.

One

Clarinda was fourteen when she met Rufus McCloud for the first time. She and Alexander had been down the mountain to the store. On their homeward climb, they stepped from the narrow path to let a young man with a big team of horses pass, but he stopped. The stranger and Alexander began talking horses, fox hunting, sawmilling and timber.

Clarinda stole a quick glance at him and her heart did a dipsy-doodle. Without a doubt, he was the most handsome young fellow in all God's creation. His brown hair tumbled in a wave across his forehead. What beautiful eyes, she thought. She'd seen violets that deeper color of blue. They grew around mossy water-splashed stones. He caught her eye and bedazzled her with the most fetching grin. Blushing, she turned her face away to hide her pleasure and watched him on the sly. She wondered how he kept from singeing his long curly eyelashes when he lit up the pipe sticking out of his overall bib. He caught her staring and winked. Pshaw... what a flirt! She hurried up the path.

Five minutes later, Alexander fell in step with her stride. They walked in silence for several minutes."Well, ain't ye gonna tell me who that feller was?"

"That was Rufus McCloud. His daddy bought the old Calvin Gunther farm. He's shore got some purty sisters."

"Have you seen any of 'em?"

"Yeah, the one named Sylvia ..."He gave a low whistle."Every single feller in the country is pullin pranks to git her attention."

"What kind a-pranks?"

"Well, I know of two fellers who went to their house. One feller knocked on the door and ast if he could speak with Sylvia. When she stepped out on the porch his friend jumped from behind the house with a woman's corset an' hat on."

Clarinda laughed."Why, that was plumb foolish. That ain't no way to git a girl to take notice."

"The heck it ain't. She hollered for her sisters an' they all swarmed out the door." Alexander chuckled."Ol' corset boy is a-callin on purty Sylvia ever Saturday night. Anyway, Rufus is comin to our house Friday night. We're goin fox huntin."

Clarinda's heart leaped.

Alexander gave her a stern look."I saw him a-rollin his eyes at ye. He better not git any notions 'bout comin to see you. Mother will put him around the bend."

But Alexander was wrong. Within a month, Rufus' winsome ways won Mary's approval. Who could scold a handsome fellow who brought wildflower bouquets and quart jars of sourwood honey?

Late one afternoon he showed up with his homemade groundhog banjo. Bowing like a true gentleman, he brought forth a bouquet of artificial crepe paper roses that he'd swiped from a cemetery along the way. Clarinda plucked one from the arrangement and tucked it in his lapel."Hey, the roses are fer you."

Clarinda giggled as she accepted the bouquet and seated herself on the porch steps. She eyed the instrument he carried."Are ye gonna play me a purty song?"

"Yeah, I shore hope to." He seated himself on the steps beside her."How 'bout this'n?"

"She tuck me in the parlor,
She fanned me with a fan;
She said I was the sweetest thing
In the shape of mortal man.

Git along home, oh Sindy, Sindy,
Git along home, oh Sindy, Sindy,
Git along home, oh Sindy Sindy,
Git along down home.

Sindy went to meetin;
So happy she did feel,
She got so much religion
She split her stockin heel.

Git along home, oh Sindy, Sindy,
Git along home, oh Sindy, Sindy,
Git along home, oh Sindy, Sindy,
Git along down home.

Although reserved in manner, Clarinda couldn't keep her feet still. She watched his long nimble fingers dance up and down the neck of that banjo and her heart swelled with happiness."I ain't never heerd that song before," she said, tapping her feet to the rhythm.

"Well, did ye like it?"

She nodded that she did.

He laid the instrument in her lap."Now, le's heer you play."

"No... no ... I cain't play a lick a-nothin." She tried to push it away, but he snuggled close.

"They ain't nothin to it. I'll show ye how." He took her left hand and moved it to the neck of the instrument. After placing each of her fingers on a different string he said, "That's the key of C. Now pluck the top string with yer right thumb and brush yer fingers down acrost the strings. Move yer hand from thumb to fingers like a dog a-scratchin fleas."

She giggled, and gave it a try. The sound was indescribable. She glanced at Rufus. He had turned his face away to watch a bird in the cherry tree nearby.

"You're a-laughin at me."

He ran his fingers through his hair nervous like. When he turned toward her, he couldn't conceal his amusement. She dropped her head and blushed.

Laying the banjo aside, he reached out and pulled her head to his shoulder."Aw... it wasn't that bad." His fingers played through her long raven tresses like a zephyr breeze. They were silent for a breathless moment.

She felt his shoulders shaking. Frowning, she pushed him away."What's so dern funny?"

"Well, it was the choke-hold ye laid on it. You purt nigh broke that banjer's neck."

She burst out laughing and Rufus pulled her back in his arms."You don't know how purty you are, do ye?"

"Hush, Mother will heer ye."

He nuzzled her neck and whispered, "Yer mother's busy at her spinnin wheel an' it's time fer a kiss."

"Clarinda! Come here and help me git these knots outta this wool!"

In haste, she jumped to her feet to obey her mother.

Rufus muttered, "Damn!"

All of a sudden, an urge seized her and she stooped and kissed him firmly on the lips. As she rushed inside — heart dipsy-doodling like a crazy June bug — she heard Rufus' joyful whoop.

20229921

With downcast eyes and rosy cheeks Clarinda worked the wool with the cards. Had her mother been watchin? Would she put Rufus around the bend? Oh, there was so much to worry about. Rufus continued his serenade with one rollicking tune after another. Clarinda forgot that her mother was even in the room, and who could fault her?

> Sindy in the spring time,
> Sindy in the fall,
> Sindy at the ballroom
> A-dancin at the ball.
> Git along home, oh Sindy, Sindy...

Mary studied Clarinda's face."Have ye got Rufus in yer heart, Rindy?"

"Huh... uh, aw... what?"

Mary took a handkerchief from her apron pocket and dabbed at her eyes."I've been expectin it. But you're too young to even think about gitten married."

"I'll swannie, I ain't been ast yit."

Clarinda was three weeks shy of age fifteen, and Rufus barely eighteen on their wedding day Feb 8, 1913. With eyes the color of wildwood fern and long black hair held in place with a white ribbon that matched her dress, she was a lovely bride. Rufus brought her a lacy-looking bouquet of an evergreen vine with sprigs of red wintergreen berries woven through it. He told her that evergreens were a symbol of everlasting love and kissed her cheek—smack dab in the presence of Alexander!

It was a five mile walk to the preacher's house, and Alexander went along with them to witness the ceremony. Occasionally, Rufus would kiss her cheek. Alexander turned red with embarrassment."Why don't you'uns cut that out?"

"Now, Alexander, in another mile or two Clarinda will be my wife. I'm a-gonna kiss 'er when I feel like it—and that'll be a lot."

"It's a good thing you're gitten married today. Mother would thrash both of ye with a switch fer actin that a-way."

"I'll risk it, brother." Rufus stopped walking and gave Clarinda a passionate kiss on the lips.

"For cryin out loud!" Alexander averted his eyes and moved ahead.

They found the preacher sitting on a block of wood in the woodshed putting the set in his crosscut saw. He had an anvil before him and the crosscut saw lay across it. He hammered away at the jagged saw-teeth.

Rufus spoke first."Rev'rent, have ye got time to marry us today?"

"By crackies, I shore have." The Reverend, a tall man with a ruddy complexion and a deep booming voice, laid his hammer down and rose to his feet."You're a McCloud ain't ye?"

"Yes, sir."

"I know yer pappy. He bought the Gunther farm didn he?"

Rufus nodded."Yep, we're new around here."

"Well, I heerd tell that yer pappy makes moonshine. He needs to git on down to the church. I'm a-fixin to start a protracted meetin next week."

"My papa don't make liquor nor drink it neither."

The Reverend puffed himself up and hooked his thumbs in his overall galluses."You ain't disputin a preacher's word, aire ye?"

"Heck, we come here to git married. We didn't come to git in a row."

The Reverend leaned forward with a twinkle in his eye."What's yer hurry? Aire ye skeerd she'll change 'er mind?"

Rufus pulled Clarinda close."No, sir, not in my lifetime. Now, le's git on with it."

The Reverend frowned. He'd take this young whippersnapper down a notch or two. Jabbing his forefinger toward a patch of snow-free ground, he bellowed in his pulpit voice, "Stand 'ere an' jine hands."

The bride and groom shuffled to the spot.

"Do ye promise to love, cherish, and honor one another?"

They looked at each other and nodded.

"I now pernounce ye man an' wife."

"But-but," Rufus spluttered, "That cain't be it. You didn't even have the Bible in yore hands."

The Reverend heaved an aggravated sigh."Young feller, I've marrit more couples than you've got toes 'n fangers. I reckon I know what I'm a-doin. Yer names are already jot down in holy wedlock."

Rufus shook the preacher's hand and gave him the marriage license that he'd procured at the county seat."Well, we gotta be goin. Thank ye, Rev'rent."

The Reverend held out his hand, palm up, and wiggled his fingers."That'll be a dollar ye owe me, young feller."

"Oh, I plumb fergot." Rufus fished a crumpled bill from his pocket.

On their way home, Clarinda discovered that Rufus had a hot temper because he called the preacher 'a damn nit-witted fool.'

"Well, Rufus, if the preacher is a fool maybe we ain't married, maybe we need to find another preacher and git it done right."

"Aw... I reckon he's got sense enough to record the marriage."

Clarinda giggled."You've got a aincher fer everthing, ain't ye?"

"Purt near it." He chuckled.

FRANKLIN COUNTY LIBRARY
906 NORTH MAIN STREET
LOUISBURG, NC 27549
BRANCHES IN BUNN.
FRANKLINTON & YOUNGSVILLE

The newlyweds set up housekeeping in a five-room log cabin in Lonesome Hollow near Clarinda's home place. Their first child was born on Clarinda's sixteenth birthday. She named him Rufus Claude. He was a big healthy baby and her days were full of joy and contentment as she tended Claude, and kept her cabin neat and clean.

Soon Rufus became known as a skilled sawyer who could turn out more lumber in an ordinary day than any two men. He stood five-feet-ten, lean and muscular—fleet of foot with the reflexes of a cat. He was a good husband and father and worked from daylight till dark to provide for his growing family.

The babies kept coming every year or so and Clarinda made Rufus speak to the doctor about birth control. The doctor informed Rufus of an operation that he might attempt, but he wouldn't recommend it, because it would destroy their marriage.

Rufus looked puzzled."I don't understand how it could do that."

"Fer heaven's sake, man, yore wife would never have any desire fer you agin."

Rufus' jaw dropped."Lordy mercy, you can fergit that I ever mentioned it."

As Clarinda put supper on the table each evening the little ones watched the path. They squealed with joy when they saw Papa coming through the sedge field, his old felt hat shoved to the back of his head, swinging his dinner bucket and bringing the scent of new lumber home. He always stopped at the bottom of the porch steps and brushed the sawdust from his overall cuffs.

After a hearty supper he'd rest for awhile, and then reach for his banjo. The little ones danced around his chair, clapping their hands even before his fingers touched a string.

> Shoulder up your gun and whistle up your dog,
> Shoulder up your gun and whistle up your dog,
> We're gonna hunt for the old groundhog. Oh Groundhog!
>
> Here comes Sally with a ten foot pole,
> Here comes Sally with a ten foot pole,
> Gonna twist that whistlepig out of his hole. Oh Groundhog!

The toddlers tried to join the fun too. They tottered around his knees, staring at the amazing instrument, and one always reached out a dimpled hand and touched a string while looking up in Papa's face with wonderment.

While Rufus played, the weariness of a hard day's labor at the sawmill vanished. He moved with the rhythm of the music, feet tapping, shoulders dipping left and right.

> Meat on the table, butter in the churn
> Meat on the table, butter in the churn.
> If that ain't groundhog, I'll be durned.
> Oh, Groundhog!

Watching him entertain the children, Clarinda settled down in her favorite ladder-back chair and worked her rag rug by the oil lamplight. When the little ones danced themselves dizzy, he turned his attention to Clarinda and teased her with his songs.

She would become overly interested in her rug craft, as if she didn't hear a word he was singing, but Rufus knew her heart was soft as goose down. He'd lay his banjo aside and rise to his feet. He'd take her rug hook from her hand and coax her from the chair. They'd go high-stepping around the room whilst the children laughed and clapped.

"Stop this foolishness, Rufus McCloud," she'd scold, but her smile was warm as sunshine.

Clarinda stored those wonderful times in her treasure chest of memories. They were sorely needed when bad times came a-callin. Their first twins, Joey and Julie were born healthy and robust. She and Rufus lavished them with love and affection. The entire family adored them. Clarinda's friends competed with each other as to who could knit the prettiest caps, bonnets, and booties for them. Little Joey's black hair curled up around his face like a cherub. Little Julie had her papa's blue eyes.

Whooping cough raged throughout the community at that time and four of Rufus and Clarinda's school age children came down with it. Within days, the twins had it too. The doctor came, but there was little he could do for babies so young.

Little Julie died in Clarinda's arms at sundown on June 22, 1932. She was two months old. Clarinda kept rocking her in the old mahogany rocking chair.

Rufus laid his hand on her arm."Clarinda, le's take the baby to the bedroom." She rose and followed him. She laid the baby on the bed and sank to her knees by the bedside. Rufus knelt by her for awhile, trying to comfort her as best he could. Then he left her alone to say goodbye to their baby.

Their oldest daughter, Eva Jean, entered the room. But she paused at the door and waited as her mother hovered over Julie, stroking her head and rubbing her tiny feet. Clarinda closed her baby's eyes with a caress and kissed them."Little angel, I'm a-gonna lay ye in the Arms of Jesus, now. He will take ye to a beautiful place where they ain't no sickness nor pain. A white cradle with a pink rosebud in the headboard is waitin fer ye. I've ast Jesus to spread a purty quilt over you, just like the one I made ye with the little rabbits an' bluebirds on it." She went to her knees with a groan, too grief-stricken for tears. Eva Jean rushed to her.

In the settin room ten minutes later, little Joey's labored breathing ceased. He died in his papa's arms. Rufus turned him this way and that way and sprinkled cold water in his face in a desperate effort to get him to breathe, but the grim reaper was determined to take his toll this day. A neighbor, who had come to lend a hand, looked upon father and son with tears in her eyes."I'll go git Clarinda."

Rufus raised his hand and stopped her."No. Leave her alone, she cain't take no more right now."

Skilled woodcraftsmen in the community made the pinewood coffins for their burial. At Clarinda's request, they carved a single rosebud on the lid of each. She laid her babies to rest in the family cemetery near her old homestead. It was not her nature to let others see her deep feelings, and some might say she took her loss well. But close friends and family saw her shrink in stature and her eyes darken with grief.

The day after the funeral, Clarinda returned to the cemetery her arms laden with wildflowers. After arranging the bouquets she knelt between the graves and placed a hand on the wooden crosses with "Joey" and "Julie" carved thereon. Died June 22, 1932. She bowed her head and her grief gushed forth. She asked the Lord to set aside a rocking chair in heaven so that she could rock her babies when she got there.

She closed her eyes and accepted the cool silence of sleep around her. A verse of scripture came to mind: "But they that wait upon the Lord shall renew their strength; they shall mount up with wings as eagles; they shall run and not be weary; and they shall walk, and not faint." (Isaiah 40:31).

A refreshing summer breeze came winging down Levi's Mountain. It passed through the cemetery, touched her face and dried her tears. She leaned over to sniff the bouquets and rearrange the beautiful orange-colored blossoms of the pleurisy root—a butterfly had found its favorite flower. With a lighter heart, she rose and set her feet on the homeward path. She knew that Joey and Julie were safe in the Lord's Care. In Matthew 19:14, Jesus said, "of such is the kingdom of heaven." Yes indeed. She'd see her babies and hold them again someday.

Two

Lonesome Hollow • 1934

Most mountain men and boys enjoy hunting. Rufus and Clarinda's eldest son, Claude, was no exception. Come Friday night, he'd bring out the lantern, whistle up Ol' Limber and head for the mountainside. As a general rule, his fox hunting friends went along with him. And thus they did one mid-October night.

The weather was perfect for coon hunting. A big harvest moon peeped over Chinky Pin Ridge and smiled down on Claude and his friends as they rambled through the woods with their yapping hounds. Every hound strained at his leash, wasting energy, except Ol' Limber. The large Bluetick Coonhound trotted alongside Claude as cool as a tin cupful of spring water. He'd run his heart out for a hambone and a bowl of sawmill gravy. Although he belonged to Rufus, he was just as devoted to Claude. Frequently, he'd look up at Claude with adoring eyes. Claude paused and tickled his ears.

At the head of Bowman Branch, the boys set their dogs free.

"Go git 'im, Belshazzar!"

"Put 'im up a tree, Rags!"

"Cornpone! Run that corn-eatin rascal plumb to Tennessee."

Claude dropped to one knee, cradled Ol' Limber's muzzle in his hands and looked into his soft brown eyes."Listen, ol' feller, I want you to show these sissy dogs how to tree a coon. You're still king of the mountain. Now, go git 'im!"

Ol' Limber whirled around and took off so fast he kicked autumn leaves in Claude's face. When he passed the pack he let out a deep chesty bawl. Claude shouted, "Go boy, go." Ol' Limber heard him and bawled again. With nose to the ground, he doubled back a few yards. Limber was not to be deceived. He knew every ring-tailed trick in the history of the creature. In no time he picked up the scent again. With a raucous bellow he brought the pack in line and led them up the mountainside and down through the Bear Wallow. Claude tilted his head to one side."Listen boys... Ol' Limber is singin his own song now."

The boys stopped in their tracks and argued as to whose hound was in the lead, then rambled on. Suddenly a moving shadow passed over them. They looked up and saw a large bird of prey glide across the face of the moon with a limp creature dangling from its talons.

"What the—"

"That was a great horned owl with a coon in its claws," said Claude.

"That wadn no coon," another argued, "A coon would a-fit to the death."

Claude chuckled."I guess it did. It looked purty dead to me."

High on the mountaintop a wildcat squalled."Dang, I hope Ol' Limber don't tackle that thang," said Claude, "it'll rip 'im to pieces."

Shortly thereafter, they came upon a cornfield. The farmer had planted his crop in new ground on a steep hillside. Here and there, stubborn stumps squatted on roots too deep for grub-hook and plow. It would take dynamite to move them. The corn stood in the shock with a neat pile of pumpkins around each upright bundle.

With a gesture of the hand, Claude beckoned, "Come on, fellers, le's jump some corn shocks."

Loud whoops went up as the boys took their jumps. They rattled fodder and scattered pumpkins left and right. Claude yanked a four foot stick from a brush pile and shouted, "Hey, you puny squirts, stop ridin over the man's fodder. Just watch an' I'll show ye how it's done." Holding the stick aloft, Claude ran at top speed toward the tallest shock. Jabbing the stick in the ground, he shot skyward and cleared the top with a foot to spare—he crashed on a granite rock and tumbled sideways. The impact sliced his tongue and knocked a lower front tooth out of socket. He lay twisting on the ground—blood pouring from his mouth.

"Mama... Mama... ," he cried, and fainted.

Scared half out of their wits the boys managed to carry him home. Rufus and Clarinda awoke at the sound of scuffling feet."Hey, Rufus!" rang out from the front porch. Flinging the covers aside they rushed forth and opened the door.

"Claude's hurt bad!"

Rufus carried Claude to his bed and pointed his finger toward the door."Boys, go fer Doc Butler—and don't let no grass grow under yer feet!"

Shortly before daybreak Dr. Butler arrived on horseback. Claude could barely endure the examination. With a nod of his head, the doctor signaled that he wanted to speak to Rufus and Clarinda in private. The three stepped into the kitchen. Clarinda braced herself for the worst.

"Well, yer boy is hurt bad, folks. He's got to go in the hospital today. His hip is busted all to pieces. All I can do is give 'im some morphine fer the pain."

Rufus quickly made arrangements for Claude's transportation to the hospital. Automobiles were scarce, but his employer owned one. They moved Claude on his straw tick to a horse-drawn sled that carried him to the nearest road. There a car waited to take him on the thirty mile trip to the hospital. Although transportation to and from the hospital was difficult to obtain, family members made every effort to be at his side.

Claude remained hospitalized for weeks with little improvement. One morning Clarinda and Rufus arrived to find Claude in terrible condition. His injured hip had shrunk and his leg was drawn backward so severely that his heel touched his buttock and had frozen there. He was skin and bone.

She stepped from the room and wept."Rufus, we're gonna git Claude outta here. He'll die if we don't. They cain't do any more fer him here."

Rufus agreed. They moved Claude to a more modern facility better equipped to treat his injury. Infection had set up in his hip. He needed surgery. Tubes were inserted to drain away the infection. The slow, painful method of straightening his leg began with a steel pin in his heel. Months passed before he was able to come home.

The family pitched in to help take care of him. Wild herbs were abundant in the woodland, so the children gathered galax and wintergreen by the sack and traded them at the store for special food for Claude. At first, Clarinda's neighbors dropped in frequently to lend a helping hand, but as his recovery stretched into months and years they came less. Always grateful for kind neighbors, Clarinda knew they'd helped her all they could.

Despite tonics and the best food available, Claude remained frail. Occasionally a large abscess broke out on his body. Dr. Butler told Clarinda it was infection in his system caused by the hip injury. Clarinda applied poultices of plantain and burdock leaves that drew the abscess to a head then she lanced it. Eva Jean, though only fourteen, helped with his care more than any other. One night she rushed to her mother who was tending baby, Lee."Mama, Claude's a-talkin outta his head, I'm afraid he's gonna die."

Clarinda hurried to his bedside.

He was burning up with fever. He raised his arms and mumbled, "Angels, take me home. I want a-see Gran'maw."

Clarinda sponged him with cool water.

Eva Jean paced around the bed wringing her hands."Is he gonna die, Mama?"

23

Clarinda took her firmly by the shoulders and turned her toward the door."Go to bed and git some rest. I'll take keer of him... he'll be all right." Clarinda was worried to death, but she kept it to herself. Along toward daybreak, she lanced the abscess between his shoulder blades and his fever fell. His senses cleared, and he took nourishment for the first time in two days.

The rays of a pale winter sun broke through the bedroom window and woke Eva Jean. She dressed quickly and hurried to Claude's bedside. She took his hand and kissed his brow."Yer lookin better this mornin."

He smiled weakly."I'm shore a-feelin better since Mama lanced that abscess."

She stroked his head."You must a-been dreamin last night. You talked about angels and heaven and stuff."

"No, I wasn't a-dreamin. Angels hovered over my bed and I heerd the purtiest harp music. I know you won't believe me, but they carried me to heaven, Eva Jean. I even dainced the streets of gold. I saw Gran'maw Mary, too."

"Course I believe ye. But I'm glad yer still with us."

The doctor told Clarinda that Claude's body would expel slivers of bone from his hip. Claude usually removed them himself. When she fussed about it, he said, "Aw... Mama, they ain't no use a-fussin over a little scrap of bone."

Frequently, Eva Jean invited her friends over for games of rook and checkers and his spirit soared. He was a pleasant fellow when he felt good, and the girls enjoyed his company. On warm sunny days Eva helped him to the porch and settled him in his big rocking chair. While he strummed his guitar, she combed his hair, tended his feet and sang the latest songs of the day. He loved to hear her sing. She had a beautiful voice and a warm nurturing spirit.

"Eva Jean, how comes you're so good to me?"

She tapped his head with the comb."Because you're my brother, silly, and besides, I'm the only one in the family who'll put up with yer temper."

"Well, I just want ye to know how much I appreciate all you've done fer me... in case I die tonight ... uh, I just want ye to know."

"Aw... Claude, you ain't a-gonna die till yer old and gray. You havta be the best man at my weddin." She fought back tears, remembering the nights when death lurked in the chimney corner like a red-eyed vulture, waiting... to snatch him away.

Three years later, Eva Jean married and moved out. Claude wasn't at her wedding because he wasn't able to walk the five miles to the preacher's house, but his health had improved to the degree that he could walk with a cane.

ꟷᕋhree

Lonesome Hollow • 1937

*T*he Death Angel called Rufus one evening. The day was winding down. The little ones played quietly on the floor. Rufus sat in his ladder-back chair by the lamplight reading the Bible aloud to the family. As he paused to turn the page, an eerie, unearthly voice spoke from the chimney corner, *"Rufus . . Rufus ... Rufus."* The entire family heard it. The little ones ceased their prattle. They looked at Papa with wide questioning eyes then ran to their mother. The Bible slipped from Rufus' hands."What in the world do ye reckon that was, Clarinda?"

"God only knows, Rufus... only God knows." She'd heard all her life that a spirit would sometimes call a soul when death was near, but she didn't mention such to Rufus.

Six months later, November 22, 1937, Rufus complained of being uncommonly tired and spent most of the day on the couch resting. Clarinda went about her chores with a worried mind. It wasn't like Rufus to spend the day around the house. After supper, the little ones begged him to play his banjo, but he refused."Papa's got a headache, Billy Dan."

Clarinda was getting the little ones ready for bed when Rufus rose from the couch. His flushed face and pained expression alarmed her. He clutched his head and cried out, "Oh God! My head is killin me — do somethin!"

She dashed to the kitchen, returning with a pan of cool water which she splashed on his head by the handful. The pan clattered to the floor as he collapsed in her arms. His eyes rolled up.

Claude called out from his sick bed, "Tom... Olus, come quick! Somethin's wrong with Papa!"

The boys rushed into the room and helped their mother get Rufus to the bed. Clarinda tried everything she knew of to bring him around.

Claude watched them work with his Papa."Olus, you an' Tom go fer Doc Butler as fast as ye can, this ain't no faintin spell."

Clarinda agreed.

She had seen enough death in her life to know that Rufus might not survive. The doctor arrived on horseback at daybreak. After examining Rufus, Doctor Butler confirmed her fears."He's suffered a fatal stroke. You all better say yer goodbyes now because his time is short."

Everyone left the room except Clarinda. She sat by his bedside and held his hand."Rufus, if you can heer me, squeeze my hand." She felt his hand twitch. Leaning down, she spoke in a low intimate voice."Lissen, doctors don't know everthing. I'm gonna pray an' ast the Lord fer a miracle. But if it ain't the Lord's will to grant one, I want you to know that I've loved ye from the day I first laid eyes on ye. I'll never love anybody else." She bent over and kissed him. When she raised her head, his pillow was damp with her tears. She left the room and the children came to his bedside two at a time to say goodbye.

Rufus slipped into a deeper coma as the hours passed. Clarinda returned to his bedside and stayed till the doctor gave her a sleeping aid. Two hours later, Eva Jean woke her."Mama, the doctor says Papa ain't got but a few minutes left."

Clarinda sprang to her feet, but her legs failed her. She sank down on the bed."Oh Lord, I cain't watch him go. I just cain't."

Eva Jean sat with her and spoke words of comfort."You don't have to watch him go, Mama. Most of the boys and Gran'maw Tana are with him."

Rufus stepped into eternity on November 24, 1937 at two-thirty in the morning. He was forty-two-year old.

Word of Rufus' death spread. Neighbors and kinfolk arrived in droves, carrying food for the wake. Men folk in the community prepared Rufus' body for burial. When they left the room, Clarinda moved to the bedside with hairbrush in hand. With gentle hands she brushed and stroked his brown hair which had grown thinner over the years. She added pomade to the brush."Rufus, it's gonna be mighty lonesome in this ol' hollar without ye. I'm dependin on God to git me through the days ahead—I shore cain't make it alone." Ten minutes later, she rose from his bedside and slipped away to the spring to pray. There on her knees she received strength to carry her through the hours ahead.

Around noon, two neighbors arrived bearing Rufus' pinewood coffin. They'd worked all night to get it finished on time. Four men laid him gently inside and arranged the artificial flowers upon his chest. Later, Clarinda rearranged the flowers, removing all except one red crepe paper rose on his lapel."He looks more like hisself, now," she said.

Two family members stayed by the coffin at all times.

The nearest church was five miles away. The only road to speak of was a narrow plank road that zigzagged down the hollow so she decided to have the funeral at home. The two coffin makers constructed a bier from two sawhorses and three wide boards. They covered it with a sheet and set the coffin thereon. Due to limited space in the cabin, the bier and coffin were moved to the porch for the funeral. A large crowd filled the porch and yard.

Shortly before the funeral service, Rufus' mother made a request."I want to heer the younguns sing the hymns in this service. I know it would please Rufus."

So the boys brought out their instruments and the younger children gathered around the bier. Their voices soared over the crowd as they sang, "Amazing Grace."

Clarinda leaned over and whispered in five-year-old Howard's ear."Sang "Rock of Ages" for everbody." Henry tucked his fiddle under his chin and drew the bow across the strings slowly. Little Howard's voice rang out as clear as a church bell on Sunday morning."Rock of Ages, cleft for me, let me hide myself in Thee;"

Lumber jacks and sawmill men wept openly as the melody touched their hearts.

Grandma Tana wept on Clarinda's shoulder."Let it all out, Clarinda. You'll feel better."

But Clarinda could not. She knew that once she let her emotions hold sway she'd never be able to keep herself together through the funeral.

The minister stood on the porch steps and spoke to the crowd."Brothers and sisters, life is like a vapor." He gestured toward the coffin."Here lays brother Rufus, one of the best sawyers that ever cut a chestnut tree down to size. In the prime a-life he 'as called to his final reward. It behooves us, brethren, to be ready when our Maker calls. They ain't no promise of tomarr in this ol' wicked world. Yer just a heartbeat away from eternity... a heartbeat away."

After a congregational hymn and the benediction prayer, four older sons carried their Papa's coffin down the steps and gently set it on a horse-drawn sled for the trip to the family cemetery. Avery and Robert rode the sled and held the coffin steady over the rough narrow road. The rest of the family and the congregation followed on foot. Rufus was buried beside Joey and Julie, their infant twins.

Clarinda's brother, Alexander, spoke frankly to her at the cemetery. "Clarinda, they ain't no way under the sun that you can raise all these younguns and take keer of Claude too. Times are the hardest that anybody has ever seen. If you'll let me, I'll go over to the Grandfather Home and talk to 'em next week. I'm sure they'd take yore four youngest—"

She raised her hand and silenced him. "My younguns ain't goin in no orphanage as long as I'm alive. I brought 'em into this world an' it's my place to raise 'em. I'm keepin the family together."

"Why don't ye be sensible about this?" he argued. "All of ye will starve. Yore married younguns have their own younguns to support."

Clarinda's eyes flashed fire. She poked Alexander in the chest with her finger. "I ain't puttin my younguns in no orphanage nor givin 'em away to be scattered over the country and mistreated. If we starve, we'll all starve together."

Alexander shook his head sadly and walked away.

Four

Lonesome Hollow • 1939

Clarinda's Song

Until we meet again, my love,
My heart shall sing sweet songs of you —
Shall sing of sunsets, wild bouquets,
And banjo tunes that tease and woo.
I'll picture you with outstretched arms,
A playful twinkle in your eye;
"Come, dance with me," I'll hear you say,
"The clock's a-tickin' — don't be shy."
The lamplight flickers and the moon
Shines through the open cabin door.
You charm me from my rocking chair
And you and I are young once more.
Our feet move perfectly in step
With our old favorite Irish rhyme —
I'll hear you whisper in my ear,
"I'll love you, dear, through all of time."

*T*he snow was knee deep and it had grown colder. Clarinda pulled on her coat, swathed her head in a woolen rag, and looked out the cabin window at the worsening weather. It was time to do up the night work. She dreaded facing the wind, but she had chickens to feed and a cow to milk. Ol' Pied would throw a conniption fit if she didn't get her rations on time. "Younguns, I'm goin to the barn," she called. "Be shore an' button this door behind me." As she eased the door open, an icy blast wrenched it from her hand and slammed it against the wall. With milk bucket in hand she stopped on the porch and opened a large tin can of scratch feed. She ladled two scoops into a paper bag, tucked it under her arm and waded into the storm.

The stinging wind shoved her from side to side as she trudged through the snow to the chicken house. The rickety outbuilding leaned into the hillside like a feeble old man with a snowdrift on his shoulder. She unbuttoned the door and looked inside. Four young hens lay dead on the floor. Her big Dominique rooster hung upside down with one foot frozen to the roost."What a pity... what a waste," she muttered. Somber-faced, she scattered out the grain and called the flock, but the bleary-eyed fowl clung to the roost. Stepping inside, she nudged them from their perch."Eat yer grain fore ye drap dead," she scolded. She fastened the door and slogged on to the log barn.

Ol' Pied peeped through a chink in the wall and rattled her hayrack at sight of Clarinda on the snowy pathway. The familiar squeak of the door hinge sent a surge of joy through Pied. Clarinda stepped over the doorsill and moved to a small grain storage bin in the barn shed. She turned the wooden button and tilted the hinged bin forward. Reaching inside a sack of sweet feed, she filled an empty tin coffee can that held a quart. With tin of sweet feed in hand, she stepped to a wooden feed trough nailed to the wall and dumped the aromatic mixture inside. It smelled of ground wheat and corn mixed with molasses. Pied rattled the stable door with her horns. Clarinda raised the door latch, opened the door and stepped aside. Ol' Pied lunged forth, her nostrils blowing steam. She rushed to her feed box and shoved her muzzle inside.

"Good gracious, Pied, you act like ye ain't never seen a bite."

Clarinda moved to Pied's right side. The left side is known as the calf's side. Pied allowed nothing on hoof except a frisky calf to lean its shoulder against her left flank. Clarinda laid her hand on Pied's right hip and spoke softly, "Back yer leg, Pied." Obediently, Pied moved her right hind leg back a step. Clarinda settled herself on a low stool and milked the cow in ten minutes.

Pulling a clean white cloth from her apron pocket, she covered the top of the milk pail and fastened it with a safety pin. She set the milk outside in the snow and climbed a crude fixed ladder to the hay loft. After pitching down hay and a sack of autumn leaves, she filled the hayrack and scattered the leaves in Pied's stable for bedding.

Feeling her sweet feed, Pied kicked Ol' Whiskers into the corner and jumped out the door. She took off in a lope for the branch nearby. The deep snow put a hitch in her get along, but she made the twenty-five yards in good time. Lowering her muzzle to the gurgling ice–rimmed branch, she took deep draughts and quenched her thirst. She followed her own trail back to the barn in a whirling white-out. At the stable door, she paused and nudged Clarinda with her nose. Clarinda stroked Pied's neck and spoke in a soft voice."You're a good cow, Pied, but ye kicked the daylights outta Whiskers. He's a fine mouser, so leave 'im be." Satisfied that her precious cow was safe and comfortable, Clarinda fastened the barn door, picked up her milk pail and headed for the cabin.

Three days the storm had been raging. It began with freezing rain which quickly turned to sleet that rattled at the windows all day and night. By midmorning the following day, the sun came out then slid behind dark, ominous clouds moving in from the west. They sagged into the hollows, their big gray underbellies dropping acorn-sized snowflakes that covered the ground within minutes. Snow thunder rumbled through the heavens. A wicked wind arose. Along toward evening of the third day, the wind increased to an endless roar, piling coves and hollows full of snow.

The wind staggered Clarinda twice before she reached the cabin. As she stomped snow from her feet at the door, her teenage sons Olus and Tom, climbed the porch steps with buckets of water in hand. Henry, two-years-younger than Tom, carried firewood from the woodshed and stacked it on the porch.

"Git in plenty of wood," Clarinda called, "It looks like this storm's gonna be a bad'n."

Olus and Tom set the water buckets in the kitchen and pitched in to help Henry.

"Henry, you owe us big fer helpin ye out," said Tom.

"Oh, yeah?" Henry threw a snowball. A fight broke out and it wasn't fluffy little flakes down the shirt collar.

Clarinda heard the ruckus and poked her head outside."Younguns, stop that foolishness an' git in the house fore ye ketch newmoany!"

Laughing like crazy, Olus and Tom seized Henry and pitched him in a snowdrift with a loud, "Yee-haa!"

She closed the door with a sigh."I'll swanee, they cain't do a lick a-work 'thout gitten in a romp."

The delicious aroma of cornpone, rutabagas, creamed corn, fried potatoes, leather-britches beans and coffee filled the cabin as Clarinda's daughter dished up supper. Although she wouldn't be fourteen until June, Mary Ann cooked and kept house as well as a grown woman."Supper's ready," she called.

Ten of Clarinda's seventeen children gathered around the homemade table that Papa Rufus had sawn from a mammoth chestnut. The older children, with the exception of Claude, had married and left home. The four youngest—referred to as the little ones, took their places with two older children on a long bench. They were spoiled by their siblings—especially the three-year-old twins, Andy and Mandy.

31

"Supper's gitten cold, Mama," said Mary Ann.

"Don't wait fer me. I've got to take keer of the milk."

The little ones snatched their sparkling clean Bruton Snuff glasses and climbed down from the bench. They hurried to Clarinda with glass in hand. She set the four glasses on the milk table and spread a snowy-white straining cloth over them. She poured milk from the pail through the strainer until each glass was full."Mama's sweet babes are gonna be drinkin cold milk this time," Clarinda said, putting a glassful in little Andy's hands.

He sipped it and smacked his lips."Mmm... g-good, mighty g-good." Looking up at her with a milk moustache he said, "I-I ain't no babe, Mama. I'm a b-big boy."

"Course ye are. I musn't fergit it agin." She bent down and hugged him close.

"S-stop, Mama, I-I'm 'bout to s-spill my milk."

She released him with a pat on the rear. He walked slowly to the table, his shoulders hunched forward and both hands squeezing his milk glass. When the milk threatened to slosh over the brim, he'd stop, take a sip and announce its goodness again.

The children loved milk and drank it throughout the day, but the little ones preferred it warm from the cow. Clarinda strained the remaining milk into a two-gallon crock, covered it with a wooden lid, and stored it away on the milk table. In ordinary weather she would take it to the dairy box at the spring, but it would be foolish to go out in the storm again. Anyway, when the fire died down the milk would freeze there. After washing and rinsing the strainer she hung it to dry on a line behind the cookstove.

The storm had brought on early darkness so she lit the kerosene lamp and carried it to the table. A ladder-back chair at the head of the table awaited her. Two years earlier, her late husband, Rufus, occupied that place of authority. But now, she seated herself there and looked around the table at her brood.

Rambunctious teenagers, Olus and Henry and Tom could eat their weight in mountain fare and never gain a pound. Olus looked down at his heaping plate."Wisht I had a punkin pie fer dessert."

Mary Ann rolled her eyes at her mother."Did he say a piece of pie?"

"Heck no. I want a whole pie. When are ye gonna bake three or four?"

"Fer the love of Pete, what a pig!"

Clarinda helped herself to the rutabagas and changed the subject."I seen smoke a-curlin to the ground tother day. That's a shore sign of bad weather."

Olus nudged Tom grinning."Well, Mama, look out the winder. It's here."

Tom pushed a black wavy lock from his forehead and flashed his handsome white teeth in a broad grin."Are you a weather prophet, Mama?"

She sipped her coffee."Humph, I heerd the mountain a-roarin, too. When ol' Levi speaks with a roar, ye better lay in lots of firewood. I shore hope we've got enough on hand."

"Don't worry. We've got plenty." Olus chuckled and reached for the cornpone.

Tom snatched a chunk from the platter and tossed it to him. Little Howard copied him."Ketch it, Andy."

Claude, the oldest son, leaned forward and smacked Howard's hand."Mind yer manners, squirt."

"I ain't no squirt—am I, Mama?"

"Course not. Now hush, an' eat yer supper."

Tom turned the conversation back to the weather."Nobody believes in them ol' timey weather signs these days."

Mary Ann rose from her chair and left the table. She replenished the empty milk glasses from a large blue pitcher on the milk table."Well, I didn't hear no mountain roarin," she said, taking her seat again.

Clarinda frowned."Maybe ye wasn't listenin."

The little ones giggled at the banter between their mother and older siblings and swung their legs happily under the table. Mandy drained her glass and plunked it down with a thump."Mama, did Ol' Pied find her calf yit?"

"No... she'll find it in the spring."

Mandy puckered up to cry."Le's go git it. It'll freeze."

A loud burst of laughter made the lamplight flicker. Olus reached over and tweaked her nose."Yeah, Pug, tell Mama to git that calf outta the spring, right now!"

She grinned at her handsome fun-loving brother.

Clarinda tried to explain."Mandy, I meant in the spring time... when the wildfl'ares bloom. That's when Pied will find her calf."

"Oh... ," Mandy said, and poked her fork in a bean.

Table talk returned to the weather and Clarinda continued, "When the shuck on the corn is thicker'n usual and the yaller jackets build underground, ye better fill the woodshed an' git ready for a bad winter."

Billy Dan slid mischievous blue eyes at Olus and Tom."Did the doodle bugs say it was gonna snow?"

Olus reached out and knuckled his head in a playful manner."They ain't no doodle bugs, buddy, you caught 'em all last summer."

Henry picked at his vegetables."I don't like ol' leather-britches beans an' I hate rooty baggers. When're we gonna have some chicken'n dumplin's?"

Clarinda put her fork down."Well, ye might as well learn to like 'em. It'll be next summer fore we see another pot of chicken."

"Why?"

"Ol' Dominick's deader'n a door nail—that's why."

"Did he freeze?"

"Stiffer'n a board. If this blizzard don't let up soon, we're apt to lose the whole flock."

A sudden gust of wind rattled every window in the cabin. The lamp blazed bright and died. Mandy squalled."Mama, I'm skeerd!"

Clarinda rose from the table and made her way to the kitchen cabinet. She took a box of matches from the top shelf and lit the lamp.

Olus leaned over and patted Mandy's head."See, Pug, we're all still here."

After supper, the family congregated in the settin room and the boys tuned up their instruments. Clarinda washed dishes to the sound of the wind and mountain music. When Henry limbered up his bow, the rhythm picked up. Andy snatched Mandy's hand."Le's kicka coon." They danced themselves dizzy.

Whirling a dishrag overhead, Clarinda did a do-si-do across the kitchen floor. It appeared that she might lasso the butter churn. She made a graceful turn to sashay back then stopped. Mary Ann and Lee and the little ones hung around the door watching her.

"What?"

They giggled.

"Did ye think yer mama had fergot how to daince?" She held out her hands and the little ones joined her. Mary Ann and Lee returned to their checker game, grinning ear to ear. They hadn't seen her dance since their papa died.

Claude reclined in his rocking chair and strummed his guitar. Although frail, he never whined about his situation. His attitude and tolerance for pain amazed all who knew him.

Olus had barely turned fifteen when Rufus died, but he laid his hands to the plow and took on a man's work. Clarinda and Tom worked alongside him, and together, they kept food on the table and wood in the shed.

Clarinda finished the dishes and joined her children in the settin room. She took up a rag rug and tried to work it, but the wind whistled through the cracks in the walls and the lamp flickered constantly. She set her work aside, rose from her chair and shoved three sticks of seasoned hickory in the stove. Settling down in her old mahogany rocker she took Mandy on her lap. The sweet melody of "Rock of Ages" from Henry's harmonica and the smooth rhythm of Claude's guitar, softened the sound of the wind. Mandy drifted into dreamland and Clarinda nodded off. Suddenly the lamp sputtered out.

"Are we out of oil agin?"

"Dang it," said Tom.

Olus said, "Damn!"

"Quit that cussin and go to bed. Ten gallons of oil couldn't keep our lamps a-shine tonight."

"Okay, Mama."

Olus lit a candle.

The dim candlelight and the scream of the wind made Clarinda uneasy. One of these nights the wind's a-gonna blow this shack to Kingdom Come, she thought. She rose to her feet."Mary Ann, pull Mandy's bed out fer me." Mary Ann put the checkerboard aside, knelt by her mother's bed and pulled a little trundle bed from underneath it. Clarinda lowered Mandy into it and tucked her in.

The boys put their instruments away. Olus scooped Claude up in his arms and carried him to his bed. He helped Claude undress down to his long johns, and settled him in for the night.

"Can I git ye anything?"

"No, I'm okay."

Olus dashed across the room to the bed he shared with Tom. All the boys slept two and three to the bed, except Claude. His withered hip was too sensitive from surgeries to share a bed with a brother. The adjoining bedroom contained two beds. Henry and Lee slept together, and Billy Dan and Howard and little Andy slept in the other. Mary Ann slept in a hall situated across the front of the cabin. Clarinda and Mandy slept in the settin room.

Clarinda bundled the little ones off to bed. Returning to the settin room, she eyed the stovepipe. A square space of ceiling had been sawn out to prevent the planks from touching the pipe. Previously, a piece of tin filled the space, but the hot tin scorched the planks so it was removed. After closing the stove dampers, she slid her hands along the wall behind the stove. The hot yellow pine boards would cool down as the fire burned low. She took a flat iron from the stovetop, wrapped it in an old flannel shirt and hurried to Claude's bed. She slipped it under the covers at his feet."Claude, do ye need another quilt?"

"Yeah, I believe I do."

She chose the thickest quilt from a stack in the corner and added it to the five that covered him.

"Thanks, that arn is already a-gitten my bed warm."

"Wake me if ye git cold an' I'll put another'n to yer feet." She reached down and caressed his head, smoothing the hair from his brow.

"Don't worry 'bout me, Mama. I'll let ye know if I need anything."

"See that ye do, son." But she knew that he wouldn't. She remembered Doc Butler tellin her that Claude could endure more pain than most people.

She returned to the settin room and wound the clock. It seemed later than eight o'clock. She snuffed the candle, undressed in haste, and slipped between icy-cold sheets topped with layers of quilts. Curling into a ball on the straw-tick, she shivered in her flour sack petticoat. Warm flannel nightwear for the family was beyond her means, but homemade quilts kept everybody warm—after the body warmed the bed. The heavy supper made her drowsy and despite the noise of the storm, she fell asleep within minutes.

While the household slept, the storm unleashed its wrath. A rebel wind barreled down Levi's Mountain. It exploded at the foot—rolling and twisting it changed course and whirled north into the mouth of Lonesome Hollow. It went on the draw, the further the faster, throwing snow and howling like a hellhound in the dead of night.

Olus awoke to a deafening roar and sat up, but dropped to his pillow and dozed off again. The wind struck. The old ramshackle cabin breathed deep, drawing in jets of snow through every chink. Walls trembled—rafters cracked. It heaved out—the stovepipe flew in a shower of sparks. Three inches beneath the roof, the decapitated stovepipe wobbled as wind-driven snow whooshed down and sizzled in dancing droplets on the hot stove top.

An hour later, the edge of the stovepipe hole was aglow and shooting sparks. Little tongues of flame sprang forth, leapfrogging across the roof, devouring shingles and licking the eaves!

Clarinda tossed and turned in her sleep. Suddenly she cried out, "Rufus don't leave us!" Bolting up in bed, she stared at the window. All outdoors had an eerie glow that lit the room. The sun's up, she thought. She grabbed the clock—ten minutes past one o'clock in the morning! Hearing a sound like sheets flapping in the wind, she looked up and saw sparks falling around the stovepipe where it entered the ceiling. She sprang to the floor."Fire! Git up, younguns! The house is afire! Oh, God, help us!"

Within minutes, every soul in the cabin except the four little ones was awake and scrambling. Olus and Tom, pulling up their britches whilst they ran for the door, shinnied up the porch post and began yanking the burning shingles from the roof.

As fast as she could move, Clarinda wrapped her four little ones in quilts and carried them two at a time to the porch bench. Their screams joined the howl of the wind. The bitter cold bit into them and they cried even louder. Andy and Mandy wiggled from their covers and clung to her for dear life, but she pried their fingers loose and dashed inside for Claude. She met him making his way to the porch on crutches. Snatching up an armload of quilts she raced outside again and wrapped them all up tight.

Mary Ann and ten-year-old Lee ran for the spring with buckets banging. They found the path blocked by a snowdrift ten feet high! Lee cried out, "Mary Ann, I'm freezin to death!"

"Come, this a-way. Foller me!" She turned and squinted into the blinding snow—he wasn't there. She opened her mouth to call his name—the wind sucked the air from her lungs. Stumbling sideways she disappeared in a whiteout.

Lee fell forward into the icy spring. He thrashed about, yelling. Mary Ann found him soaked to the skin—teeth chattering—stupefied with cold. She removed her coat and wrapped it around him. The wind shot through her flimsy cotton dress straight to her bones."Uh-uh-uh," she gasped, and tried to get inside the coat, too. They heard a roar like two locomotives coming from opposite directions—east and west! It swallowed them up. Their clattering water buckets tumbled up the snowy sedge field. When the fury passed, Mary Ann struggled to her feet and pulled Lee upright."Git behind me and hang on. We'll make it. Don't cry." She set her eyes on the blazing rooftop, leaned into the wind and they slogged toward it.

Flaming torches arched into the whirling blackness as the boys hurled the burning shingles. Olus yelled over the roar of the wind, "Hey! Give us some snow up here!"

"Take keer of the little ones, Claude," Clarinda shouted, and leaped into the yard.

A large tub hung on the wall outside the kitchen door. She wrenched it free and ran behind the cabin where the edge of the roof hung low. She found Henry throwing snow on the roof with a dish pan.

"Drop that pan an' help me!"

A huge snowdrift covered the kitchen window. They stomped it down, using it as a means to reach Olus with the tub. The force of the wind drove him to his knees. He crawled, dragging the tub of snow to the flames."My hand's numb! I cain't feel a thing! Look out!"

The tub shot off the roof like a bullet, grazing Henry's shoulder and landing at his feet with a thud. His guardian angel was watching over him that night.

Clarinda froze in her tracks as Tom—a human torch—skidded down the roof. He fell backward and landed in the yard with a muffled thump. She grabbed the dish pan and in one swoop, covered him with snow. He came up sputtering, "Good Lord, Mama, don't kill me." A few minutes later, he was back on the roof, pulling shingles with all his might.

With clenched teeth, eyes and noses streaming, Clarinda and Henry kept filling the tub till a shout from the rooftop proclaimed the fire out. Exhausted, they slumped to their knees. Mary Ann and Lee shivered and whimpered under the quilts with the little ones. Claude stood off to the side, leaning on his crutches, sheltering a sputtering lantern with his quilt.

Olus and Tom jumped from the roof, scooped the little ones up in their arms and carried them inside. The rest followed. The dish pan slipped from Clarinda's hands as she reeled against the porch post."Thank ye, Lord, fer bringin us through this awful time," she whispered, and sank to the floor.

Mary Ann poked her head out the door."Mama, are you all right?"

"I'll be there soon'es I rest a spell."

Five minutes later, she gathered her strength and regained her feet. She picked the dish pan up, scooped it full of snow and carried it to the settin room. As she raised the stove lid Mary Ann cried out, "Mama, what are you doin?"

"We cain't have a fire till the stovepipe's fixed."

A jet of steam and ash shot upward as the snow struck the fire. Mary Ann swatted the ashy cloud with a corner of the blanket she'd wrapped around herself."Look at the sut! Here we stand nearly froze to death and you dump snow in the stove. Couldn't you leave a few live coals?"

"No. Yer brothers are hurt. They cain't fight no more fire tonight."

Clarinda scraped the last icy remnants from the pan and threw it in the stove. Another pouf of ashes arose.

"Mama... ," Mary Ann whined.

Lee stood shivering by the stove, his teeth chattering and his lips blue.

Clarinda filled a hot water bottle from the large teakettle on the stove."Henry, help Lee out of his clothes and git 'im into some long underwear. Git 'im in bed as fast as ye can and put this to his feet." She placed the towel wrapped bottle in his hands with care.

Mary Ann joined the little ones on the couch where they sat peeping from their quilts like nestling birds.

"Is the farr out, Mary Ann?" Little Howard asked, rubbing his teary eyes.

She tousled his light brown wavy hair."Yes, the farr is out."

Tom and Olus had burns—their scorched clothes and shoes still smoked. Tom walked the floor, swinging his arms back and forth to ease the pain in his hands. Suddenly he stopped, leaned forward and peeped in Olus' face.

"What're you gawkin at me fer?"

"Well, brother, I doubt if you'll be makin eyes at the girls fer awhile."

"Why'd ye say that?"

"Yore eyelashes are singed off."

Olus rushed to the looking glass and held the lantern near his face. The long curly eyelashes that lapped into brows and framed his gorgeous blue eyes were frizzled stubs. He flinched."I'll be damned! I look like a carnival freak. I'm ruint—plumb ruint!"

"Bridle yer tongue, son."

"Will they grow back, Mama?"

"Shore they will."

Tom laughed in spite of his pain."Ye know somethin, Olus? You're a sissy. Did ye git yore bloomers singed too?"

"Keep it up, brother. I'll shell yer teeth like corn."

"All right, younguns, this ain't the time to commence fussin," Clarinda said, pouring hot water from the teakettle into a pan. She stepped outside and returned with more snow which she dropped in the pan by the handful. When the water was lukewarm, she stirred in a lump of baking soda and knelt at Olus' feet. He clenched his teeth and trembled and tears of pain spilled over his stubby eyelashes as she rendered aid. She reached up and touched his cheek."Hang on, son—this'll hep ye."

The wonderful herbal fragrance of balsam poplar filled the room as she applied her homemade balm of Gilead salve and bandaged their burns with strips of clean white flour sack. And thank God for the salve this night. Its comfort took away the scent of burned clothes and shingles and eased their pain. Olus held up a bandaged foot for everyone to see."Well, don't reckon I'll be a-hoofin to Barkin Creek any time soon."

Little Howard took his thumb from his mouth."What's a Barkin Creek?"

Mary Ann laughed and tickled his feet."It's a place, Howard, an' I betcha one of these days you'll be a-hoofin there, too."

"It ain't Barkin," Mandy argued, "its Sparkin."

"N-n-no, it's Fahtin Cuh-Creek," Andy said.

Mary Ann tickled his ribs."Why you little rascal, I'm a-gonna warsh yore mouth out with soap."

He kicked and squealed.

"Hush." Billy Dan gouged him with an elbow.

"M-M-Mama, make Billy Dan stop!"

"Fer heaven's sake, Mary Ann, git 'em all riled up and we'll never git 'em in bed agin."

When Clarinda was satisfied that the fire was completely out and that further flare-ups were unlikely, she and Mary Ann bundled the little ones off to bed again. After she'd put the rooms back in some semblance of order and checked on the children one more time, she trudged to her own bed, exhausted.

What a long night it had been. Would this night and its troubles ever end? They had been frozen, burned and driven to the limit of their endurance, but thank God they were all alive. The good Lord willing, she'd get her family out of Lonesome Hollow before another winter set in.

Five

Clarinda stretched her weary body out on the straw mattress and closed her eyes, but troubling thoughts kept slumber at bay. The image of Tom falling from the roof with his clothes ablaze flashed through her mind. She forced her thoughts to something pleasant, lest she sink into despair. She pictured her spring garden, but the wind wailed around the cabin like a lost child crying for its mother and the image vanished. Her hand trembled as she reached out in the darkness and took her Bible from the bedside table. The feel of it in her hands was comforting and a verse of Scripture came to mind. "Come unto me, all ye that labour and are heavy laden, and I will give you rest." (Matt 11:28). She prayed softly and the storm in her soul passed over.

Mandy awoke and heard her mother praying. "What's a-matter, Mama? Why're you cryin?"

"Oh ... Mama's not cryin now. Mama's fine." She laid her Bible on the table, reached over the edge of the bed and gave Mandy a reassuring pat in her trundle bed.

"Is the house gonna fall down, Mama?"

"Are you afeared?"

"Uh-huh."

She turned the covers back. "Come, you can—"

Mandy scrambled into Mama's bed.

"I'll swannie, youngun, yore feet's colder'n ice."

"Is the house gonna fall down?"

"No, honey."

"Promise?"

"I promise."

"Are you goin to heaven like Papa did?"

She pondered the question for a brief moment. "Mandy, you mustn't worry. I'm not a-goin anywhere. I havta take keer of my sweet babes." She hugged her child close and Mandy stopped shivering.

41

From the darkness a quivery voice called, "M-Mama, Billy Dan pushed me outta the b-bed."

She turned the covers back again."Come here, son. Hurry, it's cold!"

Little Andy ran across the room and jumped into her bed, leaving his footprints in the snow that had blown through cracks in the walls.

Mandy sat up in bed, leaned over her mother and pinched Andy."I'm a-sleepin on Mama's best arm."

"N-no ye ain't. This'ns the b-best." He reached out and pinched her back.

She squalled.

Clarinda gave them a gentle shake."Fer goodness sake, don't fight."

The twins settled down and fell asleep. The wind howled on and snow sifted down on their covers from the hole in the roof, but they slept warm.

Clarinda closed her eyes and her mind wandered back to the dream she was having before the fire. It was surely heaven sent to warn her of encroaching peril. In her dream she was out by the branch, scrubbing overalls on the washboard. A brisk breeze stirred the maple leaves overhead and flapped laundry on the clothesline. Along the branch, ruby-throated hummingbirds hovered around scarlet bee-balm flowers.

She straightened up from the washboard and rubbed her aching back. Pulling a clean rag from her apron pocket, she dabbed at a sore on her hand. The buckle on a pair of overalls had unroofed a scab. Homemade Red Devil lye soap and the washboard kept her hands sore, but she paid it no mind. Turning to stoke the fire under the black three-legged wash kettle she saw Rufus climbing the hill behind the cabin. He was going to work. She called out, "Rufus! Where's yer dinner bucket? Wait! I'll fetch it to ye."

He stopped, and slowly turned to face her."*I'm not goin to the sawmill today, I'm a-goin home. The Lord has called me home.*" He beckoned..."*Come with me.*"

She took a step forward and scolded him."A-goin home? You shorely don't think the Lord would call ye home when yore work on earth ain't done. Fer heaven's sake, Rufus, consider the younguns. They'll be fatherless if ye go."

He gazed at her for a long moment with the saddest expression on his face.

She held her breath, anticipating his change of mind, but she sensed something beyond his control pulling him away. She cried out his name as he turned and faded into the sedge field. Then she awoke to the fire.

Her dream, so clear and heartrending had left her with a lonesome feeling. This very night she had come close to losing everything—not only her meager possessions, but her precious children whom God had so generously given her and Rufus. Memories of her life with him occupied her mind until she dozed off in exhausted slumber.

Suddenly her eyes flew wide open. The sound of a dying wind moaned around the field-stone chimney. Andy and Mandy still slept in her arms. She eased them onto their pillows and rubbed the tingly feeling from her hands. Must be nigh four o'clock in the mornin, she thought. She turned on her side, rustling the straw-tick and closed her eyes.

Rap... rap... rap. Her eyes flew open again. She raised her head from the pillow and listened. Where did that noise come from? She turned onto her back and rose to her elbows. Rap-rap-rap, the sound came from the chimney corner—only louder this time. Her eyes probed the darkness around the disused fireplace. Someone or something was there, watching her. She heard the corner closet door squeak on its hinges. She kept matches and extra lamps there on the top shelf, out of the children's reach."Olus... Tom... is that you?"

Silence...

Rap-rap-rap. She held her breath as fear laid an icy hand around her throat. Was it the Death Angel again? Whom would he call this time in that tomb-like voice? Would it be Claude? Maybe he would call her name. She exhaled in shallow puffs and sent up a silent prayer. Lord, hep us!

Squeak... squeak... went her rocking chair.

She took a deep breath and called out in a cracked voice, "Rufus, are you here?"

The wind whistled in the chimney.

She stiffened in terror as the bedcovers moved—someone was tucking them in! Mandy stirred and whimpered in her sleep. Clarinda's fear turned to righteous anger. What being, be it mortal or spirit, would try to scare a widow and her little ones? As she gathered herself for a leap to the floor, a gentle hand touched her forehead and smoothed the hair from her brow. *Rufus!* She reached up to touch him, but his spirit had moved away.

Seconds later, the twang of an old time banjo rang out from the front porch. Clarinda settled down and her smile was warm as sunshine. She lay there and listened to her favorite song.

Git along home, oh Sindy, Sindy,
Git along home, oh Sindy, Sindy,
Git along home, oh Sindy Sindy,
Git along down home.

She wondered if the boys heard it. She'd tell them about it at break-fast—but she changed her mind. She had a feeling that it was meant for her ears only and that he was still there...

I did not leave the day I left,
I've been here all along.
You'll see me in our children's eyes,
You'll hear me in their songs.
I'll sing you through your autumn years,
And as you slumber, dear,
I'll occupy your sweetest dreams —
You'll know that I am near.
And when you walk death's gloomy vale,
Though it be dark as night —
Fear not; I'll take your hand and we
Will run toward the light.
We'll climb that winding mountain path
To where we met, and then,
I'll sweep you up and we shall go
A-dancing on the wind.

Six

Clarinda turned the covers back and set her bare feet on the cold floor. She dressed in haste and hurried to the kitchen. The big Home Comfort cookstove stood in the corner. It would have to serve double duty till the stovepipe for the heater in the settin room could be fixed. She raised the lid of the firebox, dropped a handful of pinecones on the grate and struck a match. The pinecones flamed up instantly, rosin sizzled, and fresh mountain air carried their fragrance from room to room. A few added sticks of locust to the firebox completed the task. While the cookstove heated, she stepped outdoors for a peek at the roof and a trip to the cellar. Her eyes widened. A gaping hole in the center of the roof showed charred rafters and the decapitated stovepipe."I'm a-gitten my younguns away from here fore we all perish," she muttered.

With plans in mind she descended the steep cellar steps underneath the cabin. Hundreds of jars of vegetables were arranged on shelves that lined the cellar walls on three sides. Corn, beans, peas, beets, tomatoes, pumpkin and squash were abundant. A smaller section contained jars of apple and pumpkin butter, berry jellies and preserves. Potatoes and rutabagas filled a bin at the base of the back wall. To the left of the cellar door, four wide shelves had held quart jars of sausage, tenderloin, and half-gallon cans of pork lard. But only a few jars of sausage and pork lard remained.

The sausage would last for a couple of weeks. After that, an occasional chicken would have to suffice, provided any chickens survived the storm. Mostly, chickens were a staple commodity for barter. Fat hens and eggs kept flour and pinto beans in the cupboard. The family loved squirrel, but they hibernated during winter. Due to the voracious appetites of owls, rabbits were scarce during the winter months. There had been no deer or wild turkeys in the area since the early settlers killed them off.

Clarinda took a jar of sausage and a half-gallon of wild blackberries from the shelf and hurried up the steps. She fastened the door securely against the weather and returned to the kitchen. The teakettle danced a jig on the stovetop. Frost slid down the window pane as she washed and dried her

45

hands. Soon she pulled a large pan of fluffy biscuits to the oven door. She loved making bread and was a good old-fashioned cook.

The aroma of frying sausage, cream gravy and hot berry jam, drew everyone to the kitchen like a magnet. Claude dressed himself and came to the table on his cane. Olus and Tom came limping. Olus tried to be his jolly-old-self, but gave it up and sat down.

Claude stood on one foot and offered his cane."Do ye want a-borry this, brother?"

Olus grinned."By gosh, if I'd a-fell through the roof last night, I'd be a-needin a wheelcheer."

Clarinda carried a large bowl of steaming gravy to the table."I'll change yer bandages after breakfast, younguns."

Mary Ann filled the wash pan with warm water and chased Andy and Mandy around the kitchen."Come 'ere ye little stinkers. You ain't goin to the table till yer hands are washed."

Mandy stopped, and raised her hands for her big sister's inspection. "Looky... my hands is clean."

"No, they ain't, little Missy. I saw you a-pickin yer nose not more'n five minutes ago."

Mandy stamped her foot and made a face."You ain't my boss."

Mary Ann picked her up like a sack of potatoes and carried her kicking and squalling to the wash pan. When it was all over, Mandy's hands were clean and her face too, except for a few teardrops smeared on her cheeks. She ran to Olus for comfort. He sheltered her in the crook of his arm."What's wrong, Pug?"

"Mary Ann's mean to me."

Olus glared at Mary Ann."You stop bein mean to her."

Mary Ann glared back."Fer the love of Pete, you have spoiled that youngun rotten—Andy too."

When all the children had been fed, Clarinda removed the bandages from the boys' hands and feet. Olus had a large blister on the ball of his right foot. Both boys had singed hair and blistered hands. Clarinda sterilized a needle by holding it in candle flame. She pierced the blisters and drained them.

Olus closed his eyes and sighed."Ahh ... that feels better."

Clarinda applied more balm of Gilead salve and fresh bandages. The boys declared themselves in top notch shape again.

"Keep them bandages dry, younguns. You'll heal quicker."

Before the boys left the table, Clarinda revealed her plans."Younguns, we've got to git outta Lonesome Hollar. And the only way we can git out, is to cut some timber off that property on Levi's Mountain and build a house."

Claude looked surprised."I thought you sold that land to Uncle Alexander?"

"I did. But I'm still payin the tax on it. He said I could use it. I'm a-goin to buy it back someday... if I ever git the money."

Claude cleared his throat and caught her eye with a solemn gaze."Mama, did you sell yore inheritance to help Papa pay my hospital bill?"

Silence... All eyes turned to Clarinda. She looked down and brushed crumbs from the daisy-flowered tablecloth with the palm of her hand. She raised her eyes and looked toward the yellow-curtained kitchen window. She could see the frosty top of Levi's Mountain glistening in the first rays of morning sun."Son, it was a blessin that I had that land to sell. I used the money to bcnefit the whole family."

Olus and Tom exchanged knowing glances. They had the feeling that every dime of the land money went to the hospital bill. But they knew that their mother did what she had to do.

Claude sighed."Well, I'm just glad you didn't sell it because a-me."

Clarinda continued, "We'll cut enough timber to build the house and a few trees extra to pay the sawmill. I'll write Alexander and ast 'im if it's all right."

Tom leaned forward."Mama, cuttin enough timber to build a house will be a mighty hard job."

Olus nodded in agreement."Yeah ... we'd need a big team of horses, loggin chains, and a cant hook to turn logs—and we ain't got 'em."

Clarinda sipped her coffee."I know it'll be hard work, but we havta try. I'll git one of the older boys to help us. I've worried with this ol' cabin fer years. I'm tard a-workin in the fields to pay the rent. I can use that time to put up canned stuff fer winter."

Olus snapped his fingers."Hey, I know how we'll git that house. Me an' Tom are gonna work at Mr. Colliday's sawmill this spring. We can take our wages in lumber."

"Yeah ... Mr. Colliday is a mighty fine feller. I know we could cut a deal with him." Tom shoved the lock of heavy hair from his forehead and leaned back in his ladder-back chair.

Clarinda studied on it for a moment."Are ye shore?"

"Yeah."

"All right. That's what we'll do."

Immediately, the boys began poking fun at each other."Olus, you look plumb skeery in daylight... like somethin from Star Springs."

Shifting his weight in his chair, Olus swiveled around and laid a frosty gaze on his snickering brother."So ye think I look skeery, huh?"

Tom dropped his head and his shoulders shook with suppressed laughter."Claude... don't he look spooky?"

Claude chuckled."Hey, I ain't gitten mixed up in yer arguments."

Olus leaned over and shoved a bandaged fist under Tom's nose."One more squeak outta you, and—"

"And what?"

"That little buck-toothed girlfriend of yores won't know ye next Saturday night."

Tom's grin withered."Shut yer mouth, she looks better'n that big bureau you're a-datin."

Clarinda hid a smile behind her hand."Younguns, stop yer foolishness fore ye end up in a fuss."

The boys were so frolicsome it was hard to keep a straight face. Her mouth turned up at the corners and the ever present shadows around her eyes faded. Even Claude brightened up and joined in their joking."If ye ast me, both of them girls is uglier'n mud."

Clarinda looked at the two boys and her heart swelled with pride. Olus was the spittin image of Rufus, same dazzling smile, same big blue eyes— and did he ever know how to charm the girls with them! She found it difficult to scold him when he flashed his Papa's grin and turned on the charm. Indeed, Olus was a handsome young man with winsome ways. He loved life and fun and frolic. When all the family got together and the boys played their games of horse shoe, boxing, and wrestling, Olus always won. But she wished he wasn't such a dare-devil. Even as a small boy, she'd seen him go up the big blackheart cherry tree like a cat. When he poked his head out from the topmost branches, she'd yell, "Hey, little Rufus, git yoreself down from 'ere."

Tom resembled her, and his stature, six-feet-two and still growing, came from her maternal grandfather who was reported to be nearly seven-feet tall. Tom's jet black hair, green eyes and chiseled features were handsome for certain. He carried himself with pride and confidence, but he was more reserved in manner than Olus.

Clarinda never complimented the boys on their looks because she didn't want them to grow up vain and arrogant. When someone told her that she had some mighty handsome boys, her face lit up. She'd fold her arms and slip a hand to her chin and hide her smile, but the light in her eyes could not be concealed."Aw... they look fairly common," she'd always say.

She couldn't stand vanity."Yore character is what counts. If ye lose yer character you're ruint... plumb ruint. If ye do the right thing and keep yer nose outta other people's business you'll save yoreself a peck a-trouble." But she never failed to tell her boys how proud she was of their accomplishments and how she appreciated their sacrifices.

And now, the boys must help their mother get the family out of Lonesome Hollow. With Clarinda's determination they'd be moving out of their old ramshackle cabin before the leaves turned in September.

Suddenly, Olus grew very serious, "Mama, there's just one hitch in yore plan."

"And what's that?"

"Who's gonna build our mansion?"

"We are. The good Lord willin, the saws will be a-singin on Levi's Mountain, come spring."

Seven

Lonesome Hollow • 1940

Wildflowers

From hollow, hill, and rugged slope
They rise from leafy beds,
And bloom in rainbow-colored hues
Some nod their dappled heads.
Mayapples lift their emerald hats
Like gallant little skippers,
An orchid waltzing with the breeze
Shakes dewdrops from her slippers.
Honeysuckles are dressing up
In flaming tangerine,
Minty catnip scents the air
Along the rushing stream.
Honeybees are buzzing around
A lofty sourwood tree,
Crimson berries nestle amidst
The leaves of mountain tea.
Majestic pines are whispering
'Cause wrens are nesting there,
The dogwood trees are snowy white
And God is everywhere!

*T*he robins whirled into Lonesome Hollow on the wings of a fickle March wind. Wild brooks broke their icy chains and tumbled from granite heights, flinging crystal swords against boulders and rocks. Evergreen fern quaked and trembled where the waterfalls roared. Creeks danced the two-step. Speckled trout leaped. Larks sang harmony in the budding cherry tree near Clarinda's cabin door. It was springtime in the mountains.

This Saturday morning found Clarinda with basket in hand and Andy and Mandy at her heels. Wild creasy greens grew in her garden plot, and she looked forward to having a delicious bowlful on the supper table. She and the older children loved them, but the little ones hadn't acquired a taste for the popular dish as yet. Andy tugged at her apron strings."Mama, d-do we havta eat them n-nasty greens?"

Clarinda paused to tie her apron."They ain't nasty, son, they're clean and good fer ye."

Mandy made a face."They smell like cow fritters."

"Ewee..." they said in unison.

Clarinda smiled. Greens weren't the only thing that occupied her thoughts. Come Monday, Olus and Tom would start work at the sawmill. Their employer, Mr. Colliday, had agreed to pay their wages in lumber for the new house. The boys, eager to get the new house started, cut two huge oaks on Levi's Mountain. Mr. Colliday let them use his team to pull the logs down to his mill. The oaks would be sawn into foundation sills. By the last of April they'd be ready to start construction.

Clarinda and the twins returned to the cabin and found that Mary Ann had a visitor. Cousin Charlotty had stopped by on her way to the store. Of course, Mary Ann wanted to go with her.

Clarinda agreed."Ketch two fat hens and carry 'em to the store. We need a few things, too."

Mary Ann groaned."I'd like to have a nickel fer every chicken I've packed to the store. I'd be rich."

Charlotty giggled."Well, what about me? I havta carry a poke of aiggs."

"Charlotty, aiggs don't peck and poop. Come with me, you havta help me ketch 'em."

Charlotty was fourteen—a year older than Mary Ann, but she wasn't as tall. Mary Ann stood five-feet-eight inches. She had beautiful honey-colored hair and big blue eyes like her Papa Rufus. Charlotty was pretty, too, with dark brown curly hair and sparkling brown eyes. They were as close as sisters.

The path to the store led through a hillside pasture. A barbed wire fence reinforced with heavy woven wire divided the field vertically. The grazing cows paid no attention to people passing through, but an ill-tempered Hereford bull with a head as big as a washtub, kept the turf pawed up along the fence. He'd gouged out big holes in the woven wire and put many a person on the run.

Naughty boys full of derring-do made matters worse. If the bull wasn't in sight, they'd climb over the fence and venture out into his territory. They'd mimic his high-pitched bawl and yell, "Hey! Bugle, where y'at?" In a hollow nearby, Ol' Bugle would toot his horn. Within seconds he'd pop up on the hilltop. The bravest boys waited till he kicked the clouds then they'd yell, "Whaa-hoo!" and skedaddle.

Mary Ann and Charlotty moved through the field talking in whispers, keeping a keen eye out for him. The cows looked at them with ho-hum expressions and returned to their grazing. The girls breathed a sigh of relief when they reached the locked steel gate. They scampered to safety and continued their journey. The path led into the woods again.

"Mary Ann, le's go see the new schoolhouse. We'll stop at the store on the way home."

"Might as well, but what am I a-gonna do with these dern chickens?"

They pondered the problem. Mary Ann's face lit up, "Hey, help me tie 'em to a tree. We can pick 'em up later."

Charlotty frowned."Shewt, we ain't got no string to tie 'em with."

Mary Ann handed her chickens to Charlotty. Reaching down she grasped her skirt and hiked it up slightly. She started unraveling the hem of her petticoat.

"What the heck are you a-doin?"

"I'm a-gonna tear some strings off this petticoat."

"Fer goodness sake, you'll ruin the purty lace on it."

Turning her back to Charlotty, she flipped her circle-tailed skirt over her shoulder blades."Would you worry 'bout tearin up a petticoat like this one?" The image of a beady-eyed black hog's head stared at Charlotty. Underneath the picture, a large caption read, Hog Chop 100 lbs. net wt.

Charlotty doubled over laughing.

"Mama boiled this petticoat and scrubbed it with Red Devil lye soap and that hog's pic'cher still wouldn't budge."

Charlotty whooped.

"What turned yore tickle box over? I saw two pair of yore bloomers on the clothes line. Both pair had a red hen and chicks stamped on 'em."

"Yeah... I know it," Charlotty said with a wistful sigh."I hate wearin scratch feed bloomers."

The girls laughed and made fun of their own hard luck."If the wind happened to blow up my skirt in a crowd, I'd be disgraced fer life," said Mary Ann.

Charlotty giggled."Them purty dresses we made from that Dan River cloth won't benefit us a bit if word gits out that we're wearin barnyard underwear."

Mary Ann tugged at her petticoat with a grimace."Dang, this chop sack is tough as whet-leather."

"Well, hurry and rip it. I'm 'bout to drop these dern hens."

Finally, the cloth gave way with a zip. Mary Ann draped the first string over her shoulder. Jutting out her lower jaw she pinched her nostrils together and grunted like a pig, "umphf-umphf. That's what I'd hear from the boys at school if they 'as to git a glimpse of this petticoat."

Charlotty cackled.

She gave Charlotty a solemn look of mock concern."Are you all right? I believe ye laid a aigg that time." When she ripped the last string, the petticoat's jagged hemline reached her waist. The hog picture had been reduced to a tuft of bristle and two pointy ears. It appeared to be peeping from the rump of her bloomers.

Charlotty laughed herself into a side-stitch.

Mary Ann smoothed the goldy hair from her damp forehead and put her skirt down."Whew! That was hard work."

Still laughing, the girls tied the chicken's feet and tethered them to a sapling with petticoat strings tied end to end. The hens cut a ruckus, but finally settled down. Stooping over, Mary Ann patted the hens on the head."Stay put sweet biddies. Take a snooze or somethin. We'll be back soon." The Rhode Island Red gave her hand a vicious peck that brought the blood. Mary Ann snatched the hen up by the neck, and nose to beak, cursed her out."Dang you, I hope a fox yanks ever feather outta yore hind end while we're gone."

Charlotty settled her poke of eggs against a mossy tree trunk."They'll be okay there, won't they?"

"Why shore. Le's go."

The girls hurried up the rutted dirt road toward the new school. Holstein dairy cows grazed in the field on their left, and farmers turned sod in the rich bottomland on their right. Those who owned the beautiful farms in the valley had pretty white houses, and their children went off to college. With few exceptions, folk who settled on the high ridges and mountain slopes lived a hardscrabble life. Their boys labored and sweated on the valley farms. Eight hours in the hayfield would fetch a youth four bits. Enough for a Coca-Cola, a bag of popcorn, and a movie ticket on Saturday night—if he was lucky enough to catch a ride to town.

Mary Ann and Charlotty had received a double portion of pride and gumption to make their way in this world. As they came around the next bend, they stopped and stared at the most beautiful building they'd ever laid eyes on. It stood on a knoll, completely surrounded by deep green bottomland and verdant pastures. The Work

Projects Administration, a New Deal agency created by Franklin Delano Roosevelt's presidential order, had constructed it from native stone. It would provide elementary and high school education for a five-school consolidation. Of course, most of the five schools had only one classroom. Anyway, it was the biggest school the girls had ever seen.

"Oh ... ain't it purty?" they said in one voice.

"I wisht we could peep in the winders," Charlotty said.

Mary Ann pointed to a farmer turning sod in the meadow."It's too chaincy. He's keepin a sharp eye on the school grounds."

"Yeah, he'd sic the Tin Badge Dep'ity on us," Charlotty said with a giggle.

The Tin Badge Deputy was a new neighbor in the community who went to the county seat and got himself deputized. With a shiny badge on his overall bib he puffed out his broad chest and bragged, 'Now, I've got the 'thority tuh slap you hell-raisers behind bars. I'll put a stop to yore pranks around the churchyard at night. '

During protracted meeting, the snickering mountain boys drove him crazy. They'd hide amongst the cars and trucks and let air out of tires. When they heard his heavy footsteps on the gravel they'd shout, "Here comes the Tin Badge Dep'ity. Le's skedaddle!"

Mary Ann laughed."Yeah, he promised Henry a badge if he'd help chase the rebel rousers down, but Henry wasn't interested."

"I'd hep 'im chase down the pranksters fer enough money to buy five pair a-shoes. It'll take a lot of shoe leather to git us through school next winter," Charlotty said.

Mary Ann pondered that for a moment."Yeah ... it's twice't as far to this school as it is to the old 'un on the ridge. And no little fairy's gonna wave a magic wand and leave five pair a-saddle oxfords under our bed. We'll havta grabble 'em out in the woods."

"Grabble 'em out in the woods?"

"Yeah, grabble, grub, dig yarbs... whatever ye want a-call it."

"Mary Ann... they ain't yarbs. They are called, herbs."

"I knowed that, Miss Hoity Toity."

Charlotty poked her lightly in the shoulder."Aw, hush." Then raising one foot, she showed Mary Ann the quarter-sized hole in the sole of her shoe."Maybe we'll git lucky and find some ginsang. My uncle dug two pound last year and got a hunderd dollars fer it. He said he dropped a couple of roots in the tea pot and brewed up a heckuva love potion. He swore that he was gorged to the gills with ginsang tea when he married his ugly wife."

The girls snickered.

"Well, I shore hope yore uncle didn't dig all the ginsang. I'd like to dig enough to buy a pair of boots too."

"We better git back to them chickens. No tellin where they're at by this time," Charlotty said.

The girls turned and hurried down the road. When they reached the trees, lo, the hens had vanished — the eggs had disappeared too. They searched the surrounding woods and found nothing, not even a petticoat string. Mary Ann called, "Chick-chick-chickieee..." A woodpecker knocked on a tree nearby.

Charlotty looked worried."How are we gonna git the lamp oil an' stuff?"

"We'll go in debt fer it. I think the store clerk will let us have it. We'll dig *herbs* and pay fer the goods later. I ain't tellin Mama we lost them chickens."

Mr. Hedgeweth, the store clerk, looked surprised when they gave him their grocery list and asked for credit."Why yore brothers was here not more'n thirty minutes ago with a load of chickens. Why didn't they buy the groceries?"

Mary Ann's face turned beet red."Which brothers are ye talkin 'bout?"

"Henry an' Lee." He turned to Charlotty, "And yore brother, Eddie Jack."

"We didn't know they was comin to the store," Charlotty said.

Mary Ann folded and unfolded her arms impatiently."What did they buy?"

He counted the items off on his fingers."Two sacks of Stud tobacco, a dozen bottles of Coca-Cola, and they wiped out the candy counter — just two sticks of peppermint left."

"Yep, that was them all right."

Mr. Hedgeweth reluctantly gave the girls credit. They left the store carrying five pound of sugar, one pound of Arm & Hammer baking soda, twenty-five pound of Bristol Maid flour, a gallon of lamp oil, matches, a spool of thread, and a glass of Dental Sweet snuff. As they climbed the mountain path, they fretted and fumed. The muscles in Mary Ann's jaw worked as she gritted her teeth."Just think, we carried 'em lousy hens nearly to the store and they stole 'em and spent the money on junk. I'm a-gonna break ever bone in Henry's body. I know it was his doin."

Charlotty set her groceries down and climbed over the locked pasture gate."They ain't worth a cuss."

"Triflin, good fer nothin, scamps," Mary Ann added. She muscled their bundles over the gate to Charlotty then climbed over the gate too. They rearranged their load and trudged on.

The noonday sun had grown quite warm for late March, and Charlotty paused to wipe her brow."Do ye reckon Ol' Bugle's close't by?"

"Nah, it's too hot. He's over in the hollar at the waterin hole."

Charlotty's eyes scanned the woods at the edge of the field."I'm afraid of that rascal—he's danger'us—le's hurry."

"Fer the love of Pete, I ain't no pack mule. I'm a-climbin as fast as I can."

Suddenly three high-pitched bawls split the air in rapid succession. The girls froze in their tracks. Ol' Bugle appeared on the hilltop—pawing clumps of turf over his back—slinging slobber. The fence separated the bull from the girls, but it wouldn't hold him if he chose to break through.

Charlotty turned pale as hickory ashes."Lord, have mercy, what a bull! Is that Ol' Bugle?"

"Shore is. He's a lot bigger an' meaner now."

"What're we gonna do?"

Mary Ann took a deep shaky breath."We'll havta fight that sonofagun."

"What?"

She put her foodstuff down. While keeping her eye on the bull, she reached out and tugged at Charlotty's grocery bag."Give me that glass a-snuff."

Charlotty's voice rose like a banjo string stretching for high tune."Snuff? You're gonna fight a bull with ssnuuff?" She took a step backward and hugged her grocery bag."You ain't gitten my Mama's snuff—you're crazier'n a June bug!"

Ol' Bugle lowered his muzzle to the ground—brought forth a loud guttural bellow—and kicked the clouds. He thundered down the hill toward them in a whirlwind of dirt clods.

The girls gasped. Mary Ann pounced on Charlotty."Give me that dern snuff!" Wrestling the bag from Charlotty's arms, she came up with it.

Ol' Bugle charged the fence like a baseball player sliding into home plate, head first. Barbed and woven wire flew—a staple dangled absurdly from his nose ring. With great agility he gathered his powerful shanks, sprang to his hooves and rammed his head through the fence again.

With heart pounding, Mary Ann lunged forward and threw the contents of the glass—aiming for his mean red eyes."Have a dip, dang ye!" His head disappeared in a rusty-brown cloud. What a conniption fit he threw! Two-thousand-pounds of raging bull jarred the ground. Bellowing and snorting he destroyed the fence in fifteen seconds.

The girls clutched their goods tight and ran for dear life. They reached the hilltop gate and flung bundles and themselves over it. Gasping for breath, they turned to look back. Ol' Bugle was on his knees—boring his head in the ground—bellowing like low thunder.

Breathing hard, Charlotty put hands on her hips in a huffy manner."I don't know... what Mama's gonna say. She gits... she gits a headache when she ain't got snuff."

Mary Ann rolled her eyes heavenward."Lord... please excuse this pore girl—and thank ye fer the snuff." She pointed her finger toward the bellowing bull."Look at 'im, Charlotty, that could be us he's a-gorin." He'd attracted a herd of curious cows, but he seemed unaware of their presence. With head against the ground, his hooves tore up turf as he went around in a circle.

"Aw... I know that. I just hate to hear Mama fuss."

"Let 'er fuss. She can trot over the hill and borry a dip of snuff from my Mama."

"She don't like Aint Clarinda's brand."

Mary Ann snorted."Fudge! She'll use it or do without."

"Do ye reckon Ol' Bugle might be blinded?"

"Heck, no. It'd take more'n that. He'll bore 'is head in a waterin hole an' chase somebody else before dark."

They gathered up their supplies and finished the last stretch of their journey. When they arrived at Mary Ann's house, Charlotty stopped for a rest before going home. The girls put the groceries away and flopped down on the couch. Henry and Lee and Eddie Jack sauntered in, sucking on peppermint candy. Henry wore boxing gloves with an extra pair slung over his shoulder.

Mary Ann couldn't hide her anger."Did ye give the little ones any candy?"

"Andy an' Mandy ain't here."

"Where are they?"

"They went with Mama to Aint Etta's."

"Well, did ye give Billy Dan an' Howard any?"

"What's it to you?"

"Shame on ye. How can you walk around here a-eatin' candy and drinkin Coca-Cola and not give yer pore little brothers any?"

"How'd you know we got Coca-Cola?"

"Mr. Hedgeweth told us he sold ye twelve bottles. You stole our chickens—and ye pestered Ol' Bugle too."

Eddie Jack snickered.

Henry tried to keep a straight face."Oh... did he put ye on the trot? Wait till I tell Mama you tied them chickens to a tree."

Mary Ann sprang to her feet."I've got a good mind to—"

"To what? Le's settle it right now." Henry dangled the boxing gloves in her face."Put 'em on or keep yer big mouth shut."

She snatched the gloves. With a blazing eye on Henry, she yanked them on and thrust her hands toward Charlotty."Tie 'em fer me."

"He'll beat the tar outta you," Charlotty whispered as she laced and tied them.

"I don't give a dern. I ain't takin no sass off a-him."

Sibling rivalry had reached its peak. Henry and Mary Ann slugged it out. Henry had the advantage of being a boy, two years older, muscular and quick. Mary Ann stood three inches taller—strong-framed and tough as a pine knot. She could swing an ax and hold her end of a crosscut saw better than Henry.

They spilled into the yard.

Claude and Olus and Tom had gathered on the porch for a music session. Eddie Jack and Charlotty took a seat on the porch steps. Giggling with excitement and sucking noisily on sticks of peppermint, little Howard and Billy Dan joined them.

Henry danced around, shadow boxing and flexing his muscles."You're a-gonna git a bruisin."

Mary Ann didn't respond.

Lee scratched a large circle in the grassless yard with a stick. A rusty cowbell rang out. Ol' Limber sat up on his haunches and gave a half-hearted "aarroof" then flopped down for another snooze. The old Bluetick hound had seen it all a hundred times before.

Lee cupped his hands to his mouth and shouted, "The fite is about to start. Listen to the rules. No buttin, no spittin and no bitin."

Henry leaned over and whispered in his ear, "And no punches below the belt."

Mary Ann heard him and snickered.

His upper lip curled in a sneer."You hit me down 'ere, and I'll pound yore bosom flatter'n a hard times fritter."

"You ain't gonna pound nothin. You'll be a-layin in the butterweeds a-pukin."

"Why would I puke?"

"I'm gonna destroy yer family jewels."

"Oh, yeah?"

"Yeah."

Henry began his fancy footwork the second they stepped inside the circle.

Lee called out, "Foul! You're s'posed to wait till the bell rings!"

Henry continued his nerve-wracking dance. Shoving his chin in Mary Ann's face, he jeered."Hit me. I double dare you to hit me if ye can."

She clenched her teeth and struggled to stay calm—one careless move and she'd be mouse bait.

"Knock 'im out, Mary Ann—keep yer eye on 'im." Lee played coach to perfection.

The older boys kept their musical instruments quiet and watched the fisticuffs closely. Olus' face showed a trace of concern."He might really hurt her."

Tom shook his head."Nah, she can take keer of herself."

All of a sudden, Claude struggled to his feet and slapped his cane aside. Swinging his right fist in a high arch he called out, "Give 'im a right hook, Mary Ann!" His fist struck his left palm with a smack.

Olus and Tom's attention darted to Claude. They reached out, anticipating his fall. Leaning against the porch railing, Claude pummeled the air with jabs, punches and haymakers."Hey, Mary Ann, ye gotta fight mean. Knee 'im in the gr'ine. Chatter 'is teeth with a uppercut!"

Henry bobbed to the left and made a feint to the right. He gave her quick taps that did little damage other than bush up her hair and increase her fury. He was setting her up for the kill—and she knew it. And yet, she stood as if stuck in a puddle of cold molasses, gloves held at bosom level, eyes moving back and forth, watching every move.

He flicked his gloves within a hairbreadth of her face."There's a fly on yore nose and a gnat on yore chin."

She didn't even see the blow coming that snapped her head back and split her lip—blood trickled down her chin.

Olus and Tom jumped to their feet. The bloodshed must be stopped.

"Kick 'im where it hurts, Mary Ann," Claude shouted."Lay 'im out on the coolin board!"

Lee dropped the cowbell and hid his eyes in the crook of his arm."Oh, m'gosh, she's a-gonna git slaughtered."

The clatter of the dropped cowbell distracted Henry for a second—and Mary Ann sprang to life. The image of his smug face sucking on a peppermint stick flashed before her eyes and spurred her on. Bobbing low to the right, she plowed her way upward with teeth gritted in pent-up rage. A left punch to the stomach bent him over—a right uppercut to the chin straightened him up. He tried to backpedal, but a sharp left hook to the temple, followed by a nose-crunching right, took him out.

His knees buckled—he saw stars falling—and going down he escaped the left haymaker that would have floored Max Baer. Unable to check her swing, Mary Ann stumbled over him and fell to the ground with a grunt.

Lee and Eddie Jack grabbed Henry by the ankles and pulled him to a grassy spot. Little Howard and Billy Dan ran to the branch. They returned with an old rusty Jewel lard bucket full of branch water and dumped it on his head. He gasped and sat up. When his world stopped spinning, he rose on wobbly legs.

Mary Ann wore a smug grin."Do ye wanna go another round, huh?" She danced a jig.

Henry glared at her with his one good eye."I'll gits ye fer this! I'll gits ye if it's the last thing I ever do!"

She hooted—her bloody lip throbbed.

Lee rang the cowbell so hard the clapper flew into the butterweeds. He tossed the bell aside and cupped his hands to his mouth."Listen, all you boxin fans, this has been one heckuva match! Mary Ann come out a-sluggin, and tough Henry went down a-blubberin. Mary Ann is champi-on of Lonesome Hollar!" He grabbed her wrist and tried to raise her arm in a victory signal, but she boxed his ears and pumped both fists skyward under her own power.

The fans whooped and hollered. Claude laughed himself into a side-stitch."I knowed she could whup 'im."

Tom tightened a string on his guitar and struck the chord of G."Yeah, and she didn't even havta kick 'im where it hurts."

Claude eased into his chair and took up his guitar. The boys struck up a lively folk tune and Mary Ann trotted around the circle, punching the air to the rhythm of the music.

"Shoulder up your gun and whistle up your dog,
Shoulder up your gun and whistle up your dog,
We're gonna hunt for the old groundhog.
Oh Groundhog!

Here comes Sally with a snicker and a grin,
Here comes Sally with a snicker and a grin,
Got groundhog grease all over her chin.
Oh, Groundhog!"

Little Howard and Billy Dan wiped sticky peppermint fingers on their patched overalls and jumped into the ring. Barefooted, bare-knuckled and eager for a fight, they sparred like Henry and Mary Ann.

Lee dashed to ringside and called out, "Listen, all you boxin fans, it's a doubleheader. Little Howard and Billy Dan are goin at it fist and skull!"

Charlotty pointed toward her homeward path."Look, yonder! Aint Clarinda and the twins are comin."

The yard emptied in seconds.

Clarinda saw it all with one sweep of the eye. The half-erased circle, the rusty lard bucket lying in a wet spot, Mary Ann's swollen lip and Henry holding a bloody washrag to his nose. She took possession of the boxing gloves right away. Accompanied by The Crawdad Song from the front porch, she gave them all a tongue-lashing."What has got into you younguns? Ever time I step over the hill to see my sister a fight breaks out. Ye ought a-be ashamed—fightin and a-scratchin like brutes. I better never heer of this agin!"

"You get a line and I'll get a pole, my honey,
You get a line and I'll get a pole, oh babe,
You get a line and I'll get a pole,
We'll go down to the crawdad hole,
Honey, sugar baby mine."

Clarinda's face remained calm as all the siblings jabbered at once, trying to justify their behavior. When they ran out of steam, a deep frown darkened her face and she raked Henry over the coals."Listen, son, I ain't never raised a thief and I'm not aimin to start now. You go find a sack and git to the woods. You're gonna pull enough mountain tea to pay fer them groceries."

Still holding the bloody washrag to his face, Henry pointed to Eddie Jack and whined through his nose."He was in on it. He gobbled as much candy as any of us. He's gotta help me."

Leaning casually against the door jamb with his thumbs hooked in his front overall pockets, Eddie's dark brown eyes bored into Henry."Don't try to drag me into this."

With his good eye flashing, Henry started to rise from the couch. Clarinda set him down with a slight lift of the hand, "Henry, it ain't yore concern whether he helps or not, that's fer his mother to say. Now git on the move and do as I told ye."

"How will I git the mountain tea to the store? The wheelbarr's broke."

"Fix it."

"It cain't be fixed."

"Tote it."

Henry groaned.

"Wake up Sal you've slept too late, Honey...
Wake up Sal you've slept too late, babe,
Wake up Sal you've slept too late,
This crawdad man done passed your gate,
Honey, sugar baby mine."

The boys pulled mountain tea for two days straight. As they rolled the rickety wheelbarrow down the hillside pasture to the store, they cursed its squeaky wheel in whispers lest Ol' Bugle hear and put them on the trot.

Eight

Levi's Mountain • Late April, 1940

*T*he sun touched the top of Levi's Mountain as Clarinda and fifteen-year-old-Henry stepped into the clearing. She saw and counted twelve apple trees in full-blown beauty. She listened to the drone of bees and the twitter of birds among the branches. Her eyes traveled to a patch of daffodils then on to a stream nearby. Moving to the stream bank, she stooped down and trailed her hand in the crystal flow. Her feet stirred a clump of mountain mint. She picked a sprig and straightened up. Holding the peppermint to her nose she closed her eyes and drew in its essence."My mother planted these fl'ares and mint when I 'as a little girl, Henry. She called the fl'ares Easter lilies because they bloom around the time when Jesus rose from the tomb. I'm home, Henry. This place shall be my home agin."

Henry turned and looked at her in surprise."You've lived here before?"

"Lawzy, yes. My daddy bought this land by gover'ment grant. He paid twelve cents a acre fer it." She raised her right hand and pointed toward the mountaintop."The tract stretches plumb to the Tennessee line. My dad was yore Gran'paw Enoch, but he named this land Levi's Mountain in mem'ry of his father."

She walked to a pile of rock in the center of the clearing."Our log house stood here and these rocks was the chimney." Clarinda looked at Henry with a wistful expression on her face."I was nine-year-old when Dad left us. Mother and us younguns lived here alone till her parents got old and feeble. It was hard on her a-walkin a mile ever day back and forth to Chestnut Grove to take keer of 'em. Finally, she give it up and we moved in with 'em."

"Who moved here, after y'all left?"

"My sister, Mina and her husband lived here till the house burnt down. I inherited the land when Mother died."

"How comes Uncle Alexander owns it now?"

"I sold it to 'im, but I'm gonna buy it back some a-these days."

"Where did Gran'paw Enoch go?"

She poked around in the rock pile with her hoe and didn't answer his question.

Henry wouldn't let it be."I heard he left Gran'maw fer a sawmill whore."

Her jaw dropped."Son, who told you sech?"

"Uncle Fred told me and Olus and Tom about it. He worked at the loggin camp with Gran'paw Enoch. Did ye know that?"

She let out a long sigh."Yeah, I know all about it."

Henry crouched, sprang up and grabbed hold of an apple tree limb. He did three quick chin-ups, turned a back flip and dropped softly to the ground."Uncle Fred said a young, good-lookin, loggin camp cook laid a hex on Gran'paw."

Henry didn't see the flash of anger in his mother's eyes."Ain't no bigger fool than a ol' fool," she muttered.

"Uncle Fred swore that them loggers and sawmill men strutted around her like banty roosters—arm wrestlin and kickin coons. He declared they lost ever grain a-sense they had when that redheaded gal dainced acrost the floor with a big pot of pinto dumplins. He said Gran'paw let out a whoop and commenced untyin her apern strangs an—"

"Hush!"

But Henry wouldn't hush."Gran'paw looked acrost the table at Uncle Fred and says, 'Freddie, this ain't no place fer a boy. It's time you 'as gitten on home.'"

"He should a-been gitten home hisself," Clarinda snapped."It's a lowdown shame—him a-carryin on that a-way—in front of his own son!"

Oh, you ain't heard it all, Mama, Henry thought. He decided he'd drop a hint and see if she wanted to hear the rest. With the recklessness of a lively youth, he picked up a rock, wound up his pitching arm and centered a hole in a dead chestnut at the edge of the clearing."Boy! You should a-heard what Gran'paw done next."

Clarinda pressed her lips into a thin line and chopped a weed asunder."I don't want a-heer no whoremonger tales about yer gran'paw. It ain't no snickerin matter, the way he treated my mother. I'm gonna have a talk with Fred next time I see 'im. He runs 'is mouth too much."

"Well, I like him better'n any of my uncles."

"Humph. I wonder why."

Clarinda reached into her apron pocket, brought forth a small tin, and took a dip of snuff. Nothing settled her nerves like a pinch of Sweet Bruton tucked in her cheek. She leaned on her hoe, raised her eyes to the mountaintop and looked down through the years.

"Henry, I think ye need to know the truth about yer Gran'paw Enoch, and, yer Great-Gran'paw Levi. Now that yer old enough to understand, I'm gonna tell ye as best I know it so ye won't believe ever tale ye heer about 'em.

"Way back in Civil War times, yer Gran'paw Enoch was a young man. He had two older brothers named David and Canada. They joined up with a gang of other rowdy fellers, an' all of 'em fought fer the Union. The Confederates went after 'em, but couldn't ketch 'em so they hanged the boys' father.

"Great-Gran'paw Levi was hung?"

"That's right. He lived down on the Watauga River 'bout half a mile shy of the Tennessee line. That was wild country back in them days. The smoke curlin outta them hollars shore wasn't groundhogs a-smokin their corncob pipes."

"Who hung 'im? What was their names?"

"I don't rightly know, but Mother said some lowdown members of the Confederate Home Guard done it. Early one mornin they come a-gallopin into his yard. They kicked the door down and yanked 'im up by the shirt collar from the breakfast table. They accused 'im of harborin outlaws. Yer Great-Gran'maw Lucy wrung her han's and pled fer his life. They told 'er that he could finish his coffee, that only heatherns would hang a man with a empty stumick. One big rascal put a gun to yer great-gran'paw's head an' told 'im to start suppin. He tried, but his han's shook so hard he couldn't even hold his coffee cup. They led 'im a little ways from the house and swung 'im from a apple tree. Yer great-gran'maw never got over it."

Clarinda didn't tell Henry that whilst his great-grandfather swung from the tree, the Confederates beat him with clubs until his head separated from his body and rolled down the hill.

"What did Gran'paw Enoch and his brothers do about the hangin?"

"It was mouthed abroad that ever man that stomped through yer great-gran'paw's door that mornin was wiped off the face of the earth."

"How'd that come about?"

"Well, yore Gran'paw Enoch an' his brothers knowed who done it, so they laid in wait at a cornfield. When the leaders of the hangin party come to gather the crop, they shot 'em down in crossfire."

"Did the Confederates hang any more of our kinfolk?"

"Yeah, a short time later they captured yer Gran'paw Enoch's oldest brother, Canada, near Tamarack. They hung 'im from a sycamore tree. It was shoot and hang, back and forth fer years."

"Why didn't the Confederates hang Gran'paw Enoch?"

"He out-foxed 'em. You cain't hang what ye cain't ketch."

Henry puffed his chest out."I wisht I'd a-knowed Gran'paw Enoch. I'm glad he was a Federal."

"Son, I ain't certain he 'as a Federal. I think plain ol' outlaw describes 'im best. I ain't nairy bit proud of his wicked deeds."

"Well, where's he buried at? He ain't in the fam'ly cemetery, and Great-Gran'paw Levi ain't neither."

Clarinda turned and pointed south."Yer Great-Gran'paw Levi is buried down yander on the river bluff—'bout twenty yards from the hangin tree. And yer Gran'paw Enoch headed west when he killed that man in the loggin camp."

"What did he kill 'im for?"

Clarinda sighed."The man washed his han's and wiped 'em on that redheaded cook's apern."

Henry looked puzzled."Heck, that ain't no reason to kill a man."

"I agree, son, but the cook was a-wearin the apern when he wiped his han's on it."

"Oh ..."

"They say my daddy set at the table and watched 'im do it without a word. When the loggers went back to the sawmill to work, my daddy picked up a cant hook and knocked the man's brains out. Uproar broke out in the camp. Them loggers would a-strung him up, but like a fox he got away. He took a train west and settled in Stevens, South Dakota."

"Did he take that strumpet with 'im?"

"No."

Probing the weeds with her hoe, Clarinda unearthed an old rusty stove lid. She carried it to a large apple tree and leaned it against the trunk."This cast arn will benefit the tree." She reached out and snapped off several water sprouts along a lower limb. Looking up through the leaves she saw a nest of robins."This ol' Rebel apple tree shore is kind to birds and younguns. When I 'as a little girl..."

Henry detected a tremor in her voice and looked at her closely.

"I hid in this tree when my daddy went on a tear. But it broke my heart to set here and listen to 'im throw my brothers aginst the walls. They never done nothin to deserve sech treatment."

Henry waited until she settled her emotions."After Gran'paw Enoch left, didn't he ever come home agin—even fer a visit?"

"No. He took up with another man's wife. He remarried and had another fam'ly. Us younguns despised Dad because he mistreated our mother. He was a man of few words—mean-hearted as they git. He showed no mercy when he whupped us. He left my mother fer that redheaded strumpet. Mother cried a lot, but she 'as better off without 'im. I always feared that he'd come home."

"Was Gran'paw a cowboy out there?"

Clarinda smiled."I don't know 'bout that, son. Anyway, on his death-bed he sent fer my brothers. Alexander and Fred went to see 'im. They said Dad told his wife to leave the room. He ast my brothers about each one of us younguns, and wanted to know how mother fared. They said he wept when they told 'im that mother had passed away. He told 'em that he could die easy if he could lay his head on the path to Levi's Mountain." Clarinda started to say something more, but hesitated.

"What... what?"

"He told 'em that he dreaded to see night come..."

"Why?"

"Because the man he killed in that loggin camp appeared at the foot of his bed ever night with 'is head caved in."

"Was it a ghost?"

"I doubt it—more'n likely yore gran'paw had a troubled conscience. Anyway, my brothers was fixin to leave when Dad's wife stepped in the room. She shoved a pic'cher under Alexander's nose and said, "'Here's a pic'cher of yore mother. I know yore dad would want you to have it.'"

"Alexander put it back in her han' like a gentleman and said, "'That redheaded whore ain't my mother!'"

"It was a pic'cher of that camp cook?"

"That's right. Alexander said her face turned whiter'n the underbelly of a goose. Some'ers in Stevens, South Dakota," Clarinda concluded, "I've got two halfbrothers."

"I saw Gran'paw's pic'cher on Aint Etta's wall. You look a lot like 'im, Mama."

She didn't comment. After a long silence she spoke and her voice was husky with emotion."I had as good a mother as ever lived. I never heerd a harmful word spoke aginst her. She knowed how to manage a homestead. She raised sheep and geese and chickens. We always kept two milk cows. And right fore the first snow, we slaughtered two big hogs. They ain't nothin better'n home-cured ham and fried aiggs on a cold winter mornin. I've got a lot a-mem'ries of this place, and we'll make plenty more when we git our house built."

Henry picked up his ax and started chopping sprouts."Are we gonna chop down these ol' apple trees?"

"No indeed." Clarinda pointed them out and named each one."That'n is a Ben Davis, it's a good keeper, and right below it is a Jonathan Winter. There's a Limbertwig, and that Polecat apple makes the best red jelly ye ever put on a biscuit. Over yander's a Rusty Coat. It's a good apple too, but this'ns the best." She reached overhead, broke a twig off the Rebel tree and sniffed the blossoms."In the fall, its limbs bend plumb to the ground with red-striped apples as big as a pint cup. Oh... they make the best stack cakes and apple butter I've ever eat." She pointed to their dinner pail that she'd placed on a chimney stone."Son, fetch our dinner here, and set it in the fork of this tree. Sow bugs have wintered under them rocks. We don't want 'em crawlin in our dinner bucket."

Stooping down, she picked up a rock and walked to the center of the clearing."Our house shall stand right here." She dropped the rock."The house Dad built had four rooms and a loft. I remember sleepin in the loft with my little sister."

"Was you afraid?"

"Why no, but one moonlit night, two bears moseyed offa the mountain. They'd caught a whiff of fresh pork in the meat house. Me and sister peeped through the chinks and watched 'em. One of 'em stood up and scratched its back on the house corner. We hurried down the ladder and told mother. She opened the door and set the hounds on 'em."

"The dogs put 'em up the mountain—eh?"

"No. Them bears slapped our dogs all over the yard. They'd a-killed ever hound we had if it hadn't been fer mother. She retch up and took yer gran'paw's musket from the wall."Them varmints ain't gonna lay nary paw on our hams and middlin's," she said, and stepped out on the porch. When the smoke cleared, the bears was gone."

Henry laughed."Did she really do that?"

Clarinda frowned."I said she did, didn't I?"

His laughter fizzled."Ol' Limber would a-put 'em up the mountain."

"Son, Ol' Limber wouldn't stand a chaince aginst a five-hunderd-pound bear. The chestnut trees bore heavy crops and bears had plenty to eat in them days."

"Was they paint'ers around here in olden times?"

"Lawzy, yes."

"Did you ever see one?"

"Yes, I've heerd a-plenty, too. The one I saw was after the cows—it 'as tan colored. But them black paint'ers squalled on the mountainside in the dead a-night. They sound exactly like a woman a-screamin. Me and sister pulled the bed kivers over our heads. We didn't sleep much on 'em nights."

She picked up her hoe."Son, it's time to git to work. Le's go find the spring."

Thirty yards from the home site, she heard its voice amongst a patch of trembling fern. It chattered and gurgled around rocks down the mountainside. Clarinda reached up and broke off a twig of dogwood in full bloom."It's the same spring I carried water from when I 'as a youngun, but it needs tendin." Of all the tasks she turned her hands to she enjoyed tending her spring the most.

While Henry chopped sprouts and moved the pile of stones from the home site, she set to work. She headed up the spring, digging, trenching and gathering pretty rocks. She lost track of time until Henry called, "Hey, Mama! When do we eat?"

She removed her straw hat and squinted at the sun through the dogwood blossoms."Good gracious, its way past dinnertime. Go fetch our dinner. We'll eat here by the spring." She spread a square of oil cloth on a flat rock, and they had fried eggs in biscuits and large slices of the best stack cake ever baked in the Blue Ridge Mountains. They quenched their thirst with a tin cupful of the purest water ever to flow from the bosom of the earth. When they finished their meal, she stood back and inspected her work.

"What do ye think? Ain't it purty?"

Henry had never thought of springs as pretty. In fact, he never thought of them at all unless he was thirsty. But he hardly recognized it as the same spring from a few hours earlier. Deep and crystal clear, she'd framed it with pretty flat rocks. It flowed unhindered, rushing and singing down the mountainside.

"Yeah, it's purty ... Hey, look!" He plunged his hand into the spring and brought up a fierce-looking crawfish, pincers snapping.

"Leave it be, son. Wherever a crawfish lives the water is pure."

All afternoon they worked, clearing a path to the spring and moving every hindrance from the housesite.

"We'll save scrap lumber from the house buildin fer a spring box. That'll be a good job fer you, Henry."

"Do ye want it built like the one we've got in Lonesome Hollar?"

"Yes, but it'll havta be stronger. They's still plenty of varmints in these woods. They'll try to git to our milk and butter in the night."

"Me an' Ol' Limber will take keer of the varmints."

"We've got to see about the old barn, son. I know it'll need some mendin." They walked across the branch to a three-stable log barn. The roof had collapsed and the door hung lopsided on one rusty hinge, but it would shelter Pied with a new roof in place.

The sun was sinking behind Levi's Mountain when they shouldered mattock, ax, scythe and hoe. They headed back to Lonesome Hollow bone-tired and weary, but satisfied with their day's work.

In her mind, Clarinda pictured her new house. It would have four spacious rooms and a nice front porch with steps and railings descending to the side. She'd plant a rambling red rose beside the porch steps. It would climb the railings and frame her porch in beauty. She'd bring her mother's lilac bush from Lonesome Hollow and plant it near the kitchen door. Its fragrance would drift all around the house and yard. She'd plant wild azaleas, mountain laurel, and wildflowers of all kinds around the foundation. It would take time and hard work to fix it to her liking, but she loved work and patience was one of her virtues.

Twilight had set in, and the twins were picking violets along the branch when Clarinda and Henry reached home. Clarinda knew that Ol' Pied would be butting the bars to get to her new calf because milking time had passed. But when she stepped through the kitchen door, she saw Mary Ann washing the milk strainer. Not only had Mary Ann milked the cow, she had their supper waiting in the stove warmer.

"Mary Ann, I shore do thank ye fer milkin Ol' Pied and fer this good supper. These creasies are the best we've ever had. What kind a-seasonin did ye use?"

Mary Ann's face lit up with pleasure. "Oh, I used butter instead of fatback."

"Well, I guess we'll season 'em with butter from now on."

Suddenly the twins burst through the door with a pint jar full of violets. Mandy climbed on her mama's lap, poked out her lip and sniffled. "Mama, Mary Ann whupped me today an' almost whupped Andy too!"

"Yes, I did, and I'll do it agin." Mary Ann wrung water from her dishrag with a vigorous twist. "Andy and Mandy fight all the blessed time. When pore little Howard tries to stop their squabbles they both turn on 'im."

Clarinda took little Howard on her lap too. Mandy jumped to the floor, and she and Andy ran into the settin room. They hid behind the door and whispered their plans to whip little Howard.

Clarinda looked toward the open kitchen door. "Where's Lee an' Billy Dan?"

"I guess they're feedin that dern crow."

"Crow?"

"Yes, they rigged up a chicken coop and captured a crow. They named it Cornbread. I've chased 'em outta the kitchen a dozen times fer snatchin the cornpone I baked fer supper."

"I'm a-gonna call 'at crow Spud 'cause it likes spuds, too," said Howard.

"Why you little scamp, I wondered what went with all the taters I peeled, the crow got 'em—didn't he?"

Howard snuggled close to his mama.

Mary Ann turned from the cookstove. "Is the housesite ready now?"

"It's as ready as we can git it," Clarinda replied.

"When are ye gonna start buildin?"

"Soon as the lumber gits there."

"Olus an' Tom come home early fer supper, but they went back to the sawmill. They said they 'as gonna load a wagon with lumber—gitten it ready to haul to Levi's Mountain first thing in the mornin."

Clarinda's face shined with happiness."Well, Henry, I guess our day was well spent—don't ye think?"

He beamed at her across the table."I'm gonna draw me a plan fer that spring box tonight."

"Good. All of us can pitch in and work together. We'll have that house built in no time."

Minutes later the children danced around her chair, asking questions, wanting to go to the home place. She knew it was important to keep the family interested in this project. Their future depended on it. It was her responsibility to provide for the family and keep them together, and with God's help and guidance she would continue to do so. She could hardly wait to pound in the first nail.

Nine

Clarinda's Prayer

Dear Lord, bless this cabin,
Foundation to rafter
And brace all four corners
With patience and laughter.

The first Saturday in May, 1940, a large wagon-load of lumber arrived on Levi's Mountain and construction on Clarinda's new house began. Clarinda made arrangements with David, an older son and carpenter by trade, to lay the foundation. Due to a full-time construction job, he'd be available for weekend work only. Olus and Tom worked at the sawmill five days a week so the house would be built on Saturdays.

Clarinda took the little ones with her to the housesite when Mary Ann had sewing or other important things to do. While the hammers pounded and the saws sang, the children swung through the apple trees like monkeys and climbed over the lumber pile. When they grew bored with that, they sneaked the ax into the woods and chopped a wild grapevine off near the ground. What fun they had soaring over the treetops on their grapevine swing!

The second weekend in May, David and the boys finished the foundation.

"Well, boys, are ye ready to nail in the floor joists?"

"Bring 'em on!" Their voices rose in unison and each grabbed a piece of lumber.

Olus and Tom were eager helpers. David could hardly keep them reined in."Don't nail in that 2x6, Olus. I ain't took a measurement yit."

"Git busy, ol' man, we ain't got all day to do this job," Olus teased.

David grinned."I'm twenty-nine, boys, and feel it."

They worked together like the happy family they were, with humorous chitchat amongst themselves. Clarinda carried lumber and stacked it within the boys' reach. The twins retrieved every pinged nail from the grass. It kept them out of mischief and saved money. The morning flew by and construction moved forward till David's wife, Rhoda, showed up with her baby on her hip.

Doubtless she'd had a hectic morning. Her home permanent resembled a bird's nest pummeled by an ill wind. Picking her way through the construction site, she kicked every obstacle in her path."Dad-gummit, I ain't never seen the like. What a godforsaken place to build a house!"

Olus nudged Tom and whispered, "Pore David's gonna ketch hell."

David laid his tools down and straightened up to greet her. The baby kicked and bounced on Rhoda's hip, stretching his chubby arms toward Daddy. David took him in his arms and tossed him up in play. He squealed with delight.

Rhoda watched the happy scene and didn't crack a smile. Instead, she uncorked her spite bottle and the bitter bile of resentment spewed forth."Don't you think it's high time ye done a little work around our place? I'm gitten tard of you a-workin on this dern hut fer nothin."

David's face turned red."I havta hep Mama and these younguns git this house started."

"Hep Mama, hep Mama," she mocked, rocking her head from side to side."I'm the one who needs hep." She snatched the baby from his daddy's arms.

The baby wailed... then suddenly turned on his mother. Quivering with rage, he buried his cherub fingers in her fuzzy hair and pulled with all his might.

Rhoda's face twisted in pain. She slapped his hands."Cut that out!"

He released her hair and cried like his heart would break.

David reached out and stroked the baby's head with a tender expression on his face."Rhoda, why don't ye go on home? The bees are swarmin around here. Little Buster might git stung."

"I ain't a-goin nowhere till I'm good and ready." She hitched the baby higher on her hip and unfastened a couple of buttons on her flour sack blouse. A breast as big as Ol' Pied's bag bounced through the milk gap. Little Buster caught it on the rebound and wrestled it under control. Then with a critical eye on foundation timbers Rhoda meandered around the worksite. Suddenly she stopped; and pointed her finger like a bird dog's tail."Whaa-hoo-urf!"

Tom flinched."What the devil was that? Is they a hoot owl around here?"

Olus chuckled."Nah, the chief outhouse inspector thinks she's found a crooked turd."

Still pointing, Rhoda turned, her eyes traveling around till they settled on Clarinda."Whoever set this lopsided thang was blind in one eye and couldn't see good outta the other'n." She glared at the boys, her eyes throwing pitch-forks, upper lip a-twitch—a sure sign of trouble afoot.

Clarinda ignored Rhoda's remark and continued her work. Go ahead, woman, jabber till ye turn blue, she thought. Rhoda's shenanigans didn't bother Clarinda, but her dominating influence on her son, David, did.

Olus straightened up, thumbed his nose and sniffed."As a matter of fact, Rhoda, I set that sleeper. Who made you the straw boss of this job?"

"Humph! Don't git smart with me." She flashed a message to David with her eyes. Are ye gonna just stand 'ere and let 'im talk to me that a-way?

David went to the foundation timber in question, bent down, and applied his level. Rhoda leaned over his shoulder, squinting, trying to read the bubble. She straightened up with a gotcha snap of the head and looked at Olus with a smug smile.

David dropped to one knee and took two more readings, moving the level back and forth. Behind Rhoda's back, he gave Olus the okay sign by raising his right hand with thumb and forefinger forming a circle. Without a word he returned to his work.

At that moment, Olus lost respect for David. What a dang coward, he thought. He gritted his teeth and started to speak, but Clarinda caught his eye and shook her head slightly from side to side.

Clarinda saw David's cowardice too, and her heart sank. She knew this would be David's last day of work on the house."David, I don't intend to be takin ye from yore work at home. We can finish nailin in the floor joists and take it on from there. I appreciate everything you've done fer us."

"I know ye do, Mama. I wisht I had more time to help you'uns out, but you know how it is."

"Don't worry, son. If there's anything we can do to repay ye, let me know."

"Well, it's about time," Rhoda shouted."It wouldn't hurt ye to pay David in cash fer the work he's done here. It's all he can do to pervide fer his own fam'ly. He ain't got the means to do charity work fer ye."

Tom straightened up with his green eyes blazing."Shut yore damn whopper-jawed mouth!" He raised the hammer in his right hand and shook it at her."Git or I'll knock yore brains out!"

"Fer heaven's sake, settle down," Clarinda coaxed, taking the hammer from Tom's hand.

Rhoda commenced bawling."He's just like his ol' Gran'paw Enoch." She turned on David."He was a-fixin to hit me. And you didn't even thank enough of me to stop workin."

Why she's tryin to git my boys into a fight, Clarinda thought. Rage surged through her and a sudden desire to strike Rhoda almost overpowered her good judgment."David, git Rhoda away from here. I've heerd enough of her foolishness."

David picked up his tools and headed down the path with Rhoda and the baby following. Clarinda watched them go. The weary slump of David's shoulders wrenched her heart. Her eyes filled with tears. Rhoda's naggin is breakin his spirit and there's nothin I can do about it. They ain't no use a-frettin over things that I cain't change. She returned to work.

The boys watched them go, too. Olus shook his head from side to side and clicked his tongue."David must a-been drunk when he married that ol' lantern-jawed heifer."

"Yeah, she fell from the top of a ugly tree and struck ever limb on the way down," Tom added.

Clarinda frowned."Younguns don't be talkin that a-way."

"I cain't help it, Mama," Olus said."I despise that woman."

"Well, son, I know how you feel, but I won't have ye quarrelin with Rhoda. It'll cause hard feelin's between you and David."

"If we havta put up with her ol' long waggin tongue to git his hep, we'd rather he stayed at home. We can do this job—ain't that right, Tom?"

"Yep, no doubt about it."

"David won't be back."

"Good," the boys said in one voice.

"Well, we'd better git to work—time's a-flyin." Clarinda headed for the main lumber stack which was thirty feet from the construction site.

The children had been playing on it and it was a mess. The 2x6's were mixed in with the 2x4's, and odd pieces of lumber lay scattered around. In her opinion, the lumber should be kept in order at all times. Suddenly, she veered to the left and picked up the water bucket that she kept close at hand. She emptied the contents which had been sitting for some time. She passed the lumber stack and headed for the spring with the twins at her heels.

From the high branches of the Rebel apple tree, Billy Dan and Lee and Howard saw two teenage girls on the wooded path that led to the housesite. They didn't know the girls by name but knew right away they were on the prowl for Olus and Tom."Le's stay here an' watch," little Howard suggested. Hidden by thick foliage, they had a snooper's perfect view of sparking mountain style. They anticipated action. Had they not overheard their big brothers boast of romantic exploits time after time?

Tom took a measurement on a 2x6.

Olus poked Tom with his hammer and whispered, "Look down yonder. Who's that a-comin up the path?"

Tom straightened up and stared."Well, I'll be hanged if it ain't them purty gals from Mossy Gap."

Olus looked at Tom with a puzzled expression."Which girls?"

"Gosh a-mighty, shorely you ain't fergot C. J. an' Madge—ye know—the marshmallow roast last Friday night?"

Olus let out a low whistle and brushed the sawdust from his pants with his hands. His ego soared."Well, now, ain't we two lucky rascals. They're carryin baskits of somethin good, too."

The boys glanced at the lumber stack. Their mama was nowhere in sight. They knew she'd gone to the spring and wouldn't be back for a spell.

Tom reached in his back pocket for the comb he always kept handy."Hey, do I look all right in these dern overalls?"

"You look like a skeercrow on stilts."

Tom poked him in the shoulder."Well, fer a chunky feller, you look about as good as ye ever will."

"What do ye mean by chunky? I ain't—"

"Shhh! Here they come."

The girls approached the construction site acting real bashful.

The boys dropped their carpentry tools and swaggered toward them, grinning ear to ear.

"Ain't you girls lost up here in the woods?" Olus feasted his eyes on tall, willowy Madge.

"Why, no, you silly gander, we know exactly where we're at. Ain't ye glad to see us?"

"You know we are, Sweetheart."

Madge wore a white ruffled off-the-shoulder blouse with a red full-circled skirt. Her strawberry-red lips matched her skirt. She smoothed her high pompadour with her hand and tossed her long, brown wavy hair, giving him that special look that she'd doubtless practiced before the mirror.

Olus' breath caught in his throat as he sidled up to her and laid an arm around her shoulders. The fragrance of Blue Moon perfume enveloped his head. His starry eyes lit on the heart-shaped locket adorning her neck and his hands followed his gaze."Is my pic'cher in here?"

She slapped his hand."Mind yer manners."

C. J. folded her arms, dipped her chin toward one shoulder, batted her big brown eyes at Tom and purred like a tabby cat itching for a scratch. "My ... ain't yew han'some in them overalls?"

Tom blushed."Aw, shucks."

She scooped up a handful of sawdust and tossed it in his hair. He nudged her in a playful manner and reached for his comb. She took it from his hand and pointed to the foundation timber."Set down and I'll comb it out. I really didn't mean to throw it in yer hair."

Tom obeyed, then closed his eyes and surrendered to her petting.

C. J. ran her slender fingers through Tom's jet black mop."Ooh... what a gorgeous head of hair." The heavy wave tumbled down on his forehead."Oou... wee ... have mercy," she gushed. She stooped over, kissed the top of his head and whispered in his ear.

"Look! She must a-said sump'n good," Billy Dan whispered from his perch in the rebel tree.

Lee chuckled."Yeah ... he's a-grinnin like a possum."

Suddenly C. J. straightened up and stiffened. Tom looked up at her startled face. She had seen Clarinda and the twins emerging from the woods."Who's that woman? We thought y'all were alone up here."

"Aw, that's Mama, she'll be glad you're here, but ye better watch out, she might put ye to work."

C. J. smiled, but looked anxious."Well, we thought y'all would be hungry 'bout now so we brought some food if ye want it."

Tom chuckled, slapped his hands together and rubbed his palms."Oh, boy! Bring on the chow!"

Olus, the handsome, smooth-talking rascal already had Madge under his spell."What's in yore baskit, Sugar Babe?"

"Oh ... just some fried chicken, tater salit, and chocklit cake," she murmured, gazing into his eyes like a sick cow foundered on little green apples.

Olus kissed her."Mmmm ... is that cake as sweet as you are?" He nuzzled her ear and lifted the napkin on the food basket. Ka-pow! Like magic a big chicken leg appeared in his hand.

From his perch in the apple tree little Howard slipped. Billy Dan and Lee caught him by the seat of the britches and saved him from a nasty fall. They gave him frowns and a shake of warning lest he give their hiding place away.

Clarinda stopped at the lumber pile and stared."My stars! I cain't turn my back fer even a minute," she blurted out. Well, them girls ain't gonna hang around here. No siree! I'll send 'em back where they come from, she thought."Olus, Tom, it's time to git to work."

Olus dropped his arms from Madge and grinned at Clarinda."Mama, meet the girls. This'n is Madge and that'n over there is C. J. — ye want some chicken?" He held up a gnawed-on chicken leg."They brought us two big baskits of all kind a-good stuff."

"No. I've got work to do and so have you."

"I do. I do. I want some chicken!" Billy Dan dropped from the Rebel tree with Lee and Howard in hot pursuit.

Madge and C. J. looked stunned.

Clarinda's stern expression didn't change."Girls, it's time to git goin. Olus and Tom havta git back to work."

The girls sprang to their feet—and so did the boys. Olus put his hands on Madge's shoulders and gently pressed her down on the foundation."Why you ain't leavin, Sweet Thang. There's plenty a-food left in that baskit, and I'm still hungry." He turned and gave Clarinda a rebellious look."Mama, these girls' walked all the way from Mossy Gap to bring us this feast, and we ain't strikin another lick a-work till we finish eatin."

Clarinda sighed."All right, I'm a-callin it quits. There'll be little work done here fer the rest of this day. It's been one aggravation after another since early mornin." She turned and started down the path."Come on, younguns, le's go home."

"Wait a minute." Olus beckoned the children near. He brought a large piece of chocolate cake from the basket and held it out to Mandy."Want some cake, Pug?" She nodded and held out her hands."How 'bout some chicken too?" Her eyes shined with gratitude as he laid cake in one hand and a chicken thigh in the other. The boys stepped forward and received a generous portion.

The little ones went home smacking their lips."I hope C. J. an' Madge comes agin tomarrah and brangs more chicken 'n stuff." Mandy shoved the cake and crumbs into her mouth.

"Humph!" Clarinda retorted. She knew the girls had probably planned a picnic for the boys and themselves. They might not be so keen to bring food again since Olus and Tom had passed it around so freely.

After supper, Clarinda worked a rag rug till the boys came home." You're gitten in mighty late, ain't ye?"

Olus looked sheepish."Yeah ... by the time we finished work it was gitten dark. We walked the girls through Dark Hollar. You know how girls git spooked in the dark."

"Humph! I don't know nothin of the sort. They should a-stayed home in the first place. How many joists did ye git nailed in after I left the site?"

The boys looked at each other quizzically."Oh, three, maybe four?"

"Aw, Mama, we didn't work any more after you left," Tom confessed."Olus tried to show the girls how to drive a nail, but they couldn't git the hang of it, so we took 'em to the top of the mountain and showed 'em the view. They 'as amazed. You'd think they 'as on top of the world the way they raved about it."

"I'm amazed that ever time we start workin on the house, somebody shows up. It's late. I'm a-goin to bed," she snapped."Tell them girls to stay away or I'll tell 'em myself."

"Well, Brother," said Tom, "it's gonna be a *long time* before we git any more chocklit cake."

"Damn!" Olus stomped off to bed.

A week later, Rhoda came by the construction site. Her home permanent still looked frightful even though she'd drenched it with David's Bryllcreme to dampen the fuzz. She wore new penny loafers, yellow anklets, a green pleated skirt and white blouse.

She looks better'n usual, Clarinda thought, stepping a short distance from the sound of hammers to greet her.

"Howdy." Rhoda plopped her foot on the stepping stone that Clarinda had pulled down the mountainside. With hands on hips and nose aloft, Rhoda watched Olus and Tom and Clarinda's son-in-law, Joe, at work. Turning to Clarinda she stated, "David won't be here to hep ye today nor next Saturday neither."

"That's all right. We'll manage." Clarinda stooped and picked up a piece of scrap lumber.

Rhoda gestured toward Joe with a nod."Is that yer new carpenter?"

"He's lendin a hand."

"Whaa-hoo-urf!"

Clarinda dismissed her with, "I've got work to do," and turned toward the main lumber stack.

Tom nudged Joe and whispered, "Look at Rhoda. She acts like she owns this place."

Joe, a tall, lanky, quiet sort of fellow had a satchel full of homespun humor. He rolled his big sleepy-looking blue eyes at Tom and mumbled, "Why don't ye give 'er yer comb?"

"Why?"

"Her head looks like a stump full a-crawdads. Do ye reckon she combed 'er hair with a table fork this mornin?"

Tom snickered.

Olus didn't say a word, but he watched Rhoda like a hawk.

Rhoda's eyes bored into Joe."Why he couldn't build a chicken coop," she remarked in a loud voice.

Joe chuckled."She must a-seen that chicken house I tacked up."

As Rhoda took her leave, she came upon a wild azalea seedling at the edge of the yard. Upright sticks encircled it to protect it from wayward feet. Looking over her shoulder in a sneaky manner, she raised her right foot and brought it down hard on the beautiful flame of the wildwood, destroying it with one stomp. She walked away with a smug expression.

From the corner of her eye, Clarinda saw Olus leap from the house floor and go running. He grabbed Rhoda's shoulders from behind, and spun her around."You damn devil! I saw you stomp that bush Mama set out. You done it on purpose. You ain't gitten away with it!"

Rhoda stepped backward and drew her right hand."Why you little Friday fart, you jist strike me one time, an' I'll sue you fer 'sault an' batt'ry."

Olus drew his fist. Clarinda stepped between them and caught his wrist in mid air."They ain't gonna be no fightin around here." She turned and faced Rhoda."If you cain't come here and act like a decent human bein—stay off this property!"

Tom sat down on a floor joist and egged Olus on."Slap that twitch off her upper lip. Give 'er a knuckle san'wich fer me."

Joe stood up and shoved his hands in his overall pockets. His long homely face labored to conceal his amusement.

Rhoda glared at Tom."Haw-haw-haw," she mocked, wagging her head from side to side."I hope ye die fore daylight, you long-leggit varmint."

Tom's laughter fizzled—a solemn expression dropped over his face."Gosh, Rhoda, yer plumb purty when ye wobble yer noggin that a-way."

Joe lost control. His shoulders almost touched his ear lobes as he folded himself inward and shook with low wheezing laughter.

Rhoda let loose a string of curses like a heathen.

Clarinda pointed toward the path."Didn't you heer me, Rhoda? I told you to go. I ain't gonna tell ye agin!"

Something in Clarinda's voice and eye put Rhoda on the move. She took off in a lope, slinging snot and throwing threats."When David heers how I've been treated today, somebody's apt to git hurt."

"I'm so skeerd I'm a-shakin in my boots," Olus shouted.

Clarinda laid a hand on his arm and squeezed it."Hush."

"Ever last one of ye will regret this," Rhoda flung over her shoulder.

Olus cupped his hands to his mouth and hollered, "Ye want a-bet?"

"I told you to hush up." Clarinda stooped down, picked up a trampled pokeweed and lashed him over the head.

Tom whooped.

Joe went back to work.

Olus rubbed his stinging ears."Dang it, Mama, why'd ye do that?"

"When I say, hush, I mean it."

He reached out, took hold of her wrist, and pulled the pokeweed from her hand."Mama, I'm seventeen-year-old now. I know you're the boss here, but I ain't gonna let you swarp me over the head agin. That hurt."

She looked into his angry eyes with a solemn expression."Be thankful it was a weed instead of a switch."

He turned away and left the housesite. She let him go without a word. He needed time to think about his behavior and she needed time to consider her own actions.

Tom returned to his work, but every now and then he'd pause and laugh.

Clarinda let out a long weary sigh. Ever time Rhoda shows up, my day is ruint, she thought. I wisht she could be a little more agreeable. She's a good cook, a fine seamstress, and puts up enough canned stuff to feed Pharaoh's army. But her selfishness is a millstone around her neck. She'll never lend a hand or allow David either, except to accommodate her own kin. She's the bitterest pill I've ever had to swaller.

I knowed David wouldn't be here today. Joe is willin to hep us, but he ain't the carpenter that David is. Oh, well, a little hep is better'n none at all. We shall finish this house if we havta work by lantern light.

Ten

The Rug Maker

She pulls the string through burlap
With a rug hook that she fashioned from
A coat hanger and seasoned hickory.
Her sketch takes on color
As a yellow Lady's-slipper
Blooms under her calloused hand.
The lamplight flickers...
The oil is low.
She turns in her ladder-back chair,
And reaching out,
Rolls up the lamp wick.
The flame smokes then sputters and dies—
The moon has stolen away from the window pane
To set behind the mountain.
The hour is late...
The wall clock strikes two—
Her creations adorn grand homes
In faraway places
That she will never see.

There weren't enough hours in the day for Clarinda to finish all the tasks at hand. Besides daily chores, there was the garden to tend, blackberries and cherries to can, and rag-rugs to hook.

She spent most evenings from supper to bedtime working on her rugs. She purchased Pied's sweet feed in burlap sacks, and when emptied, she unraveled the seams and washed them. As needed, she stretched and tacked the burlap to a frame of narrow wood strips. She drew her pattern on the burlap with a tiny brush dipped in ink. She used pokeberry dye when she didn't have ink. She'd sketch pastoral scenes, farm animals, log cabins, and her most requested pattern, the flower basket. The design required at least three different colors which she didn't always have on hand. In that case, she made do with what she had. She never made an ugly rug.

She fashioned her rug hook from a wire coat hanger and a short piece of hickory. She'd take a piece of broken glass and shave the wood into a handle that fit comfortably in her hand. With pliers in hand, she heated a short piece of coat hanger wire red hot, and then shaped it into a hook. When she had smoothed it with a whetstone to her liking, she made a hole in the wooden handle with awl and screw. The procedure was tedious. The hole must be sized for a snug fit. She then inserted the wire, shoved it through and secured it with a twist.

Many a night Clarinda worked on her rugs by the kerosene lamp until the wee hours of morn to clothe her children. Tom and Olus came in from fox hunting one Friday night and found her slumped over her rug. They rushed to her side and gently shook her."Mama, are you all right?"

She jerked awake, rubbed the sleep from her eyes, and winced in pain.

The boys looked alarmed."What's wrong?" they asked in unison.

"Oh, nothin, just a kink under my shoulder blade from settin in this cheer."

Olus rubbed his Mama's back and helped her to her feet."Go to bed, Mama. It's way past midnight."

"I havta finish this rug, Olus. It hasta be mailed today or I might lose my buyer."

Two ladies in Baltimore, Maryland, purchased every rag rug that Clarinda hooked. She acquired her customers from a neighbor, who, because of failing health could no longer make the rugs the ladies wanted. The Baltimore ladies sent Clarinda secondhand children's clothes as payment for the rugs.

After a refreshing splash of cold water Clarinda returned to her rug. By mid-morning she had it in the mail. When Clarinda received a large box from Baltimore it was like opening up a gift at Christmastime. Everyone gathered around to see the goods. Clarinda gave out the clothing.

"Mandy, this dress will fit you. Howard, this coat looks like a perfect fit fer you. Billy Dan, these overalls and shirts are fer you and Andy."

The clothes were always secondhand, but they still had plenty of good wear in them. One of her buyers was more generous than the other. She sent bigger boxes that always contained clothing, whereas the other lady sent curtains, bedspreads and the like. Clarinda preferred clothing, but she didn't complain. A nice pair of curtains draped around sparkling window-panes always lifted her spirit.

Oftentimes, a box contained a useless article of clothing. Such was the pink silk dress with flounces and a big artificial rose on the shoulder."My lands," Clarinda exclaimed, "I cain't even use that in a rug. The knots would fall out as fast as I pull 'em through the burlap." She tossed it on the useless pile.

Mary Ann, in a spurt of fourteenth-birthday joy, snatched it up and hurried to the bedroom. Two minutes later, she poked her head around the doorjamb and yelled in her best Minnie Pearl voice, "Howdee... ain't I jest the purtiest thang?" With silk swishing she did a scissor-leg dance across the room.

Everyone whooped.

Henry dropped into an attack crouch and mutely mouthed the words, "Now's the time."

Lee caught the signal and nodded.

An old mountain custom gave siblings the authority to pitch a brother or sister under the bed or dining table on birthdays. If Henry and Lee could shove Mary Ann under the table, her dominance in the household would be diminished. The boys had pre-planned their moves for the takedown. Lee would grab her ankles and jerk her off her feet whilst Henry laid a head-lock on her from behind.

Henry maneuvered around behind her and gave Lee the nod. The attack surprised Mary Ann, but she didn't go down. The pink silk dress so appropriate for Minnie Pearl looked ridiculous on her as she sprang into action. Her ribcage expanded, popping the long back zipper. Henry's head-lock-hold looked pathetic as she drove her elbow into his stomach and twisted out of his control with ease. A number nine shoe sent Lee sprawling. She yanked Henry off the floor, and pitched him kicking and sliding under the table.

Clarinda straightened up from her boxes."My stars! What's a-goin on?"

"Nothin," Mary Ann replied."These two squirts just tried to put me under the table."

"Oh ..." Clarinda returned to her sorting chore.

Mary Ann stooped, picked up her pink silk rose and tossed it under the table."There's yer souvenir."

With a crooked grin and a red face, Henry crawled forth."That's all right. Next year you're a-goin down."

"Oh, yeah? That'll never happen."

And it didn't.

Another box contained a large corset with staves. Clarinda held it up for inspection with a critical eye."I'll swannie to goodness! Do ye reckon somebody really wore this?" She tossed it aside. Five minutes later, Billy

Dan pranced through the room wearing it. Howard and Lee pounced and wrestled him to the floor.

When Clarinda expected a clothes shipment from Maryland, she always walked to the main road and waited for the postman. But one day the postman arrived earlier than usual and left her package beside her mailbox. She found the shipping cord cut and knew her mail had been pilfered.

She wrote the lady in Baltimore and asked for a list of all the items she had shipped. When her list came, Clarinda found that two pair of blue organdy parlor curtains with tiny white dots, and a brown, wool coat had been stolen. As soon as she read the list she knew who the thief was. A certain lady's organdy polka-dot curtains were described down to the last ruffle."If I'd a-caught that thief a-pilferin through my stuff, I'd a-wiped the ground with her," Clarinda declared. She considered confronting the thief, but the rogue was linked by marriage to the family and Clarinda decided the curtains weren't worth the trouble. But from that day forward, she kept a closer watch on her mail.

Clarinda's rugs adorned beautiful homes in faraway places. Occasionally, the ladies would write and tell her how lovely the rugs looked on their varnished parlor floors. Of course, that made Clarinda happy because the more rugs they wanted, the more clothes her children would receive. Mary Ann read the letters aloud because Clarinda didn't know some of the big words like "magnificent" and "contrasting colors."

Mandy loved to hear Mary Ann read the letters."Mary Ann, what's a parlor?"

"It's a room with a fine velvet couch and cheers and a mahogany piano. It's got a fireplace with a fancy fireboard like Aint Etta's. It's where uppity folks sup tea and set around gabbin and thankin their lucky stars they ain't got a settin room like pore people."

"Will we ever have a parlor?"

Mary Ann snorted."Yep, when Uncle Riley gits outta the pore house."

Clarinda kept a rug or quilt in the frame at all times. Mary Ann helped with the quilting, but she shunned rug making."I cain't hardly bear to set fer hours pullin strings through burlap. It gives me a crick in my neck. I'd druther dig spuds with a table fork."

Clarinda sighed."Sometimes I hate it too, but it hasta be done."

During winter, every quilt was in use because the cabin was so cold. Clarinda determined that her new house would be warmer than the old shack in Lonesome Hollow. Maybe she could slacken up on her quilting for a year or two.

In late August, Clarinda and the boys laid the tarpaper roof on their new house."I wisht I had some tin to lay over the tarpaper. I always liked to heer the sound of rain a-fallin on a tin roof," Clarinda said.

Olus and Tom bought the windows and set them in. Clarinda inspected their work."Younguns, the winders look mighty fine."

"Of course they do, Mama. We're good builders. We just might give up sawmillin and take up carpentry," Tom bragged.

"Hey, Mama, take a look at this!"

Clarinda leaned on her post-hole diggers and looked up. Olus had his head poked out a kitchen window."How do ye like this slidin winder? Come in here and have a look."

"I've got to git this post set fer the clothesline."

He wouldn't hush until she came inside and looked it over.

"The winder looks fine, but I don't believe we had to have one that slides."

"Why, this winder is handy as can be. You can keep a-eye on the younguns and never havta step outside." He slid the window open and poked his head out."Hey, younguns! Git yore hind ends outta them apple trees!" Within seconds, the children were standing at the door. Olus looked at Clarinda and grinned."See how easy that was."

"I'm proud of ye, Olus. You done a good job."

The house had two bedrooms, and each bedroom was large enough for three beds. The settin room would also have a bed. The kitchen and dining room were combined and spacious enough for the big Home Comfort cookstove, dining table, homemade dish cupboard, and cabinet which stored meal, flour, seasonings and lard.

A rough porch stretched across the front of the new house with steps descending to the side. Clarinda insisted that railings be added to the porch and steps. She wouldn't risk another little one falling and breaking a limb as Mandy had broken her arm in Lonesome Hollow.

They really needed another bedroom, but that would have to wait for another year. Mary Ann would have to sleep in the settin room on a roll-away bed until another bedroom could be built. She fussed about it."Charlotty's got her own room. Am I ever gonna have a little corner where I can hang my stuff?"

"Next year we'll build another room fer you and Mandy," Clarinda said."She's out-growin her trundle bed and she's gitten too big to sleep with me or you. I talked to the man on the Rollin Store and he said he'd sell me two roll-away beds purty cheap."

The Rolling Store was a peddler's truck that passed through the mountains once every three months, weather permitting. It carried various household items for sale. Folk walked out of the hollows and coves to the main road to meet it at designated stops.

Clarinda continued,"Mandy will like sleepin on a roll-away bed."

"Thank the Lord. I don't want her sleepin with me. She kicks like a mule," Mary Ann said, and began planning new blue organdy curtains for her future room.

"I want pank curtains," Mandy said.

"You're big enough till yer wants won't hurt ye," Mary Ann retorted."My curtains are gonna be blue."

Mandy squalled."Mamaa... I want paannk!"

Mary Ann rolled her eyes toward the ceiling."Fer the love of Pete, that youngun is spoilt rotten."

Clarinda didn't have the money to buy doorknobs and locks, so she carved a strong wooden button for each outside door. As she put them to the test she smiled with satisfaction, "That'll keep the varmints an' thieves out."

Olus let out a big guffaw."Heck fire, we ain't got a thing anybody would wanna steal." Clarinda smiled."Maybe not, but I'll sleep better with a good button on the door." She hung curtains on all the inside doorways for privacy.

There was a large decayed stump in the front yard. Clarinda dug all around it trying to loosen it up. She worried with it for half a day, but it refused to budge. Finally, she straightened up and tossed her mattock aside."Stay there, dang ye, I'm not wastin another minute on ye." She planted a red rambling rose beside the stump. In a year or two it would be covered.

After they finished the house, they built a small shelter with poles and scrap lumber for the chickens. The new barn roof would keep Pied comfortable and dry."Well, younguns, we've got one more thing to build before we can move to our new home."

"The outhouse," they all chorused.

"Where are we gonna put it?" Olus inquired.

Clarinda pointed to a spot at the edge of the woods."How 'bout there?" They all pitched in and dug the pit and by sundown the following day, the outhouse was done. It had two seats with covers and a corner shelf for catalog paper. Olus had carved The Stump above the door.

Clarinda fussed."Olus, that's abomination. Git rid of it, right now."

"Aw, Mama ..."

"You heerd me."

"Oh, all right," he groused, but he was determined to carve something naughty. When he finished, the wording had been replaced by a grinning moon with one star-shaped eye. He said he wanted the building to look like the genuine article lest somebody think it was a tool shed.

The first Monday in September they moved to their new home. Olus and Tom borrowed Mr. Colliday's team and wagon to transport their household possessions. At sunrise the wagon rattled into Lonesome Hollow and came to a squeaking halt at the cabin door. Olus went tramping from room to room."Roll outta bed, ye little squirts. This is movin day! We need to load yore beds on the wagon."

The little ones tumbled out and ran to the window to see the big horses that Tom and Olus had brought to haul their house plunder away. As usual, Andy and Mandy argued."Th-th-that big red hoss is mine and I'm a-gonna ride it."

"You are not-so, that'n is mine. You can have the grimy-colored 'un."

It took five trips to get all their stuff moved to Levi's Mountain. With the last chair on the wagon, Tom and Olus set the four little ones on the horse's backs. Of course, an argument broke out."I wanna ride the red horse," Mandy whined.

Olus turned toward the red horse and raised his hands to Andy."Do you wanna change places with her?"

"Nooo ..." shaking his head he tightened his grip on the horse's hames.

Mandy squalled."I don't like this grimy horrssee..."

Tom shook his finger at her."Shut up, Pug, or you'll be a-ridin the tailgate."

Mandy hushed, but she looked at Andy and gritted her teeth. He snickered and stuck his tongue out at her.

Finally they started with a jolt. Clarinda raised her hand and brought the procession to a halt. Tom looked puzzled."That's everything, Mama. They ain't a scrap of nothin left in the house."

Clarinda pointed to the maple tree beside the branch."One of ye fetch my washboard. It'll never do to leave it behind."

Henry dashed away and snatched it from the nail on the tree trunk. He gave it a careless toss toward the wagon. Clarinda caught it and gave him a scolding."Be careful with our stuff, son. A damaged washboard means dirty clothes fer all of us."

"Yeah, watch what yer doin, pea brain," Tom added.

Mary Ann had arrived at their new home with the first wagon-load of furniture. She set to work putting things in order while the boys returned to Lonesome Hollow for another load. They rattled into the yard with the fifth and last load of house plunder at sunset. They were greeted by wood smoke curling from the kitchen stovepipe. Loud whoops of joy erupted."Mary Ann's got supper ready!"

"Thank goodness," Clarinda said, with a grateful heart. The family hadn't eaten since daybreak and they were famished. They gorged themselves on potato soup, milk and lots of butter with delicious crusty cornbread.

After supper, Clarinda and the boys unloaded the wagon while Mary Ann did the dishes. When the last bed had been made and every household item put in its rightful place, Clarinda stepped out on the porch and raised her eyes toward heaven."Thank ye, Lord, fer our new home. My cup of joy is full tonight." She felt a tug at her apron.

Billy Dan looked up at his Mama's face in starlight."Mama, we're rich now, ain't we?" Looking down, she laid her hand on his head and stroked it."We've got a new house, but that don't make us rich, son. Someday you'll know that we're rich in ways that the world don't understand."

He reached up, took her hand and squeezed it."Yeah, I know. I've got more brothers to play with than anybody."

The sound of Henry's harmonica pulled them indoors. Clarinda paused on the threshold. "Are all the younguns in?" She scanned the room as she made a mental count. There's Olus, Tom, Henry, Lee, Billy Dan, Howard, Andy and Mandy and Mary Ann in the kitchen. She smiled and closed the door on the outside world. All the family was in the fold except Claude. During the summer he'd met and married a country nurse from Tennessee. He and Beatrice were settled in their own cabin a couple of miles away.

The following day, Clarinda and Henry returned to Lonesome Hollow for Pied. As Clarinda walked around in the empty cabin, memories of the past flooded her mind, and her eyes grew misty. She stood looking down at the plank floor near the settin room window. It showed rocking chair and cradle wear from countless days and nights of rocking babies. She smiled at the remembrance of suddenly coming awake to find a toddler prying her eyes open.

Henry's call from the yard startled Clarinda from her reverie."Hey, Mama! Are ye ready to go? Ol' Pied's gitten tard a-standin out here."

"I'll be there in a minute." She looked around the room. The outline of Rufus' banjo was still visible on the faded wallpaper. She had given the treasured instrument to Claude because he begged for it so. She walked to the door then turned and spoke to the empty room, "Well, Rufus, I won't be a-livin here anymore. I've moved into the house we planned to build years ago. I wisht we could a-built it together, but the good Lord had other plans fer ye. I'm takin all my mem'ries with me, the good times and the bad too, because that's the way life is. I've come to a bend in the road and I havta see what's around the curve. The younguns depend on me. I know you'll be a-waitin fer me at the end of my journey." She closed the door softly behind her and didn't look back.

Eleven

October • 1940

Froggie Went a Courting

Froggie went a courting and he did ride, uh huh, uh huh
Froggie went a courting and he did ride, uh huh, uh huh.
Froggie went a courting and he did ride,
Sword and pistol by his side uh huh, uh huh, uh huh.
He rode up to Miss Mousie's door uh huh, uh huh.
He rode up to Miss Mousie's door uh huh, uh huh.
He rode up to Miss Mousie's door,
Seemed like he'd been there before uh huh, uh huh, uh huh.

–Traditional Folk Song.

Clarinda stepped through the kitchen door into the early morning sunshine. It had rained during the night and a fleecy mist hung over the stream that chattered nearby. Raindrops lingered and sparkled like diamonds on the mountain laurel that she had dug up in the woods and planted by the front porch steps. The yard sloped gently from the kitchen door for thirty feet before dropping into the stream. She took a deep breath of fresh mountain air and released it slowly. The autumn woods smelled like her first cup of morning coffee, rich and delicious.

She ambled into the yard and turned to gaze at her new house. It stood dwarfed by towering poplars and giant muscular oaks that surrounded the clearing. She raised her eyes to the mountaintop and scanned the horizon. Bare trees etched the blue sky, but half-way down the mountainside, the timber still wore a mantle of color.

She turned her attention back to the house. Four rooms with a front porch and steps descending to the side. The entire house was built with oak and pine, straight from the sawmill. She preferred well-seasoned lumber for her house, but she'd been unable to find it. Thank the Lord, she wouldn't have to lie awake at night and worry that the roof would fly off with every storm. The mountain rising to a height of 4600 feet sheltered their home from the fierce north and west wind. Although the land on which her house stood wasn't legally her own as yet, it doubtless would be, and soon. Her dear brother, Alexander, would see to it.

The orchard surrounding the house was ready to harvest. She expected to gather at least fifty bushels of quality fruit. Yes indeed, she had a bountiful crop of apples, praise the good Lord who grew them, and thanks to her mother who had the foresight to choose the best.

Fog rose from the hollows in wispy veils as she turned indoors. Mary Ann had set up the ironing board to do some touch up pressing for Olus and Tom.

"I've arned their clothes already," Clarinda said.

"I know ye have, but they want a sharper crease in their pants. You know how fussy and proud they are."

Olus came from his bedroom carrying pants."Sis, see if you can git these dang wrinkles outta my pants." Tom followed with a pair of khaki pants draped over his arm.

"Are you younguns goin somewhere?" Clarinda asked."I was plannin on gitten all the family together this weekend. We'll fix a big supper, have music-makin and just have a good ol' time a-celebratin our new home."

"That'll havta wait, Mama. Me and Tom are goin to Sweetgum Creek. We're goin today and won't be back till Monday or Tuesday."

"Why are ye goin over there?"

"Why, girls, of course. We heard they're thicker'n rabbits—a purty girl behind every bush—yee haa!" Olus danced a jig across the kitchen floor.

Mary Ann looked at Clarinda and gave a slight sideways nod toward Olus."How long has he been in that shape? He's plumb batty."

Olus laughed and bushed her hair."Hush, and git my shirt pressed. I'm in a hurry."

She set the iron down and smoothed her hair. She couldn't stand for anyone to bush up her hair."Don't git so dern bossy or you'll press 'em yerself."

Clarinda sighed. It was difficult getting them all together, now that they were older. Two of her married sons had even considered moving to Ohio where work was more plentiful. If she was going to have a family gathering it would have to be soon.

"You younguns better be keerful a-goin that far from home. Ye never know what might happen."

Tom rolled up his sleeve and showed his log-turning muscle."We built this house and we hold down a job at the sawmill. We ain't youn-guns no more — we are men!"

Clarinda turned her head and looked away. She couldn't stand to hear her children brag."Many a man a lot tougher'n you has been killed in them moonshine hollars, son."

Tom stretched himself to his full six-feet-two."Don't you worry one bit, me 'n Olus can take keer of ourselves."

Olus strutted over to the looking glass, stroked his hair and grinned at himself."Now, Mama, tell me, have you ever seen me with a black eye? Have you ever seen this face momicked up?"

"Well, fer a fact I ain't, but maybe that's because yer either lucky or a fast runner."

Tom whooped.

Olus bristled up."They ain't no rabbit blood in this ol' boy."

"Well, yer Aint Berthie lives on Sweetgum Creek — that's where you're goin — ain't it?"

"Yep, we're spendin the weekend with Aint Berthie, but we're goin to Hackaway Hollar to see some girls, too," Olus said.

"You younguns stay outta there. Do ye heer me?"

Mary Ann set a flat iron on the stove and picked up a hotter one."I've never heard of Hackaway Hollar — and how come it's called that?"

"We asked some girls that question," Olus said with a chuckle, "and they told us their great-gran'parents hacked into the hollar, and they was too tard to hack a-way out so they just settled there."

Clarinda's eyebrows shot upward, "You've been there?"

Olus couldn't meet her eyes.

"Well?"

"Olus, ain't you never gonna learn to keep yer mouth shut," Tom scolded.

Clarinda gave the boys a stern warning."Stay out of Hackaway Hol-lar — it's a rough place — whiskey makin — murders — bad houses."

"Where did ye hear that?"

"Bad news travels like a feather on a fast wind, Olus."

Clarinda worried about her boys' safety. It wasn't uncommon for mountain boys to be ambushed with clubs and rocks when they strayed into distant communities with a roving eye for pretty girls. Why she re-membered the time that three boys called on Rufus' three sisters. While on the homeward path, they were ambushed by a malicious gang and beaten. One of the boys escaped and made a run for the nearest farm. When he climbed the barnyard gate, a man stepped from the shadows and knocked him unconscious with a club. His companions found him and they all took refuge in a barn till daybreak.

Olus and Tom were handsome and frolicsome. The girls swarmed around them at every social event. Yes indeed, she had good cause to worry. It wasn't their going to Sweetgum Creek that concerned Clarinda. It was the homeward journey, and the danger that lurked in every patch of laurel.

"Mary Ann, have ye got my shirt ready?" Olus inquired.

She held it up for his approval.

He whistled."Sis, you're gonna make some feller a good housekeeper one a-these days." He snuck up behind her and tried to plant a brotherly kiss on her cheek.

"Skedaddle, before I brand ye." She raised the flat-iron and chased him around the kitchen.

Tom winked at Olus."Mary Ann, do ye want us to bring you a Tennessee feller home?"

"No, thank ye, I can git my own sweetheart I'll have ye know." She gave Tom a pair of khaki pants with a crease as sharp as a razor blade.

Mary Ann had blossomed into a mighty pretty girl and Tom had no doubt that she could get her own sweetheart."You sure know how to make a feller look good, sis. Thanks a bunch."

The boys hurried to their bedroom. When they emerged a few minutes later, Mary Ann inspected their appearance with a critical eye."Well... maybe Aint Berthie won't mistake ye fer tramps."

Olus winked at Tom and chuckled."That means we're lookin good, brother."

"Ha!" Mary Ann barked—she turned her head to hide a smile.

Clarinda listened to their jovial gab with a twinkle in her eye. Sometimes their banter would turn to anger in a flash, but the common thread of love that binds a family together was ever present and their spats didn't last long.

Olus wore a sky blue shirt that made his eyes look as blue as a deep ocean. Khaki pants, brown belt, and shiny brown shoes completed his outfit. His stunning smile, sun-streaked brown hair, and deep tan would stop the girls in their tracks on Sweetgum Creek.

Tom looked spiffy in a snowy-white shirt, ironed to perfection. He, also, wore sharp-creased khaki pants, brown belt and shiny brown shoes. Before shoving his comb in a hind pocket, he ran it through his thick, jet black hair. A heavy, wayward lock dropped down on his forehead again and again even after repeated strokes of the comb and a dab of Bryllcreme."Mary Ann, have I got hair on my collar?"

She inspected his collar and brushed his shoulders with her hand."Fer the love of Pete, are you'uns gonna primp all day."

He picked up the suitcase she'd packed and headed out the door."Come on, Olus, le's hit the trail."

Clarinda tried to hand a paper bag of food to Olus, but he refused it."I ain't goin down the road a-totin no dern paper poke a-biscuits."

Tom reached for the poke."I'll carry it, and you ain't gitten none of it."

They headed down the path—whistling and acting silly—primed and ready for fun and frolic in the grand old state of Tennessee. They'd have to walk every step of the way, but that didn't matter. They were healthy and full of the sap of youth.

They'd been walking a couple of hours when a flat-bed milk truck stopped."Hey, yew fellers wanna ride?"

"Shore do." They climbed in amongst the five-gallon metal cans. Tom settled himself as comfortably as possible and opened up his lunch poke. He brought forth a biscuit almost as big as a flapjack. It was stuffed with streaked fatback, fried crispy, and a fried egg. His beverage was a pint jar of black coffee.

Olus eyed the biscuit as Tom ate with gusto."Well?"

Tom stopped chewing."What?"

"Ain't ye gonna offer me a biscuit? I know you've got two more in 'ere."

"Damit, Olus, Mama packed yore dinner and you 'as too proud to carry a poke. And now ye want mine. You can starve fer all I keer."

"Well, gimme some coffee."

Tom drank half the coffee and passed the jar to Olus who was jiggling a milk can.

"What do ye think you're a-doin?"

"I like cream in my coffee," Olus said, and opened it up. It was three-fourths full. He filled the pint jar to the brim and drank it all without taking a breath.

"You want me to pour ye some?"

"Well... yeah, I'll take a couple of swallers."

"Fork over one a-them biscuits first."

Tom reached for the milk can."I can pour my own milk."

Olus put his arms around it and tilted it backward."You ain't gitten none till ye hand over a biscuit."

Tom gritted his teeth and shoved his lunch poke in Olus' face."There, eat it, ye dang pig. I could take that milk away from ye if I's a mind to."

Olus laughed."Oh, yeah? You want a-start hoofin agin? If that truck driver hears us in a squabble, he'll put us offa this truck. Its untellin what he'd do if he found out we opened and slobbered in his milk can."

Olus surrendered the milk can. He reached deep into the paper poke and brought up a mouth-watering fried apple pie. He took a bite and smacked his lips."Mmm... good. Ain't nothin better'n fried apple pie. Makin love to Madge is purt nigh as good, but not quite."

"You better keep yer mouth shut, brother. If Mama hears tell of yore shenanigans, she'll—"

"She'll what? Take a hick'ry switch to me? You ain't no saint, Tom. The only difference between me and you is you're sneaky and I ain't."

The truck came to a squeaky halt and the driver called out, "Okay, boys, there's the path to Sweetgum Creek. This is as far as I go in this direction."

The boys jumped off the truck and went to the driver's window."How much de we owe ye?"

"Not a thing. Yew fellers have a good time, heer?" He shifted into gear and took off in a cloud of dust.

The boys headed up the path to their Aunt Berthie's with renewed energy. They snickered about their adventures with C. J. and Madge, but looked forward to meeting some Tennessee beauties.

Aunt Berthie was a small woman and frisky as a kitten."Well, I'll swannie, if it ain't Olus an' Tom! Come in an' pull up a cheer. I know you youn-guns are starved plumb to death." She piled their plate high, chattering non-stop.

The boys tried to eat the delicious food on a stomach full of biscuits, fried pies and sweetmilk."Aint Berthie, we sure do appreciate this food, but we've already had dinner," said Olus.

"Ye have?"

"Yeah, Mama packed us a poke a-food."

"Well, I know ye can eat some fruit cake." She set ten layer slices before them.

Aunt Berthie had a son and daughter about the same age as Olus and Tom. Within the hour, word spread in the community that Berthie's nephews had come all the way from Levi's Mountain for a weekend visit. Young folk came in droves. The house rang with music, games and laughter all weekend.

By Sunday afternoon, the boys knew they should head home, but Aunt Berthie begged them to stay another night.

Early Monday morning, she cooked a huge breakfast and offered to pack them a basket of food for their journey.

"Nah, we don't want to put ye to all that trouble. We'll be home by dinnertime," said Olus.

"Ah, tain't no trouble. That's a long walk over the mountain, at least twenty miles, maybe more, wouldn't ye say?"

"It's somewhere's around twenty-five if we take a short cut," Olus said.

"Why, boys, you'uns will faint by the wayside fer certain. I've got plenty of biscuits and streaked meat left from breakfast. I can skeer up half a stack cake too. It won't take me but a few minutes to git it ready."

Olus rubbed his stomach."Thanks, Aint Berthie, but we better git goin. We put away enough biscuits 'n gravy to last all day."

Tom gave Olus a look that plainly said, 'Hush yore mouth and let her fix us some vittles!'

Aunt Berthie sighed."Well, you'uns tell yore Mama to come and see me while I'm still alive an' kickin. Seems we never git together anymore till there's a death in the fam'ly."

"Yeah... seems that way." Tom looked disappointed. He pictured the mountain trail they'd have to travel with no food—and all because of Olus.

"Thanks fer feedin us, Aint Berthie," they said in unison.

"You're mighty welcome, boys, and have a safe journey home."

For some reason the homeward hike seemed especially tiresome or perhaps they had frolicked too much. Olus decided to take a shortcut even though Tom had misgivings. He veered off the trail and Tom followed. They waded through a patch of trembling fern."Me and Papa walked this way when I 'as ten year old."

"Yeah, but a lot can change in that length of time—like the path could be long gone."

"Hush yer complainin. We'll be home in half the time it would take us to walk the long way."

For more than an hour, they zigzagged around boulders, stumbled over protruding roots, and got nowhere. Suddenly they stepped into a patch of sunlight and found themselves standing on a precipice. They looked down on a deep, dark, foreboding hollow that hadn't been touched by a ray of sun in ages."Damit, Olus, you've brought us to the rim of Hell."

A gentle breeze stirred the scarlet leaves of the maples. Olus sniffed the air."I smell whiskey, don't you?"

"Yeah..."

"Look!" Olus pointed to a thin wisp of smoke curling up from the hollow. Behind them, a dry twig snapped. They whirled around. Two beardy, dirty, bushy-headed backwoodsmen emerged from the undergrowth. Oh, Lordy, Olus thought with a quiver in the pit of his stomach. We've stumbled into a viper's den.

A red-faced fellow with a neck as thick as a shorthorn bull thumbed his nose and sniffed."Whut 're yew sonofabitches sneakin round here fer?" He slid his eyes at his grubby companion and winked."Nubs, hit looks like we got two danged idjits treed."

Scrawny, hatchet-faced Nubs nodded in agreement."Yep, shore as shootin." He eyed the boys with two of the meanest-looking black eyes ever set in a human head."Ain't yew idjits gonna ain'cher Hard Rock's question?"

Trusting their gut instinct, the boys sidled from the edge of the cliff and walked backward while keeping their eyes on the men. They stopped with a boulder at their back."We'll havta fight or die, brother," Olus whispered.

Hard Rock brought forth a chesty wheezing chortle that whistled through a gap in his lower front teeth. Swaggering toward them, he flexed his meaty fingers."Nubs, we're gonna teach these two piss-willies a lesson."

As if by magic, a straight razor appeared in Nub's hand. He brought it to his beaked nose and scratched with the blunt side, revealing two missing fingers."Are yew idjits ready to die today?" He hitched up his baggy britches and followed Hard Rock.

For a brief second, Olus and Tom's eyes locked and each knew the other's thoughts. Then they moved as one. Leaping forward with the speed and agility of a timber cat, Olus whipped Rufus' pistol from his hind pocket and brought the butt down on Hard Rock's head. Blood spurted, arched, and sprinkled the autumn leaves underfoot. He swayed and fell like a big chestnut snag.

Nubs moved like greased lightning. His skinny arm snaked out—his straight razor hissed. Tom's Stud tobacco pouch fell from his shirt pocket severed in half. In the same instant, Tom's right fist, adorned with steel knucks, caved Nub's mouth in. He went down and lay still. Tom picked up Nub's wicked-looking weapon and threw it over the cliff.

Breathing hard, the boys looked at each other."Are ye hurt, brother?" Olus asked, tugging at Tom's bloody shirt.

"Nah just nicked a little."

"Nicked, hell, he nearly shaved yer armpit. I guess yore reach is a bit longer than his or you'd be in bad shape fer certain."

Nubs groaned, then rolled on his side and gagged. Bloody vomit and teeth gushed forth. Hard Rock didn't move.

Tom cautiously stepped to Hard Rock's side and stared down at him."Lordy, do ye reckon he's dead?"

Olus stooped and pulled a six-inch knife from a leather sheath attached to the big man's belt."Nah, he's still a-breathin. I guess he thought he'd kill me with his bare hands." Olus straightened up and threw the knife over the cliff too."Sorry to let ye down—you big tub a-dung."

"Are we gonna just walk off and leave 'em?"

Olus shook his head in disbelief."Yer too soft-hearted for yer own good, brother. But, if it'll please you..." He dropped to one knee and put a finger on Hard Rock's neck."He's got a good heartbeat. We'd better git goin before he wakes up, but first ..." Leaning forward, he picked up a small strip of dead birch bark and broke it in half. He laid a piece over each eye of his foe.

Tom's eyes widened."Why'd ye do that?"

Olus chuckled."Because I'm a danged idjit. Now, le's skedaddle."

The boys scrambled up the mountainside, keeping a keen eye out for more bushwhackers. Before they disappeared around the bend, they looked back and saw the moonshiners sitting upright.

Somewhere on the western side of Levi's Mountain, the boys realized they were nowhere near any sort of trail. They took their shoes and socks off and waded across miry bogs and teeth- chattering streams. The only good thing about the afternoon hike was the ever-changing landscape. The autumn leaves overhead and underfoot made their journey seem surreal, like they were walking a glowing path through a dreamworld.

The sun pulled its last rays from the mountaintop when the boys stepped from the forest into a little sedge field. Tom plopped down on a flat rock."I cain't go another step till I rest. I'm as tard as Ol' Limber after a Saturday night fox hunt."

Olus slumped down beside him and took off his shoe to check the big blister on his heel."Yeah... me too."

"Dang! I'm hungry! My stumick has quit barkin and started growlin," grumbled Tom.

Olus picked up his shoe and smashed a black spider that had crawled from underneath a rock."Dang spiders give me the creeps. Ye know what I'd like to have? I'd like to have a big heapin platter a-fried chicken."

"Well, we could a-had a baskit of somethin good, but what did ye tell Aint Berthie? 'Oh, don't go to all that trouble, Aint Berthie, we'll be home by dinnertime,'" Tom mimicked in a nasal tone.

Suddenly Olus stood up and pointed to a small cabin at the foot of the hill. Smoke curled from the stovepipe sticking through its roof."Stop yore complainin and look down there."

Tom rose to his feet, hitching his belt in a notch to ease his hunger pains."So, that's a cabin down there. It ain't no benefit to us." He sat down again and gingerly took off a shoe to check his own blisters.

Olus gestured toward the cabin with his shoe."I'll bet you a buffalo nickel that a good Christian woman lives there. Why don't ye mosey down the hill and buy us some supper?"

"With what? I ain't got a thin brownie to my name. Why don't ye mosey down 'ere yoreself? You're the one with the gift of gab. Git goin!"

"All right, don't git yore bowels in a uproar. I'll go, but what'll I say?"

Tom brought forth a sound that was somewhere between a chuckle and a grunt."Beg, dern ye. Git down on yore knees 'n cry and snivel if ye have to. I'm-a tellin ye, brother, I ain't takin another step till I've had some vittles!"

"Well, you don't havta git so damn huffy about it."

Tom waved him away and blew on his raw heel. Olus slipped on his shoe and ambled down the hill. Every few steps he'd pause and look over his shoulder, but Tom ignored him.

Olus was the proudest son that Clarinda had. He'd never beg for food. This handsome fellow with the dreamy blue eyes and infectious toothy-grin had never begged for anything. Aunts, uncles, and folk all around, flung their doors wide when he passed their way."Well, I'll be hanged if it ain't Olus. Come in, boy, and pull up a cheer. Marthie has made chicken n' dumplins and aigg custard pie." No indeed, no beggar was he. He'd think of some way to get the food they needed.

At the edge of the yard, he hunkered down in the tall sedge to get a closer look at the cabin and surrounding area. Would there be dogs to contend with? Most mountain cabins had at least two short-tempered, mangy, sore-pawed hounds. They lolled around the kitchen door waiting for leftover biscuits and gravy. In his opinion, the meanest of hounds had sissy names like Rosebud, Queenie or Buttercup. Didn't his right ankle carry the dental imprints of an old yellow-fanged bitch named Pearl? Anyway, Ol' Pearl and all her kith and kin could smell a stranger a mile away. They'd take the seat out of a man's britches in two wags of a sheep's tail.

He scanned the porch and yard and didn't see a sign of a dog anywhere, not even a doghouse. He saw a washboard hanging on the trunk of a walnut tree and two upside-down laundry tubs on a bench under its spreading branches. Someone had been scrubbing laundry, because the tree trunk had a wet spot below the washboard. White sheets, shirts, and a pair of overalls flapped on a clothesline stretched between two maples. It appeared to be a peaceful place so he stood and eased out of the sedge.

He paused and pondered his next move. How should he begin his begging act? Play sick—nah, she'd think he was drunk. He pictured the lady of the house as a beautiful Christian maiden a-pinin to meet a handsome, hungry, wayfarin stranger. He chuckled at the thought and walked into the yard.

He stepped lightly in case the dogs were snoozing under the porch. The kitchen door stood wide open."Hello! Is anybody home?" No answer. He knocked and called again. Still no one stirred. He peered around the door jamb. The table was set for two. A three-legged cast iron pot of bubbling pinto beans drew his attention to the stove. Black-skillet cornpone rested on the stove's reservoir. His mouth watered like a hound dog waiting for table scraps.

He turned and scanned the yard with a quick glance. Caution be damned. Them vittles are goin up the hill, he thought. Quicker than a fox at the henhouse door he entered the room. He snatched spoons from the table and shoved them in his pocket. Grabbing two pot rags from the oven door handle he was out the door with the food in thirty seconds. Up the hill he ran, laughing like a fool.

Tom rose to his feet with a lopsided grin."You must a-done some humble beggin to git that feast."

"No, brother, I didn't even havta say please."

"Well, how did ye git it?"

Olus thumbed his nose and sniffed."Charm, brother, pure charm."

"That's a bunch a-bull."

Tom reached for the beans."Where's the milk? Didn't ye ast fer any?"

Olus frowned."How could I carry milk? I ain't got but two hands, ye know."

The boys fell silent as they tore into their supper. Hambone seasoning made the beans lip-smacking good. They complimented the cook by wiping the bean pot clean as a whistle. Tom scooped the last chunk of cornpone from the pan "Them was the best beans I've ever had, but I'd give my eye teeth fer a cold glass of milk. We're gonna havta find a spring soon or we'll be spittin blazes with heartburn."

"All right, brother, I went down to that cabin with my tongue a-hangin out like a half-starved dog and carried yore supper to ye. Now the least ye can do, is take the empty vessels back and thank the lady fer bein so obligin."

Tom sighed and rose slowly to his feet, expelling gas.

Olus frowned and fanned the air."Dangit, ain't ye got no manners?"

Tom laughed."Git use't to it. Them vittles are workin up steam fer the battle of the year." He raised his leg and let another one rip. Picking up the empty vessels, he strolled down the hill real lazy-like with spoons jangling in the cast iron pot.

The cabin door was now shut, but an eye watched him through a knot hole. As he set foot on the porch the door flew open. Tom saw a brown streak and felt the sting of broom straw across his face as she flogged his head."So! You're the low-down, sorry, good-fer-nothin daylight robber who stole my man's supper!"

Dropping the clattering vessels he flung his arms up to protect his head — to no avail. What a wildcat! With every blow her feet left the porch."A body cain't even go tuh the spring tuh fetch a bucket o' water 'thout bein pilfered. Soon'es my man gits here he'll kill ye — iffen I don't kill ye first!"

Tom staggered backward into the yard. He squeezed his eyes shut and lunged for the sedge field with rocks thumping his backside. When he reached the hilltop, Olus stood grinning ear to ear with a buttermilk moustache. While Tom was getting thrashed, Olus had slipped to the spring and filched a gallon of buttermilk from the spring box.

"Damn you! I could a-been killed. I've been broom-whipped by a witch!"

Olus slapped his thigh and doubled over laughing."I saw her whoppin ye. She could whip a dozen fellers like you."

Tom rubbed his head with a pained expression."I guess you'd a-laughed if I'd a-got shot, huh? We better git while the gitten's good. Her husband will be home any minute."

A blast of buckshot riffled the sedge around them. Tom snatched their suitcase and they headed up the mountain like the devil was after them. The jug of buttermilk hindered Olus speed, but he refused to leave it behind. The boys didn't stop till they crossed over the mountaintop."We're in North Ca'lina now," Olus said, panting hard.

With mock seriousness Tom leveled his green eyes on Olus."Yeah, them crazy hillbillies are gonna foller us to the mountaintop. They'll stop and her husband will say, "Shoot farr, womern, we cain't go no furder. We'uns done retch the state line."

Olus chuckled.

After catching their breath, the boys raced on till darkness overtook them. Stumbling over a large mossy log they lay there — and couldn't stop laughing.

"Give me a swig a-that buttermilk, Olus. Them beans are a-burnin my gizzard out."

Olus handed over the jug. Tom lifted it to his mouth and guzzled a quart without stopping.

"Dang! Don't drink it all, ye big glutton. Save me a few swallers."

Tom smacked his lips, breathed a sigh of satisfaction and passed the jug."Now gimme a smoke."

Olus pulled a can of Prince Albert from his hind pocket.

Tom frowned."Why do ye keep buyin Prince Albert when Stud is better?"

"Well, I happen to like it. You can take it or leave it."

Tom fingered his severed shirt pocket."I guess I'll take it."

The boys took cigarette papers from their pockets and rolled their own cigarettes. A bright harvest moon rose through the trees. They leaned against the mossy log and blew smoke rings. For a long time neither boy spoke; then, Tom sat up."Olus?"

"Yeah?"

"Does Mama know you're carryin Papa's gun?"

"No. Does she know you're carryin knucks?"

"No."

"She ain't gonna know neither. She'd never trust us agin. I couldn't find any bullets, but that pistol saved our lives, along with yore knucks and that sack a-Stud in yore pocket."

"Yeah, no doubt about it."

By the time they finished their cigarettes they were overcome with drowsiness so they curled up in a beautiful bed of autumn leaves and fell asleep. Their slumbers, however, were far from peaceful. The gassy beans and buttermilk transformed them into human balloons and they rolled and kicked all night long. Despite that, even the noisy owl in a tree nearby couldn't get them fully awake.

At daybreak, they were awakened by the chatter of a chipmunk sitting on the end of the log, watching them. Tom stared at the frisky critter and it stared back. He yelled, "Boo!" The chipmunk sprang through the air and hit the ground running. Tom whooped, and fell backward in the leaves, "Olus did ye see that? I've never seen anything move that fast."

Olus sat up, yawned, and raked the leaves from his hair."Stop playin peep-eye with the squirrels and le's git goin. Maybe we can make it home in time fer breakfast."

"Olus, did ye sleep easy last night?"

"No, cain't say I did."

"Did ye have nightmares?"

Olus laughed."No, did you?"

"I never had such a skeery dream in my life. That hatchet-faced Nubs chased me from tree to tree all night long. And that little pop-eyed witch was right behind him a-hollerin, "'Kill 'im. Take a straight razor to 'is roguish hide!'"

Olus chuckled."Why brother, you just foundered on beans."

"Didn't yore conscience bother ye last night?"

"Heck, no. Why'd ye ast?"

"You stole that woman's supper. Don't stealin bother ye?"

Olus sighed."It ain't stealin if yer starvin. I heard a sermont preached on that subject not long ago. The preacher said, "'Sisters, fail not to feed the stranger at yore door 'cause that pore hungry wayfarin feller may be a angel in disguise.'"

Tom chuckled."That preacher wasn't talkin about you, because you damn sure ain't no angel."

Tom removed his bloody shirt and shoved it into the log. The wound across his ribs looked like a long briar scratch.

Olus gave a low whistle."Well, a angel must a-been lookin out fer you."

Tom took a dirty shirt from their suitcase and slipped it on. It would never do to let their mama find out they'd been in a fight. No indeed, their mama must never know of their shenanigans.

It was ten o'clock Tuesday morning when the boys got home. Clarinda immediately wanted to know how the kinfolk fared on Sweetgum Creek.

"How was yore Aint Berthie?"

"Oh, she was fine. Everybody's fine. She said to tell you to come see her while she 'as still alive and kickin."

Clarinda chuckled."That sounds like Berthie all right. Did she say anything else?"

"No. That's about it," Olus said.

And that was all the information they gave their mama about their trip. Comes wash day and Tom's new shirt was nowhere to be found. Clarinda questioned him about it. He said he left it at Aint Berthie's. Clarinda never did hear of the fight with the moonshiners either.

Twelve

"Well, younguns, you've been to Sweetgum Creek. If we're goin to have a gatherin, it's high time we put the chicken in the pot. The snow will be a-flyin soon."

"Set the date, Mama," said Olus, "and ye better plan fer two extra because me and Tom are bringin our girlfriends."

"Which girlfriends?"

"C. J. and Madge."

"That'll be just fine, but they're a-gonna act like ladies."

Tom winked at Olus. "They are ladies. How could they act any other way?"

"Humph, ain't they the same girls that come here a-waggin baskits of vittles when we 'as buildin the house?"

"Yep."

Clarinda frowned. "Nice girls don't go out searchin fer boys."

"Aw, they're okay. We like our gals wild and sassy." Olus snickered.

"Well, them girls had better not come here and commence that huggin and kissin on ye amongst the fam'ly. It's ill-mannered and shows they ain't had a drap a-raisin."

This sort of talk was difficult for Clarinda because she was brought up in a time when open displays of affection were absolutely forbidden and never discussed.

"Yeah, we know the rules," Olus said, "but fer the life of me, I cain't understand what is wrong with huggin an' kissin."

"You'll behave, if ye know what's good fer ye."

The boys laughed. They knew their old-fashioned mama would never see things their way.

The following Saturday at sundown, Clarinda stood in the yard on a carpet of beautiful autumn leaves and waited to greet her married children, their wives and her grandchildren. She heard them on the homeward path laughing and singing. Olus and Tom strummed their instru-

104

ments with a girlfriend at their side. The girls' sang, "You get a line and I'll get a pole, honey..."

Everyone talked at once as they all filed through the door. Rhoda handed Clarinda a large platter of fried fish. Clarinda lifted the paper wrapping."Oh, it's speckled trout. I shore do thank ye. We ain't had a good mess a-fish fer a time and a time."

The daughters-in-law wore pretty cotton dresses. They ambled through the rooms inspecting every crack and crevice.

Mary Ann sniffed the air."Somebody's had a new perm. I smell wavin lotion."

Beulah and Rhoda grinned and patted their fuzz balls."I put Rhoda's in, an' she done mine, but hern curled better'n mine."

Mary Ann reached out and touched Beulah's hair."I'd never a-noticed it if ye hadn't told me."

The new house was spotless. Starched, ruffled white curtains adorned sparkling clean window panes. The lamp globes gleamed. The Home Comfort cookstove stood proudly in a corner of the kitchen, its cooking surface shiny from a rub down with a pork skin. A new kindling box made from scrap lumber sat snug against the wall. The big homemade chestnut dining table wore a new green-checkered oil cloth. The house smelled of allspice, vanilla and fried chicken.

Within minutes the dining table groaned with platters of fried chicken and vegetables of all kinds prepared plain and simple. The enameled kitchen cabinet shelf held stack cakes, pumpkin, apple and berry pies. The children's eyes grew big as they gazed upon a chocolate cake with white frosting baked by none other than Alena, the best cook among the daughters-in –law.

Clarinda asked the blessing and the feast began. Mary Ann and Charlotty filled sparkling snuff glasses with grape juice. The packed house spilled onto the porch. The rafters rang with laughter and fellowship. All the daughters-in-law exchanged small happy talk. But being a prickly bunch, they seldom got together without a tiff.

"That pie I brought ain't fitten to eat," remarked Beulah.

Parlee sniggered."Well, why did ye bring it?" Everyone laughed and Beulah blushed. She thought her pumpkin pie was doubtless the best dessert in the house.

Rhoda reached for a piece of cornbread but withdrew her hand."Who baked this dody bread?"

Dora June stared at her."I did. What's wrong with it?"

"It ain't done and it's got too much sody in it. You must a-used a whole box of Arm & Hammer."

"I didn bake it fer you." Dora left the kitchen in a huff.

Andy and Mandy and their niece and nephew, Punkin and Avery, sat on the porch steps and ate and giggled and told silly jokes. Punkin and Avery were actually two months older than Andy and Mandy.

Soon every ladder-back chair, bench, and nail keg was occupied. The overflow came in from the porch for second helpings. With plates piled high, they returned to the outdoors where they ate by the light of a harvest moon that lit up the mountain almost as bright as day.

Cool refreshing night breezes carried the aroma of the forest and Clarinda's apple orchard. From atop Levi's Mountain a screech owl's cry rippled down the mountainside and echoed through the hollow. The bejeweled night sky twinkled with God's brightest stars—it was a night to remember for a lifetime.

The strum of a guitar, the melodic ring of the mandolin, and the trembling note of a fiddle floated out the open door. Henry tucked his fiddle under his chin and limbered up his bow on "Sourwood Mountain." The children on the porch came to their feet and commenced dancing. Music and dancing were as much a part of their lives as eating and sleeping. Every child in the family could sing at an early age, and the majority played an instrument as well. They never had music lessons they just picked up an instrument, plunked on it a few days and started playing. Henry could play five instruments, but the fiddle was his favorite with the harmonica second. When he cut loose on the "Orange Blossom Special" with his fiddle, a body just couldn't keep the feet still.

Little Howard made a dash for the back bedroom where he kept his beautiful Gibson guitar. It was a gift from Aunt Amanda, a kind and wonderful lady who was dearly loved by all the family. She recognized Howard's talent and bought the guitar for him as a reward for helping her with chores. He'd been playing it for several weeks, but his older married brothers didn't even know that he had it. When Howard eased into the room with his guitar the music stopped. Clyde laid his mandolin aside and gave a low whistle."Little Howard, that guitar is bigger'n you. Where did ye find it?"

"Aint Amanda bought it fer me." Howard stroked the gleaming gold-colored instrument and began tuning it with their instruments. His long slender fingers danced from string to string.

"Well, buddy, do ye know the keys yit?" Big Avery asked.

Howard didn't reply—he just leaned into his guitar and began playing and singing.

"There's a rabbit in the log and I aint got my dog,
How will I get him, I know.

106

I'll get me a briar and I'll twist it in his hair,
That's how I'll get him, I know,
I know, I know,
That's how I'll get him, I know,
I'll get me a briar and I'll twist it in his hair,
That's how I'll get him, I — know."

What wonderful rhythm he had for a seven-year-old. His older brothers looked at each other, nodded their approval and joined in. Howard showed Big Avery that he knew all the keys with a lot more in between. He earned his brothers' respect as a musician that night. He could play any tune they suggested. His talent wasn't confined to the guitar, his tenor voice climbed the music scale as clear as a bell.

One might imagine the screech owl ceased its crying to listen to the beautiful harmony of Olus and Henry and Mary Ann singing, "Rock of Ages." Clarinda knew the good Lord was listening because she could feel His Presence. The family's love for Clarinda and music had brought them home where they could all be together.

They played instrumentals, sang train songs, love ballads, harmonized as duets, trios and quartets. Mary Ann and Lee even danced a jig or two. Then someone called out, "Who's gonna kicka coon?"

"O-lus, O-lus," the children chanted.

Olus jumped to his feet, loosened his belt a notch, and dropped to a squat. He began with left heel forward and right toe back. As the boys played a lively tune, Olus sprang up and down, right heel forward and left toe back, left heel forward and right toe back. With his brown, gold-streaked hair flying and pearly white teeth flashing, he clapped his hands after each move in rhythm with the music."Yip-yip," he hollered."Now this ol' coon's a-gonna travel." He kicked the coon through the kitchen and back to the settin room. Everyone clapped their hands and stomped their feet to the rhythm of the music. The little ones scattered as he circled left and right, and then came to his feet in one huge leap.

But he wasn't out of steam. He did a buck-and-wing across the floor to his sweetheart, Madge. She rose and waited till Henry tightened a fiddle string. When he cut loose on another hot tune, she gave a sassy kick and danced a jig that sent her skirt flying. The daughters-in-law gasped. The musicians commenced playing off-key.

Rhoda puffed up like an old setting hen because David's face shined with happiness as he watched Madge. He even forgot the words to the "Crawdad Song." Rhoda slapped Madge's twirling skirt down as she whirled by."Yore chop sack petticoat's a-showin."

Madge turned her back to Rhoda, leaned forward, and gave her skirt a quick flip over her rump. Her pink satin petticoat and garter belt showed. Rhoda gasped and nudged Beulah."Did you see what that floozy done?"

"No. I was gittin a dip a-snuff. What did she do?"

"She threw her skirt over her head and showed her hind end as plain as the nose on yore face."

Beulah almost lost her snuff."Shorely not. Clarinda will put that strumpet out the door."

"Humph, she won't do no such a-thang. Look! She's a-settin over there in the corner a-laughin her head off."

Beulah craned her neck and saw Clarinda wiping tears of joy from her eyes. As Olus danced near Rhoda, he stooped over and said, "Hog chop don't come packed in pink satin, Rhoda."

"I know it don't, but trollops do."

"I never seed the like," Beulah whispered, tugging her cotton dress down over her knees as far as it would go.

Rhoda and Beulah stewed and fumed, but nobody paid any attention to them. Shortly after midnight, Tom broke a guitar string and didn't have a spare so the boys called it quits. They had enjoyed themselves immensely and made plans to meet again soon. The moon was dropping behind the mountain when the gatherin came to a close. Clarinda's married sons carried their sleepy little ones down a starlit path toward home.

Before she closed her eyes in slumber that night, Clarinda thanked the Lord for her family and her new house on Levi's Mountain. Come Monday mornin, she thought, we'll gather the apples and git ready fer winter. She dozed off, happy and content.

With the last of the late beans in her lap, Clarinda sat on her porch and broke them. The garden in Lonesome Hollow was finished. She and Mary Ann had returned to the old homestead and gleaned every vegetable from the garden before the wildlife consumed them. They dug the potatoes, rutabagas and carrots. Tom borrowed Mr. Colliday's horse and sled and hauled them to Levi's Mountain. They stored them in a deep pit in the ground. With a board over the pit and dirt mounded upon it, they would keep fine. She and Henry dug ditches three-feet deep and lined them with leaves and straw. Placing the late cabbage heads in the ditch with roots up, they buried them. It was a no-fail method of keeping cabbage through the winter. The cold ground improved the taste and color. Clarinda and her children worked like beavers. They buried bushels of apples in the same manner as the potatoes. She and Mary Ann made apple butter, applesauce and dried them by the bushel. Mary Ann said she was sick and tired of apples.

"You won't be sayin that when the snow starts flyin." Clarinda said.

She wished she had a hog to slaughter. The streaked side meat and sausage were mighty good on cold winter mornings. The good Lord willing she'd buy a pig next year. The boys hunted grouse, squirrels, and rabbits, but pork was the preferred meat. They had plenty of milk and butter. And the combination of dried beans with canned vegetables and fruits completed their diet.

It was a comfort to know that her family would eat well when the blizzards roared through the mountains. Why, a family could survive a year or two with a cellar chock full of a bountiful harvest. The good Lord willin we'll dig a root cellar next year, she thought.

Clarinda finished the beans and sat dozing in her rocking chair, enjoying the warm late autumn afternoon. Forty-three-year-old and not one gray hair could be seen in her jet black hair. Her skin, smooth and pretty kept its youthful glow because she always wore a big-brimmed straw hat when out of doors. Her hands were strong, rough and calloused from years of toil, but they were gentle when tending her children. She had a sense of humor and loved to play with her children and grandchildren. Always generous, she never turned a borrower away empty-handed if she had the item one needed. Patience she possessed in abundance, but she could be blunt and forthright with an iron will too. Respected and loved by her children—a Baptist who believed every word in the Holy Bible, she tried to live by its teaching and principles.

Clarinda awoke to the barking of Molasses the pup. Rhoda, with her baby on her hip, walked toward the cabin. Clarinda sighed. Rhoda always brings bad news, she thought. When Rhoda reached the porch, Clarinda rose to her feet and offered her the rocking chair.

"No, I don't want to set down. I've got to git home soon," Rhoda snapped, tugging the baby higher on her hip.

Rhoda's spittin foam about somethin, Clarinda thought, it ain't her nature to come by fer a friendly visit. There must be a reason.

"Well, come in, and I'll make us some coffee. I baked a stack cake this mornin." Clarinda went inside with Rhoda following.

"I didn' come here to sip coffee and nibble fruit cake," Rhoda retorted.

Clarinda set the coffee pot on the stove firmly and turned to face her, "Well, what did you come fer?"

"I come here to tell you that Alexander gave me and David the authority to be keertakers of this place, and more'n likely we'll buy it next year."

Clarinda looked her straight in the eye."I don't believe a word a-that."

"Humph! I guess you'll believe it when I git the deed to this property!"

Clarinda took a large fruit cake from the cupboard, cut a generous slice and seated herself at the table. Rhoda stepped into the settin room, laid her babbling baby on the bed and let loose her signature chortle."Whaa-hoo-urf! Since I'm now in charge of this place, I'd better not hear tell of you'uns gatherin the apples, especially them Rebel apples."

Suddenly, Olus appeared at the door."What the hell is goin on around here?"

Rhoda whirled around and spluttered, "Why, I-I-I was just a-tellin Clarinda ..."

"I heard exactly what you said!" Olus moved across the room with amazing speed. He slammed Rhoda against the wall and held her there with his left hand around her throat. With his right hand he slapped her jaws back and forth—actually slapped the spit out of her.

"Olus, stop it!" Clarinda demanded, tugging at his arm.

He gave Rhoda's throat a final squeeze and a warning through gritted teeth."If I ever see or heer of you comin around here aggravatin Mama agin, I'll choke the hell outta you!"

When Olus stepped back, Rhoda slid down the wall in a slobbering faint."Git my baby," she squawked hoarsely and flopped to the floor.

The baby had rolled to the edge of the bed and was in danger of falling. Clarinda caught it in the nick of time. With the baby on her hip, Clarinda walked slowly to the kitchen and took a dipperful of water from a bucket. She carried it back to the settin room, and holding the dipper at arm's length she dumped the contents in Rhoda's face.

Rhoda squawked and sprang up."You'uns ain't a-gonna git away with this!"

Olus' handprint stood out on her jaws. She snatched her baby from Clarinda's arms and dashed out the door. Down the path she loped, sobbing and holding her head sideways like a chicken with its neck half-wrung.

The next few days were worrisome for Clarinda because she expected David to take sides with Rhoda, but it didn't happen. Rhoda's daddy came around instead."Clarinda, where's Olus?"

"I don't know."

"Ye might as well tell me."

"Are you callin me a liar?"

"Why, no." The old man eased himself down on the porch steps then pulled a knife from his overall pocket and commenced carving little notches in the steps.

"Well, Clarinda, since Olus ain't here, I'll jest tell you. I'm a-gonna sue him fer 'sault and batt'ry. Rhoda cain't speak above a whisper, and I'm not about tuh let him git away with chokin my girl."

Clarinda looked at him and her eyes squinted ever so slightly."Well, I'll tell you to quit whackin on my porch steps with that knife. And the next thing you can do is saddle yore carcass down the road."

Rhoda's daddy folded his knife and put it in his pocket. He rose to his feet and glared at her."You'll come down offa yer high horse when the sheriff comes here and slaps the han'cuffs on 'im."

Clarinda took a step toward him."I'll give you the count of ten to git off a-my property. You can walk or be carried—don't matter a hill a-beans to me which."One... two... three..." The old man moved faster than he had moved in years.

Clarinda didn't tell Olus that Rhoda's daddy had come looking for him, making threats. She knew that would only make matters worse. Every day for a week or more, she expected the sheriff or a deputy to come looking for her son. But they didn't show up. For a month the incident was fodder for the gossip mill. Most folk said Rhoda got what was coming to her. Within a few months it was seldom mentioned. But Rhoda didn't forget. She kept her distance from Olus and neither of them would speak in passing.

Thirteen

Winter • 1941

Winter brought snow by the foot instead of inches. Although Clarinda's new cabin was sheltered from the fierce west wind by the mountain, the family suffered anyway. Clarinda had been unable to obtain cured lumber to construct the cabin so Olus and Tom bought green lumber with their own labor at the sawmill. The second winter in their new dwelling, cracks appeared in the floors and walls as the planks seasoned out.

Mary Ann complained bitterly."Mama, the cracks in these walls and floors are wide enough to pitch Ol' Whiskers through."

Mary Ann had hated cats ever since the night Ol' Whiskers climbed through an open window, jumped on her bed and marked his territory across her pillow. The stench of cat poo and a scratching sound invaded her dreams. Groggy-headed she wobbled up on one elbow and punched her pillow. Phfftt! Gagging, she kicked the covers to the ceiling and leaped to the floor. That cat barely escaped with his life.

Ol' Whiskers was a good mouser, though. He'd kept the house and barn free of vermin in Lonesome Hollow. But Levi's Mountain was too wild for a barn cat. Great horned owls swooped down nabbing rabbits. Screaming hawks snatched Clarinda's baby chicks. Wild cats squalled on the mountainside. Black bears growled in the apple trees. Tooth and claw ruled the night, and Ol' Whiskers was too domesticated to survive. Big cat tracks in the snow around the barn led Clarinda to the hayloft where she found Whiskers stiff as a board. She didn't tell the children of his demise because he'd been their cat for several years.

The next storm came without warning. Dark snow-laden clouds boiled over the mountaintop and rolled down over Clarinda's cabin. She and the boys rushed outdoors and stacked a good supply of wood on the porch. Day after day the north wind roared through the timber, gobbled up their wood and spit the ashes from his teeth on Chinky Pin Ridge. They were down to their last cord when the south wind brought a warm spell.

"Younguns," Clarinda said, "we havta cut more wood, and we'd better make it snappy. Another storm's a-comin."

Tom chuckled."Look outside, Mama, the sun's a-shinin the snow's a-meltin—"

"And I seen a hazy ring around the moon last night," Clarinda interrupted."Olus, go sharpen up the ax. Tom, you can set the saw."

Tom sighed, and put away the shot gun he'd been oiling up for a rabbit hunt."Ever time I plan a good hunt, somethin happens. If it ain't a moon sign, it's the call of a whippoorwill." Taking a steel file from a corner shelf, he headed for the lean-to that served as a woodshed. Clarinda followed with hammer in hand. Tom laid the crosscut saw across an anvil and pounded the jagged teeth on each side. This task removed rough edges and kept the saw running true through the log. Nothing started a fuss quicker than two frustrated sawyers yanking at a dull saw. Clarinda inspected his work.

With sharpened crosscut-saw, ax, and steel wedges in hand, Clarinda and the boys headed up the mountain. They slogged through mushy snow searching for dead wood. Yanking fallen dead timbers from snowy undergrowth is a grueling task. Olus and Tom worked as a team. They slid, fell and cursed. Clarinda scolded them."Younguns, that cussin ain't gonna hep matters a bit."

"Maybe not, but it makes me feel better," Olus said, wiping snow from his face. As each block of wood dropped from Olus and Tom's crosscut saw, Clarinda and Henry loaded it on a small sled. With the sled piled high, they pulled it down to the cabin. They cut wood from daylight till dark for three days.

"Remember, younguns, a hazy ring around the moon means bad weather's on the way. Don't ye fergit it."

The boys rolled their eyes at each other and grinned. New falling snow had rendered them speechless.

While Clarinda and the boys worked on the mountain, fifteen-year-old Mary Ann kept the housework done and tended the little ones. Clarinda had channeled the spring's overflow, via wooden trough, into a wooden barrel some fifty feet from the cabin door. This handy water supply was used for laundry, bathing, and house cleaning. Mary Ann decided to take advantage of the sunny day and do laundry. It had stacked up during the bad weather.

She began by stoking the fire in the big Home Comfort cookstove in the kitchen. Next, she carried water from the wooden barrel and filled a large tub she'd set on the stovetop. While the water heated, she pulled the bench from behind the eating table and set an empty tub on it. Hot water from the stove's reservoir filled the tub three-quarters full. She stepped outside and took the washboard down from a nail on the wall. Returning to the kitchen, she set the washboard in the tub and placed a bar of

113

homemade lye soap in its soap holder. Like her mama had taught, she separated the clothes by type and color. Beginning with white sheets and pillowcases then towels, shirts etc.

She attacked the laundry with gusto. Pulling one article at a time onto the washboard, she slathered it with soap and scrubbed it on both sides. After wringing the water out, she tossed it into a tub of rinse water. She changed the laundry water as needed. Her poor hands suffered from the lye soap, but she didn't stop till the job was done. She looked out the kitchen window, admiring the snowy-white sheets and shirts flapping in the breeze.

On the third day, Clarinda and the boys came down from the mountain to a hurried dinner of potato soup and cornbread that Mary Ann had prepared. An hour later, they returned to their wood cutting. After washing the dishes and tidying up the kitchen Mary Ann scrubbed the floors. Steam rose from the planks as she rinsed them with hot water from the stove reservoir. She swept the water through the floor cracks and the planks dried fast.

Streaks of sunshine fell across the floors through cracks in the walls. The little ones stood at the settin room door and waited for permission to set foot on the scrubbed floor.

Mary Ann stood with hands on hips and stared at the wall cracks."Billy Dan, gather up all the old catalogs and rags ye can find. We're gonna chink these walls." They worked like fighting fire. Billy Dan tore the catalogs apart and rolled the pages into tubes then handed them to her.

"I'm gitten tard a-wakin up ever mornin with a snowdrift on my bed," she muttered, pounding the tubes in place with a hammer.

Billy Dan leaned toward her and whispered, "Mary Ann, look behind ye."

She whirled around and caught the twins with their fingers buried in the cracks. Coils and wads of paper lay in neat piles along the base of the wall. They'd cleared every crack as high as they could reach.

"I'll be—" Mary Ann nabbed them but they slipped through her clutches and fled to their favorite hideaway—behind a stack of quilts in the bedroom. Disgusted, she didn't pursue them. Although her energy flagged, she finished the walls.

Soon Andy and Mandy grew tired of their cozy corner and ventured out. The house was quiet. The task of stacking wood in the shed had the rest of the family outdoors. The noise of chickens under the floor grabbed their attention. They dropped to their knees for a peek through the floor cracks. They giggled. Mary Ann's scrub water had drenched the flock.

"Le's m-make 'em fite."

"Okay."

They ran to the kitchen and snatched chunks of leftover cornbread from a platter on the stove reservoir. What fun they had! The chickens fought like the dickens for every crumb. Then the spoiler opened the front door and stepped inside.

"Stop feedin them chickens! The house will stink like chicken dung!"

Andy's blue eyes studied Mary Ann through his cotton-white bangs. He pinched his nose and made a face."Shewee."

Mandy raised her chin defiantly."Who keers?"

Mary Ann grabbed her, but she jerked loose and fled to the kitchen with Andy at her heels. They scrambled under the dining table. Mary Ann gave chase, but stopped and stared at the kitchen floor."Good gosh a-mighty! It looks like a horde of mice had a shindig in here. I'm a-gonna whip yore hind ends this time." She gritted her teeth and dove under the table.

What a racket arose!

Olus stepped through the doorway."What's goin on? Why are y'all under the table?"

"Mary Ann's gonna whup us," Mandy squalled.

"No she ain't."

The salt and pepper shakers danced a jig across the table as the twins overwhelmed Mary Ann and scampered to safety. They ran to Olus. He scooped them up in his arms, then took a good look at the floor and made a face.

Mary Ann regained her feet and stomped from the room in a huff. Moments later, she saw Olus with a broom in hand, showing the twins how to clean up their mess.

Darkness came early as another blizzard struck. Day after day, the snow kept falling. The temperature hovered around zero. The children awoke one morning to find an owl perched on a curtain rod. The creature had flown in under the eaves seeking shelter. They squealed with delight. Howard claimed ownership. He coaxed Screech onto a broomstick and carried him from room to room.

The flour gave out first then the lamp oil. Three days in a row they ate cornbread and cornmeal gravy for breakfast.

"Mama, can I have a biskit, please?" Mandy begged.

"M-me too," Andy said, "a-a great big 'un with apple butter on it."

Solemn-faced, Clarinda turned away and swallowed the lump in her throat.

Comes night, Mandy cried with an earache. Andy barked with the croup. Clarinda arose and lit the blizzard lamp. The simple apparatus consisted of a string coiled in a small dish of hog lard. The string acted as a wick, drawing in the melted grease as it burned. She spooned warm ashes onto a flannel rag, tied it securely, and laid it on Mandy's ear. She brought out a round tin of Watkins Medicated Ointment and rubbed it on Andy's chest. Then she applied a warm flannel cloth which made the remedy comforting and more effective. Soon they returned to their slumber.

Three hours later, Mandy awoke to the sound of her mama softly praying. She sat up in her roll-away bed and rubbed her eyes. Mama was kneeling at the foot of her bed. She could have reached out and touched her, but she didn't. Mama's voice shook as she prayed. Mama's skeerd—somethin bad is happenin, Mandy thought. Tears rolled down Mandy's cheeks, but she didn't make a sound. Instead, she chewed on her fingernails and listened. She heard her Mama ask the Lord for bread to feed her children. Mandy loved her dearly and couldn't bear to hear her troubled voice another minute."Mama, I ain't hungry no more."

Clarinda rose from her knees, gathered Mandy in her arms and took her into her bed."I'll swannie, yer a-tremblin like a leaf. You musn't worry. Yore mama asts the Lord fer bread ever day." Mandy settled down and both dozed off.

Toward daybreak, four young roosters commenced honing their crowing skills under the floor. Congregated under the bedroom where Olus and Tom slept, the noisy cocks seemed to be in competition.

"What the hell—?" Olus leaned over the edge of the bed he shared with Tom. He snatched up his shoe and thumped the floor."Stop that damn racket!"

Tom slammed a pillow against his head."Damit, why don't they roost in the barn?"

"Hush yer cussin, younguns." Clarinda eased from bed and dressed in haste. She hurried to the kitchen and built a fire in the cookstove. The roosters stopped crowing when they heard her moving around. While the stove heated, she set the table and brought out her wooden bread bowl—cornbread would be the fare again. Then she picked up a water bucket and stepped outside.

She always brought in fresh water for their morning coffee. She paused and listened to the silence. The eastern sky was aglow. Long icy swords sparkled from the edge of the cabin roof. Wood smoke from the stovepipe curled upward into the frigid air. That's a shore sign of fair weather, she thought. She raised her eyes heavenward just as the sun kissed the mountaintops and ridges. The scene brought Scripture to mind. "And God said, Let there be light: and there was light." (Genesis 1:3). All outdoors shone so bright she had to shield her eyes with her hand. The summit of Levi's Mountain wore a frosty crown that shimmered against the deep blue sky. Her spirit soared. Joy cometh in the morning!

She made new tracks in the snow to the spring. Stooping down, she shoved her bucket into the clearest, purest water that nature can provide. Little snow buntings flew from a tree branch overhead dusting her hair with snow. With bucket brimming full she returned to the cabin and made breakfast.

The children loved eggs, but the hens hadn't laid an egg since the first cold spell. The little ones climbed on the bench and found their place at the dining table. Howard looked at the gritty-tasting, cornmeal gravy on his plate then turned his big blue eyes up to Clarinda."Mama, I was wishun fer a biskit."

Andy chimed in, "I-I was wishun fer a bunch a-biskits."

Howard's next remark kept Clarinda's eyes from welling up."Mama, can me and Billy Dan crawl under the floor and squeeze some aiggs outta them hens?"

Clarinda knew her children could read her expressions."Bless yore hearts my darlins, you shall have biscuits fer supper."

"Yea!" They clapped their hands with joy.

An hour later, she and Henry wrapped themselves against the cold and headed down the mountain to Hedgeweth's Store. She needed flour, lamp oil, matches, and sweet oil for Mandy's earache. This day she would have to ask for credit. She hated being in debt. She knew that Olus and Tom would help her pay it when the sawmill started up in spring. But it bothered her. It wasn't fair to put burdens on their young shoulders. On the other hand, she knew they were tired of cornmeal gravy too.

Mr. Hedgeweth owned the store, but his middle-aged daughter, Myrtle, looked after the business from time to time. Clarinda hoped to see Mr. Hedgeweth. It took him longer to fill an order, but his friendly smile was worth the wait. His moody daughter was sour as a green possum grape.

Clarinda sighed and her shoulders drooped as they entered the store. Myrtle worked behind the counter arranging stock on the shelves. To further add to Clarinda's dismay, a crowd of lazy loafers had congregated around the potbellied stove. She considered walking out the door, but the voices of her children echoed in her ears. I was wishun fer a biskit, fer a bunch a-biskits. She couldn't go home empty-handed.

In order to get Myrtle's attention, she moved toward the tally counter. This maneuver brought her within six-feet of the jabbering men. They fell silent. She kept her composure despite their stares. You rascals ain't got a speck a-manners, she thought. Henry moved to her side and pointed to a new crosscut saw hanging on the wall. They chatted quietly. The men returned to their gab.

The men folk enjoyed tobacco in all its forms. Their favorite pastime was chewing, dipping, smoking, baking their shins by the stove, and spinning yarns. Lank, a tall, slender stalk of pure Appalachian corn, sat in their midst. He appeared to be an average loaf-about. His plaid flannel shirt, overalls, and brown brogues laced with leather strings were common wear. But his gray slouch hat and easy smile set him apart from the rest. Behind his sleepy-looking brown eyes, the cog-wheels of a remarkable memory worked like a clock. In a split second he could snatch a tale from yesterday or yesteryear or make one up in his head.

Clarinda didn't like Lank. Some of his tales were condescending to women folk. He told a story about the day he persuaded his wife to go with him to town."I drapped 'er off at the Five and Dime and told 'er to stay there whilst I took keer a-business." Lank swore—but not on the Bible—that she headed for the underwear counter on the trot. She plowed through a stack of bloomers three-feet-high trying to turn up a pair made from a chop sack. According to Lank, she was mighty particular about her underwear. That tale dried up his wife jokes. Lank declared that sleeping on a floor pallet for a month had bridled his tongue.

Lank's wife would be spared this day, but Myrtle the store clerk would not. Lank spat a stream of ambeer toward the spittoon with the accuracy of a sharpshooter.

"Damn, Lank, how'd ye do that?" one scruffy fellow asked.

"Practice, fellers, practice." Lank stretched out his long legs, tilted himself back in his ladder-back chair, shoved his hat forward to a jaunty howdy-do and twined his fingers behind his head."Ye know fellers," he began in his slow lazy drawl, "I feel plumb wretchit tuhday—never slept a peaceful wink last night. I fit the kivers till midnight, and then I had one a-them... uh... whatsyecallits?" His eyes roamed the circle of captivated listeners as he waited for a response. He liked a participating audience.

"Nightmars?" someone suggested.

"Yep, that's it, a nightmar. I drempt I died an' went tuh Hail. And right smack-dab in the middle o' Hail set a big black three-lagid kittle. And all around that kittle was purt nigh a hun'ert little demons. They 'as jest a-laughin an' a-daincin an' a-pokin the farr with their red pitchy forks. By the grannies, they 'as shore a-makin the sparks fly. From the corner a-my eye, I seed the big muckety muck."

One fellow unloading his jaw in the spittoon paused."The big muckety muck?"

Lank looked irritated."Dayum, Ode. Shorely ye know who that is?"

Ode shook his head."Nope, never heerd of 'im."

Lank brought the front legs of his ladder-back chair to the floor, leaned forward and raised his voice."He's the head-knocker o' Hail—the gran-pappy of all devils—Ol' Lucyfear hisself."

"What was he doin?"

Lank settled back in his chair and breathed out slowly."Ay... he 'as jest a-standin 'ere in the flickerin shadders with his arms crost. Dayum! He 'as a mean-lookin booger. Well... atter a bit, I sidled over tuh that ol' scalawag and I said, 'Howdy... what's ye got a-bilin in this here pot?' I put out muh hand tuh lift the lid. And like a blue streak, that wickit devil whipped his forkid tail acrost my knuckles and hissed, 'Don't tetch that pot! I've got ol' Myrtle Hedgewitch in 'ere!' He ground his teeth and a puffa blue smoke shot outta his nose an' he said, 'I'm a-gonna brile her dayum stingy hide till it crackles like a chitlin.'"

The guffaws rattled the rafters and the spittle flew. Lank paused till everyone reset their cuds and wiped their chins on their sleeves. Every man except Lank craned his neck toward Myrtle. She ignored them and continued her work. She hadn't noticed Clarinda and Henry waiting for service—but Lank had. He acknowledged them with a polite nod and called out, "Hey, Myrt, are ye gonna keep these folks a-waitin all day?"

Myrtle straightened up."I'll be with you in a minute, Clarinda."

Lank spat over his shoulder and, of course, hit the spittoon dead center. Then he continued his tale."Fellers, I tell ye, it was a skeery thang tuh see... mighty skeery. Why these puny shanks a-mine was a-quiverin like two leaves of tremblin fear'n." He reached down and wrapped his long skinny fingers around his thigh, as if to quell the malady.

Ode snickered and scratched his stubbly neck."No wonder yer shanks trembled they ain't no bigger'n two rye straws."

"That's right, Odie, they ain't quite as big as that sweet tater a-stickin betwixt yore eyes."

The men whooped.

Ode just grinned and wiped his snoot on his sleeve.

"What happened next, Lank?"

"Well... , atter my knees quit knockin I picked up the nerve tuh ast that ol' devil another question. In a squeaky-like voice I ast, 'Mister Lucyfear, what in tarnation has ol' Myrt done tuh make ye so vengeful, tuh make ye render her out o'er the gritty grates?'"

One fellow peeped around the stovepipe at Myrtle and snickered.

Lank continued."Well... 'at big muckety muck shifted hisself over tuh one clovent hoof, leaned on 'is pitchy fork and looked down on me like

119

I's a warty toad. 'Listen, ye little botch a-Egypt, I don't know why I'm a-tellin ye this, but Myrtle Hedgewitch come a-stompin through here a-snatchin up lawyers. She tried tuh steal my shaykels of gold, tried tuh take over my tarrytory, and gen'ly speakin, dayum nigh tore Hail all tuh pieces!'"

An explosion of laughter erupted around the stove. One short fleshy man leaned back and cackled like a hen, and then his chair slipped. For a brief moment there was a possibility that his brains might be dashed out on the anvil behind him. With a flurry of arm waving he regained his balance, put his trotters on the floor and commenced coughing.

The nearest fellow slapped him between the shoulder blades."What's a-matter, Luther, did ye swaller yer cud?"

"Herrumpffhh, herr... uummppffhh! I'm all right," Luther replied, pulling a kerchief as red as his face from his hind pocket.

All the men, except Lank and Luther, stole glances at Myrtle.

"Lank, you are the biggest fool that ever darkened the door of this store," Myrtle declared.

Lank grinned ear to ear."Aw... hold yer cork, Myrt." He leaned toward her with outstretched hand and wiggled his fingers."Pitch me a chaw a-that Chattanooga Chew. My gizzard's a-gitten dry."

"You'll wait your turn," she snapped, and turned toward Clarinda and Henry.

Lank withdrew his hand slowly."Dayum, she's a mite tetchy tuh-day, ain't she?"

The men puckered their lips in a useless effort to contain their spittle. Their shoulders shook with suppressed laughter, their eyes danced with delight.

One fellow brought forth a plug of homegrown tobacco and leaned toward Lank."Try this — g'arnteed tuh wet yer craw."

"Dayum, 'at twist would choke a wild hawg." Lank declined the offer."Myrt will brang me a chaw terrectly."

Clarinda felt sorry for Myrtle, but couldn't understand why she allowed the men to hang around the store. If it was my store, she thought, I'd send them rascals down the pike even if I never sold another plug of tobacca, but then, I'm not Myrtle.

Myrtle waved Clarinda toward the candy counter where they could conduct business without having to shout over the loud men."What can I help you with today?"

The soft tone of Myrtle's voice took Clarinda by surprise."Before I give ye my grocery list, I need to know if you can let me have credit."

"We'll see what we can do." Myrtle took the list from Clarinda's hand."Do you want fifty pounds of flour?"

"No, twenty-five will be enough. Oh, by the way, would ye happen to have any fresh aiggs on hand?"

"Yes, I have several dozen. How many do you need?"

"Three dozen."

As Clarinda and Henry left the store they heard Lank begin another tale."Did I ever tell you fellers 'bout the time ol' Fudge Hockeydoo got lost on Lost Ridge?"

On the way home, Clarinda pondered on Myrtle's behavior. Had Lank's story softened her up? Not likely, yet, something had sweetened her attitude. She had even dropped two handfuls of peppermint candy in the bag, saying, "That's for the children—no charge."

I'm just thankful I've got my younguns some bread, Clarinda thought, and lengthened her stride with renewed energy. They had three hard miles to climb. She'd promised her children a big breakfast for supper and she'd keep that promise.

Suddenly she saw something sticking up in the snow. She had almost stepped on it. Stooping down, she picked up a small tobacco pouch. This was no ordinary Stud tobacco pouch, this one had a roll of money inside.

Henry's eyes widened with excitement."How much is it, Mama? How much is it?"

"I don't know yit. I ain't had time to count it."

She pulled out $150. 00.

"What are ye gonna buy with it?"

"Nothin."

Henry couldn't believe his ears."What! You're not gonna spend it?"

"It's not our money. It belongs to somebody else."

"Ain't you ever heard of finder's keepers, loser's weepers?"

She ignored his remark."Listen, Henry, and listen good. You are not to tell a livin soul about this money. Do ye heer me?"

"Oh, all right."

"Now, le's git home."

When they came in sight of the cabin, Clarinda saw her children's faces in the window. They scampered to unbutton the door for their mama. They danced around her as she gave out the candy. She wasn't going to make them wait for their treat—no indeed.

Howard tugged at her sleeve."Do we git biscuits and gravy too?"

"I promised, didn't I?"

"Yea!" They all yelled as one.

Mary Ann already had the cookstove hot so Clarinda put her coat away, rolled up her sleeves, washed her hands and went to work. The kitchen was warm and cozy. The little ones climbed on the bench and took their places at the table. They sucked peppermint sticks, giggled, and watched their Mama knead dough. She worked fast. She pinched off a lump of dough and rolled it into a ball. She placed the ball in the biscuit pan and flattened it with the heel of her hand. Each biscuit had her handprint on it. When she commenced breaking eggs in a skillet the children clapped their hands for joy."I want two aiggs, Mama," Howard called out.

"You cain't have none," Mandy said.

"Mamaaa... , I can have two, cain't I?"

"Yes, you can have all the aiggs ye want."

The children's eyes shined with happiness as Clarinda put the food on the table. The large green platter of golden brown biscuits, and a big white china bowl of steaming gravy, had them swinging their legs from the bench and making happy sounds.

"Is that a swarm a-bees I heer?" Clarinda teased, as she spooned eggs onto their plates from the big cast iron skillet. Olus, Tom, Henry, Mary Ann and Lee served themselves.

With their plates loaded, all the children fell silent. The only sound around the table was the tap of forks and spoons as they filled their empty bellies with the food they loved. As Clarinda settled herself at the table she gave her apron pocket a pat. The money was still there. After supper, she stashed it under her straw tick.

Clarinda held the money for two weeks. Then she dropped word in the community that she'd found a substantial amount of cash. The first claimer said he had lost a billfold with $35. 00 inside. Clarinda turned him away. The next inquirer was a deacon of the church. She asked him to describe how his money was carried, how much he had lost, and when.

"Well, about two months ago I sold my terbaccer crop. I put most of the money in the bank, but I kept back $160. 00 which I rolled up and put in a Stud terbaccer pouch. When it commenced snowin, I figured we was in fer a blizzard so I put the pouch in my pocket and headed down the mountain tuh Hedgeweth's Store. I walked the same path the gen'ral public does. I spent $10. 00 at the store, and put the rest a-my money back in the pouch. I shoved it deep in my coat pocket. I didn' miss it till I got home. I tried tuh foller my tracks tuh the store, but the snow had kivered 'em up. Anyway, $150. 00 is the amount that I lost."

Clarinda gave the man his money.

"I shore do appreciate ye holdin my money fer me. I promise ye fair and square that I will give you a twenty dollar reward as soon as I git one a-these fifties changed."

She never received a cent.

When the next protracted meeting commenced, the old deacon took his customary seat in the amen corner of church. He loudly encouraged the visiting preacher, "Amen brother! Hallelujah! Tell 'em 'bout it, brother!" His eyes, with a holier than thou gleam, roamed over the congregation and lit on Clarinda. Their eyes locked.

Clarinda's expression revealed her thoughts. Why you ol' two-faced lyin hypocrite, I'd like to slap ye off a-that bench. The deacon blinked and looked away. The preacher shouted on, but the deacon was mute—the gleam in his eye snuffed out. As Clarinda watched, he seemed to shrink before her eyes...

Suddenly, her attention swung to the preacher.

"How can ye call yoreself a Christian and hold a grudge against yer neighbor?" he shouted.

Her conscience smote her hard—He's right and you know it, Clarinda McCloud.

After the sermon, the church members congregated around the altar for fellowship. As the choir sang "Standing On the Promises," Clarinda walked over to the old deacon and shook his cold bony hand warmly."God bless ye, brother."

His lower lip quivered.

She turned away with her eyes full of cleansing tears and raised her voice in song..."By the living word of God I shall prevail, standing on the promises of God."

Fourteen

Spring • 1942

Ol' Clyde

Howdy, kids, my name is Clyde —
I'm here to stay — so I've been told —
But I cannot as yet decide,
If I should move into this fold.
Have you a stable, big and warm?
My joints all tend to stiffen up ... ,
And how are vittles on this farm?
I take my sweet feed by the cup.
For breakfast, give me corn or oats,
Then turn me out to pastures green.
Don't barn me in with sheep and goats,
I never could endure the things.
Yep, I'm a logger, a horse with pride —
Tickle my ears — I'll give you a ride.

*A*t last, the long cold winter gave way to spring. Wildflowers poked their fragile heads through a carpet of moist brown leaves and raised their faces to the sun. Wild azalea and dogwood bloomed in profusion on the mountainside. Songbirds warbled amid the blossoms in the old Rebel apple tree — and Olus fell in love.

Clarinda's sister, Etta, had been a widow for years when she met a man from Kentucky. He was a widower who had no children, but he made friends easily with Etta's four. After a brief courtship, he and Etta married. Soon after the wedding, the groom's relatives from Pennsylvania arrived for a visit. Among the group was a girl named Margie.

Clarinda knew something was afoot when Olus and Tom went whistling down the path carrying their instruments of music, dressed in their Sunday best on a Wednesday."Where do you younguns think yer a-goin?"

"Aint Etta's. She needs us today," Tom replied.

"Fer what?"

"To cut wood. She's got a house full of comp'ny to cook for."

"Ye cain't cut wood with a guitar and a fiddle. Besides, yer Aint Etta's got a husband to cut her wood," Clarinda snapped.

The boys looked at each other and quickened their step. They wanted to get around the bend before Mama found a chore they must do."Whew! That was a close shave," Olus said as they disappeared from her sight.

The next day, they dressed up at twilight, and gathered on the front porch for a music session. Olus' fingers danced up and down the neck of his Gibson guitar in a rollicking ditty.

"Are ye gonna play that tune fer Margie tonight?" Tom asked.

"Maybe... damn, that girl's stacked like a—" He raised his hands and brought them downward in a slow curvy gesture. The boys let out a raucous guffaw. Olus started to make a rowdy comment but clammed up when he saw Andy and Mandy listening.

Observing that the boys had dressed up again, Clarinda bent her ear to their conversation and overheard them. The next afternoon, she moseyed down the path and over the hill to Etta's house. She found her sister in the kitchen on her knees with her head in the oven. She had a bucket of sudsy water at her side. Etta was a finicky housekeeper. From ceiling to floor, throughout her house, not one spot of dirt could be seen.

"I expected to find you cookin up a storm," Clarinda said."The younguns said ye had comp'ny."

Etta pulled her head from the oven."I did have. But they all left this mornin... except Margie. She's stayin a couple of weeks longer."

"Where's Charlotty?"

"She's tote'n water. Tomarr's warsh day."

"Where's Margie?"

"She's piled up in the dern bed." Etta rose to her feet, pitched her cleaning rag in the bucket and wiped her sweaty brow with her apron tail."I oughta go in there, throw back the kiver and drench her sorry hind end with this lye water." She gritted her teeth and snatched up the bucket.

Clarinda smiled."Aw... Etta, put the bucket down. You shorely wouldn't treat yer husband's kinfolk that a-way."

Etta reluctantly set the bucket aside. She had a temper and didn't shilly-shally around a subject when she got riled. She yanked a ladderback chair from the table, plopped down and fanned her red face with her apron."She ain't worth a tinker's damn. She spends most of the day a-primpin fer Olus."

"I'll put a stop to Olus a-comin here till she leaves."

Etta let out a cynical chuckle."It's too late fer that. Olus is crazy 'bout 'er. As the old sayin goes, she'll dole out the corn—and choke 'im on the cob."

Suddenly, Margie emerged from a bedroom and passed through the kitchen. The sisters almost lost their snuff. She wore red shorts and a white blouse tied in a knot that bared her stomach. She'd caught her blonde hair up in a red scarf that matched her shorts. Her dark brown eyes and shy smile were beguiling indeed. If she'd overheard Etta's remarks she didn't let on.

Clarinda didn't like that girl, no siree. She seemed older than Olus—sly—maybe even dangerous. Clarinda questioned Etta about the girl's reputation.

"She's my husband's niece, and that's all I know to tell ye," Etta said, then added, "What if she traps Olus? You know... gits in the fam'ly way?"

Clarinda leaned toward Etta with a wry smile."Etta, you always did have a way of puttin my mind at ease."

Clarinda worried and counted the days for Margie's departure. Before the happy day arrived, Olus walked in the kitchen and announced his plans."Mama, I'm goin to Pennsylvania to find work."

Clarinda ladled up a large brown bowl of cream gravy. What about the sawmill? Are ye gonna just quit Mr. Colliday?"

Olus turned his back to Clarinda and paced the floor in silence.

"Does that Pennsylvany girl have anything to do with this?"

"Why heck no. Where'd ye git that notion?"

With a firm voice she warned him."Son, you ain't never been away from home. You'd better be keerful who ye run off with."

"Yer right about one thing, I ain't never been away from home." He whirled around and faced her, his blue eyes flashing with anger."I'm eighteen now, and I'm goin to Pennsylvania. I ain't workin myself into the grave at no damn sawmill like Papa did."

"I didn't say ye had to."

He strode out the door and went down the path at a fast clip. Clarinda knew he was headed straight for Margie. Suddenly Clarinda's anger shifted to her sister."Etta should a-sent that girl home with her family two weeks ago," she muttered.

Later in the day, Olus returned and apologized for his outburst of temper."Don't worry, Mama, I'll find a job and a place to stay. If I don't, I'll come home."

Two days later he was gone. The family missed him terribly. The little ones asked about him often."Mama, when is Olus a-comin home?"

"I don't know, Mandy. Soon I hope."

126

Two weeks passed, and then his letter came. He'd found work on a dairy farm. The farms in Pennsylvania were beautiful. Margie's folks provided room and board. Of course he paid them because he was no bum. He doubted he'd get married. He didn't like farming that good and was looking for a job that paid more money.

The little ones danced around her as she read the letter."Did Olus mention us... did he?"

"Yes, he says fer Howard and Billy Dan to keep the wood box filled. And he sends kisses and hugs to Cottontop and Pug." Clarinda pulled four dollars from the envelope."He sent each one of ye a dollar. We'll go to the store tomarr and you can spend it."

The children returned to their play, chattering about the candy and gum they'd buy with their Olus money.

Despite Clarinda's concern for Olus, life went on. Garden time was at hand. According to the Farmer's Almanac the moon was on the wax. Potatoes and all manner of root crops should be planted before it moved into another phase. She and Henry cleaned out the log barn and scattered manure over a patch of ground nearby. Tom borrowed Mr. Colliday's team and laid his hands to the plow.

"Son, ye done a good job," Clarinda said, reaching down and scooping up a handful of soil."This ground is soft and rich. It'll grow good taters and beans."

Tom looked over the ground with satisfaction."Ain't you gonna plant any Tommy Toe 'maters? I really like the yellow ones."

"Shore I am. I sowed 'em in a bed six weeks ago. They're nearly two inches high already. I'll set 'em in the garden when the sign is in the Balance."

"Where did ye learn about signs and stuff."

"It's been passed down through the generations. Don't plant nothin when the sign is in the Secrets. You'll git lots a-blossoms but little else."

Clarinda saved her garden seeds from year to year. She was eager to get her seedlings in the furrow. Shouldering her hoe she called, "Come on, younguns, le's git these taters planted."

"Le's wait till tomarr, I'm goin fishin today." Henry stood barefoot in the branch with a rusty can of worms in hand.

"It's goin to rain tomarr. Our taters are goin in the ground," Clarinda stated.

Henry threw his can against a rock."How do ye know it's a-gonna rain?"

"The grass was dry this mornin."

"What?"

"There wasn't a drap of dew. That's a shore sign that rain's on the way."

Henry knew it was useless to argue. By dinner time they had the potatoes planted as well as beets, carrots, rutabagas, turnips and parsnips.

"We'll plant beans and corn when the sign is in the Breast," Clarinda said.

Henry wiped the sweat from his brow."Mama, we need a horse."

"I don't have the money to buy a horse."

"We wouldn't have to use the hoe so much if we had a horse. We could grow a patch of corn to feed 'im. I'd use 'im to pull logs off the mountain fer firewood. He'd be good comp'ny fer Ol' Pied."

"I told you, Henry, I ain't got the money to buy a horse so ye might as well hesh."

Henry dropped the subject. I'm gonna git a horse if I havta buy one myself, he thought.

A week later, Tom announced that he would be leaving home too."Mama, Mr. Colliday is movin his sawmill to Caldwell County. He wants me to work as his sawyer. It pays twice't as much on the hour as turnin logs and stackin lumber."

How in the world would she manage without her boys? Oh, a mama's heart just has to let go, she thought."Where will you be stayin? Who's gonna wash yore clothes? Who's gonna cook ye somethin to eat?"

Tom chuckled."I can take keer of myself. But to answer yore questions, I'll be boarding with Mr. Colliday's sister and she'll cook me somethin to eat. She don't do laundry though. I'll havta git out under the old shade tree and scrub my own duds."

"Why, you ain't never scrubbed a rag of clothes in yore life."

"Well, I guess it's time I did."

The day Tom moved away, Clarinda went to the spring, sat down on a rock and cried. She knew he'd never move back home. He wanted to leave the nest. I shain't be a whiney mother and hold him at home. No siree, I havta let go, she thought. Somehow I'll manage without him.

Henry occupied Tom's chair at table, now. Although of a temperamental nature, he proved to be more helpful to Clarinda than any of her sons. He had a head for management and always looked for ways to make their work more productive and easier.

Tom came home for a visit six weeks later.

"My stars! Yer a sight to behold." Clarinda broke her own rule of never complimenting her children on their appearance."If ye git any more han'some, some girl's gonna ketch ye fer certain."

Tom blushed, flashing his dazzling smile. "Mama, will you hush that?"

"I worried about ye fer nothin. Somebody's shore been a-lookin out fer ye."

From the top of his head to the sole of his shiny black shoes, he was groomed to perfection. Black pants, and a long-sleeved white shirt with thin black stripes showed his knack for style. Of course, the jet black wavy lock still fell down on his forehead.

"Well, it looks like the flatland is agreeable to ye," Clarinda said.

"I don't reckon I've got any complaints."

"Have ye learned how to scrub yer clothes?"

A lopsided grin spread across his face.

"Well... ?"

He looked at the ceiling and whistled a little ditty.

"Tom?"

"Aw, Mama, I've got somebody a-fixin my clothes."

Clarinda teased him."Well, I'll swannie. Is she young and purty?"

He chuckled."You ast too many questions."

He spent the weekend catching up on all the news and playing music with his brothers. The forty dollars he gave Clarinda would buy the little ones' shoes. At first, she refused the money, but changed her mind when she saw how disappointed he looked. She was grateful for his help, because Howard and Billy Dan were barefooted.

"Have you heard from Olus lately?"

"I got a letter from 'im last week. He wants you to write." She gave Tom his address.

"Well, I gotta go, Mama. I havta be on the job early in the mornin." He gave her a big hug and went whistling down the path.

"Be keerful goin down that Blue Ridge, son," she called out.

He turned and waved and was gone.

Monday was always wash day. Clarinda carried water and filled the tubs. She was sorting clothes when she heard a commotion in the yard. She dashed to the front door with heart pounding. Henry stood in the yard, holding the lead strap of the ugliest plug-of-a-horse she'd ever laid eyes on.

"How do ye like my horse, Mama?"

"Where did you git that beast?"

"He got 'im offa No'es Ark," Howard said with a giggle."Ain't he a beaut?"

Clarinda sighed."Yeah, he's a beaut all right."

Henry stroked the horse's neck."You said ye didn' have the money to buy a horse, so I decided to buy one myself."

"Well, you can take 'im right back where ye got 'im."

"I worked three days in a hot field a-bustin clods fer this horse."

"Well, you've been cheated."

"How?"

"Because he's half-dead with old age, that's how."

"No he ain't. The man that sold me this horse said Ol' Clyde was eleven-year-old and proved it." Henry beckoned."Come here, I'll show ye." Clarinda moved around to Ol' Clyde's head and looked into his eyes. He looked peart enough.

Henry pointed to the corner of the animal's eyelid."Do you see them three wrinkles?"

"Uh-huh."

"The man told me that you judge a horse's age by the wrinkles in the corner of his eye. When he's nine-year-old he gits his first wrinkle, and every year after that he gits another'n. Ol' Clyde has got three wrinkles, so he's eleven."

Clarinda smiled, she wasn't convinced, but she didn't argue about it.

"The man told me that Ol' Clyde was a trained loggin horse with a lotta good years left in 'im. Heck fire, just think of the logs he can pull off the mountain. Why, we'll never run out of firewood agin—will we, ol' buddy?" Henry tickled his ears. The brute lapped it up.

"Mama, the man also told me that he wanted to keep a clear conscience so he confessed that Ol' Clyde had one bad habit."

Clarinda's eyebrows shot up."Hmm... I wonder what that could be?"

"He said Ol' Clyde was a cribber."

"What's a cribber?"

"It's a fancy name fer stump sucker. His teeth hurts and he gnaws on fence posts and cribs and stumps to stop the pain. While he's doin that, he's swallerin gobs of air."

"My stars! That's why he's so pot bellied."

Ol' Clyde turned his head and looked at Clarinda with his big sad eyes as if to say, 'Gee, I know I ain't no prize colt, but I'm a bargain fer three day's wages.'

Clarinda looked closer at the animal. She didn't know much about horses, but she could see that he had been worked hard. His ribs were sticking out."Lee, go to the barn and git a quart of Ol' Pied's sweet feed. This pore brute is starved."

And so, Ol' Clyde came to live on Levi's Mountain. He wasn't much to look at, but he had personality. The children loved his old weathered hide and spoiled him rotten. They gave him apples, biscuits... Whatever they ate, Ol' Clyde received a portion too. When he saw them playing in the yard, he'd toss his mane in the air, let out a loud whicker and gallop to the gate. Billy Dan carved spectacles from a pumpkin and Ol' Clyde wore them for half an hour before he ate them. They'd turn their backs and ignore him as a tease. He'd nip and tug at their clothes to get their attention.

The following spring, Henry borrowed David's horse, and teamed him with Ol' Clyde. He plowed up the wild strawberry field on the top of Levi's Mountain. The entire household climbed the mountain and planted the field in corn.

Three weeks later, the corn was up amid Johnson grass that grew faster than the corn."Younguns, we've gotta git that grass outta the corn," Clarinda said.

Henry appointed himself chief overseer. He was tough after Clarinda left the field to cook dinner. The corn stood ankle high, and the sun sizzled their heads from a cloudless sky. Henry brought Ol' Clyde to a halt and shouted commands at his siblings."Stop leanin on yer hoes. Quit lollygaggin. Git to work before the grass grows through yer shoe soles."

Little Howard held up a bare foot and gave a feisty kick."Grass cain't grow through my shoe soles."

Everyone giggled except Henry. He didn't see the humor in it. He pointed to the western side of the field located over the state line in Tennessee. The grass was knee high there."Howard, git yore hind end over in Tennessee and start diggin."

Little Howard looked at Mary Ann and puckered up to cry.

Mary Ann stood ram-rod straight, jabbed her hoe against the ground and glared at Henry.

Henry glared back."What are ye buggin yer eyes at me fer, Pokey-hontas?"

"Why you little wormy-lookin squirt, you ain't the boss."

"You shut yore mouth! Mama put me in charge of this cornfield. When I say dig, the lazy little scamps are gonna dig."

Mary Ann mocked him."In charge? Haw-haw... You'll find out who's in charge when I bust yore dang noggin with a rock!"

There was no scarcity of ammunition so a rock fight broke out. The little ones scattered as missiles flew back and forth. When a fritter-shaped rock whizzed between Ol' Clyde's ears, he took off across the field.

"Whoa, Clyde, whoooa!"

Henry brought the horse to a heaving halt at the edge of the woods."Now look what ye caused Ol' Clyde to do!" He pointed to a long swath of uprooted corn.

"Hah! It ain't Ol' Clyde's fault that you don't know how to plow."

Henry gritted his teeth and straightened up the corn.

Despite the squabbles, the corn grew tall and the harvest was abundant. Clarinda had planted her favorite old timey sweet potato pumpkins in the corn. Andy and Mandy enjoyed arranging them in a big pile.

They were in a quandary as how to get the corn shocks off the mountain. They didn't have a sled and wouldn't even bother asking a neighbor to lend them one because they always got the same old song."We would lend it to ye fer awhile, but I declare we'll be using it all week to haul wood."

"Younguns, we'll just havta pull the shocks down the mountain ourselves. It won't take us long. We'll pull some every day till we git it all," Clarinda said.

Henry took matters into his own hands when she wasn't around."I'll git the corn off the mountain—just watch me," he bragged, and headed for the edge of the field with an ax. He chopped down several saplings then he and Lee lashed the butt ends together with a rope and spread the limbs out. They piled shocks of corn in a high mound on the brush. Henry hitched Ol' Clyde to the apparatus and tried to hand the lead lines to Mary Ann."It's all yores—take it down the mountain."

"You shorely don't think I'm fool enough to ride a brush pile down the mountain."

Henry's face turned red with fury. He looked at Lee."Here, take these lines and climb up ere!"

Lee backed away, shaking his head."Heck no! I don't wanna git killed."

Henry took a threatening step toward Lee and spoke in measured tones, "I said, climb on the corn pile."

Mary Ann stepped between them and raised her chin defiantly."He will not climb on that botched up mess!"

"I'll be danged if you'uns ain't the biggest bunch a-cowards that God ever put breath in," Henry snapped. He climbed on the corn, took the lines in hand and clicked his tongue."Giddy up." Ol' Clyde didn't move. Instead, he looked back at Henry as if to say... 'who, me? Bruise my hocks with a fool's load like that?'

"Giddy yap," Henry shouted, giving the lines a snap. The old logger took off with a jerk. Down the mountain they went in a cloud of dust."Heigh ooohh Clyiiideee! Yee haa!" Henry disappeared as the whole kit and caboodle turned over. Ol' Clyde kept going, sliding on his hocks while the empty brush pile swung left and right. He didn't stop until the brush lodged against a tree.

"Oh, Lordy!" Mary Ann cried. She and Lee ran down the mountain as fast as their trembling legs would allow. They found Henry crawling from the fodder, grinning like a fool.

Mary Ann yelled, "You ain't got the sense that God allowed a goose!"

He came to his feet and pulled a can of Prince Albert tobacco from his hind pocket."Would ye look at that? I didn' git a scratch, but my tobacca can is bent double."

They all pitched in and pulled the corn down the mountain on brush. It wasn't hard to pull once they got it going. And, the little ones carried a pumpkin down every day until they got them all.

Before hauling in a winter's supply of wood, Ol' Clyde took a two week vacation. He lolled around the pasture, indulging himself with his disgusting habit of sinking his upper teeth into a fence post and drawing great gulps of air into his stomach. Henry smeared Jewel lard on the posts as a deterrent, but Ol' Clyde ate it.

One Saturday the children had friends for the day. They brought Ol' Clyde from the pasture for rides and fun. As each child finished his ride, Ol' Clyde received an apple or plum. By mid-afternoon the children grew bored with horseback riding and put him back in the pasture. Well, Ol' Clyde either had a belly-ache from cribbing, or from foundering on snacks, or both, because he threw a conniption fit. He kicked the latch off the gate and came across the yard trying to kick up his heels. He trotted lickety-split through a flower bed, almost beheading a black hen dusting herself there.

Clarinda and Mary Ann heard the chickens squawking and came on the run. Mary Ann maneuvered around Ol' Clyde. She was waiting with a big switch when he reached the edge of the yard. He came to a sudden stop, his eyes bulging. He knew Mary Ann would lay the lash to his hindquarters so he turned, snorted, kicked up his heels expelling gas and headed for the woods.

Clarinda stood on a mossy log waving her apron."Shoo, Clyde! Go through the gate, Clyde!" She felt a sudden weakness in the pit of her stomach when she saw him speed up and head straight for her. He swung his head sideways and batted her off the log into a perfect somersault.

"Go ye darn rascal! Take to the woods! Hope ye never come back!" she shouted as he disappeared into the bushes.

Mary Ann doubled over laughing.

"What's so funny?"

"Go look in the lookin glass, Mama!"

She hurried inside. She hardly recognized herself in the mirror. Her hair was bedecked with twigs, and one black braid stood straight up on the back of her head like a crow's feather. A black and white smear on the bridge of her nose turned out to be chicken manure. The log she'd tumbled from was a favorite chicken roost. She dashed through the kitchen, snatched the steaming teakettle, and headed for the wash-up bench on the back porch.

When Henry came home he went in search of Ol' Clyde and found him nonchalantly nibbling leaves off the bushes a quarter mile away. The old logger returned as gentle as a lamb.

"The pore ol' feller was just aggravated because the younguns yanked on his bits all day," Henry said.

Clarinda stepped into the yard with hands on hips and she and Ol' Clyde stared at each other."Well, I see the ol' hayseed's back," she grumbled."Git yer cantankerous hide in the pasture where ye belong. You better stay there, too, ye ol' potbellied windbag or I'll cut yer rations down to a nubbin."

Ol' Clyde hung his head over Henry's shoulder and whickered softly. Henry stroked his head and tickled his ears."Come on, ol' feller, I'll see that ye git plenty to eat." As Ol' Clyde approached the pasture gate, he neighed, flapped his lips and tossed his mane.

Clarinda smiled."Well, I'll swannie, I believe he's a-laughin at me."

As Clarinda watched Ol' Clyde head for his favorite gnawing post, Lee arrived with three speckled mountain trout.

"Well, it looks like ye had a good day at yer fishin hole, son."

Lee raised the fish high."Ain't they purty? Will you clean 'em an' fry 'em."

"I shore will. We'll have 'em fer supper."

Lee handed Clarinda the fish, then searched his pockets."I stopped at Aint Amanda's on the way home. She sent ye a note but I must a-lost it."

"Search yer overall bib pocket."

Lee unsnapped his pocket and pulled out a crumpled piece of paper."I guess it's got worm slime on it."

Clarinda took the note and went indoors to read it and clean the fish. The reaping season was now at hand, and field hands had hearty appetites. Aunt Amanda needed Clarinda's help to cook the big meals. She wrote that her laundry was piled up, and she also needed some house cleaning done. Clarinda was glad to get the work. She'd never worked for a kinder lady than Aunt Amanda.

Although Aunt Amanda wasn't a blood relative, Clarinda and her children loved her as if she were. She always welcomed the little ones with open arms. One by one she scooped them up and showered their faces with kisses. If she had a favorite, it was Howard."Oh, would you just look at those big blue eyes!"

Howard smiled and touched the pretty silver-colored combs in her gray hair. Billy Dan and Andy and Mandy tugged at her apron strings and looked up at her with adoring eyes. Indeed, Aunt Amanda was a wonderful Christian lady and a good friend. Clarinda worked for her at harvest time for many years.

Fifteen

Summer • 1942

The Wayfaring Stranger

I am a poor wayfaring Stranger,
While traveling thro' this world below;
There is no sickness, toil, nor danger
In that bright world to which I go.
I'm going there to meet my father,
I'm going there no more to roam;
I am just going over Jordan,
I am just going over home.

–Traditional Folk Song

Clarinda hadn't seen Olus for nearly two years and for a brief moment she stared curiously at the handsome young man standing at the door."Mama, don't you know me?"

"My stars! Why shore I know ye, but you've filled out and changed so much." She hugged him with misty eyes.

"Are you tellin me that I'm fat?"

"Why, heavens no, I ain't sayin no sech a thing."

More than any of his twelve brothers, Olus bore a likeness to Rufus. Vigorous outdoor work had broadened his shoulders. Tanned, muscular and a picture of health, he was as handsome as handsome gets.

"Tom's been astin 'bout ye. I'll put a letter in the mail tomorrow and let him know yer here. We'll have a fam'ly gatherin this weekend."

"That'll havta wait fer another time, I'm on my way to join the army, I cain't stay long."

"Oh, Olus, shorely you're not a-goin to do that. Pearl Harbor's been bombed, a war has broke out."

"Aw, Mama, somebody's gotta go to Germany and kill ol' Hitler. You wouldn't want me to shirk my duty—would ye?"

136

"I want you to stay alive. As sure as I stand here today, if you enlist in the army, yer brothers will foller ye."

"I ain't gonna git killed, Mama. I can shoot a gnat's eyelash off at thirty paces." He raised his imaginary gun to his shoulder, took aim and, "Pow!"

"You'll change yore tune once't you git in there. I pray you won't do it."

Olus didn't change his mind, and within two weeks his boots were on the march in boot camp. Shortly thereafter, Clyde enlisted. Tom made comments about joining, too, but his new wife threw a conniption fit and put a stop to it.

"Well, I'll be drafted anyway," Tom argued.

"Maybe not. We've got a baby on the way."

Tom wasn't drafted.

When Olus finished boot camp, he came home on furlough. Everyone raved about how handsome he looked in his uniform—especially the girls. He'd be going across the waters in a few weeks and Clarinda prepared a farewell dinner. All the family came together for a regular old time hoedown. When they all sang, "Will the Circle Be Unbroken," Clarinda had to leave the room to cry. They played their music and just enjoyed being together until way past midnight.

Olus visited all his older brothers and their families while home on leave, but he spent more time with Tom. Barely fourteen months difference in age—they'd grown up together. Wherever one happened to be, the other was nearby.

Olus spent the last evening of his furlough with Tom. They sat on Tom's front porch making music. Suddenly Olus stopped playing and turned solemn. Reaching out, he laid a hand on Tom's guitar strings to still the sound."Ye know, this might be the last time we play music together—in this life."

"Don't be talkin that a-way, brother. Hush that, do ye hear?"

"Well, I havta face the truth because the war's gitten hotter all the time. I'm in infantry, trained and ready to go. More'n likely, I'll be servin under General Patton, and from what I've heard he's a general that loves to fight. If I'm under his command, I'll see a lot of action—and some of us won't be comin home."

Tom hung his head and couldn't bring himself to speak.

Olus sensed Tom's misery, but he had to have his say. "I want you to promise me that you'll go see Mama every chance ye git."

"I will. You know I will."

"Write and let me know how they're farin at home. If Mama was to git sick and die, I don't know what would become of the little ones."

"Yeah ... I've thought of that many a time. Don't worry. I'll keep a-eye on things."

Olus stroked his Gibson guitar, the only instrument he'd ever owned."I'm leavin my guitar with ye. I know you'll take good keer of it." He poked Tom in the shoulder, strummed a line or two of "Ground-hog" and led Tom out of the doldrums. The last hymn they sang together was, "Leaning On the Everlasting Arms." They harmonized perfectly.

"What have I to dread, what have I to fear,
Leaning on the everlasting arms;
I have blessed peace with my Lord so near,
Leaning on the everlasting arms."

The next morning, Olus hugged his Mama and playfully poked her under the chin."Don't worry, Mama, yore blue-eyed boy will be back, and I might bring a purty fraulein home with me."

Clarinda tried to smile, but her face crumpled and tears rolled down her cheeks.

"Aw ... don't cry, Mama, I'll be back."

Clarinda wiped her tears away with her apron."I'll pray ever day that ye do come back safe."

"I know ye will, and that's why I know I'll be home agin." He walked to the looking glass hanging on the wall and cocked his army hat to a dashing angle. He saw Mary Ann leaning against the door jamb watching him. She looked like she might burst into tears.

He turned and beckoned."Come 'ere."

Mary Ann straightened up and took a hesitant step forward."What fer?"

"Cat fur." Olus yanked her into his arms. He gave her a big bear hug, stepped back and dropped into a boxer's stance with a mischievous grin."I'm ready fer anything ye want a-throw at me."

"Don't tempt me, brother." She smoothed her hair in place. She never could stand to have her hair messed up.

He chuckled."Now you can tell people that you've been hugged by the handsomest man in North Ca'lina—even if he is yer brother." He picked up his satchel and went whistling out the door. Mary Ann thought he certainly did cut a mighty fine figure in his dress uniform that she'd pressed to perfection. Full of tears, she hurried to her bedroom. She had a dreadful feeling that he'd seen his Blue Ridge Mountain home for the last time. Later, she found forty dollars and a note tucked into a corner of her dresser mirror."Thanks, Sis, for fixin my clothes," it read.

Clarinda stood on the porch and watched him quick-step down the path. The light in her eyes dimmed as she sank into a well of pain."Goodbye, my precious son, may God watch over you and keep ye from harm," she whispered. He stopped on the path, turned and waved then disappeared into the trees.

Sixteen

Autumn • 1942

Clarinda was busy making changes on secondhand clothes when her sister, Etta, dropped by for her weekly visit. Mandy stood by the sewing machine watching her mama sew."Mama, will I have a new dress fer the first day of school?"

"You'll have a purty dress, but it won't be brand new."

"Oh ..." Mandy let out a long sigh.

"Would you just look at that pouty face," blared Etta."You ain't the only youngun that won't have a new dress fer the first day of school. My younguns never did."

"Aint Etta, I think it's milkin time."

Etta chuckled."Youngun, I believe you're tryin to git rid a-me."

Mandy left the room, but she ambled back and hung around the door because she wanted to hear every word Etta said.

"Well, it really is milkin time, so I'd better be goin—oh, by the way, do ye still want me to go with ye to Hedgeweth's Store tomarr fer that vaccination clinic?"

"Yeah ... we'll start about ten o'clock."

A little alarm went off in Mandy's brain. Vaccination Clinic? She remembered her older brother, Howard, telling her and Andy that they'd have to be vaccinated before they started school. He also told them a nurse would stick a needle as long as the devil's darning needle in their arms. Mandy had seen the insect known as the devil's darning needle. It skimmed over their crawfish pond catching gnats. It looked dreadful. Black, with a long pointy mouth and it had a sharp stinger on its hind end.

Clarinda noticed Mandy leaning against the door jamb, listening. She made big eyes at Etta and tilted her head in Mandy's direction with a slight nod. Etta caught the signal and buttoned her lip.

As Etta went out the door, Mandy overheard her Mama whisper, "Lord, I dread tomarr."

Pity tugged at Mandy's heartstrings. Oh, pore Mama was goin to git vaccinated."Mama, you don't need Aint Etta to go with ye to Hedgeweth's Store. Me and Andy will go."

Clarinda's eyes widened."Well, I'll swannie," she muttered and put her sewing away.

It would be a long time before Mandy forgot that dreadful day at Hedgeweth's Store. Young mothers walked down from the hills with drooling babies bouncing on their hips and preschoolers in tow. It sounded like every unhappy child in the world had congregated at the store. She'd never heard such horrid screams or seen the like of tears and snotty noses blowing bubbles.

The store smelled of rubbing alcohol and medicine. As the twins watched the general disorder around them with fearful eyes, a little blond-haired boy in striped overalls and blue shirt walked over to the nurse with his sleeve rolled up."I'm weddy fuh my shot," he chirped.

His mother beamed with pride."That's my brave boy."

Everyone standing nearby praised the cute little fellow too, but his bubble of courage burst when he saw that long spitting needle coming at him. He broke free of the nurse and ran squealing like a piglet. He hid behind a wooden keg of dried soup beans, and no amount of coaxing could bring him forth. Finally, the boy's teary-eyed mother yanked him out and held him tight as the nurse stuck him.

Saucer-eyed, Andy and Mandy clung to Clarinda's skirt and whimpered."Oh, Andy, Mama ain't gonna git a needle stuck in her arm—we are!"

The nurse turned to Clarinda."I'm ready for your children now."

A big uproar broke out.

"No, Mama, no! Pleeeaassee don't let her stick me," they screamed in unison.

"Now, Andy, show Mama what a brave little man you are," Clarinda coaxed.

"Nuh-nuh-no! I-I-I don't wanna die."

"Ma-maaaa! I don't wanna die eeeither."

"Hush yer squallin." Etta huffed and pulled Mandy's fingers from Clarinda's skirt. Mandy turned and tried to bite and kick her, but Etta was strong and held her at bay."If you 'as my youngun, I'd turn you acrost my knee and scorch yore bloomers."

Finally, Andy took his shot with a loud squall that trailed off to a whine, but Mandy ended up stretched out on the dry goods counter with Clarinda, Etta, and Myrtle Hedgeweth holding her down.

"My, my, she sure has got a strong set a-lungs," the nurse remarked and shoved the needle in the inside of Mandy's forearm.

A red-hot pain shot straight to Mandy's armpit. She peed in her bloomers—on the counter—and Etta's hand. Etta let go of Mandy's thigh and jumped backward."If you ast me, that's what I'd call, gitten the piss skeerd out of ye." She held out her dripping right hand and stared at it—like it was leprous."Myrtle, ain't you got a wash rag or somethin that a body could use to clean their hands with?"

Myrtle either didn't hear Etta's request or else she ignored it because she was under the counter tossing boxes left and right."This'ns ruint, that'ns ruint, this'n will do," she muttered as urine poured through the cracks like a hard spring shower off a steep tin roof.

Etta shifted her weight to the left and held her right arm away from her body. Her hand dangled from her wrist like a limp noodle as she tapped her right foot impatiently."You'd think they'd have a big tub of soapy water handy as many snotty-nosed younguns as they got in here. Why, I'd bet my last brownie that half the babies in this store have got a hippen full a-poop."

"Etta, why don't you go outside and warsh yer hands at the water spout?" Clarinda suggested.

Etta touched the side of her nose, gingerly, with the fingers of her left hand."That cold water will set off my neuralgia."

"Maybe not. Don't hold yer hands under the water too long."

Afflicted with a case of facial neuralgia, Etta had been in pain for years. She wore a turban or scarf on her head at all times because cold air brought on sudden attacks."Well, if the pain starts, I guess I'll just havta grin and bear it because I've just got to warsh this piss off a-my hand."

"Shh ... don't talk so loud," Clarinda chided."Somebody will heer you."

"Well, I don't give a-shit. They ain't nobody in here but women folk and skeerd younguns."

"Etta, I declare, the way you clatter on about a little pee. If yer that skeerd of it, how in the world did you put hippens on yore babies."

"It wasn't easy," Etta flung over her shoulder as she headed for the water spout.

Clarinda helped Mandy from the counter and held her close to her side. She could feel her trembling. Andy was clinging to his Mama's skirt, whimpering. She stroked their heads and murmured, "Now... it's all over and done with now." Their sniffling ceased.

Myrtle Hedgeweth's head popped from under the counter.

"Myrtle, I'm shore sorry about the mess. If you'll git me a mop, I'll clean it up," Clarinda said.

"No, I'll clean it up. It wasn't yore fault. It was my idea to put her on the counter."

"Well, jot down the damage to yore goods, an' I'll pay ye soon as I can."

"Aw, the only damage I saw was a pair of number fourteen shoes that I ordered five-year-ago for big-footed Bob Jessup. He died before the shoes got here."

"Well, would you happen to have any underwear that would fit my youngun? I've just got to clean her up, she cain't walk home in wet underclothes."

"I think I've got a box or two around here somewheres," Myrtle said. She fumbled through a couple of boxes and came up with two pair of underwear.

"I'll need a wash rag and some soap and water too," Clarinda added.

When Etta returned from the water spout, Clarinda had a pan of water, towel, washcloth, and new underpants for Mandy in her hands. Etta's jaw dropped."How in the devil did ye git a-holt of that stuff? Nobody offered to help me when I needed it," she said, loud enough for Myrtle to hear.

"You should a-had some patience," Myrtle snapped and beckoned to Clarinda with her hand, "Come with me."

Clarinda followed her to a small room in the back of the store. There, amid sacks of hog chop and new horse collars, she bathed and changed Mandy into fresh underwear.

When she returned to the clinic, Etta was still grousing."I wisht somebody else would set up another store around here. It would serve Myrtle right — bet she'd be a little more accommodatin to folks."

Clarinda went to the candy counter and bought Andy and Mandy a small poke of candy. This was a special treat because they seldom had sweets other than stack cake and molasses. Their eyes lit up and they loosened their hold on Clarinda's skirt.

"Andy didn' cut half the shine that Mandy did today," Etta said.

But Clarinda wasn't listening. She watched Andy and Mandy with a mother's love-light shining in her eyes. She nudged Etta."Look at 'em, Etta, ain't they sweet? They're crazy over peppermint candy."

As Etta watched, Andy and Mandy consoled each other in whispers and swapped candy sticks — they slurped it up, happy and content. They showed each other their vaccination spot. Etta studied them for a full minute with a far-away look in her eyes."Yeah ... I know," she mused, "but the pokes of candy have been few and far between fer my younguns as well as yores."

"Well, we do the best we can, Etta." Clarinda took the twins by the hand and they all left the store.

The first Wednesday in September, the school bus came to a screeching stop where a steep woodland path met the road. Five children climbed aboard. Andy and Mandy were the youngest in the group. This was their first ride on the Doodle Bug, as their brother, Howard, called it. They were excited, but anxious too. They could hardly wait to get to their first grade class and meet their teacher.

They sat on a long low seat in the middle of the bus that ran all the way to the back door. Older children sat on long seats along the inside of the bus next to the windows. Mandy pulled her pretty dress primly over her knees, sat up straight like a little lady and tried to remember Mama's instructions."Obey the teacher, an' show her you've got some manners." The twins were fortunate to have big brother Howard show them to their class. The day evidently went well, because after school they all got off the bus jabbering and laughing.

Mandy bounded through the door talking non-stop."Mama, my teacher's name is Miss White. Look-looky, see the purty book she give me!"

Clarinda took the book and settled in her rocking chair with Mandy on her lap. She read it aloud from beginning to end."I declare, I like this book as much as you do." Clarinda gave her a hug. Mandy took her book and sat on the porch steps. Clarinda heard her pretending to read it until suppertime.

For six years Mandy had been a very happy child. She had a mother who loved her, big brothers and a big sister to look up to, and a twin brother to play with every day. But her whole life changed the second week of school. The teacher separated her from Andy at recess."Now, Andy, go play with the boys in your class, and Mandy, you must play with the girls."

Mandy stood on the playground and watched her classmates play their games of tag, hop-scotch and jump a rope. She had never played those games before. She and Andy loved to swing on wild grapevines in the forest, catch crawfish in the branch and play "toad in the treetop."

They captured the biggest, fattest, toads they could find. With a spool of Clarinda's sewing thread they bound them to the end of a long plank. They balanced the plank like a see-saw on a rock or chunk of wood. They took turns jumping on the end of the plank opposite the toad. They fell-down laughing as the threads broke and the toad went flying through the timber. The toads, all expert swingers, grabbed twigs and turned somersaults.

But now, she must learn new games. She wandered over to a group of girls playing hopscotch, hoping to join them. The leader of the group, a little girl with bouncy brown curls named Patty, bossed her playmates around. When Patty said, "Le's jump rope," her playmates jumped, other-wise, her patent leather slippers did a temper dance on the concrete walk.

"Can I play?" Mandy inquired.

Patty's face turned red with rage."No, you can not play — git away from here!"

Mandy didn't budge.

"What's yore name?" Patty hissed through a gap in her front teeth.

"Puddin tame, ast me agin, I'll tell ye the same."

Patty jutted her pointy chin out and did a rat-a-tat stomp. All of a sudden, she shoved Mandy hard. Mandy backpedaled with a shocked look on her face. Regaining her balance, she gritted her teeth and slapped Patty so hard her red hair bow flipped in the air. Pandemonium broke out. The little tattler went squalling to the teacher with all her friends following. They yakked and pointed their spiteful fingers at Mandy.

When Mandy saw the teacher walking toward her she almost keeled over. Oh, I'm gonna git spanked with that big paddle she keeps in her desk.

"Mandy, did you slap Patty?"

She dropped her head and nodded. She wanted to tell Miss White why she had slapped Patty, but she didn't utter a word.

"You must not strike your classmates. If you do that again, I will punish you. Do you understand?"

Mandy nodded.

As Miss White turned away, Patty stuck her tongue out at Mandy and laughed. Mandy turned her back to Patty and made a circle in the dirt with her big toe. She raised her foot and brought her heel down in the center of the circle again and again. In her mind she was stomping Patty. Slowly, she wandered off to the edge of the playground and leaned against a shade tree. Inching her way around it till hidden from view of her classmates, she squatted down and laid her head on her knees. She felt like crying, but didn't want to draw attention to herself or be called a crybaby. So she sucked in her hurt feelings and buried them in the deepest pocket of her heart. She stayed there till the class bell rang.

The next day, Mandy spent recess in the bathroom. She stood on tiptoe, looked out the window and watched her classmates play their silly game of "Ring around the Roses." One little girl with goldy-colored hair, always wore a pretty bow on top of her head. She wore a new one every day.

Mandy looked down at her bare feet. She and Andy shared one pair of shoes during winter, but they couldn't do that in school. Oh, how she wished for a pair of shiny patent leather slippers like Patty's. She'd show that hateful girl how to dance. Why, I could kicka coon from one end of that concrete walk to the other, she thought.

She touched the white embroidered pocket of her green secondhand dress. It had little yellow daisies embroidered on the white collar too. She'd thought it beautiful until she saw the dresses her classmates wore.

She wondered whether she should tell Mama that all the other little girls wore their dresses above their knees and didn't go barefooted to school.

Gazing at herself in the looking glass she saw straight dark hair combed to the side. But it now hung over one green eye because she'd lost the bobby pin that held it in place. She stuck her tongue out at her reflection. I'm the ugliest girl in school—maybe in the whole world. My classmates ain't never gonna play with me, she thought.

For two weeks, Mandy spent every recess in the bathroom. She always stood on tip-toe, looked out the window and watched Andy playing marbles with his friends. Tears rolled down her cheeks. She'd wash her face and dry her eyes before returning to class. Once she forgot to dry her tears, and one smart aleck told the teacher."Miss White, Mandy's been a-cryin." The entire class turned and stared at her—and she stared at the floor. Andy rushed to her side.

"Andy, return to your seat," Miss White said. After the teacher had given the class an assignment she walked to Mandy's desk, stooped down and whispered in her ear, "Mandy, will you tell me why you've been crying?"

"I ain't been a-cryin. I'm fine."

"If something is troubling you, be sure and tell me, all right?" Mandy stared at her desk and nodded that she would.

The next day she spent recess in the bathroom as usual. Suddenly, the door opened and two girls from the sixth grade entered. She would never forget their big mean faces as long as she lived. They looked at each other and grinned mischievously.

"Le's put 'er in the toilet," the black-haired one said. They put a hand over Mandy's mouth and held her hands behind her back. They shoved her into a stall, shut the door and held her there. She could see their shoes when she peeped under the door. She tried to crawl out, but they stepped on her fingers and kicked her in the face.

She heard the bell and children returning to their classes. Surely they would leave now—but they didn't. She panicked. The teacher would paddle her for being late. She dropped to the floor and tried to crawl out under the door again—a black and white saddle oxford kicked her in the mouth and stepped on her fingers again. She knew the girls wanted to see her cry, because every minute or two they cracked the door and taunted, "You're gonna git a whuppin. Your teacher is comin with the paddle—ha ha."

For the first time in her young life she experienced hate. Oh, how she hated them! If I was bigger, she thought, I'd take ye by the neck and slam yore heads together so hard you'd be cross-eyed fer a week.

At last, she heard the bathroom door open and a student told the girls that their teacher was looking for them. Before they left, the big dark-haired girl poked her head in the stall and said, "You better not tell the teacher about this, or we'll shove yore head in the toilet tomarrah."

Mandy entered her classroom as quietly as possible. As she headed for her seat the teacher called out, "Mandy would you come over here, please?" Mandy came slowly with her head down, she could feel her classmates staring. She wanted to turn around, stick out her tongue and say, 'What're ye lookin at — you little pop-eyed nit heads?' But the teacher had that paddle in her desk.

"Why were you late for class?" Miss White asked in a gentle voice. Mandy didn't utter a word. The teacher put her hand under Mandy's chin and lifted her head so that Mandy had to look at her. The teacher had big pretty blue eyes that saw everything."What happened to your lip?"

Mandy tucked in her lower lip and tasted blood. The teacher's kind eyes and gentle voice disarmed her completely. She burst into tears and fled to the back of the room. She hid behind the screen where the students hung their coats and caps. Burying her face in a sweater she cried her eyes out. The teacher followed her and dried her tears, but Mandy still wouldn't tell her anything. She knew she'd be shoved in the toilet if she tattled.

When Mandy returned to her seat, she looked across the room at Andy. He had his head down on his desk, crying. A big lump of hurt rose in her throat. She felt his anguish, and wanted to rush over and stroke his head and comfort him. Oh, it hurt more than anything to see Andy cry because she loved him so.

The next morning, she complained of a stomach ache and stayed home. Sometime up in the day, Clarinda noticed her playing happily with her paper dolls. The following morning, she had the stomach ache again, but Clarinda made her go to school anyway.

"Mary Ann, will you try to find out why Mandy don't want to go to school? She won't tell me."

"I already know — Andy told me — I'll take care of it today," Mary Ann said, and then told Clarinda about Mandy's tormentors at school.

"I'm a-goin down to that school this very day."

"No, Mama, fer heaven's sake, don't do that. It'll just make matters worse. I'll report it to Mandy's teacher."

Mary Ann had a good view of the playground from her classroom window. She watched the first graders during recess and saw Mandy standing off to herself, leaning against the playground shade tree, biting her fingernails. Tough Mary Ann swallowed a lump in her throat. The bell rang, ending recess. First graders would be spilling into the bathroom before heading back to their class. Mary Ann waited a few minutes then asked her teacher to be excused.

When she entered the bathroom she found two girls holding a stall door on Mandy.

"What do you girls think you're a-doin?"

"It ain't none a-yore business," the black-haired girl replied.

Mary Ann sprang forward and grabbed a bushy head in each hand."I'm makin it my business." She hurled the girls against the wall with all her strength."You damn bitches have picked on the wrong youngun this time," she said through gritted teeth.

Mandy heard the scuffle of feet and recognized Mary Ann's voice. She peeped out the stall door. She saw one bully-girl cringing in the corner and Mary Ann had a black bushy head under her arm in a vise-like hold.

"Let me loose," the girl cried. Mary Ann clenched her fist and frogged her head. Her knuckles struck the bushy noggin like a jackhammer in full throttle. Mandy tucked in her lower lip and winced. Last week, Howard had knuckled her head like that. She'd never mess with his stuff agin.

"Ooow! Aiieeoowwee, I'm choooaakin'!" The girl writhed in agony, but Mary Ann didn't let up.

"Yeouw, I'm gonna faint!"

"Faint away, bitch." Mary Ann blew on her knuckles and used the heel of her hand to sand the frogged spot—which she did vigorously. The bully-girl sagged to the floor, but Mary Ann brought her up by the hair. The girl in the corner tried to escape. Mary Ann stopped her with an elbow to the nose. The blood flew. Taking each girl by the scruff of the neck she slammed their heads together and shoved them toward the door. Before the girls could open the door, she kicked their hind ends.

Mandy had never seen her big sister fight so hard. She looked up at her with a heart full of gratitude.

"Come on, squirt, le's go to class." Mary Ann told the teacher about the bullies. Miss White said she'd see that it didn't happen again. Mandy just smiled because she knew it wouldn't happen again.

The children attended school through the winter, but when the big snows came, Clarinda kept them home. The school bus stalled more than once on Levi's Mountain due to the weather. The children came near freezing on one such occasion.

The day dawned clear and cold as the children climbed on the school bus that morning. By noon, snow fell an inch an hour. School adjourned.

The buses headed out on their treacherous routes with their precious cargo.

The Levi's Mountain bus lurched and slid from side to side, then stalled. The driver, a young fellow barely old enough to have a license, flung the bus door wide."Git out, younguns, yer gonna havta walk. I ain't crawlin under this bus to put on chains in this weather."

With clothing insufficient for such weather, four teenagers and six little ones stepped into the wind and drifting snow. The smaller children stood in their tracks and screamed as the wind yanked their clothes. Mary Ann, Charlotty, and two other teenagers sheltered them under their coats as best they could and kept them moving. Finally, they found shelter at a little cabin by the roadside. One little girl's boots had frozen to her feet. The kind lady of the house thawed them loose by the fire. Clarinda's children had no boots.

Clarinda paced the floor and watched the path. Darkness would fall early, and she couldn't rest with her children out in the storm. She wrapped herself in several layers of clothing, grabbed extra wraps for the children and set off around the mountain. Visibility was limited to a few yards. She heard the children crying before she saw them. Mary Ann and Charlotty carried Andy and Mandy on their backs. They were exhausted. Then they heard the jangle of horse's harness as a neighbor came around the bend with a sled. The lady at the cabin had sent him. He stopped and they all piled on and rode the rest of the way.

Andy and Mandy cried out in pain as Clarinda thawed their feet in warm water and wrapped them in flannel rags. A few days later, their heels turned a sickly yellow, cracked open and bled. Clarinda applied herbal poultices and salves and their feet finally healed. The bitter snowy weather kept the children home for most of that winter.

Seventeen

1943

Wayfaring Stranger

I know dark clouds will gather o'er me
I know my pathway's rough and steep;
But golden fields lie out before me,
Where weary eyes no more shall weep.
I'm going there to see my mother,
She said she'd meet me when I come;
I am just going over Jordan,
I am just going over home.

–Traditional Folk Song

larinda met Mr. Wadell Dudley at a church social. He ate a slice of her stack cake and returned for a second helping. He cleared his throat and spoke in a gruff voice, "I'm here a-beggin fer another slice a-fruit cake, Ma'am. It shore is mighty good."

Clarinda served him a generous portion.

"My name's Wadell Dudley. I ain't had nothin fit tuh eat since my wife died."

They chatted amiably for the rest of the meal. Before he went his way, he asked if he could call on her at some future time. She said she'd have to think about it.

Clarinda told Etta about the man she met at the church social.

Etta was impressed."Oh, my, did ye know that Mr. Dudley is a wealthy man?"

"Well, he told me that he had a farm."

A smug expression crossed Etta's face."Oh, I heer things. I git out and about more'n you do. Why, if you married him, you'd never have to worry 'bout where the next meal was comin from."

"There you go a-tryin to git me hitched agin."

"Well, as you know, I lived in widderhood fer years. It's a hard life, especially when ye got younguns to raise. I'm glad I found a good man and I don't regret marryin 'im one bit. He likes my younguns. He's a good pervider."

Clarinda couldn't dispute that."Oh, I know you married a good man, but I've never seen anybody that could take Rufus' place."

"Clarinda, Rufus is dead."

"I know, but I spent twenty-five-year with him and that's a long time."

"Well, I'm a-tellin you, sis, Mr. Dudley ain't some old maid's last hope. I'll bet many a widder would give her eye teeth to ketch him."

"Oh, I'll probably never see or heer tell of him agin."

But the very next Sunday, Mr. Dudley arrived at Clarinda's place in a fine carriage drawn by a shiny black horse. The children dropped out of the apple trees, abandoned their crawfish ponds, and came on the run to greet the stranger.

Mary Ann looked out the window."Mama, there's somebody a-settin in the yard in a carriage. Do ye know who it is?"

Clarinda peeped out the window."My stars! That's Mr. Dudley." She rushed to change her apron to a fresh one.

Mary Ann looked at her Mama with a puzzled expression on her face. What the heck is this all about, she thought? It didn't take her long to find out because Mr. Dudley took Clarinda and the children on a carriage ride.

The following week, the community was a-buzz with chatter of Clarinda and her beau. Clarinda's older married children fumed about it. Memories of their Papa remained fresh. They'd never accept a stepfather."Papa would turn over in his grave if he knowed this," David said.

"Well, I was Papa's pet," said Mary Ann."I don't know how Mama can even think about goin on a carriage ride with that ol' man. Papa ain't been dead but five year."

The next Sunday, Mr. Dudley showed up again. Clarinda invited Mary Ann to go along with them to his farm. She refused."I ain't ridin down the road in no carriage. Nobody travels around like that these days. Anyway, why's he takin you to his farm? I'll tell ye why. He sees we're pore as whip-poor-wills and he wants to show off his property. He's lookin fer a wife to cook and wait on his sorry carcass. As sure as I'm a-standin here, Mama, you'll marry him and that'll be the biggest mistake of yore life."

The little ones enjoyed the carriage ride to Mr. Dudley's farm. They admired the brown leather seats and the way he drove his horse. He stopped the carriage at a large wooden gate with a sign attached. Twin

Meadows, the sign read. Rolling onto the farm, they could hardly believe their eyes. Sleek horses trotted around the fields and foals kicked up their heels. White-faced cattle grazed and lolled in green pastures. Sheep and lambs watched them curiously. Wide blooming meadows and fields of grain waved in the breeze.

"Come on in and rest a spell," Wadell said, leading the way up the stone walk. The big weathered farmhouse was old and beautiful. It had a wide wrap-around porch, a portico on the second floor, and two swings with a lovely wisteria vine in full bloom twining along the edge of the porch roof. Mandy reached out and touched a drooping blossom. Wadell noticed her admiration of the flower and snipped it with his pocket knife for her pleasure.

While Mr. Dudley showed Clarinda and Billy Dan and Howard around the farm, Andy and Mandy explored the house. They climbed the stairs and saw two big bedrooms on the second floor. Between the rooms a narrow stairway led to a spooky garret."I ain't goin up 'ere,"Mandy said, "Mama might give us a whippin if she ketches us up here." After a quick glance in each bedroom they returned to the porch.

As Mandy swung in the porch swing, lavender wisteria blossoms brushed her cheek and perfumed her hair. Oh, everything looked big and rich and marvelous to her eyes.

On the other hand, her big sister, Mary Ann, being nine year older and much wiser, wasn't the least bit impressed with Mr. Dudley."I don't like ol' Wad. I don't keer if he's got a farm as big as Tennessee and half a-Georgie."

"But Mary Ann, he's got big shiny horses, lots of cows and sheep ... I even seen some guineas."

Mary Ann laughed."Heck fire, that just means he's got more manure than most folks."

"Well, he's rich. I know he's got a million dollars."

Mary Ann spread another shirt across the ironing board and took a hot flat-iron from the stove top."Fudge! I'd bet a Yankee nickel that he never spends a wheat penny on you or Mama either."

"Well, I hope Mama marries him. I liked his fine house. I wouldn't ever havta go barefooted agin."

Mary Ann slammed the flat iron down on the ironing board."You don't know what you're talkin about. The next time Wad comes to see Mama, I want you to take a good look at his thumbs. They curl back to'ard his wrists like a chittlin. Do you know what that's a sign of?"

"No."

"Stinginess. Why, that ol' stingy devil wouldn't buy you a pair a-shoes or a thread of clothes if you was necked as a plucked chicken. You'll find out I'm right—wait and see."

The farm evidently impressed Clarinda because she married Wadell Dudley eight months later. Etta and her husband witnessed the marriage ceremony at the Magistrate's Office.

"I'm a-packin my chop sack petticoats and goin to live with Eva Jean," Mary Ann stated.

Mandy giggled."But Mary Ann, if you move with us to Mr. Wad's farm, you won't have to wear them ol' chop sack petticoats and scratch feed bloomers. You'll have lacy petticoats with ribbons and eyelet."

Mary Ann ground her teeth."I'd rather go in tatters and rags than live on that farm."

"Oh, I'll have purty pinafores and shiny black patent leather slippers and all kinds of purty hair bows. I'll dress up like a princess ever day."

Mary Ann rolled her eyes toward the ceiling and sighed."You better git yore head outta the clouds, little girl."

"Oh, you'll be jealous—wait and see."

Mary Ann chuckled."Okay, we'll see."

Their brother, Lee, walked through the doorway."What's so funny?"

"Oh ... this pore youngun thinks she's gonna turn into Cinderella when she moves to Happy Acres."

"Well, I ain't a-goin to that ol' farm. I'm a-gonna stay with Claude and Bee," Lee stated.

"Mama, did you hear what Lee said?" Mary Ann called.

"Yes, I heerd," Clarinda replied from the kitchen.

Claude, and his wife, Beatrice, had no children and from the day they moved into their own home, Lee tagged along. Since Papa Rufus' death, Claude had been the man of authority in Lee's life. Claude, being sick much of the time, was grateful for Lee's help with the crops. The brothers enjoyed fishing and hunting together and that kept them close. So, it didn't bother Lee that his mother had married Mr. Dudley. Claude would see to it that he didn't have to go anywhere that he didn't want to.

Clarinda hung her dish rag to dry on the string line behind the kitchen stove. Stepping out into the warm sunshine she let the screen door slam behind her. Storm clouds boiled over Levi's Mountain as she walked to the woodshed for her hoe. When Clarinda had a decision to make or a troubled mind to settle, she'd head for the spring. This day, she climbed the path using her hoe like a staff. She cast it aside and sank to her knees when she reached the spring.

Mandy, always attuned to her Mama's feelings, followed at a distance. But she stopped in her tracks when she saw Clarinda kneel in prayer. Wait ... leave her alone, an inner voice whispered. Although she couldn't see Him, Mandy knew the Lord stood beside Mama with His Hand on her head. Instead of returning to the cabin, Mandy sat on a rock and listened. Growing heavy-hearted, she bowed her head on her knees and prayed too. She asked the Lord to comfort Mama. A warm breeze stirred the dogwoods blossoms around the spring. Mandy raised her head and saw Mama wiping her eyes with her apron. Mandy rushed forward and patted her shoulder."Are you all right, Mama?"

"Mama's fine." Clarinda used the hoe to regain her feet.

"Mandy, run to the house and git me a water bucket."

"Okay."

When Mandy returned, Clarinda was busy cleaning the spring and all traces of tears and worry had vanished from her face. While on her knees in prayer Clarinda had received divine guidance. She knew Mary Ann was no ordinary sixteen-year-old. She had the maturity of a grown woman. No amount of urging would change her mind at this time... maybe later she could be persuaded. So she'd leave her be.

As for Lee, he stayed with Claude nearly all the time anyway. Lee would help Beatrice with the crops, Claude being sick much of the time. Clarinda also decided to leave her house plunder with Eva Jean. If things didn't work out at Wadell's farm, she'd have her things near at hand for a return home. She'd take Ol' Pied though. Wadell had acres of pasture land. She'd keep a prayer in her heart that Mary Ann and Lee would decide to join her.

Mr. Dudley was born back in the early 1880's. Twenty-one-years Clarinda's senior, he didn't look his age. His coal-black hair showed only a trace of gray. And no one had seen him wearing spectacles. His black eyes counted sheep in distant pastures without a squint. Clarinda's children giggled at his strong old-fashioned dialect."Look a-thar," he'd say, "this paith is narr. Fotch the bucket hyar."

Clarinda didn't ask her older married children their opinion about marriage to Wadell Dudley because she knew they'd object. Her sister, Etta, however, gave advice and offered her opinions freely."Clarinda, if I 'as you, I wouldn't pay any attention to what the married younguns say. They've got their own fam'lies to take keer of. They don't put food on yore table—you do."

So, Mary Ann went to live with her sister, Eva Jean, and Lee moved in with his older brother, Claude. Henry had followed Tom to Caldwell County a year earlier, and had found work there.

Heavy-hearted, Clarinda and her four little ones set out on their journey to life on her new husband's farm. They'd barely started when they met Claude in the road. Riding a sled drawn by a mule, he kept his balance by holding the handlebars of a cultivator he hauled. He halted his mule and stepped to the ground, leaving his left foot on the sled in order to make his crippled leg more comfortable. The accident that smashed his hip had shortened his left leg three inches.

"So you're really movin to ol' Wad's farm," were the first words out of his mouth.

"I reckon so. I'm hopin to make a better life fer the younguns—fer all of us," Clarinda replied, looking down and smoothing the wayward wisps of Mandy's hair in place with a calloused hand.

Claude looked toward the top of Levi's Mountain, but he didn't see the beautiful dogwoods blooming there because his eyes were full of tears.

"Claude, are you cryin because you cain't move to Mr. Wad's farm with us?" Mandy asked.

Claude wiped his tears away with his hands and shook his head sadly."You pore little youngun, you don't know what the heck you're a-gitten into."

Clarinda looked away and her eyes welled up too.

"Mama, I know you've had a hard life, but it ain't gonna be any easier on that farm." He reached down, picked up his lead-tipped cane from the sled and jammed it on the cultivator handle."If I ever heer tell of ol' Wad a-liftin a hand aginst one of these younguns, I'll kill 'im."

"Now Claude, you know I'm not goin to allow Wadell or anybody else to mistreat my younguns. You can put yore mind at ease on that matter." She glanced at Claude then looked away to a blue mountain in the distance.

"Well, you'd better make sure he understands that, otherwise—he's a dead Wad."

Clarinda met Claude's eyes steadily."Where's Lee?"

"He's settin minner traps in the creek. Trout season opens next week."

"I wisht he'd come and live with me."

"Lee's stayin with me. He ain't workin fer them damn Dudley's fer nothin. He'll be just fine with me."

Howard butted in, his big blue eyes wide with excitement."Do you know what, Claude? Do you know what?"

"Well, what?" Claude snapped.

"Uh... uh... Mr. Dudley's got a big team of horses. He said he'd teach me and Billy Dan how to work 'em."

"The only thing he'll teach you and Billy Dan is how to use a hoe!"

Feeling older than her years, Clarinda sighed, and hitched her paper bag of clothes higher on her hip.

155

"Well, I guess we'd better be a-goin. Come and see me, Claude, and bring Lee with ye."

"Yeah, I'll do that," Claude said sarcastically. They parted with heavy hearts.

It was late afternoon when Clarinda and the children reached the farm. Wadell met them at the gate, grinning ear to ear. He swung the gate wide and they all walked through. At the click of the gate-latch a melancholy feeling swept over Clarinda. Troubled thoughts raced through her mind. Oh, Lord, have I done the right thing fer my younguns? Is Claude right? Will I regret this move? Her arms ached. She wanted to sit down and rest a spell.

Wadell led the way up the stone walk with a spring in his step.

"Wadell, I hope you've had supper because I'm plumb tuckered out."

"Yeah... I had supper at my son's house." He opened the door wide and stepped aside to let them pass."I'll be 'spectin a good breakfast in the mornin though, hee-hee."As Clarinda stepped over the threshold, he gave her a playful nudge with his elbow.

Although in a jovial mood he was dead serious—and Clarinda knew it."I packed enough food fer our journey here, so we've had our supper too. I always fix a good breakfast. I've got growin younguns with big appetites."

Wadell frowned and pointed toward the stairs."The younguns can tote their stuff up thar."

Mandy climbed the stairs to the landing and chose the room on the right. Her brothers took the room on the left. She set her box of clothes on an old trunk near one of two windows. The tall window panes hadn't been washed in years and the ruffled curtains were yellowed with age. Her eyes traveled around the large bedroom. She noticed the walls didn't have cracks in them. The yellow pine planks ran horizontal. They looked smooth and old and glowed with the richness of fine timber. An ancient, oval-shaped looking glass in a mahogany frame hung on the wall between the windows. She climbed upon the bedrail and looked at her wavy reflection. She had two heads and a long crooked nose. She sat on the bed and flopped herself backward into heavenly softness. She could hardly wait to tell Mary Ann that she had a feather bed. She noticed a lovely mahogany wardrobe standing in the corner. She liked it because it had lots of drawers where she could store her stuff, and it even had a lock and key.

Her eyes traveled around the room and locked on the picture of a little boy. It hung on the wall above the headboard of her bed. The child looked to be about her age. He wore high-buttoned shoes and a black riding outfit. His coal-black hair was cropped bluntly below his ears. He carried a small whip in his hand and his expression conveyed that he'd use it on the spotted pony at his side. Mandy had a notion that this room had once belonged to that little boy. If he was dead, his ghost might appear at her bedside when the lamps went out. She ran downstairs and tugged at her mother's dress sleeve."Mama, do I havta sleep up there by myself?"

"You're a big girl now, and they ain't no reason why you cain't sleep in yore own room by yoreself."

"But Mama, that room is way up in the sky, an' what if the house ketches on fire?"

"Oh, the house ain't gonna ketch afire."

"But it did once't—in Lonesome Hollar."

"I know, but this house is lots better than the cabin in Lonesome Hollar. This'ns got strong chimneys made of stone an' mortar."

"I wisht Mary Ann was here to sleep with me."

"I wisht she was too. Maybe she will be, fore long."

"I don't like this house. It's spooky, and I don't like that pic'cher on the wall, neither." Clarinda followed Mandy upstairs and took the picture down, but it still seemed to be there, because its outline was bold.

"Now, Mandy, you needn't be afeared, yore brothers are in the next room. Anyway, I'll stay with ye till ye git use't to sleepin in here."

There wasn't a soul in the house who slept well that first night, not even Wadell. He wasn't used to hearing, "Hey, Mama! I saw a ghost in here."

"Now, Howard, you never seen no sech a-thing. Settle down an' go to sleep. It's a-gitten late."

"I-I heard somethin a-gnawin in here, Mama."

"It was prob'ly a mouse."

Silence settled in, and then a loud thump and giggling erupted from the boys' room. "Mama, Howard th'oed his shoe at a bat."

Wadell slammed a pillow over his head and grumped. "Fer gawds sake! Why don't ye all hesh so's a man can git some sleep."

The next day, the children were all over the farm exploring every stable and pen. Howard and Billy Dan followed Wadell everywhere, asking a zillion questions. They yearned to work the horses. Wadell had given them a solemn promise that he would teach them. 'Soon'es me and yore mammy gits married and she moves tuh my farm, I'll show you boys how tuh work a team a-hosses. '

The boys watched Wadell bring the big red team from the stable. He led them to a wagon and started hitching them up. Billy Dan nudged Howard and they grinned with excitement. Any minute Mr. Dudley would say, 'All right boys, jump on the wagon. I'll show ye how to drive this hyar team. ' But Wadell said nothing. He went about his work and ignored them.

"I'd like to learn how to harness a horse," said Howard.

"Yeah, me, too," added Billy Dan.

Wadell spat a sluice of ambeer on the ground and didn't respond. The boys looked at each other, puzzled."Maybe he don't hear good," Billy Dan said.

"Mr. Dudley, what are the names of these horses?" Howard asked in a loud voice.

Wadell tugged at the trace chains and hitched them to the double-trees.

"Mr. Dudley, what—"

"Plug an' Jug," Wadell interrupted in a gruff voice.

Billy Dan leaned against the wagon and watched him adjust the harness."Does Plug work better'n Jug or is it the other way 'round?"

"I'll be dad-gummed. Do you'uns allus ast this many questions?"

Howard and Billy Dan looked at each other with Claude's warning ringing in their ears. 'The only thing he'll teach you an' Billy Dan is how to use a hoe!' They could plainly see that Wadell didn't want to be bothered so they ambled away. They petted the frisky calves and foals. Howard tried to pet a lamb, but the ewe put him over the fence.

"Why, you danged ol' dumb sheep, I wasn't hurtin yer precious lamb," Howard scolded, and began imitating a frightened lamb."Blaaa-aat-aat!"

The ewe started pacing back and forth with one loud "baa" after another.

Wadell's face turned dark as a thundercloud. He rushed from the barn toward Howard."You listen hyar, boy! Stop tarmentin muh yo."

"I ain't hurtin that ol' yo. I just wanted to pet the lamb."

Wadell looked down on Howard with clenched fists and dentures clicking."If you stay around hyar, you'll do as I tell ye, boy."

Howard climbed to the topmost fence rail, sat down and looked Wadell straight in the eye."Ol' man, you lay a hand on me and I'll tell my big brother, Claude. He'll knock a pump-knot on yore noggin bigger'n a goose aigg."

Wadell ground his teeth."I ain't afeared a-Claude."

"You'll be afraid when my big brother Avery gits a-holt of ye. He's seven-feet tall. He can pop yer eyeballs out with one hand."

Wadell cleared his throat and muttered, "Damn hellions." As he turned away, he saw Billy Dan peeping around the corner of the barn with a tobacco stick in his hand."Whut do you thank yer gonna do with that stick, boy?"

"Ain't none a-yore business."

"Well, you boys leave muh stuff alone or I'll tell yer mammy."

Howard corrected him."She ain't mammy, she's our Mama."

Wadell returned to his work, but every now and then he'd look over his shoulder.

Howard climbed down from his perch."He's gonna tell Mama on us."

Billy Dan shrugged."Who gives a damn?"

The following day, Andy and Mandy went exploring."Andy, le's go to the garret."

"O-okay." They climbed the stairs that led to their bedrooms. At the second landing, they took the steep, narrow stairway that led to the garret. Mandy hesitated."Oooh... it looks spooky up 'ere." Andy tugged at her hand."C-come on." They climbed the dimly lit stairs, arm in arm. One step ... stop and listen, two steps ... stop and listen some more.

"Andy, I believe I seen a shadder a-movin around up 'ere." They stopped and waited until their hearts quit pounding. Andy put his arm around her shoulders, "I-I didn't see nothin. Don't be afraid, I won't leave ye." Mandy thought of the little mean-faced boy in the picture on the wall—maybe that shadow was his ghost.

"Le's go back downstairs... I'm skeerd."

"N-no, I'm goin on up. We might find a big chunka gold."

They took another step and the stairs curved sharply to the right. In the gloom they stumbled against a crock full of something. Naturally, they just had to see what was in it.

They removed the wooden lid and white cloth."Oh, it's 'lasses," Mandy exclaimed, and poked her finger in the glossy ooze. They seldom had molasses so they gorged themselves. With sticky chins and fingers they climbed another three steps and found an open area with two big windows. Suddenly, from the rafters above, a yellowish something streaked over their heads and struck the landing with a plop.

"Wh-what was that?"

"I think it was a cat." Indeed, Wadell always let his big calico cat in the garret when the mice started keeping him awake at night.

Mandy sneezed."Shewee! It's dusty up here." They poked around awhile longer and found nothing but empty canning jars, old crocks and baskets.

"Le-le's go. They ain't no gold up here."

They left the spooky place in haste. On their way downstairs they stopped at the landing and stared at the molasses crock."Oh, Andy! We plumb fergot to put the lid on the 'lasses. It looks like the cat done fell in!" They tracked the cat down the stairs and out the kitchen door.

"We gotta git the 'lasses off the stairs," Mandy said. She brought the mop and bucket and they cleaned up all the cat tracks or so they thought.

Clarinda found the trail of molasses and followed it to the crock. She wondered why any body would put molasses in such a place. The younguns have been in 'em, she thought.

The following morning, she set a white pitcher of molasses and a big platter of flapjacks on the table. The children wouldn't touch them. Andy and Mandy had passed the word on to Billy Dan and Howard that the 'lasses was nasty.

"Younguns, ain't you gonna have some flapjacks an' molasses?"

Andy giggled."I-I don't like 'em anymore."

Mandy kicked his shins under the table and gave him a mean look.

Billy Dan and Howard snickered.

"Why, I thought you'uns loved sweetnin."

"We've plumb outgrowed it. Don't like 'lasses ner syrup neither," Mandy said, avoiding Andy's eyes.

Clarinda didn't look convinced. She didn't think anybody would turn their nose up at such a treat.

Wadell certainly didn't. He wolfed them down like he hadn't seen a flapjack in months."You younguns don't know what good eatin is. Muhlasses is good fer ye — got arn in 'em." He reached for the white pitcher again and smothered another stack of flapjacks.

"Wadell, how come you stored the molasses in the top o' the house?"

"Aints was a-gitten in 'em."

Howard leaned toward Andy and Mandy and whispered, "They got cat hair in 'em, too." That remark brought on a fresh outburst of giggling.

"Younguns stop the foolishness an' eat yer breakfast," Clarinda scolded.

Wadell handed her the white pitcher and she generously smothered her flapjacks in molasses. The children looked at each other and winced.

Mandy wrinkled up her nose, "Mama, them 'lasses looks nasty — you ain't gonna eat 'em, are ye?"

Clarinda brought a forkful to her mouth."Sometimes you younguns are a puzzlemint to me." She polished off two whole flap jacks.

After breakfast, Clarinda washed the dishes and headed toward the hog pen with a big bucket of swill. Suddenly, she saw a weird-looking creature come creeping from the oat field. She set her bucket down and ran to the house for Rufus' pistol. She'd brought it from Levi's Mountain as a treasured keepsake.

"Whar ye headed with that gun?"

"I'm a-gonna kill a varmint."

"Put yore gun away. I'll take keer of it." A few minutes later, Wadell stepped into the yard with a twelve-gauge shotgun. Clarinda and the children followed. The creature now lapped swill from the hog's bucket. Two huge wads of cockleburs covered its ears. Drooping sprigs of oat straw trailed from its whiskers to the ground. It was covered from the tip of its nose to the end of its tail with oat stubble and burrs.

"Clarinda, you better take yore younguns in the house, this ain't gonna be purty tuh look at," Wadell advised.

Clarinda coaxed the children inside, but they ran to the window to watch, despite her orders to stand back. Wadell brought the shotgun to his shoulder and started tamping his feet like a golfer getting ready to putt. The creature dropped from the swill bucket and looked straight at him with a piteous, "meow."

"Good gawd a-mighty! It's Ol' Tab!" Wadell walked closer to get a better look. Clarinda and the children spilled out the door for a look, too. Wadell stooped and touched Ol' Tab then straightened up and glared at the children."Which one of ye besmeared muh cat with axle grease?"

The boys looked at each other, shrugged and shook their heads."We ain't touched yer cat," Howard replied.

"Didn't even know you had a dang cat," Billy Dan stated.

"Do you'uns 'spect me tuh believe that?"

Clarinda butted in, "Wadell, the younguns are tellin the truth."

Mandy turned pale and cast a furtive glance at Andy's ashen face. She licked her lips and swallowed hard because her mouth had suddenly turned dry as cotton."Mr. Wad," she squeaked, "that ain't axle grease on yer cat, it's 'lasses. Uh ... er ... me an' Andy was the cause of it. We tasted 'em an' fergot to put the lid back on. Somehow or 'nother we skeerd the cat an' it jumped outta the garret and landed smack-dab in the 'lasses crock."

"An'-an' we heard it go ker-plop," Andy stuttered.

Clarinda's hand went to her throat as her stomach tumbled.

Wadell looked like he smelled a skunk. Good gawd, I devoured purt nigh a pint, he thought. He handed his gun to Clarinda and made haste to get away. As she and the children turned to go inside they heard him gagging and heaving behind the smokehouse. Clarinda managed to get the gun put away before she lost her breakfast. Later, Wadell penned the cat up until it could rid itself of the trash clinging to its fur.

Eighteen

Twin Meadows

Since moving to Wadell's farm, Clarinda didn't have a spare minute to call her own, much less time to hook the rugs that she traded for the children's clothes. They were ragged. When she asked Wadell to buy Mandy a pair of shoes, he acted like she'd asked for his last dime. He rose from the supper table and instead of pushing his chair back in place he kicked it and stormed out the door.

A week later, he brought a pair of brown slippers to Clarinda and growled, "She'll make do with this parr. Whuther they fit or not, ain't no concern a-mine."

Mandy cried when she had to wear them to school. They were two sizes too big and the soles resembled tractor treads. Clarinda spoke to Wadell about it."Wadell, why didn't ye give the money to me? I'd a-bought her shoes. I don't expect ye to know what little girls like to wear."

"She's too dad-gummed puhtickler. I guess you'll be 'spectin me tuh buy shoes fer the boys next."

"It wouldn't hurt ye to buy 'em shoes. They're barefooted now. Billy Dan chops all the wood an' keeps the wood box full. Howard an' Andy keeps plenty a-water on hand. You keep 'em on the tramp the blessed time a-fetchin this an' that fer ye."

Wadell scowled and cleared his throat."They're jest a-earnin their keep."

"My work on this farm earns my younguns keep. I'm a-gitten tard of you a-watchin ever bite they eat at the table, too. What kind a-man are you anyway?"

"I'm the same man I've allus been."

"No, ye ain't. You promised me an' my younguns a good home if I'd marry you. Well, it shore ain't turned out like I expected. My understandin of a good home is more'n food on the table an' a roof over our heads. It's lookin out fer each other an' bein kind to'ard one another. You act like you despise my younguns. They ain't done nothin spiteful to ye."

Wadell turned his back and stomped out the door.

162

The following week, the children worked on a sled in the woodshed. They'd found old scrap planks around the farm and decided to put them to good use."This sled will take us down the hill like a bullet this win'er," Billy Dan said.

Howard scraped a runner with a piece of broken glass like he'd seen Mama do when making hoe handles."Look how smooth this runner is, Billy Dan. Run yer hand over it."

Billy Dan rose from his knees and turned toward Howard. He reached out to inspect the sled runner and his hand froze. Nelson Dudley, Wadell's grandson, stood in the woodshed doorway. The children had seen Nelson a couple of times and named him, Whistlepig, because he resembled a groundhog. Nelson Dudley, however, was no cute harmless woodchuck. One could accurately describe him as a stumpy-necked—coldhearted—rodent from Hell—and he brought three of his own kind with him.

"Git in the house, Mandy!" Billy Dan commanded.

Mandy knew by the sound of Billy Dan's voice that she'd better make tracks, and so she did as fast as her legs would go. Breathing hard, she dashed through the kitchen doorway. She found her mother already aware of Nelson's presence on the farm. Clarinda stood at the kitchen window watching the boys through a gap in the curtain. Mandy darted to her mother's side and stood on tiptoe trying to see out the window, too.

"What do ye see, Mama?"

"Shhh ... be quiet," Clarinda whispered, laying a hand on Mandy's head.

Mandy watched Mama's eyes follow every move the boys made. When Mandy saw her eyes widen and her teeth clench, she knew trouble was afoot on the farm.

Clarinda saw Nelson laughing and chatting with her children. Abruptly, they all headed for a stand of pines beyond the hog lot. As soon as they were out of sight, she threw her dish rag aside and headed out the door at a fast clip with Mandy at her heels. She thought of ordering Nelson and his gang off the farm, but Wadell would say, 'Aw... they didn mean any harm to yore younguns. ' So, she'd follow them on the sly and see what they were up to. Suddenly, Howard dashed from the pines, his eyes wide with fear."Mama! Whistlepig is beatin Billy Dan to death!"

Clarinda broke into a hard run. As she neared the hog pen, her eye lit on a stick leaning against the slop chute. Without slowing her speed she grabbed it and struck a fence post—testing its strength. It felt strong as a limb from the old Rebel tree. Her racing footsteps fell silent on the spongy ground beneath the pines. She broke from the trees and paused at the top of an embankment just long enough to take in the scene below.

Seventeen-year-old Nelson Dudley had twelve-year-old Billy Dan by the hair of the head. Blood gushed from Billy Dan's nose as Nelson struck him back and forth across the face with his free hand. Nelson's companions hee-hawed and shouted, "Pick 'im up by the heels—shake the sourwood whistles outta his pockets!" Although Billy Dan fought back with all his might, he couldn't land a blow because his arms were too short. He only boxed air under Nelson's arm pit.

Seven-year-old Andy, tugged at Nelson's shirt tail crying, "Leave my brother alone—leave him alone!" Nelson slapped Andy down without taking his hand or eyes off his captive. He took Billy Dan by the shirt collar and yanked him up on his toes, and Billy Dan had to look into his beady-eyed, buck-toothed, chuckle-chop face."Git offa Granpap's farm, you little squirt! Take that and that and—"

Nelson's buck teeth plowed up dirt. He clawed the ground in a frantic effort to regain his feet. He made it to his knees, but another wallop took him down again. He didn't have enough hands to deflect the blows. He howled in pain and threw his arms up to protect his head. Clarinda brought the club down across his shoulders with all her might. It splintered to pieces, but knocked the wind out of him. He rolled on his back, gasping for breath. His eyes widened in fear. The maddest woman on earth had a foot raised to stomp him. He rolled sideways. Her foot glanced off his head. He lurched to his feet and stumbled down the path with the remnants of Clarinda's club bouncing off his noggin.

Howard joined the fray and threw a rock that struck Nelson's heel. Profanity and filthy language gushed from Nelson's mouth, but he was moving on at top speed as he said it. He didn't stop until he was well out of Clarinda's reach, then he hollered, "You just wait till I git home and tell Pap what you've done. He'll come out here and kick yore ass and put all you ridge runners offa Granpap's farm!"

"You do that, Nelson—send a whole herd of damn Dudleys out here—I ain't afeard of 'em!"

Mandy had never heard her mother say a cuss word stronger than "dang it" before, but she'd never seen her mother that mad either. Mandy saw her mother read the Bible every day and heard her pray almost every night. She remembered the day a cuss word slipped from her own lips and Clarinda boxed her ears, "That ain't no way fer a good little girl to talk. Don't let me heer you say that agin."

Mandy was a bad girl this day. While Clarinda thrashed Whistlepig, Mandy jumped up and down on the embankment swinging her fists."Bust his damn whistle, Mama—knock his front teeth out!" Lucky for Mandy her mother didn't hear that.

Clarinda picked up a stout-looking piece of broken pine limb and weighed it in her hand. She turned to Nelson's companions."Are you low-down cowardly rascal's a-lookin fer trouble? If ye are, you've come to the right place!"

"We ain't got nothin in this. It was all Nelson's idee," the tallest boy replied.

"Git yore hind ends down the road. I better not see hide ner hair of ye around here agin."

They slunk off down the path, looking sideways as if they expected her to ambush them too.

"Come on, younguns, le's go to the house."

Back at the farmhouse, Clarinda questioned her children."Why did you younguns take off with that gang?"

Billy Dan and Andy wouldn't say, but Howard tattled."We went because Whistlepig promised us a big chew of tobacca."

"Good heavens! That was a trick to git you away from the house so he could whip ye."

"We know that now, Mama, 'cause soon as we got through the pines, he shoved me and Billy Dan down the bank and started punchin and slappin us, but I got away."

"Why didn't you run, Billy Dan?"

"Cause I ain't no dang rabbit."

Clarinda's voice took on a very somber tone they hadn't heard her use with them before."Younguns, I want you to listen to me and listen good. That Nelson Dudley is meaner than a striped snake. He's might near a grown man an' ain't got no business here except to see Wadell. Don't be talkin to him or any of his buddies. If he comes on the farm, I want you to run an' tell me. Do ye understand?"

In one voice they said, "Yes, Mama."

"Clarinda, my son's hyar tuh to plow up a garden plot, an' he needs tuh know whar ye want 'im tuh plow," Wadell called.

Clarinda stepped into the yard and looked at the rich rolling land that stretched on and on. Behind the house, a paling fence separated the yard from a grape arbor, and off to the left of the house were outbuildings. Clarinda looked at the green level land near the kitchen yard."That's a mighty fine lookin piece of ground right there," she pointed out. Before sunset, the garden was plowed and worked down until it was as soft as a lettuce bed.

The next morning, Clarinda checked the almanac to make sure the signs were right before planting. There was no use sowing good seed when the sign was in the Bowels or Secrets. There would be blossoms, but no vegetables. She waited four days until the sign was in the Breast and then planted everything in one day. It was Clarinda's best garden, ever, and she achieved it with half the labor that she was accustomed to because Wadell's son cultivated it. Wadell spent a considerable amount of his time in the garden, too.

She gathered vegetables by the bushel instead of the peck—more than enough for the five hundred jars she filled. She carried loads of garden scraps to the two huge red hogs. They would be slaughtered and laid to cure in the meathouse before Christmas.

For the first time since Rufus' death, Clarinda didn't have to worry about where the next meal was coming from. Wadell's son did most of the farming and gave Wadell a third of each crop. Clarinda had chickens and a crib full of corn to feed them. Her children had eggs, sausage and middlin meat in addition to cream gravy every morning. Wadell's two milk cows shared the barn with Ol' Pied—Clarinda had never seen so much milk in her life. She winced when she poured a bucketful to the hogs. *So many hungry younguns in the world, and here I am pourin out milk to swine.*

She could live here on this farm and feed her children off the abundance of the land and for that she was thankful, but every time she stepped out on Wadell's front porch her eyes turned homeward. *How many weeks since she'd seen Mary Ann, and Lee? Tom and Henry will never visit me here, either,* she thought. Here on Wadell's farm she seldom saw a soul that wasn't a Dudley or related to them. Her sister Etta crossed her mind."Oh, Etta," she muttered."I cain't decide which is the worst, homesickness or poverty. I'd leave here fore the sun went down if I had a third of the foodstuff on this farm to feed my younguns."

The following Saturday, Mary Ann and Lee arrived for a visit. Clarinda gathered them in her arms even though they didn't like open displays of affection. Tears of joy coursed down her cheeks. Immediately, she began planning a big dinner."Billy Dan, I need a big fat hen. Can you an' Howard ketch me one? I'll make chicken 'n dumplins..."

Mary Ann raised a staying hand."Mama, I cain't stay, I've got to git back an' help Eva Jean can beans tomarr."

"Me an' Claude's cuttin locust fer fence posts," said Lee."I havta git back tonight."

"Tomarr is Sunday, younguns. You know good an' well they ain't gonna be no beans canned or locust cut on the Sabbath."

"I don't want to hurt yer feelin's, Mama, but I ain't stayin all night here. Wad don't want me an' Lee around. I know you noticed the mean looks he gave us."

"I've not heard him say anything against either of ye stayin here."

"Actions speak louder'n words. Come on, Lee, we'd better go."

Clarinda stood on the porch and watched them go with tears streaming down her face.

"What's a-matter, Mama? Why're you cryin?" Clarinda pulled Mandy close and hugged her."Oh, Mama was jest a-feelin sad today fer some reason, but I'll pearten-up after awhile."

Mandy patted her mother's arm."Don't cry, Mama, Mary Ann an' Lee will come back soon—won't they?"

"I hope so. Oh, I shorely hope so."

Mary Ann had brought Clarinda news of Olus. He had written Eva Jean and asked her to pray for him, saying that he had been in battle for eight days straight and might not be coming home. He had never mentioned this in the letters he wrote Clarinda. She read that he was marching across France with General Patton and might not get to write much for awhile. Clyde, who followed Olus into the army, was in Sicily. She hadn't heard from him in two months and was worried sick. She decided that come Saturday, she was going to Clyde's to see his wife, Parlee, and their two children. Parlee would have news of him.

All day Friday Clarinda cooked. She wanted to make sure Wadell had plenty to eat while she was gone. Maybe he'd take them to Parlee's in his carriage. She'd ask him at supper. Wadell sat at table with a frown on his face."Why'd you cook suh much fer?"

"Well, me an' the younguns are a-goin to Clyde's fer the weekend. Do ye mind takin us in yore carriage?"

"What're you goin over there fer?"

"I want to hear news of my son. Are you goin to give us a ride or not?"

"My carriage is broke down—got a bad wheel—needs work done."

"The wheels was a-turnin mighty fine when you come to Levi's Mountain to see me. It ain't been outta the shed since I moved here," Clarinda stated.

Wadell rose from the table with a scowl and stomped out the door.

"Hateful rascal," Clarinda muttered. She decided that she'd visit Clyde's family even if she had to walk every step of the way.

Early Saturday morning, Clarinda packed a basket of food, and she and the children set out on their journey. Wadell's hound dog, Ol' Jube, trotted along with them. It was an eight mile hike one way, but if they took short cuts they could lop off three miles.

"Younguns, we should git to Low Gap by ten o'clock. We'll stop an' rest there because we'll be in North Ca'lina. We'll eat our dinner when we git to the Signee Fields. There's a real purty spring there with big flat rocks to rest on."

Clarinda knew the mountain land like the palm of her hand. She told the children interesting stories about each hill and hollow they trod. It kept them from getting whiney."You see that big chestnut snag over yander? Mother took us younguns along that ridge in the fall of the year and we'd pick up chestnuts by the bushel."

Billy Dan gazed at the mammoth tree trunk."Was it fun?"

"Shore, especially when Mother wasn't along. I remember one time us younguns was a-pullin our sled alongside a rail fence an' my little sister stopped an' said, 'Oh, look at the purty calf. ' We all looked in the direction she pointed."

'That ain't no calf,' my brother Alexander said, 'Calves don't climb fences. '

"Wh-what was it, Mama?"

"It was the biggest black bear that ever walked on four paws. We run like the wind. Mother wouldn't let us go gatherin chestnuts without her anymore."

Howard bent over and peeped through the undergrowth."Are they bears in these woods now?"

"Not many. They ain't much fer 'em to eat since the chestnuts all died."

The children were hungry and getting fussy when they reached the Signee Fields. According to the slant of the sun, it was nigh two o'clock. They quenched their thirst at the cold gushing spring. Ol' Jube lay belly-down in the branch and didn't move for awhile.

Clarinda spread their lunch on a big flat rock and they ate ham biscuits, boiled sweet potatoes, boiled eggs, and drank grape juice from a fruit jar. They shared their food with Ol' Jube and saved the fresh apples and plums to be eaten along the way. After an hour's rest, Clarinda tidied up her picnic basket."Younguns, it's time to go, le's git movin."

"How much far'der is it? I'm tard," Mandy whined.

Clarinda took her hand with a gentle tug."Oh, we'll be there fore ye know it."

They waded into knee-high sedge then crawled through an old rusty barbed wire fence. Maneuvering around a briar patch, Clarinda and Andy and Mandy came upon a pile of weathered fence rails. Billy Dan and Howard had already passed it and were almost out of sight. Clarinda felt a prickle of uneasiness so she lengthened her stride and called out, "Younguns... wait up."

Suddenly, Billy Dan and Howard turned and came toward her on the run."Mama, they's a big bear a-comin!"

"Climb on the rail pile, younguns. Hurry! Hurry!" The boys climbed like squirrels. Mandy balked and started crying, "I lost my hair bow. Maamaa, I want my haaiirr bow!"

Clarinda swung Mandy to the top of the rail pile in one powerful swoop. Then she scrambled up—in the nick of time, too. The children shivered in fear as the bear popped over the hill. He paused— swung his head from side to side then raised his muzzle and sniffed.

He's caught a whiff of our food basket, Clarinda thought.

"Oh, Lordy, here he comes," said Billy Dan.

The bear came toward them with a lolloping gait and headed straight for Ol' Jube. Poor Jube tried to climb the rail pile too, but couldn't. So around and around the rail pile went Jube and the bear.

Mama, I'm skeerd," Mandy squalled.

"M-Mandy, hush," Andy begged.

Clarinda took Mandy by the arm and shook her."I've heerd enough outta you."

Mandy knew she was on the brink of getting spanked, so she hushed and sniffled.

The bear stood on its hind legs and took swipes at Ol' Jube with one paw and then the other. Somehow, Jube managed to stay out of its reach.

Clarinda and the children huddled on the rail pile and watched with fearful eyes."We've put up with this rascal long enough," Clarinda said, and pulled Rufus' pistol from a towel in the picnic basket. She fired one shot over the bear's head lest she hit Jube. She didn't want to wound the bear either, she just wanted it to go away and leave them be. The bear took off like a streak for the river bluff and Jube headed for home.

"Younguns, le's git off this rail pile and do some back trackin. We'll take the longer route." Clarinda figured the bear might follow them for their food, so she emptied the basket on the ground.

It was sunset when they reached Watauga River. The roar of the foaming water around big boulders frightened Mandy. To her eyes, the river looked wild and dangerous because she'd never seen a watercourse that big. Clarinda yelled several times before someone answered from the other side. It was Clyde's brother-in-law, and he came for them in a small wooden canoe. Billy Dan and Howard and Andy stepped into the canoe first. They enjoyed the smooth traverse across the sparkling water. When the canoe returned for its next passengers, Mandy balked.

Clarinda tugged at her hand."Come on, le's git in the boat, Mandy."

"No, Mama, nooo! I don't wanna git drownded!" She squalled until her nose burst out bleeding.

Clarinda took a handkerchief from her apron pocket and held it to Mandy's nose. Then she picked Mandy up in her arms and set her in the boat."I don't want a-heer another peep outta you, young lady. They ain't nothin about a boat ride to be afeard of."

169

Mandy gripped her plank seat till her knuckles turned white, but she kept quiet, it would be just awful to git a spanking and a nosebleed, too.

Clyde's wife, Parlee, lived a short distance from her folks along the river. She kept her two-roomed cabin as neat as a pin. She and Clyde had two children, a girl about Mandy's age and a boy a couple of years younger. Despite the cramped quarters, Parlee was thrilled to have Clarinda and the children. Somehow it eased the worry of Clyde's absence for them both, if only for a few hours.

The boys enjoyed playing with their nephew along the river. They waded through shallows, threw rocks, and tried to spear fish with a sharp stick. Mandy and her niece played with paper dolls and a little tea set. Clarinda found out that Clyde had been moved to the front lines. She stayed with Parlee until Monday morning. Parlee advised her to take the more traveled route home because bears were often sighted along the river bluff.

Parlee's brother canoed Clarinda and the children across the river again, and this time, Mandy behaved. She even trailed her hand in the water as they crossed. They took the longer route back to the farm.

"Mama, when are we goin to see our kinfolks agin?" Mandy asked.

"I don't know. It's a long ways to Parlee's."

"How come our kinfolks don't visit us?"

"I don't have a ain'cher fer that, Billy Dan."

Howard spoke up."I know why. My nephew said our kinfolks don't like Mr. Dudley because he broke up a happy home."

Clarinda didn't comment but she thought about Howard's saying the rest of the day. They arrived on the farm by mid-afternoon. Wadell was nowhere around, but he came home at suppertime with his usual frown in place and sat down to a hot meal. He pouted and didn't speak to Clarinda for a month because she went to visit her folks against his wishes.

At the rooster's first crow, Clarinda began her day. She kept her mind occupied with the tasks at hand, but as the months stretched on, her unhappiness increased. She had an uneasy feeling that something bad was going to happen. She kept a keen watch over her children and comforted herself with the thought that she still had her cabin on Levi's Mountain.

Nineteen

Twin Meadows

Going Home

"Come, my children, do not tarry,
The time's a-flying, we must go.
October sun is nigh a-setting,
A harvest moon is rising, slow.
"Take my hand, I'll lead you safely
Through yonder hollow, dark and deep;
We'll climb the path up Levi's Mountain,
At home sweet home we'll peaceful sleep."

Months passed and Wadell grew even more aloof. He frowned and grumbled about every trifle. Each evening he'd rise from the supper table and give his chair a sharp kick. He'd reach for his hat and off he'd go to his son's house. He'd only come back home after everybody was abed.

Clarinda tried to talk to him at the supper table. "Wadell, are ye done with shearin the sheep? The boys would love to learn how to shear sheep an' harness the team. I'd like fer 'em to learn how to do sech as that."

He cleared his throat, rose from the table and gave his chair the usual kick. She thought he was hard of hearing till she heard him grumble, "Dad-gummed noisy younguns ain't worth a-hill a-beans."

Comes wash day, Clarinda built a fire under the black three-legged wash kettle in the back yard. She'd scrubbed several loads of laundry when the wood gave out. She hurried to the woodshed to gather an armload. There, stretched across the chopping block she found Billy Dan's checkered coat. Ten swings of the ax had slashed the front and back and one sleeve hung by a thread. It stank of ambeer. She perceived that the doer of this wicked deed had murder in his heart. It was the only coat that Billy Dan had.

She waited till supper to confront Wadell. The children had finished eating and were doing their evening chores. She held up Billy Dan's coat."Wadell Dudley, did you do this?"

He looked up from his plate—his black eyebrows took a nose dive. Slamming his fork down, he ground his teeth and gave her a menacing stare."I never done no sech a thang!"

"You're the only person on this place that chews tobacca."

"That don't mean I done it."

"Well, what about yore grandson, Nelson. Has he been a-sneakin around here agin?"

"Naw... Nelson didn' do it... he's a good youngun."

"How can you say that, Wad? You know he tried to beat my little younguns to death."

Wadell rose from the table. He kicked his chair so hard it skittered across the floor and crashed against the wall."Them other boys was the cause a-that. They put 'im up to it. Anyway, when Nelson got home an' told his Pap about it, he got another whuppin with a leather strop."

"Well, his Pap is a better man than you are. At least he didn't uphold him in his meanness."

"I wouldn't put it past Billy Dan a-choppin that coat. He knowed you'd blame me fer it. The dad-gummed little devil needs a leather strop took to his hind end!"

Clarinda sucked her breath in sharply and rage shook her from head to toe."If you so much as look cross-eyed at one of my younguns, I'll wrap a cheer around yore head, Mister."

Wadell lunged for the door. Clarinda grabbed the ladder-back chair he'd kicked and threw it with all her strength. It crashed into the door jamb, but a broken slat flew sideways and clubbed his shanks. He made tracks for the barn, looking over his shoulder. When he reached a safe distance, he yanked his britches legs up and examined his pipe stems."Damn!" he muttered, "I got a knot down thar bigger'n a guinea aigg. How can a peaceable woman fly into sech a fit?" He limped down the lane looking like he could bite the head off a ten-penny nail.

The following morning, Clarinda rose early as was her custom. While she cooked breakfast, the children dressed. After they ate, they headed down the path to catch the school bus. Wadell ate his breakfast and went to the barn to groom his horses. Clarinda milked the cows, stored the milk in the springhouse and went about her morning chores.

She worked with a dark melancholy cloud hanging over her head. The house seemed haunted. *Git out! You don't belong here.* Yes, indeed, she felt unwelcome for certain. She fixed Wadell's noon meal of potato soup and cornbread."Wadell, try some a-this grape jelly I made yister-dey. It'll go good with the biscuits leftover from breakfast."

He ignored her. In moody silence he ate his potato soup then rose from the table and returned to the outdoors.

For a brief moment, a wave of self-pity rolled over Clarinda. For two-and-a- half years she'd tried to make her marriage work but her efforts had failed. I'm homesick. My younguns are homesick too, she thought. I can feel it... I see it in their faces. Suddenly, her shoulders lifted as she made the decision she'd been pondering for days."I'm a-gitten my younguns away from this godforsaken place. We'll be outta here fore the sun goes down," she muttered.

She set to cooking. My younguns need a extra good supper fer the journey, she thought. Her spirit lightened and she hummed as she worked. She prepared enough food to feed a reaping crew. Soon the aroma of cured ham, red eye gravy, biscuits, green beans, boiled sweet potatoes, deviled eggs and apple cobble filled the house

The children came home from school at four o'clock. Clarinda gave them ham biscuits to take the edge off their hunger. At five o'clock they all sat down to a loaded table. Wadell wore his usual sour face. He raised his eyes from his plate and scolded Clarinda."Why'd ye cook suh much fer? Are ye tryin tuh founder the hawgs? It's a dad-gummed wasteful habit ye need tuh break."

Little Howard reached for a biscuit. Wadell stopped chewing, cleared his throat, "uh-huh huhrumm," and glared at him. Howard slowly withdrew his hand and tucked in his lower lip. His head dropped as tears flooded his big eyes. Clarinda reached over and put two biscuits on Howard's plate. Wadell shot her a look that would have withered the devil. She ignored him and asked the children about their day at school.

Wadell finished his meal, rose from his chair, kicked it and stomped off to his son's house for the seventh evening straight.

"Mama, what's Wad so mad about?" Billy Dan asked.

"I don't know, an' we ain't waitin around to find out. I want you younguns to gather up yore clothes — we're gitten the hell outta here!" She rushed around the kitchen making preparations for their journey.

The children looked at each other with big eyes."Uh-oh," Mandy whispered, "Mama done cussed agin. Mr. Wad better watch it. The last time Mama cussed, she beat the daylights outta Whistlepig."

Howard tugged at Clarinda's sleeve."Mama, where are we goin to?"

"We're goin home."

"Back to Levi's Mountain?"

"As soon'es we can git our things together." Clarinda took a burlap sack from the pantry and gave it to Billy Dan."Hurry younguns, it'll be dark fore long."

The children looked at each other with big smiles breaking out on their faces. Chattering and laughing they raced upstairs to gather their clothes.

Clarinda brought two baskets from the pantry. She'd need enough food to last till she could get her canned stuff hauled to Levi's Mountain. She filled the baskets with dried pintos, a gallon of cornmeal, flour, and a large chunk of cured ham. That ham will go mighty good with supper tomarr evenin, she thought. From the kitchen she hurried into her bedroom and snatched two pillowcases from the bed. Within minutes, she'd stuffed them with every article of clothing she owned.

She stood in the kitchen and looked down at her meager possessions piled around her feet. Two pillowcases full of rags and the baskets of food. She wanted to take some potatoes, but knew she had all they could carry.

Her eyes traveled around the kitchen that she'd once thought so pretty. Dirty dishes filled the sink. She'd never neglected her chores, but she felt no guilt. These dirty dishes belonged to the deceased first wife whose faded yellow apron still hung from a peg in the corner. Clarinda had asked Wadell twice to store it away, but he never did. It was a constant reminder that this kitchen belonged to the dead wife—always had—always would. Dead my foot, Clarinda thought, you've been a-standin 'ere in the corner a-watchin me work since the day I come here."Fer all I care, yore dishes can set 'ere till a blizzard blows through Hell!" The beautiful red geranium on the windowsill would die from lack of water because Wadell wouldn't tend it."So be it," she muttered. She didn't fret over trifles. Uppermost in her mind was the survival of her children.

She strolled into the dining room and opened the glass door of Wadell's beautiful cupboard. He had given her to understand that the dishes in the cupboard were for show only. She reached inside and chose a pristine teacup and saucer adorned with blue flowers. She carried them to the kitchen and filled the teacup with coffee.

Walking slowly to the dining room door, she leaned against the door jamb and gazed at Wadell's exquisite mahogany dining table."Ye look mighty han'some perched on yer fancy post with nairy a leg to stand on. I've filled ye with bread an' meat an' all manner of goodly things, but yer a pauper's table—a table of frowns an' woe. Compared to the big chestnut table Rufus made me—yer fit fer nothin but the ash heap. Every hungry soul who entered our door pulled up a cheer an' partook of sech as we had." A wry smile lifted one corner of her mouth."Sup sorrow from a dirty cup, Beelzebub." She threw the cup with gritted teeth. As an afterthought, she flung the saucer in the same direction. It whizzed over the table and struck the cupboard, cracking the glass door. She winced. She didn't mean to do that."So be it. That'll give ye somethin worth fussin about."

From the corner of her eye she caught movement. Turning, she found the children at the kitchen door, staring at her in amazement."Who was you a-talkin to, Mama?" Billy Dan asked.

She shouldered the hemp sack."Come on, younguns... grab a basket an' le's go home."

Laughing with relief, the children snatched a parcel and rushed outside. She followed them, pausing long enough to wipe her feet on the threshold before stepping over it. She slammed the door behind her hard. Wadell's antique wall clock crashed to the floor with a loud bong. She didn't flinch or turn back.

Wadell's meadows and rolling fields were awash in golden sunset light as Clarinda and her children turned their faces homeward. The children whooped and hollered and went leaping oat shocks. They were leaving this hateful farm where a hoot owl wouldn't even holler at night — where their only friend was a dog that belonged to the farm — where their mother had worked from daylight till dark, and it was hard to remember when last they'd seen her smile.

Tonight, they'd sleep in their shack on Levi's Mountain and listen to a screech owl cry. They'd hear a wild cat scream on the mountainside and a big bear growl in the apple trees.

"Hey, look!" Billy Dan yelled.

Clarinda turned and saw Wadell's dog running toward them. He leaped on the children, wagging his tail for joy.

"Mama, Ol' Jube wants to go to Levi's Mountain too," Billy Dan said.

"No, he cain't go with us."

Mandy stroked his head."Why not?"

Clarinda stopped and set her bundles down."Now younguns, I know it's hard to leave 'im behind, but he belongs to Wad." She took the dog by the collar and led him away from the children."Go home, Jube! Git!" Jube headed back to the farmhouse, looking over his shoulder. The children watched him go with tear-filled eyes."He's lonesome on this farm," Billy Dan said, with tears rolling down his cheeks.

"Younguns, you cain't have what ain't yore'n. You can git a dog of yore own when we git settled in at home."

"Yee haa!" Howard yelled "We'll git a hound just like Jube."

175

"Yeah, we'll name him Digger 'cause he's a-gonna dig crawfish outta the branch fer my new pond," declared Billy Dan.

"An-an he can dig out the arr'heads an' spearheads that the Indians made long ago. I'm gonna find 'em by the gobs."

"Mama, are we gonna see Mary Ann an' Lee an' all our brothers soon?" Mandy asked.

"We shore are. We'll see Mary Ann by bedtime."

"Oh, goody!" Mandy skipped ahead and joined her brothers in jumping oat shocks.

Wadell stood at the sheepfold in the lower pasture with his head tilted to the side, hand cupped behind one ear. He could hear the echo of children's laughter. He raised his eyes to his harvest fields and saw the dark silhouettes of four children dancing across a blazing sunset. One, heavy laden, stooped figure followed them.

Wadell's eyes widened, then squinted, as he recognized the figures and realized that Clarinda was leaving him. Agitated, he paced back and forth his mind in a dither."I'll be dad-gummed, she ain't a-gonna leave me," he muttered."I'll take a short cut an' head 'em off." He lit out across the fields in a lope.

"Younguns, le's hurry. We'll stop at Eva Jean's, an' stay all night. We'll go home tomarr."

"Okay, Mama."

As Clarinda and the children drew near Dark Hollow, Clarinda lit the lantern that Billy Dan carried. Virgin timber spread a thick canopy across Dark Hollow that blotted out light even on a sunny day. The children fell silent as they entered the dark quiet hollow. It seemed every creature within had stopped to listen and watch their dim lantern glow.

Mandy clutched Clarinda's arm and whispered, "Mama, I hear somethin walkin."

Clarinda smiled."It ain't nothin that'll harm us."

The boys kept a few paces ahead of Clarinda and Mandy till snorts and snuffles in the laurels sent them flying to their mother's side.

Billy Dan whispered, "Mama, le's run!"

"No, we'll just keep a-walkin like we are now."

The sound of padded feet seemed faked, but a hellacious growl stopped Clarinda in her tracks. The children clung to her skirt, quaking in terror.

Clarinda set her bundles down and reached deep in the burlap sack. She brought forth Rufus' Colt . 45 pistol."Stand back, younguns, an' don't be afeared." With a steady hand, she aimed a little high of the shaking laurels where the varmint was in the throes of a conniption fit. She squeezed off three shots. The growling stopped—not a leaf stirred.

The children tugged at her arms."Did ye kill it, Mama? Did ye kill it?"

"I don't know, but it shore ain't growlin no more."

The boys' courage soared. An abundance of rocks lay scattered along the roadside. They scooped them up and peppered the laurels. As usual, Mandy joined the action. She chose a round rock about the size of a Rusty Coat apple. She tucked in her lower lip and let the stone fly. It arched high and dropped into the bushes with amazing accuracy for one so small. She heard it land with a thunk and something grunted."I hope I killed ye—you danged ol' booger!"

Clarinda yanked the sack to her shoulder and they continued their journey, but she kept the pistol in her coat pocket until they had put Dark Hollow behind them.

Wadell lay face down behind a large decayed log until the children's voices faded into the hollow."Am I dead?" The sound of his own voice startled him. He felt his chest. His heart was still thumping. He heaved a great quivering sigh, "Good gawd a-mighty!" He ran shaky fingers through his hair."Whar's muh hat?" He staggered to his feet and found it lodged in the undergrowth. He rubbed his aching wrist and found a knot the size of an acorn."Damn little rock-throwin heatherns."

Wadell thrashed around in the bushes and fell face foremost into a hole where a dead chestnut had uprooted. He crawled out and crept on all fours toward the road. Suddenly, his right hand sank to the wrist in something warm and mushy. A dreadful stench invaded his big Roman nose."Damn b'ar dung," he muttered, reeling sideways to gag. He lunged to his feet, crashed through the bushes like a madman and tumbled into the road.

He stood on wobbly legs wondering if he'd be able to make it home. The sound of snapping twigs and the snuffle of something big coming up the hollow put an end to his shilly-shally. His feet took wing. When he emerged from Dark Hollow, he wiped his stinking hands on his cowboy hat and found a hole in the brim."Good gawd a-mighty! I've come in a-harr a-gitten kilt!"

Eva Jean and her family were surprised and happy to see Clarinda and the children—and Mary Ann was there. The children gathered around her, chattering about the booger that had followed them through Dark Hollow.

"It-it was a bear!" Andy stuttered, his eyes wide with excitement.

Mandy disagreed, "It was not so. It was a paint'er! I saw its yaller eyes a-shinin in the bushes, an' I heerd it snort."

Howard butted in,"Yeah, but I betchie it snorted its last snort."

The twins scrunched in as close to Mary Ann as they could get. She put an arm around each and listened intently as they argued back and forth. It warmed Clarinda's heart to see them together again. She knew that she'd made the right decision to leave Wadell.

Eva Jean and Mary Ann looked closely at their mother then glanced at each other. An unspoken understanding of the situation passed between them. Their mother needed clothes. Her shoes were falling apart. Her hands were calloused and stained from hard labor and harvesting the fruit of the vine. Furthermore, the October night was far too cold for the children to be going barefooted.

They talked and planned far into the night. Mary Ann, of her own choosing would be going home with her mother. Clarinda and the children fell asleep quickly in the comfortable beds that Eva Jean provided.

The following day, Clarinda sent her son-in-law, Joe, to Wadell's farm to get Ol' Pied and her canned stuff. He returned with Ol' Pied, but only three dozen jars of canned food. He said Wadell tallied the jars on his fingers and said that was it.

Clarinda looked stunned."Why, I canned over five hunderd jars of vegetables. The jars belonged to Wad. Maybe that's the reason he wouldn't let 'em go.

"Do you want me to go back to Dudley's farm an' git yore stuff, Clarinda? Five hunderd jars of canned goods is a lot to lose."

"No, leave it be. I don't want a big row. We'll manage somehow."

Mary Ann's temper flared, "Mama, I'm a-goin to Wad Dudley's farm. I'll git yer canned stuff. I ain't a-gonna let that pack a-people gobble down what you canned up."

"They ain't no use a-that, Mary Ann. I'll take keer a-things."

Mary Ann sprang to her feet."Mama, you've always let people walk all over you."

Eva Jean butted in."Don't worry Mama. I've got enough canned stuff fer two families. I'll share with you."

"You'll do no sech thing. You've got yore own younguns to feed."

Clarinda had stored her house plunder at Eva's when she moved to Wadell's farm, so they all pitched in and loaded the most needful things on her son-in-law's old farm wagon. It was two o'clock when they rattled into the yard of home sweet home.

Clarinda felt like dropping on her knees and kissing the stepping-stone at the kitchen door. She walked through the rooms, getting reacquainted with her humble little cabin. It seemed like she'd been gone for years. The roof had sprung a leak and the wallpaper sagged, but that could be fixed. She opened the sliding kitchen window that Olus installed at age seventeen. It needed lubrication to slide true. The cast-iron heater she'd left in the settin room had accumulated rust, but that could be removed. She inspected the pipe. Although rusty, it looked safe.

"Mary Ann, le's clean this house before we put the house plunder in."

Mary Ann agreed and immediately took a water bucket from the wagon and gave it to Mandy."We need water and lots of it, Mandy." She pointed to the wooden water spout a few yards from the kitchen door. While Mandy filled the wash tub, Mary Ann picked up dry limbs from the edge of the woods and built a fire in the rusty cast-iron heater. Within the hour, she had her scrub bucket full of hot sudsy water and set to scrubbing like she was fighting fire.

"Mary Ann, you're gonna scrub a hole in the floor," Mandy said.

"I'll worry about that. I need another bucket of water, so shake a leg, Missy."

"I'm tard, an' my name ain't, Missy."

"Well, I'm tard, too, but this ol' shanty hasta be cleaned an' I ain't doin all the work by myself, Missy!"

"Stop that quarrelin, younguns," Clarinda called from the roof where she was spreading tar to stop the leaks.

Mandy headed back to the water spout with two buckets. It was a heavy load for one so small and the tendons in her neck stood out as she gritted her teeth with the effort. She plopped the two brimming buckets at Mary Ann's feet."There's yore water. If you want more you'll git it yoreself! I'm tard of you a-bossin me."

"Well, don't git sassy with me, little girl." Mary Ann picked up a bucket and splashed fresh water all over the floor. Mandy headed for the door with a river of sudsy water lapping at her heels. Mary Ann knew how to clean a house and every movement she made banished dirt and germs. The floor had big cracks between the floor boards and the dirty suds were easily rinsed away. There wasn't a root cellar under the floor so the water went back into the earth. The breeze would blow the dirt dry in no time. By late afternoon, the windows sparkled and everything smelled fresh and looked neat.

Eva Jean had slipped several jars of vegetable soup into Clarinda's wagon load of stuff because she knew Clarinda would object if she tried to give it to her outright. Clarinda cooked their supper with a happy heart. Absolutely nothing smelled as homey as a big pot of beans bubbling on the stove and cornbread browning in the oven. Slices of the cured ham she'd brought from Wadell's pantry made their supper extra good. She saved the vegetable soup for another day.

When the sun sank behind Levi's Mountain and night came on, Clarinda took out her well-worn Bible and read several of her favorite Psalms. She stretched her weary bones out on the straw mattress, happy and content. Lee would be home tomorrow and Henry would visit from Caldwell County when he found out she was back. She drifted into the first peaceful sleep she'd had in months. The thought of Wadell Dudley never entered her mind.

Twenty
Levi's Mountain

Wadell

He shook the spiders from his coat
And from one boot he plucked a rat—
He stood before the lookin glass
And cocked his dusty Stetson hat.

Clarinda was glad to be home, glad to see her children happy again. But she'd spent the summer working on Wadell's farm and didn't have one penny to show for her hard labor. She could hook rugs and trade them for clothes as she'd done before, but they had to eat, too.

She could hardly stand the thought of asking her married children for help. She could almost hear the daughters-in-law talking amongst themselves... Clarinda should a-knowed Wad Dudley wouldn't provide fer her younguns. Anyway, her sons had their own families to support.

The vegetables she'd canned at Wadell's farm would have carried her family through the winter with some to spare. Why did Wadell tell her son-in-law that the canned stuff was gone? He had to be lying. He'd fork over the food or pay for it. The good Lord had always provided a way, and with His help they'd be around when the old Rebel apple tree bloomed in May.

Clarinda's sister, Etta, had given her two bushels of apples to dry. Clarinda was busy peeling them when Wadell rode up in her yard on his shiny black horse. Two years earlier, the children had dropped out of the apple trees and abandoned their crawfish ponds to greet the man with the fine horse—not so this time. Billy Dan and Andy stood in the yard, stony-faced, and stared, making no effort to greet him.

From the top of the Rebel tree, naughty Howard looked down on a stepfather he despised and muttered, "Why's ol' Wad here? This house belongs to Mama and us younguns. I'll put him offa our land—right now!"

181

Howard swung down through the tree and dropped softly to the ground. He scooped up two slushy, half-frozen rotten apples and shouted, "Hey, mister turdy wady, chaw on this!" He threw the soggy missiles with all his might. The first apple exploded on Wadell's head, knocking his cowboy hat off. The second apple struck the stallion over one eye with a splat. The animal reared on its hind legs."Whoa! Settle down hyarr," Wadell shouted, yanking the reins from side to side until he got the horse under control. The boys saw that he was a skilled horseman, but would they give him credit? "Whoo- haaa!" They yelled, and the rotten apples flew.

"Damn little heatherns," he muttered.

Mary Ann heard the commotion and rushed to the settin room window."Mama, come here, quick. Ain't that yore bronco bustin cowboy in the yard?" She tilted her head back and whooped.

Howard, who could imitate anything on foot, hoof, or wing, squalled into his cupped hands. As his wrists moved in and out, fearsome panther screams erupted. Wadell's high-spirited horse laid his ears back, rolled his eyes in terror and tore up turf.

"Howard, stop that racket, right now!" Clarinda demanded, and stepped out on the porch.

Wadell got his horse under control, dismounted, and hitched him to the porch railing. Mandy knelt down on her knees and reached through the porch railing to stroke the horse's face.

With hands on hips Clarinda faced Wadell."What brings you here today, Wad?"

"I'm hyarr tuh find out why ye walked off the farm."

"You're barkin up the wrong tree, Mister. I ain't goin back to yer farm."

Wadell leaned against his horse and wept.

Mandy had never seen a grown man cry."Mr. Wad, you've got a big drip on the end of yore nose."

Wadell pulled a blue handkerchief from his pocket and buried his face in it."Youngun... you'd have a drip... on yore nose too... if you was sad as me," he blubbered between sniffles.

Mandy's mouth drooped at the corners and her nose wrinkled up. What a cry baby! She'd ten times druther see his ol' sour face as this snotty-nosed weasel.

Clarinda spoke in a stern voice."Now Wad, you can shed a washtub full a-tears, but it won't change a thing. I'm not livin where my younguns ain't welcome. This is our home here and we can do as we please. I don't havta watch and worry that yore low-down, sorry grandson will catch my little younguns away from the house and beat 'em to death."

"That wud'n my fault."

Clarinda ground her teeth."I don't want to heer yer lies, Wad. You treated me an' my younguns sorry, mighty sorry. If I'd a-knowed you was a poutin man, I wouldn't a-married you fer yore farm an' ten more like it. I cain't stand a pouter. Why, talkin to you is like speakin to a stump. What's the matter with you? Are ye deef?"

Wadell lifted his face from his handkerchief."I know I ain't acted like I ortuh, but Clarinda, it's been yeers since I've been around younguns and it takes awhile to git use't to 'em."

"Well, Mister, that's one less worry you're gonna have. I'm home to stay, yes siree. I don't walk back'ards!"

Wadell felt his chance for a reconciliation slipping away. He'd never seen her in such a rage. 'Twas time to prime the pity pump. He sank to the porch steps and opened the flood gates.

Mary Ann heard him sniffling and poked her head out the door."Fer the love of Pete, is that ol' Troll still here a-boo-hooin around?"

Mandy looked up at her big sister and wrinkled up her nose."Uh-huh, he's still a-snubbin, but they ain't no tears a-comin outta his eyes."

"That figures—he's fakin. If I git my hands on 'im the tears'll fall by the bucket load."

Wadell clicked his false teeth together so hard he almost chomped the tip of his tongue off and that really made his eyes water. Dad-gummit, this ain't none a-her business, he fumed.

Mary Ann returned to her work, muttering to herself, "That danged sonofagun ain't nothin but botheration. Surely Mama won't take that sorry rascal back."

Clarinda watched Wadell weep, and despite his orneriness she felt pity tug at her heart. He had aged ten years in a matter of days. She'd wished a thousand times over that she'd never married him. It was the biggest mistake of her life. She didn't really love him—never would. Her late husband, Rufus, the father of her seventeen children, was the only man she had ever loved. But Wadell was getting along in years and perhaps his children didn't want him over the long haul. She had married him with the intention of staying with him for life, but her children came first. She'd told him so many times.

With trembling hand, Wadell made two attempts to pocket his handkerchief before he actually did. He turned and looked up at Clarinda with his most heartbroken look."Well, Clarinda, would it be agreeable to ye if I moved in hyar?"

Clarinda turned her back and walked to the opposite end of the porch. She stood with her arms folded, in deep thought. She'd spent all summer workin on his farm, and now, another winter was close't at hand and she had nothin to git them through it. No firewood, no food, and no money to buy any either.

She thought of the small farm adjoining Alexander's property. It was for sale. She wanted that property. She could still harvest the apples and get wood from Levi's Mountain. The farm cabin had six rooms and two porches. Her family needed the space. Furthermore, fifteen acres of tillable land lay in the tract. If Wadell would hep her buy it, she'd grow tobacca an' repay him. Oh, how she yearned for a place that she and her children could call their own.

"It's so dad-gummed lonesome at home that I cain't stand it," Wadell lamented between sniffles.

Clarinda turned and walked toward him."You should a-thought of that before you acted the way ye did."

"Well, I don't know whut's a-gonna become a-me," he blubbered into his handkerchief.

"You cain't move in here, Wadell. We ain't got enough room as it stands now. The farm next to this'n is fer sale. If you'll hep me buy it, I'll consider reconciling, otherwise, you can fergit it."

Wadell stiffened and buried his face deeper into his handkerchief.

Clarinda perceived that he'd been struck dumb, but she forged ahead anyway. She'd not daince to his tune. She'd worked on his farm long enough to pay fer a dozen acres of land."Well, Wad, the best thing you can do is git on yer horse an' ride. I've got apples to work up." She turned to go inside.

Wadell sprang to his feet."All right. If ye want that dad-gummed rock pile I reckon I'll hep ye git it. But I ain't farmin it." He sat down again and buried his face in his handkerchief.

"I didn't ast ye to farm it. It'll take seven ton of coal to git us through the winter. Seven ton costs $72. 00. Are ye gonna pay fer it?"

Wadell didn't respond.

"Well?"

He raised his head and nodded.

"You're a-gonna pay fer half the rations, too."

"Half? But they's jest one a-me."

"Yer clothes havta be washed an' arned don't they?"

He nodded."All right. I'll pay half."

"I want a big wagon load a-hay fer my cow, and I want my canned stuff brought here."

"The canned stuff's gone."

"Where is it?"

Wadell broke into a fresh spasm of weeping, declaring that every jar had been lifted from the cellar and that he didn't know who took the food.

"Didn't you lock the cellar door?"

"No, I've never had anythang stole outta there."

"Why, anybody with a grain of common sense would lock their cellar. You lock the meathouse don't ye?"

"Uh-huh."

"All right, Wad, that'll be a dollar fer ever jar of food that I put in yore cellar. My younguns have to eat this winter. I worked mighty hard a-cannin an' a-picklin food all summer. I want ten bushel of taters, too, and don't tell me that somebody carried off all the taters."

He nodded weakly.

"You'll buy ten bushel."

"All right, but I'll havta cash some bonds."

"Well, that won't bankrupt ye."

"I'll do it tuhmarr."

Wadell rode out of Clarinda's yard sitting high in the saddle and feeling smug, but conflicting thoughts raced through his mind. A mile down the road, he heaved a heavy sigh and dropped his head in deep thought. He had to think things through.

It was touch and go there fer awhile, but she had fine'ly come tuh her senses. In a spate of weakness I agreed tuh hep her buy that property that jines her brother's place. Hep? She ain't got no dad-gummed money. I'll havta buy it—havta plunk down ever penny of it. She'll pay the taxes, though. I shore ain't gonna spend a dime on that sorry Rock Pile Farm. I agreed tuh give her five hunderd dollars. Five hunderd dollars! Good gawd! I'll havta cough ever penny up tuh feed her sp'iled brats this win'er.

Still, I don't regret givin the canned stuff away. Muh conscience is cleer as a new-born babe. We growed that garden on my land. Them cannin jars was mine, empty or full they 'as mine.

So, I had tuh eat crow—dad-gummed pinfeathers an' all. I shore don't intend tuh live alone. Wadell Dudley don't set by a cold hearthstone a-gnawin on last yeers corncobs. Clarinda's a good cook an' housekeeper. I'm a-gitten old. I need tuh be tuck keer of.

Then he remembered the dream he'd had the night before. Even the thought of it in broad daylight gave him the shivers. In his dream ... a dad-gummed mouse scuttled down the stairs an' up his bed post. It dove under the kivers, and then of a sudden, there it was a-settin on his chest. It's little watery, buckshot eyes watched him even as it snuffled left an' right. It was so close't he could see the dew draps on its nose. Then it blinked an' it was bigger, blinked agin, twice't as big, third blink—its eyes popped out as big as purple grapes and red-rimmed they was. It wore Billy Dan's checkered coat. He saw the gashes whar he'd chopped it with the ax. He saw and smelt the ambeer he'd spit on it. Then the dang thang rared up on its hindquarters an' drapped its head to whar it could look him smack-dab in the eyes. It commenced slatherin at the mouth like it had hyderfobie. It twitched, an' he could see that it was a-fixin tuh blink agin.

He sprung up in bed an' screamed—soaked with sweat. His heart thumped like pheasant wings a-drummin. With tremblin han's he lit the lamp, and there sot his ol' yaller-spotted calico cat on the foot a-his bed. It stared at him and its eyes got bigger'n bigger. It tamped its paws on the kivers, an' its claws moved in an' out. Its tail commenced switchin from side tuh side like it had a mouse cornered—an' he was the mouse! Good gawd a-mighty! I dread tuh see dark come.

How did I drap down tuh this? Ain't I got one of the finest farms in Tennessee? Ain't I got horses, cattle, sheep, a dung-pot full a-money and bonds by the stack? An' now, I'm a-fixin tuh leave it all fer a shack on the side of a dad-gummed mountain. I must be plumb addled in the head. But then... there's that ol' empty house with the clock a-tickin an' the mice a-gnawin. Wadell shivered.

As Wadell trotted his shiny steed homeward, Mary Ann was raising the roof on Levi's Mountain. She kicked her scrub bucket sideways, "Mama, why are you a-takin that ol' devil back?"

"Well, Mary Ann, in two or three weeks the snow's gonna be a-flyin an' we ain't got a penny. We ain't got a stick of firewood nor much more'n a meal in the house. If you can think of a better way to take keer a-that—let me know."

Mary Ann clammed up. It was on the tip of her tongue to tell her mother that she'd jumped from the fryin pan into the fire when she married Dudley. But Mary Ann knew her mother regretted her decision so she kept her thoughts to herself. Her mother had been through hell on that farm and she wasn't about to say, I told you so. Instead, she let loose on Wadell."Well, I guess he thinks he'll move in here an' git waited on hand and foot, but that ain't a-gonna happen. I ain't cleanin after that hookid-nosed rascal." Mary Ann dipped her broom in the scrub bucket and scoured the floor so hard she raised splinters.

"Well, I don't expect you to clean after him," Clarinda retorted.

A month later, Wadell and Clarinda purchased the small farm on Levi's Mountain and they all moved in. Wadell brought two big wagon loads of hay from his farm for Ol' Pied. He bought seven ton of coal as he'd agreed to do. He came down with a dreadful headache when he had to fork over $500. 00 for the canned stuff he'd given away. Mandy heard him grumble, "I'll be dad-gummed if I'm a-spendin another brownie around here. I've paid my share fer the next five yeers." So Wadell sat by the fire, baked his shins, gazed at a flower in the wallpaper and mutely counted his money on his fingers.

Mary Ann and Wadell were mortal enemies from the day he moved to Levi's Mountain. She held a grudge against him for the way he'd treated her mother. Did he think her mother would stay on his farm and work like a slave whiles her children went barefoot and ragged? Clarinda had told her nothing about Wadell's farm, but Howard did."Mary Ann, Wad shoved me out the door one mornin because I fergot to fill the wood box."

"Where was Mama?"

"She was at the barn a-milkin the cows."

Mary Ann ground her teeth at the thought of Wadell Dudley shoving her brother. She patted Howard on the head."Don't worry, Howdy, that'll never happen agin."

Howard grinned and ran outside. It made him happy to hear that pet name from his big sister. One thing certain, she loved him and would stand up for him against anybody.

Although poverty still plagued the family, their living conditions improved. The cabin's six rooms and two porches provided adequate living space. For the first time ever, Mary Ann and Mandy shared a bedroom. Mary Ann draped blue organdy curtains around their bedroom window. The next week, Clarinda brightened up the place by hanging new wallpaper in all the rooms. Mary Ann's jaw dropped when a truck delivered a new gas-powered washing machine—compliments of Clarinda's power to get blood from a turnip.

The apparatus stood on the kitchen porch awaiting its first load of laundry. Mary Ann heated a large tub of water on the cookstove and carried it by the bucketful to fill the machine. Clarinda added the clothes and a handful of shaved homemade lye soap. Standing with the washing machine between them, Clarinda and Mary Ann looked at each other and grinned. Mary Ann laid hold of it."Well, is she all gassed up an' ready?"

"Ready as she'll ever be."

Mary Ann stomped the start pedal. It coughed and died. She stomped until she turned red in the face."Why I'd druther use the washboard as go through this rigmarole. Where's Billy Dan? He'll git it started."

Billy Dan piddled around the motor and with a squirt of gasoline he primed the carburetor. Mary Ann stomped the pedal again. Ka-boom—it took off with a roar—black smoke rolling—washing machine rolling too. She wrestled it against the wall whilst Clarinda scotched the wheels with a stick of stovewood. Within a couple of hours the clotheslines, barbed wire fence, even the trees were full of clothes. They had a house full of company too. The daughters-in-law heard about Clarinda's new purchase and came on the trot.

"Whaa-hoo-urf! I heard somebidy had set a sawmill up here," Rhoda blurted out.

Clarinda smiled."My stars! Shorely it ain't that loud."

Beulah couldn't take her eyes off the wringers."Them wrangers will make good pea busters. I'll bet I could shell a bushel in ten minutes."

In less than a week, community gossips told that Clarinda and Mary Ann had a case of big head because they had a washing machine.

Twenty-one

Levi's Mountain • "The Rock Pile Farm"

The Bean Patch

They read the Farmer's Almanac
And when the moon was on the wax,
They dropped the seeds in furrowed rows
And put the whetstone to their hoes.
Audacious weeds did bite the dust
And chomping bugs were soundly cussed —
Wood ashes put the pests to flight —
Foolhardy groundhogs shot on sight.
Beans grew and blossomed — what a crop!
They harvested around the clock.
Then perched on sacks of market beans,
They rode to town like royal queens.

"I ain't got enough clothes to wipe out a shotgun barrel." Charlotty plopped herself down on the settin room couch where Mary Ann sat folding a huge mound of laundry.

Mary Ann took a pair of raggedy bloomers from the pile and held them at eye level for closer inspection. She sighed."Me neither."

Charlotty giggled."Is that yer best?"

"I've got five pair that ain't full a-holes. It's that dang Red Devil lye soap Mama makes. It eats the 'lastic. I havta fasten 'em at the waist with a latch pin."

"Oh, you mean a safety pin."

"No, Charlotty, I mean a latch pin. Ever since you spent that weekend with yer kinfolks in Boone, you've been actin highfalutin and tryin to talk up north."

"Aw, hush." Charlotty gave Mary Ann a good-natured jab to the shoulder and snatched a blouse to fold."Mary Ann, we're as necked as two old moltin hens. We've just gotta find some work."

"They ain't no payin work around here till bean pickin time, but we might make a few measly pennies diggin stoneroot."

Charlotty slumped sideways on the laundry pile with a groan."Lord, spare me from another herb dig. Remember that herbin trip we took last summer? All we got outta that day's labor was a backache, a case of poison ivy an' a belly button full a-chiggers."

Mary Ann chuckled."Yeah, Mama daubed my belly button full of Bruton snuff. I fussed about it, but it killed 'em overnight."

Suddenly Charlotty sat up."Hey, le's grow our own patch of beans this year. We can make enough money to buy lots of clothes. If we don't start dressin up, we're apt to become old maids."

"Fer the love of Pete, we're barely seventeen."

"Yeah, an' I'm gitten tard a-pickin beans ever summer fer twenty-five cents an hour. We could just as well pick our own."

Mary Ann picked up a ragged bra."I guess we could give it a try. I've gotta have new underwear or else go around with my bosom a-bouncin."

Charlotty giggled then let out a long sigh."Aw, shewt, we can't grow beans. We ain't got no fertilize."

"Ain't you younguns ever heerd of cow and chicken manure," called Clarinda from the kitchen."I use it all the time, an' I always have a good garden."

Charlotty frowned and lowered her voice "Too much hard work in that. We don't want a- work like mules."

Mary Ann tossed a frayed petticoat in the rag pile and held up calloused hands."We 'as born a-workin like mules. It comes with the territory."

Charlotty showed her own blistered hands."But who is gonna plow an' fix our bean patch?"

"I'll ast David. He's got a team a-mules."

Clarinda poked her head around the door."You know Rhoda won't let him hep his brothers and sisters. She's too contrary. Why don't you'uns ask Eddie and Lee to fix the ground?"

"Mama, Eddie an' Lee are too lazy to draw a deep breath."

"Aw... you shouldn't judge 'em like that."

"Aint Clarinda, Mama has spoiled Eddie Jack rotten. If I 'as strong enough, I'd wrang his triflin neck."

"Now, Charlotty, you know ye don't mean a word a-that."

"Well ... maybe not, but them boys wouldn't lend us a hand or give us a drop of water if we 'as dyin of thirst."

"Well, here's yore chance to find out. They're comin in the kitchen door."

The boys ambled through the kitchen, pausing long enough to swipe a handful of fried apple pies when Clarinda had her head turned. They settled themselves in ladder-back chairs in the settin room and smacked their lips with satisfaction. Charlotty and Mary Ann glared at them which bothered them not. In fact, the boys added comments to their noisy eating."Mmm ... lip-smackin good. Good enough to make a hound dog slap his brains out with his tongue ... slurp, slurp."

The girls turned their attention to the task at hand and tried to ignore their obnoxious behavior. Charlotty folded a pillowcase and let out another wistful sigh."Oh, how I wisht I was a boy. I'd plow up creation."

The boys stopped chewing and stared at her."What fer?" they said in unison.

"Fer a bean patch. Me an' Mary Ann are thinkin 'bout plantin beans fer the market if we can git the ground ready."

"We'll fix yer ground," said Eddie with a sly wink at Lee, "fer half the crop."

"Half the crop!"

Eddie shrugged."Plowin is hard work. Danged if I'm gonna work that rocky ground fer nothin."

"That goes fer me too," Lee added.

Mary Ann stared at the smug-faced boys and wagged her finger."If you'uns thinks we're gonna beg you to plow that bean patch, ye better have another think comin. Heck, we'll plow it ourselves."

Charlotty's eyebrows shot almost to her hairline."We will?"

"Yer dang right. We'll hitch up Ol' Clyde an' turn the sod."

Eddie snickered."Cain't wait to see that."

Mary Ann snatched a corset from the laundry pile and shoved it over his head. He dashed out the door, tearing at his head gear and cursing up a storm. Charlotty grabbed a brassiere and chased Lee through the kitchen and out the back door. Clarinda peeked in the oven and muttered, "What's the use of tryin to bake anything." Her Blackberry Pudding Cake was flat as a hard times fritter.

Wadell acted like he despised Clarinda's children. He sat on the porch bench and made fun of the young folk at play. They paid no mind to his snickers behind his hand, but Mary Ann knew his kinfolk would receive another report about the heatherns he had to put up with on the Rock Pile Farm.

The girls returned to the laundry."Charlotty, don't be such a worry wart. We can plow that ground as good as them pore excuses fer brothers."

"Well ... I don't know about that."

191

The next morning, Charlotty arrived at Clarinda's early. The aroma of homemade sausage and biscuits drew her to the kitchen. She snatched a big biscuit from a pan that Clarinda had pulled to the oven door. She broke it open and stuffed it with sausage from a green platter resting on the stove reservoir. A large white enamel coffeepot percolated slowly on the back of the stove, sending its wonderful aroma throughout the cabin.

"Mmm ... , Aint Clarinda, you make the best biscuits and sausage in the world." Charlotty savored every bite as she watched Clarinda stir down a large skillet of cream gravy on the verge of boiling over.

"Help yerself to another'n youngun. There's a-plenty fer everbody."

"Oh, I want some gravy too." Charlotty took a plate from the table and crumbled her second biscuit on it. Clarinda served her from the skillet then filled a large brown bowl with the best lip-smacking, sawmill gravy in the mountains.

"Is Mary Ann still in bed?"

"No, I heerd her up an' about."

"Be ready in a minute," Mary Ann called from her bedroom. Five minutes later she appeared, wearing an old ragged shirt and Lee's pants which were four inches too short. Charlotty burst out laughing."You look exactly like a skeercrow."

"Well, you ain't no beauty, little plowboy with hat in hand."

Charlotty hitched up her overalls and cocked her straw hat sideways."Well, hush yore mouth. I think I look plumb purtyful." She removed her hat and did a graceful bow.

After breakfast, the girls hurried to the barn and fed Ol' Clyde a hasty meal. They eased the bit into his mouth. While Mary Ann fussed and fiddled with his gear, he stood quietly even though his corn nubbins and a big biscuit of spicy apple butter had his bowels in an uproar. Gas put his ribs on the rise and sent shivers of pain along his flanks.

Curiosity drew Wadell to the barnyard fence like a magnet. Working teams of horses had been his occupation since childhood. Would he lend the girls a hand—offer advice? He did not. He snickered behind his hand as they struggled with the chains.

Lee and Eddie strolled on the scene. They leaned against the barnyard gate, watched the girls and snickered, too.

"Charlotty, fasten that left trace chain to the swingletree and make it snappy," Mary Ann ordered.

Charlotty didn't budge.

"Well, ain't you gonna do it?" There was a hint of anger in Mary Ann's voice.

"Uh ... , what's a swingletree?"

Wadell snorted and tried to pass it off as a cough.

Mary Ann pointed to the wooden bar hanging lop-sided near Ol' Clyde's fetlocks. She'd already hitched one trace chain to it.

"I'm skeerd of the horse. He might kick me."

"Fer the love of Pete, you ain't a bit of help." Mary Ann stooped over, stretched herself across the plow beam and hooked the swingletree to the left trace chain. She straightened up, red-faced."See how easy that was," she bragged, leaning her right shoulder against Ol' Clyde's rump with an arrogant lift to her chin."See ... this horse is gentle as a lamb."

Ol' Clyde flapped his lips, swung his head around and his manner shouted, Git offa my shanks! He raised his tail and gave Mary Ann a blast of gas that rearranged her pompadour. She staggered sideways, fanning the air and holding her nose."You danged ol' filthy rascal! I'm a-gonna work the devil outta you fer that dirty caper!"

Wadell nearly lost his dentures. He hurried away because he couldn't conceal his glee.

Charlotty doubled over, laughing.

Eddie and Lee were fit to be tied."Hey, Mary Ann," Eddie called, "did ye git yore eyebrows singed?"

Lee raised a leg and brought forth a couple of windy toots."Did ye feed 'im moldy oats fer breakfast?"

Mary Ann gritted her teeth and picked up the lines. Her tongue gave two cheeky clicks like an expert plowman."Giddy yap." Ol' Clyde took off in a lope with the Vulcan hillside plow bouncing from side to side."Whoa! You dern fool—slow down!" Mary Ann dug in her heels and yanked hard on the lines. Ol' Clyde came to a rattling halt. She flopped over the plow handles like a wet dishrag.

The boys and Charlotty whooped.

"Hey, Mary Ann, don't you know yore gees an' haws?"

Mary Ann peeled herself off the plow with a groan. She turned and glared at Eddie through a curtain of goldy-colored hair."I'll gee an' haw you, you little squinty-eyed blatherin idiot."

Eddie knew he was getting her goat, so he kept the jeers going till Clarinda stepped from the barn with milk bucket in hand."Hey ... you boys," she hollered, "git out there and lay yore hands to that plow! You oughta be ashamed—treatin yore sisters that a-way. Git on the move before I take a switch to both of ye."

The jollity ceased, and the boys' faces turned sour."They ain't no money in it fer us," Eddie Jack muttered.

Lee groused, "Why do we havta fix the dern ground?" Nevertheless, they did as they were told. The boys spent two days of hard labor on the bean patch. They plowed, disked, harrowed—they even pulled a wooden clod-buster known as a drag over it. Last, they hitched up a small plow and made furrowed rows.

Mary Ann and Charlotty inspected their work. They knew that it would never do to criticize. The boys were already ill as hornets.

"You'uns owe us big fer all this work," Eddie Jack said, leaning on the lay-off plow."When them beans are sold, we want cash on the barrelhead."

Charlotty's face turned red."Don't worry, you'll git yer money, but if you git too picayunish, you'll not git a brownie."

Mary Ann joined in."That's right. You'll git yer money in due time an' not one day sooner."

Lee looked at Eddie with a lopsided grin."Did you hear that? They're gitten mighty sassy after the patch is fixed."

Eddie puffed out his chest and hooked his thumbs in his front pants pockets."They better watch their smart aleck mouth if they know what's good fer 'em."

Mary Ann tilted her head slightly to the side and raised one eyebrow."Are you threatenin us, you little piss aint?"

Eddie took the insult with a grin."Hah! Just wait till 'em beans start comin up. I'll roll my ol' Levi's Mountain Chariot in here in a blaze a-glory an' they won't be a bean sprout left."

Mary Ann glared at Eddie with her lower jaw moving from side to side like she was whetting her teeth. Reaching down, she scooped up two fist-sized clods."Yore blaze a-glory will fizzle in a puffa smoke!" The boys ran snickering from the patch with clods bouncing off their heads as Charlotty joined the fray.

The next morning, the girls made a hasty trip to Hedgeweth's store for bean seed. They had to get the beans in the ground while the moon was waxing if they wanted a good crop.

"We'll pay you Mr. Hedgeweth, as soon as the first pickin is sold," Mary Ann said.

"I know you will, girls. I ain't nairy bit worried about this debt."

For two months, Mary Ann and Charlotty all but slept in their bean patch. Every weed that reared its ugly head was chopped to bits before its abominable little roots could get a foothold. They side-dressed their crop with chicken manure and dusted the vines with wood ashes to keep bugs from setting up quarters and laying their tiny odious eggs under the leaves. During a two week dry spell they prayed for rain—when the rains came they besought heaven for sunshine. The good Lord surely heard their prayers because the beans hung in wads.

The girls and Clarinda picked beans from sunup to sundown that first day of harvest. They finished the following day by midmorning. The girls were proud of their crop. Twenty-three hemp sacks filled to overflowing.

Eddie Jack drove his old black pickup truck to the edge of Clarinda's yard, and he and Lee poked their heads under the hood. The Levi's Mountain Chariot had rusty fenders patched with tape and black shoe polish, but it kept the boys on the road.

Charlotty and Mary Ann moseyed over to the truck for a friendly chat."Eddie, are you gonna haul our beans to market?" Charlotty asked in a timid voice. Eddie ignored her and continued his tinkering. Mary Ann stepped to his side, leaned over and poked her head under the hood too."Listen, friendly Eddie, are you gonna haul our beans to Mountain City or not?"

Eddie nudged Mary Ann and Lee from under the hood, stepped back and slammed it down hard. He inspected his horsey hood ornament and shined it with his shirt sleeve. Mary Ann laid a firm hand on his shoulder and turned him about-face."Eddie, have you been struck dumb? I ast you a question."

"All right, I'll haul 'em, but you'uns will cough up money fer expenses an' a little extra. My ol' chariot don't roll on water."

"How much extra?"

"Oh, since me an' Lee are gonna havta load 'em, I'd say fifteen dollars each would be enough."

The girls cried, "Fifteen dollars each!"

"You dang tootin. I ain't haulin yer beans fer nothin. It'll take ten gallons of gas to git this load to market."

Lee grinned. He knew Eddie was going to bilk them out of every cent he could get.

Clarinda butted in, "How are you gonna buy ten gallons of gas when it's rationed to three?"

They all turned and saw her standing beneath the oak in the yard. How long had she been there, listening and fanning her face with her big-brimmed straw hat?

Eddie stammered, "Uh ... er, it oughta be worth a little extra to load 'em on the truck."

"What if we load the beans ourselves? Would you still charge the same?" Mary Ann haggled.

"Hah!" Eddie pointed to the biggest sack in the pile, "I'd like to see you weaklins lift that sack a-beans." It had 100 lbs. printed at the bottom and was stuffed so tight the top of the sack had been secured with a nail twisted in the hemp.

"We cain't load them beans," Charlotty blurted out.

"Shh!" Mary Ann warned.

Charlotty leaned in close and whispered, "I doubt if both of us could lift the smallest sack."

Mary Ann walked over to the bean pile and laid one hand on the sack fastened with the nail. She yanked it forward, dropped to a half squat and wrapped her lean muscular arms around it. In one smooth motion she brought it to her shoulder while on the rise then strode to Eddie's truck and tossed it in.

Wadell's jaw dropped."I'll be dad-gummed," he muttered, shifting his rear on his pouting stump at the edge of the yard.

Clarinda looked concerned."Mary Ann, ye shouldn't be a-liftin sech loads. The female vessel ain't built fer it."

Eddie stared, bug-eyed."Mary Ann, I hope you never git mad at me."

Mary Ann yanked another sack forward."Le's git these beans loaded." Within fifteen minutes the truck was loaded and ready to roll.

"Ten dollars is a fair price fer haulin them beans to market," Clarinda said.

Eddie ignored Clarinda's comment."I think you've fergot somethin, Mary Ann, you'uns owes us fer fixin the patch. You thought we'd fergit didn't you?"

Clarinda cut in, "I think you an' Lee have fergot somethin fer certain."

The boys looked at each other then stared at her."Like what?"

"Charlotty washes and arns yore clothes, Eddie. Mary Ann does the same fer Lee. They've more than paid fer fixin the bean patch."

Eddie shifted his feet and looked at Lee. He knew that Clarinda was right."Oh, all right, ten dollars it will be. That will cover my expenses, git us a Smithey burger and git us in the movie." Leaning toward Lee, he whispered, "If we wait till the movie starts we can sneak in. I've done it plenty a-times."

Lee nodded."Okay, sounds good to me."

The boys climbed into the truck. Eddie's old black International started with a bang and a puff of smoke."We'll take these beans to market in Mountain City. After the sale, we're goin to see *Gone with the Wind*. We'll give you'uns the bean money in the mornin. It'll be around midnight before we git back."

Mary Ann stepped in front of the truck and held up her hand."Whoa, now, hold yore taters one cotton pickin minute. We're goin with ye."

"What? Why you'uns ain't even ready." Lee glared at the girls and Eddie mumbled a double damn.

"It won't take us long. We wanna see *Gone with the Wind* as much as you'uns does," Charlotty said.

"If you'uns goes, I'll havta drive all the way to Boone and drop you'uns off, then turn around and drive to Mountain City and sell these dang beans."

"Well, that ain't a-gonna kill ye." Mary Ann quashed further protest with a wave of her hand as she and Charlotty hurried into the house to get dressed for town.

While the girls bathed and primped, the boys discussed their predicament. Lee slammed his hand on his thigh."Well, that throws a wrench in our plans. What're we gonna do now?"

Eddie Jack struck the steering wheel with his fist."We cain't do a damn thing. We'll just havta change our plans, that's all 'ere is to it." The boys had planned to truck on down to Carter County after selling the beans. They knew two pretty girls down there who would love a trip to Boone to see *Gone with the Wind*. Eddie blew the horn for the third time."Dang it, what's takin 'em so long?"

Finally, Mary Ann and Charlotty stepped out the door and the boys hardly recognized their sisters. Charlotty was lovely in a red taffeta dress with silver teardrops printed on the fabric. Her cherry-red lipstick was the same shade as her frock. Her accessories were white pumps with 2½" heels and a pocketbook to match. She had pinned a sprig of fragrant bubby blossoms in her curly dark hair. Her pretty brown eyes sparkled with happiness as she chewed and cracked her Teaberry gum.

The boys' jaws dropped as Mary Ann floated down the porch steps in royal blue teardrop taffeta with wheat-colored sandals and a straw pocketbook to match. Her wide matching belt accentuated her curvaceous figure and a scalloped Vneckline revealed more cleavage than she was accustomed to showing. Her honey-colored hair gleamed in a high pompadour with waves and curls spilling down over her shoulders. She had tucked a bunch of Black-Eyed Susans behind one ear. Both girls were wearing Blue Moon perfume—a gift from an old boyfriend of Charlotty's.

"What're you'uns dressed up fer?" Lee asked.

"None of yer business," Charlotty snapped, opening the truck door. She stood staring at Lee, cracking her gum, waiting for him to get out. When he made no effort to move, she heaved a frustrated sigh, put one hand on her hip and thumbed toward the back of the truck with the other."Lee, you're gonna havta ride in the back—keepa eye on our beans."

"Heck no! I ain't ridin' back 'ere. They ain't no use of you'uns a-goin anyway."

Mary Ann stepped forward and glared at him."You might as well shut up. We're goin an' that's that."

Eddie lifted both hands from the steering wheel and thumbed backward, "All right, if you're goin with us, you better be a-pilin yer hind ends in the back."

The girls looked at each other."If we havta ride back 'ere we're gonna change into somethin else," said Mary Ann.

"Yeah, our full skirts will carry us into the clouds," Charlotty added.

"No you ain't. We ain't waitin a minute longer. The movie starts at two o'clock an' I ain't missin it," Eddie stated.

Grumbling all the while, the girls climbed aboard. They had barely settled on a bean sack when Mary Ann sprang to her feet."Le's git offa here. I feel like a dern fool."

"Yeah, me too." As Charlotty threw a silk clad leg over the tail gate, Eddie took off with a roar and a jerk. She reeled sideways with one white high-heeled shoe pumping air in search of a foothold. Down the road a ways, Eddie looked at Lee with a mischievous grin and a devilish gleam in his eye."You know what I've got a mind to do?"

"What?"

"I've got a good mind to give 'em two movie stars back 'ere a ride they'll never fergit."

"Do it!" Lee tried to look through the back window, but sacks of beans blocked his view.

The road down Levi's Mountain was crooked, rutted, and steep. Eddie took the curves at a bootlegger's speed. The dust rolled and the bean sacks bounced. Charlotty fell into a gaping hole and ended up sandwiched between two sacks of beans.

"Mary Ann! Git me outta here!"

Mary Ann lay sprawled backward over a bean sack with one hand clutching her pocketbook and the other hanging on to the wood-slatted truck bed. She stretched out her six-foot frame and kicked the bean sack off Charlotty. She clawed her way forward and pounded on the truck cab."Let us off! You dern fools—we're gonna git killed!"

Eddie laughed and kept trucking. He didn't slow down till they reached the paved road. The girls were miserable and their hair—a mess. Mary Ann looked at Charlotty and laughed.

"What's so dern funny?"

"You look like somethin the cat drug outta the woods."

Charlotty had one high heel spiked into a sack of beans. Her silk stockings sagged down her legs in twisted folds.

"Well, you ain't no beaut," Charlotty retorted, then grabbed her throat and threw her head back. She made a gravelly noise and gaped like a nestling bird anticipating a worm. Mary Ann slapped her between the shoulder blades. A pink wad of gum shot from her mouth like a bullet. After a lengthy pause, she spoke in a raspy voice, "Hurrumph! Oh, Lordy, I purt nigh choked."

"Fer the love of Pete, how much gum did you have in yore mouth?"

"Just two slabs." When Charlotty recovered, she pointed at Mary Ann's face and burst into peals of laughter.

Mary Ann's smile faded. She searched her face with her hand."What is it? What's on my face?"

"Bug guts. A big bug has splattered smack-dab in the middle of yore fard. Its innards is strung out in yore hair."

Mary Ann moaned and turned pale. She leaned over the side of the truck and gagged. She had always had a weak stomach. She opened her pocketbook for her white lacy handkerchief, but the wind snatched it and it flapped away like a bird."Dang it, there goes my purty hanky."

"Don't touch yer hair, Mary Ann. That bug will be dried by the time we git to Boone. As soon as we git there, we'll go to the Ladies-Room at the courthouse and clean ourselves up."

"Oh, an' we'll jest be the purtiest thangs," Mary Ann said in a Minnie Pearl voice. She ground her teeth, "When I git my hands on them boys, I'm gonna break every bone in their body."

Ten minutes later, they were tooling along up Boone Mountain when a small gray truck with rusty fenders and a Tennessee license tag, pulled up behind Eddie's jalopy and honked ugga wugga! The truck cab was packed with laughing boys who looked to be Charlotty and Mary Ann's age.

Frantically, the girls tried to paw down their ballooning dresses which were on the verge of carrying them aloft.

"Oh, I am so embarrassed," Charlotty moaned.

"Lordy, I'm glad I ain't wearin a chop sack petticoat today," Mary Ann said. She gritted her teeth and boxed her dress tail down—it rose with a whoosh and slapped her face. The Tennessee boys pounded the dashboard in a frenzy of joy. Ugga wugga wugga!

Suddenly, two more boys popped up from behind the truck cab and shouted, "Boo!"

Mary Ann snorted—her imitation pearl choker snapped."Oh, my purty pearls," she wailed, trying to catch them, but those that didn't fall into her bra were carried by the wind. They bounced off the little gray truck like hail. The girls couldn't keep from laughing.

The boys whooped and hollered, "Hey girls! Are you'uns goin to Boone?"

Mary Ann and Charlotty looked at each other, and yelled "Yeah!"

"Meet cha at the Appalachian Theater at two o'clock? Take you to the movies?"

"We'll be there!" Charlotty shouted.

Wugga wugga wugga! The boys took off like a gray streak and passed Eddie like he was standing still. Mary Ann looked at Charlotty in wonderment."You know what we just did? We made dates with a truck load of boys that we don't even know. Mama will scold me through eternity."

Mary Ann could hear her mama now, 'You're a pore girl, Mary Ann, and all a pore girl has got is her character. So keep a guard on yore affections, an always be a lady because once't you git a stain on yore character— you're ruint—plumb ruint.'

"We're big girls now," said Charlotty."We don't havta tell our mama."

"Of course we don't, Eddie an' Lee will do the tellin."

"We ain't got a thing to worry about. I'll betcha them Tennessee fellers are halfway down the Blue Ridge by now."

"Yeah, probably."

Eddie and Lee let the girls off at Smithey's Store then made a U-Turn and headed to the bean market. The girls rushed to the Watauga County Courthouse bathroom and primped anew. When they had groomed themselves to their satisfaction they returned to Smithey's.

They stepped through the door and found themselves in a throng of storytellers. These men had graduated from the country store and had moved to town. This was the stomping ground of the best storytellers in the entire county. One fellow had told a whopper of a tale and was showing off his lying license. The girls elbowed their way through the swarm and headed to the sandwich grill in the back of the store. Their morning labors and the hellacious ride to town had whetted their appetite to a keen edge. Mary Ann sniffed the air."Mmm ... , don't that liver mush smell good?"

"I like the burgers an' hot dogs better," said Charlotty. The girls didn't have enough money to buy two sandwiches. They'd have to make one choice, divide it and wash it down with water.

"Howdy, girls."

The girls whirled around to find five Tennessee boys grinning ear to ear.

"Can we buy you'uns a burger an' somethin to drank?"

"We ain't use't to lettin strangers buy fer us," said Mary Ann.

The boys looked disappointed. Charlotty nudged Mary Ann and whispered under her breath, "Aw, le's let 'em buy us a burger."

"We ain't really strangers, are we?" said Charlotty.

The boys laughed."Heck, no. We done met you'uns back yonder on Boone Mountain," one said.

The tall handsome one looked straight at Mary Ann."Where's 'em boys that was drivin you'uns to town?"

"Oh, that was our brothers. They're gone to the bean market."

The fellow with a pencil-thin black mustache caught Charlotty's eye and grinned."Well, I don't guess they'd mind if we bought you'uns a burger an' took you to the movie, would they?"

"Nah, they're glad to be shet of us fer awhile."

The Tennessee boys bought the girls all the hot dogs, burgers, and Coca Cola they could hold. Charlotty's fellow took her hand."Are we ready to see the movie?"

She popped another slab of Teaberry gum in her mouth and rose from her chair. Laughing and chatting, they all walked down the street to the Appalachian Theatre. Tall, handsome Poley sat with Mary Ann and the mustached one, sat with Charlotty. The three pimply-faced unattached boys took seats behind them and generally made pests of themselves. During the movie they'd poke their heads over the girls' shoulders and make comments.

"Why you'uns are purtier'n movie stars—ain't they, Poley?"

"Yep, especially this'n." Poley slid his gorgeous brown eyes at Mary Ann in a way that made her blush. They sure grow handsome fellers in Tennessee, she thought.

"Hey, Sody Head, le's change seats," came a voice from the rear.

Charlotty's companion put a finger to his lips."Be quiet, Gordie, we cain't heer the movie."

Mary Ann giggled."His name ain't really Sody Head, is it?"

Poley looked solemn."Nope, that's his nickname. Ever time he gits a bowel complaint or headache, he eats a teaspoonful of Arm & Hammer bakin sody."

"What's his real name?"

"Cobb Dandy, or Dandy Cobb—I fergit which. Anyway, he's not from around here. I thank he's from some country acrost the waters." Poley snickered.

Mary Ann rolled her eyes at him, a smile playing around the corners of her mouth."That's the biggest fib I've ever heard."

Poley raised his right hand and grinned, his brown eyes twinkling.

Charlotty leaned sideways and pinched Mary Ann."Shh... we cain't hear the movie."

Mary Ann leaned toward Charlotty, wiggled one eyebrow and whispered, "You ain't watchin no movie. You're too busy sparkin Cobb Dandy." She turned her attention to the screen before Charlotty had a chance to reply.

When the movie turned sad, the boys in the back seats heard Mary Ann and Charlotty sniffling. One sympathetic fellow leaned forward and dangled a big nasty snot rag against the girls' cheeks."Here's a hankychuff, girls. The first time I saw this movie I purt nigh cried too."

Mary Ann slapped the vile object toward Charlotty—and she batted it back. Mary Ann swatted it to the floor. Poley seized the moment and slipped an arm around her shoulders. Two minutes later, he eased his hand down and squeezed her knee. Mary Ann stiffened then reached down and covered his hand with her own. His pinkie cracked—his jaw dropped. He removed his hand like he'd touched a hot stove. That had better be yore last move, Mister, she thought. Poley took the hint and acted like a gentleman the rest of the evening.

After the movie, the girls saw Eddie and Lee in the lobby. They abandoned their boyfriends and rushed to their side."Where's our bean money? How much did they bring a pound?" Eddie started to hand over the bill of sale and $297. 00 in cash, but he changed his mind and shoved the money deeper in his pocket."I'll give you'uns the money later," he said, glancing at the Tennessee boys who were standing over to the side chatting among themselves.

"Where did you'uns git acquainted with them hooligans?" Eddie demanded.

"Oh, around town," Charlotty replied, nonchalantly cracking the last remnants of her popcorn."An' they ain't hooligans, they're fine fellers."

Lee stifled a snort."Why, two of 'em done time on the chain gang, they ain't been out a month yit."

Charlotty stopped chewing and both girls cast furtive glances at their Tennessee boyfriends."How comes you'uns know so much about 'em?" Mary Ann asked.

Lee chuckled."We don't spend all our time on Levi's Mountain, ye know."

Mary Ann turned a suspicious eye in Poley's direction. He did appear older than the other boys, at least twenty-five and kind of like Rhett

Butler, tall, dark and handsome, but dangerous—maybe a bootlegger."I wonder what he done that sent him to the chain gang."

"He cut some feller's throat over a woman, missed his jug'lar by a hair," Lee stated.

Mary Ann gasped and whispered, "Really?"

"Yes, really. You ain't ridin home with that pack a-jail birds."

"Don't you be orderin—"

"Lee, is 'em steel knucks still in the truck? That's the only thing we've got to fight with except the tarr tools." Eddie said.

The girls turned pale. Steel knucks—tire tools—throat cut—chain gang! What had they gotten themselves into?

Poley looked their way."Hey, are you girls about ready to go?"

"We'll be with you in a minute," Mary Ann replied. Turning to Eddie she whispered, "Where did you park at?"

"Out front, acrost the street."

"We'll meet you there in three minutes."

The girls rushed toward the Ladies Room and slipped out a side exit. They all piled in Eddie's truck with Lee in the middle and Charlotty sitting on Mary Ann's lap. Eddie preached all the way through town, "It's a good thing you've got brothers to look out fer ye. You'uns cain't even come to Boone without gitten in cahoots with a bunch a-outlaws—you girls are somethin else."

"Shut up, Eddie, or I'll slap ye cross-eyed!" Charlotty snapped.

They were going down Boone Mountain, shielding their eyes from a blazing sunset when they heard a familiar sound, ugga wugga! Charlotty peeped out the back window and squawked, "Oh, Lordy, it's Poley an' Sody Head!"

Mary Ann craned her neck around."It's them all right. What're we gonna do?"

Eddie stomped the gas."Hang on, you bean market queens, this ol' chariot is a-gonna fly!"

"Yee haa!" Lee yelled.

"You cain't outrun 'em, Eddie, they passed you on Boone Mountain this mornin, remember?" said Charlotty.

"Just watch me." Eddie shoved the gas pedal to the floorboard. Never was there such a race—tires screaming—fenders rattling. A loose spring in the truck seat kept gouging Mary Ann in the back, and Charlotty sitting on her lap wasn't helping matters either.

"Dang it, Mary Ann, cain't you set still fer a minute!"

Mary Ann ground her teeth in pain, "Keep yore yap shut or I'll slap the bubbies outta yore hair an' pitch ye out the winder."

Lee squirmed."Will you girls be quiet? An' quit usin my head fer a dern pocketbook rack!"

Eddie's tires squealed around a curve and he lost their pursuers for a few seconds. He swung the truck to the right and down a side road. The girls looked back and saw the little gray truck flash by. They had given the Tennessee boys the slip. Everyone was relieved that the chase was over. Eddie turned around, got on the main road again and they continued on their way at a reasonable speed.

"You know somethin," Charlotty said, "they might come lookin fer us."

Lee chuckled."Naw, they won't do that."

"How do you know they won't?"

"Cause you'uns ain't *that* good lookin."

Charlotty pounded his head with her pocketbook.

Eddie and Lee didn't tell the girls that they'd never laid eyes on those Tennessee boys before or that they'd lied about them being criminals. Anyway, in their opinion it was their responsibility to see that their sisters got home safely. They also knew that if they shirked their duty and some evil befell the girls, the wrath of Clarinda and Etta would rain down on their heads.

Eddie puffed out his chest."Well, the way I see it, you girls oughta be thankful you've got brothers to protect ye from hooligans."

That remark brought a loud protest."Oh, yeah," said Mary Ann, "what we really need is a baseball bat to protect ourselves from you. You made us ride in the back of the truck. You tried to sling us off and kill us ..."

The next day, Charlotty and Mary Ann walked down to Hedgeweth's Store and paid their bean seed debt. They'd had fun growing a bean crop and after the third picking they had made over $500. 00. Yes, indeed, $500. 00 would buy them new outfits in town and they wouldn't have to wash their Smithey burgers down with water either.

Twenty-two
The Rock Pile Farm

The Old Wood Stove

I remember the winters back years ago,
The old wood stove kept a rosy glow.
It nibbled on pinecones that smelled oh, so good!
It gobbled the kindling and acres of wood.
As it baked up bread from the golden grain,
Frost would slide down the window pane—
Teakettle did dance, and then it would sing,
The table was laden with wonderful things:
A pound of butter from the spring house crock,
Moon-shaped and yellow with a star on top.
Pitcher of honey from a tall sourwood tree,
Did smother my flapjacks and sweeten my tea.
Comes evening I heaped up the kindling box
Whilst grandfather ticked and leisurely tocked.
The old wood stove brought sweet comfort and cheer
To the old home place for many a year.

*T*he afternoon sun was taking its toll on Clarinda and Wadell as they picked another row of beans. Clarinda had already canned over a hundred half gallon jars. She always put their vegetables up by the half gallon. Why, a quart with her hungry, growing boys was just enough to whet their appetites.

"I don't know why you want tuh can so many beans. I hate the dad-gummed thangs," Wadell groused.

"Green beans are good fer ye, Wad. You oughta eat more vegetables instead of so much pork."

"I like corn an' taters, an' that's all the vegetables I'd give two cents fer."

Doubtless, Wadell remembered the big bowl of mashed potatoes left-over from lunch—or dinner as mountain folk called it. He rose from his bean-picking crouch and wiped his brow on his sleeve."Whew! I've purt nigh got the weak trembles. I wonder if a man has got a chainch a-gitten a-batcha tater cakes fer supper—I'm a-hawngry."

"Mandy will fix supper; we need to git the rest of these beans picked."

Wadell looked toward the cabin, remembering the last batch of big knobby biscuits Mandy turned out."I wonder what kind a-gom she'll stir up this time."

"She hasta learn how to cook. Hesh and be thankful fer the food she sets before ye."

Clarinda saw Mandy going up the spring path and called out, "Mandy! Warm up the dinner leftovers fer supper—and be shore and make tater cakes from the mashed taters."

"Okay, Mama."

Billy Dan and Lee came home tired and hungry around two o'clock. They had been down at the creek fishing and hadn't caught a thing. They made for the cookstove warmer where they knew they'd find dinner leftovers. In two wags of a sheep's tail, a bowl of creamed corn, half a pot of beans, and two thirds of a bowl of mashed potatoes vanished.

Ten-year-old Mandy felt proud that Mama trusted her enough to cook a meal by herself. She'd already mastered cornpone, biscuits, and hard times fritters, and thus far, her only mishap was setting the kitchen afire when she tried to kill a mess of lettuce. She'd put grease in the pan but it wasn't getting hot fast enough so she lifted the stove lid and set the pan over the blaze. By the time she got the vinegar jug open, the pan was smoking. When she poured in the vinegar, grease popped on the stovetop and blazed up. In two blinks of an eye the curtains caught fire. Smoke boiled out the window and brought the family on the run. When Clarinda came through the door, the fire was going around the wall, devouring the wallpaper. Clarinda grabbed a bucket of water from the water bench and doused it with one throw. She smothered the greasy blaze on the stove top with a handful of baking soda which she flung with one huge splat.

"What a mess!" Mandy griped.

"A mess can be cleaned up, but there ain't no remedy fer a house that has burned down," Clarinda said.

Today, I'm gonna whup up the best batcha tater cakes that Mama's ever had, Mandy thought. I'm sure I can do it. I've watched Mama make 'em lotsa times. She searched the warmer and stared in dismay at the scanty portion of mashed potatoes. How am I supposed to make tater cakes from that little dab? Oh well, I'll just stir up some pone and we'll have cornbread and milk fer supper.

She got the fire going in the cookstove then went to the cupboard to get a mixing bowl. The cupboard door stuck. She bopped it with the palm of her hand and stood on tip-toe to pull it free. As she looked up, her eye lit on a white bowl on top of the cupboard. That bowl didn't belong there. Mama was particular about her dishes."Put the dishes in the cupboard Mandy," she'd say again and again.

Mandy pulled a ladder-back chair from the dining table and stepped up two rungs. She took the bowl down carefully. It was nearly full of mashed potatoes. She wondered why her Mama had put them on top of the cupboard. I must use them right away or they will spoil, she thought. They did look kind of strange, mountain-shaped with a crater on top. Inside the abyss, little green do-dads floated in a lake of whey. Prob'bly diced onion tops, she decided. She sniffed them. They smelled okay. They'd make good tater cakes. She'd mix 'em with the taters that Billy Dan an' Howard had left. She'd have more than enough fer everybody and comp'ny too, in case somebody dropped in around suppertime. But first, she must git the bread in the oven. It wouldn't be supper without cornbread.

She sifted a pint of cornmeal and a handful of flour into a bowl. She added a pinch of soda, two pinches of baking powder, and two pinches of salt and stirred it well. A heavy, black, cast-iron skillet hung from a nail on the wall behind the cookstove. She took it down and set it on the stovetop. After greasing it with a piece of pig skin she turned her attention to the mixing bowl again. With a wooden spoon she whopped a chunk of Jewel lard into the cornmeal, rolled it around a little then poured in a quart of buttermilk and stirred until the mixture was just right. She pulled a step-stool up to the stove and climbed it. Raising the bowl as high as her strength allowed, she dumped the mixture into the skillet. She came in a hair of dropping the entire conglomeration on the floor when she slid it in the oven."Whew," she said, passing the back of her hand across her sweaty forehead which left a streak of cornmeal in her dark brows. She closed the oven door with a sigh of relief."Now, the tater cakes."

First, she whopped a chunk of lard the size of a walnut in another cast-iron skillet and shoved it to the hottest section of the stove. While the lard melted, she scraped the contents of the white bowl from the top of the cupboard into the potato bowl from the stove warmer and mixed it up good. Next, she added an egg, sifted in flour, sprinkled in salt and pepper, and stirred till her arm ached. She climbed the stool again and dropped globs of potato mixture from a big wooden spoon into the hot grease. She loved to watch them sizzle. When she flipped them over she used the flapjack turner to flatten them out. Each time she lifted a big golden tater cake from the pan she whopped in another gob of lard."My tater cakes shore gobble-up lard," she muttered. Finally, the cornbread was done and she had five golden-fried tater cakes stacked on a platter.

Mandy poked her head out the kitchen window and called, "Supper's ready!"

"It's 'bout time," Wadell groused. While Wadell and Clarinda washed the garden dirt from their hands at the wash up bench on the porch, Mandy poured Guernsey cow's milk in tall glasses and set a big ball of butter on the table. Clarinda had pressed the butter into a wooden mold with a star pattern. Mandy thought it looked real pretty on the green butter plate.

She took one last look at the meal she'd prepared, hot crusty cornbread, golden- fried tater cakes, a big sliced onion and a pint jar of pickled beets. She wished she'd had time to cook a pot of October beans, but it took three or four hours to boil them tender on top of the stove. I'll cook beans tomar-rah, she thought.

Clarinda gave Mandy's shoulder an affectionate squeeze as she took her seat at the table."Somethin smells mighty good in here."

Mandy beamed with happiness.

"Mandy, fetch us a cold jug of buttermilk. It'll be so good with that pone of cornbread."

"All right, Mama." Mandy headed for the spring box.

Clarinda kept her milk and butter in a long, wooden box below the spring. An iron pipe led from the spring into the box, and cold water circulated around the gallon jugs of milk and crocks of butter and then flowed out through another iron pipe at the opposite end. The milk was continuously chilled by the cold running water and would stay fresh for several days. The spring-box also had a hinged lid and a latch to keep animals out.

When Mandy returned with the buttermilk she saw Wadell bowed over his plate, but he wasn't turning thanks, he was hogging down the last morsel of five tater cakes with a greasy smile on his face.

Mandy had to bite her tongue to keep from saying – Dang you, Wad, I wanted a bite or two of them tater cakes. She poured Clarinda a tall glass of cold buttermilk."Mr. Wad, do you want some buttermilk, too?"

"Mought as well. Maybe it'll warsh down these greazy vittles. Them tater cakes tasted like they 'as fried in lamp oil." Mandy wrinkled up her nose and the corners of her mouth drooped as she watched Wadell guzzle a glassful of buttermilk without taking a breath. His goozle bobbed up and down as he swallowed. Dang ol' rascal, she thought, nobody forced you to eat five big tater cakes. If he didn't stop complainin, the next time she'd fry his tater cakes in lamp oil fer certain.

"Fer goodness sake, Wadell, are you that hungry?" Clarinda commented as he drained his second glass of buttermilk.

Wadell cleared his throat, "Uuh-huh... huhrumm. Good gawd, you take a man out in the field an' work 'im like a mule and then grumble 'bout his rations. Yer a-gitten mighty stingy, ain't ye?"

In the middle of the night, the patter of woolen stocking feet zipped up splinters on the back porch. Wadell had a case of the back-door-trots so bad he didn't even have time to put his shoes on. The screen door opened and slammed, and then pitter-pat, zip-zip.

Molasses the pup thought a prowler was around and commenced barking. The entire household awoke when they heard Clarinda quarreling."Wadell, git outdoors this minute before you befoul the whole house!"

Mary Ann sprang from bed and went to investigate the uproar. She poked her head around the door."What the heck is goin on in here?" She staggered backward as if struck by a mighty wind.

"Oh, Wadell didn't make it to the outhouse in time and he's a mess," Clarinda grumped.

Mary Ann pinched her nostrils and trotted back to her room in haste."Shewee... open the winders!" Her paper poke hair curlers bounced and rattled as she jumped in bed and threw the covers over her head.

By that time, the entire household was aware of Wadell's affliction. The boys showed no sympathy. In fact, they made fun of him."Wad's got the scours... Wad's got the scours," they chanted then whooped and hollered."Do you reckon he's afraid of the dark?" Howard said, and giggled.

Andy was so tickled he stuttered double-time, "Do-do- do ye- do ye reckon he's skeerd of spiders in the outhouse?"

"Yeah, he 'as so skeerd he pooped in his drawers." Billy Dan whooped.

Wadell didn't think his misery a laughing matter. He felt like he'd been gut-shot with a pint of red-hot pepper seed. He stood in the back-yard shivering in his long johns – waiting for the next jolt. His bowels thundered."Its a-fixin tuh strike agin," he said, in a voice on the rise.

"Did ye hear 'im?" Billy Dan shouted over peals of laughter.

Wadell ground his teeth."Go ahead! Spread the news abroad – broad-caist it from the housetop – put it in the papers!"

Wadell's outburst tickled the boys even more. Mary Ann and Mandy joined in the jollity too.

Wadell glared at the corner of the house where the boys' bedroom was located and shouted, "Ye dad-gummed little heatherns, ye ain't got no more pity fer a sick man than – " He grabbed his belly and took off."Whoo wee!" He yelled whilst on the run.

The boys sprang from bed and peeped out the window. They saw Wadell streaking for the outhouse in the moonlight. He missed the foot-plank that spanned the branch and fell with a loud splash, but he jumped to his feet as quick as a cat. They saw him fumble with the outhouse door—he couldn't get it open. He gave a mighty yank—the door sprang from its hinges and crashed into the smartweeds. When he jumped inside and disappeared from view, the boys fell backward on their beds and laughed till they cried.

Clarinda set a galvanized tub in the backyard and filled it with warm water from the stove reservoir."Hey, Wad! Here's a tub a-water fer yore bath."

Molasses ran barking across the yard and jumped into the tub, splashing water all over her. She boxed his ears. The commotion disturbed the chickens and they commenced squawking. Finally, Wadell sat down in the outhouse and stayed there till daylight. At breakfast, he refused to come to the table and took to his bed.

Clarinda set her herb kettle on the stove and went to work, doctoring Wadell."Are you feelin better, Wad?"

"I feel like I've been gored by a bull," he whined, and brought forth a couple of weak hacking coughs that sounded like a put on.

"Well, drink as much of this as ye can," she said, offering him a glass of dark-colored liquid.

He struggled to one elbow and eyed the glass."Whut's 'at?"

"It's warm blackberry juice."

He took two sips and fell back on his pillow."I thank I've got the flux, an' I'm purt nigh shore that I've got a case a-quinsy, too," he whispered in a raspy, feeble voice that sounded like another put on.

Clarinda laid a hand on his brow "I knowed you was bad sick last night."

He sprung to life."Bad sick! Fer gawds sake, woman, I stood by the river o' Jurden all night long. I seed a herd a-camels a-comin to'ards me a-hoppin like rabbits. I come in a damn gnat's hair a-dyin. Them tater cakes wuz pizen!"

Clarinda took a step backward and blinked. She'd never heard Wadell blurt out such profanity."You better quit that cussin. You might go to sleep an' wake up in Torment."

"Don't commence preachin tuh me about Tarment. I 'as in Tarment all night long." He yanked the covers up to his ears and turned his face to the wall.

"Ain't you gonna drink this blackberry juice?"

He didn't reply so Clarinda left the room. An hour later she returned and noticed that the glass was empty.

"Wad, I've got some anjellicoe roots a bilin in my kittle. I guarantee the tea will hep ye."

He sat up, stretched his neck and raised his chin toward the ceiling."If you could git a-holt of some tar," he rubbed his neck gingerly, "an' smear it on muh neck, especially up under my yurs. It would cure me in a hurry. That tar allus laid it in the shade when I 'as a youngun."

Clarinda didn't smear tar on Wadell's neck because her herbal decoction brought him out of the kinks in less than a week. Nevertheless, his appetite for golden-fried tater cakes was kaput forever. When he smelled them frying on the stove he climbed the hill behind the house, plopped down on his poutin stump and sat there for hours.

"Mandy, have you seen my udder balm?"

"No, Mama, I ain't seen no utter balm."

"Why, I set it on top of the cupboard. It was in a white bowl."

Mandy gasped and her eyes got very big. Clarinda looked at her and knew right away that she had done something with it.

"Where is it, Mandy?"

Mandy's eyes dropped to the floor and her hand went to her mouth. She began biting her fingernails."Uh ... er ... I think I made tater cakes out of it."

"My stars an' little kitten britches! How come you to do that? You know I wouldn't put mashed taters there."

"But Mama, it looked like mashed taters to me."

"That was yellow dock root that I b'iled an' mashed up. It had chopped jimsonweed, Epsom salts, wahoo bark tea an' turpentine in it. Its good fer scratches an' scurf an' corns, but that jimsonweed causes befuddlement of the head. No wonder Wad saw camel's a-hoppin an' thought them tater cakes was fried in lamp oil."

Tears filled Mandy's eyes."Well, I guess I'll not cook any more?"

"Yes you can. It was more my fault than yores. I should a-put that udder balm some'ers else besides the kitchen. Anyway, it'll be a long time fore Wadell Dudley asts fer another tater cake."

Tewnty-three

Clarinda and her family attended a small Baptist church located three miles from their home. During the summer and fall, bees of every strain were active in the area around the churchyard. While the choir sang, hornets built a big nest under the church window near the amen corner. By late August, its contents thumped and hummed with enough power to stampede a multitude.

Inside the church, an old grouchy deacon sat by the hornet window through every service. He considered that seat his own and scolded anyone who took it."Git up from thar," he'd bark, thumping his cane on the floor. He'd settle himself comfortably, arrange his long white beard over his overall bib and sit quietly. When the pastor began his sermon, the deacon would say 'amen' a couple of times, and then drift into slumber-land.

When fourteen-year-old Howard's naughty eye fell on the hornet's nest, his face lit up. Immediately, he contrived a plot to bestir the bees. He persuaded two friends and his younger brother, Andy, to be his partners in mischief."Boys, we'll havta wait till the time's right. If we git caught, our character will be ruint. They'll kick us outta church—send us to the chain gang—an' Mama will scour my hide with a keen birch switch."

They all agreed that the fun of it would be worth the risk.

Occasionally, their pastor invited a minister from a nearby church to deliver a sermon and he, likewise, returned the favor. This kept the messages fresh and attendance high. Beginning preachers, eager to hone their skills, were always welcome. So, their pastor invited a new, young, fire and brimstone preacher to conduct their autumn protracted meeting.

This preacher had increased in popularity since his ordination and everyone was eager to hear him expound on the Scriptures. According to all accounts, he had a keen sense of perception, and had already kicked the devil out of several congregations around the country. Should it be jealousy in the choir or a grudge on the deacon board, pray and get right with the Lord or get the boot.

In the community, one fellow praised the young preacher to the skies."I heerd 'im preach once't, an' I tell ye the truth, he laid the lash tuh my back. He told me to keep my bootleg money in my pocket. He didn' want it stinkin up the collection plate."

Clarinda didn't attend the first night service. Her sister, Etta, was down with a fever and needed her. She advised her children to pay close attention to the sermon as she'd be asking questions later.

Twelve-year-old Mandy and her niece, Punkun, reached the church at twilight. A large crowd had already gathered in the churchyard."The church is gonna be packed, Punkun. Le's hurry or we might not git a seat on the alto bench." They weaved their way through the throng and up the steps. Mandy sang alto in the choir. Her big sister Mary Ann and cousin Charlotty sang soprano. The choir consisted of two benches of soprano, one bench of alto, and one bench of tenor and bass combined.

At the church entrance, Mandy turned and caught a glimpse of Howard and Andy with two of their pals. They stood under the huge oak tree in the yard, talking and laughing. Every one in the churchyard was smiling and chatting with their neighbors and friends. Joy filled Mandy's heart and spilled over the brim. Oh, we're gonna have a wonderful service tonight, she thought.

The superintendent rang the church bell and people poured through the door. Women and children took seats on the left of the aisle, and the men folk seated themselves on the right. Within minutes, every seat was taken, and still, the people kept coming. The superintendent brought ladder-back chairs from the Sunday school rooms to seat the overflow.

The crowd sat quietly... all eyes turned to the Ten Commandments and sacred pictures of Jesus on the wall behind the pulpit. They read the Sunday school record posted there as well. Fifty-three members the previous Sunday had dropped $34. 27 in the collection plate.

The church's seating capacity was seventy-five souls. Kerosene lamps glowed on small separate shelves high on the yellow pine walls. The floors and rough-hewn benches creaked with age. The wood-burning stove had been removed for the summer. It would be reinstalled in late autumn. The choir was situated to the right of the pulpit. The amen corner to the left was occupied by deacons, preachers, and the church superintendent. They encouraged and uplifted the minister in the pulpit. Directly in front of the pulpit at floor level, a table displayed a large Bible, the collection plate, and a crystal water pitcher and glass.

A cold mountain stream nearby was dammed up for baptisms. It would chatter a new convert's teeth on the hottest summer day. Scheduled baptisms were carried out regardless of weather conditions. Sometimes ice had to be chopped from the water surface. The procedure was complete immersion.

In the church, men were addressed as brethren and women as sisters. The congregation was mountain folk—the salt of the earth—reserved in manner with a distrust of the highfalutin or those who frowned on their way of life. They considered neighborliness a virtue. 'If you want a good neighbor—be a good neighbor,' was a common saying. Since pioneer days they'd endured the rigors of a rugged land by being a good neighbor and holding fast to their faith. Most could quote the Beatitudes from memory, and all church members tried to keep the Ten Commandments. But occasionally, sheep strayed from the fold. It was the pastor's duty to lead them home. Most came humbly, but others needed a lash or two. The fire and brimstone preachers laid it on.

Heads turned as the pastor and his guest entered the door. The young, new Reverend cut a handsome figure in a light gray suit, white shirt and black tie. With his Bible in one hand, he followed the pastor down the aisle. He carried himself with confidence and ease, shaking hands with the brethren and nodding to the sisters. He and the pastor took seats in the amen corner. Moments later, two visiting pastors entered the building and took seats there as well—a sure sign of the young preacher's popularity.

Seated on the first soprano bench in the choir, Mary Ann and Charlotty had a perfect view of the young preacher. Mary Ann nudged Charlotty with an elbow and whispered, "Look at that gorgeous red hair. I wonder if he's married."

"Who keers? I could never be interested in a preacher."

"Why not?"

"They seem fuddy-duddy to me. I cain't imagine 'em bein romantic."

Mary Ann stifled a snort."Have you been livin under a rock some'ers?"

"Shh... he'll heer you."

The choir leader, an elderly gentleman called Uncle Jim, rose to his feet with hymnal in hand."Turn to page 37," he instructed. Then lifting his right knee, he struck it with his tuning fork. He held the instrument to his ear to get the correct pitch."Sol-sol- la-sol- fa," he chanted."Sol-sol-la-sol-fa," the choir echoed, and then raised their voice in song."Standing on the promises of Christ my King, Thru eternal ages let His praises ring..."

The red-haired preacher joined in.

Mary Ann leaned into Charlotty's shoulder and whispered, "If his preachin is as good as his singin, there'll be shoutin here tonight." She watched the young preacher with keen interest. He'd reset his tie, look at his wrist-watch, and glance over the crowd while engaged in low conversation with the preachers at his side."He's chained lightnin," she blurted out.

Charlotty put a finger to her lips."Shh... , he's watchin us."

"Yeah... I hope so." Mary Ann chuckled.

The choir leader closed his hymnbook and took a seat. Their pastor rose and stepped into the pulpit."Brothers and sisters, we're glad to have Reverend Ode Shavers with us. As you can see from the attendance tonight, he shore knows how to draw a crowd. People are hungry fer the gospel, and this preacher will give it to ye straight. Reverend, the pulpit is yore'n."

Reverend Shavers waited till the pastor seated himself. Then he rose and ascended to the pulpit on nimble feet.

Mary Ann nudged Charlotty again."Look at 'em shiny black shoes. I can see myself in 'em."

"Hush!" Charlotty pinched her.

The Reverend read a few verses of Scripture then removed his jacket and laid it on the pulpit bench.

The congregation stirred."We're gonna git our hides tanned," someone whispered in the choir.

He closed his Bible and quoted verses pertaining to the clergy's duties, pronouncing each word in a crisp, clipped manner.

Mandy heard a deep voice on the bass bench, say, "He's a called preacher all right—shore knows the Scriptures."

The old white-bearded deacon leaned forward, belched out a hearty "Amen," and promptly fell asleep.

The preacher's voice rose and ended with a shout."Deacons an' Bishops must keep their own house in order!"

The congregation blinked.

Clasping his hands behind his back, Reverend Shavers drew himself to full height and rocked back and forth—heel to toe. He added a small bounce from the balls of his feet as his eyes roamed the congregation, sizing them up. They fidgeted under his scrutiny. The preacher's eyes locked on the slack-jawed deacon. The old man's head rested atilt against the wall. Stepping from the pulpit, the preacher tiptoed toward him.

Children giggled—the elders watched.

"I like a man with a sense of humor," Charlotty whispered.

"Yeah, me too, but they're skeerce as hen's teeth."

Reverend Shavers folded his arms and tapped one foot while looking down on the sleeping man. A titter rippled through the house. The deacon stirred, rattled his dentures and leveled his head, which dropped to his chest. His jagged snores reached the four corners of the building.

Reverend Shavers shook his head sadly... then exploded. Clapping his hands over the old man's head, he squalled, "Wake up, Brother, the Rapture's here!"

But Brother slept on—deaf as a fence post.

With arms akimbo, that red-haired preacher danced across the floor like a coiled spring coming unwound. He leapt into the pulpit and slapped the lectern so hard it wobbled."Wake up, Deacon, there's sin in the midst! Wake up, preachers, there's sinners goin to Hell!" And thus, he commenced his sermon.

Describing horrific scenes of the Lower Regions, he prodded back-sliders and sinners to the torture grates, forked them up and dangled them over the flames."Feel the heat... John Barleycorn... do ye feel the heat?"

He jumped from the pulpit, marched down the aisle and shook his finger at the sisters."You thought you'd git by, didn't ye? Well, I'll give you to understand that this preacher don't mollycoddle hypocrites an' tattlers. I've heard about yer ol' long forkid tongue a-waggin—a-goin door to door a-sowin discord among the brethren. How can ye stand to look at yoreself in the lookin glass?" He leaned toward the brethren and cupped a hand to his mouth as if to whisper."Why, most of 'em ain't seen a lookin glass in ten year," he said aloud.

The brethren laughed.

Most of the sisters knew the preacher wasn't referring to them. They had home perms. They glanced across the aisle at their husbands and snickered, their fuzzy heads bobbing like round pot scrubbers in a pan of dishwater.

The preacher straightened up, hooked a thumb in his hind pocket and looked at them with a disgusted sigh. Suddenly, he raised a shiny shoe, squalled like a wildcat and stomped the floor so hard the lamps flickered.

The sisterhood flinched and batted their eyes.

Sleeping babies awoke.

"Yore pastor oughta snatch you up by the scruffa the neck an' shake the Hell an' damnation outta every last one of ye!"

The preachers in the amen corner looked at each other with grins breaking out on their faces."Amen! Preach it Brother!"

Mothers cuddled and patted their babies, but others gave him a cold granite stare.

Mandy and Punkun looked at each other saucer-eyed.

Mary Ann rolled her eyes at Charlotty."They ain't a preacher in this congregation that's man enough to yank me up by the scruffa the neck."

Mandy heard her and snickered. The eagle-eyed preacher whirled around and pointed a scornful finger straight at Mandy."So you think that's funny, do ye? Well, young lady, there's comin a day... yes! There's comin a daaay when that smirk will be wiped off yore face!"

Mandy shrunk into her yellow frock as every eye, except the deacon's, fell on her. She swallowed her embarrassment and her anger kindled toward the preacher.

Breathing hard, but getting his second wind, the preacher turned to the brethren and spoke in a low raspy voice."What kind a-husband are YOU? Are you the head a-yore house?" His voice climbed to an ear-splitting holler."When you rise in the mornin do ye cock-a-doodle-doo, or do ye plark-arrk like a henpecked rooster?" He tucked his thumbs under his armpits and flapped and strutted then staggered across the floor like an addled rooster.

The brethren whooped.

Mandy snickered in spite of her anger.

Down the aisle the Reverend preached, chopping the air, wagging his finger in faces left and right."When you come home after a hard day in the field, is yore supper ready, brother?"

He swung around to the sisters and mocked them in a high, nosey whine."Oh, it ain't ready yit — we're outta stovewood."

He wheeled to the brethren and his voice changed to a chant."If that be the case-uh, I'll tell ye what to do-uh. You take that little wife by the hand-uh, and lead 'er out to the slab pile. You lay that ax in 'er hand-uh, an' tell 'er to start choppin. It's a wife's place to keep the home and be a helpmeet for her husband. If that husband says split wood — so. shall. she. split. wooood!" He chopped that commandment into the palm of his left hand with the edge of his right.

The cocks of the roost sprang to their feet and crowed, "Amen!" They popped their suspenders and rearranged the seats of their britches before sitting down.

One squirrelly-looking fellow leapt into the aisle and danced a jig. The dark scowl on his wife's face foretold that his cake would be dough when he got home.

Mary Ann snickered and nudged Charlotty."Have ye ever seen the like?"

Charlotty stared ahead and didn't crack a smile.

The preacher raised his voice to the rafters then dropped it to the floor."Stand up an' be a mann-uuh!" Turning about-face, he pointed a finger at the amen corner and rebuked the pastors."Do ye think you're blameless? Well, think again, preachers. Are ye visitin the sick, feedin

217

the hungry an' clothin the pore — or fleecin the sheep? Are ye goin about from house to house with yer hand out on the beg? Git yore lazy carcass to the sawmill an' put in a ten hour day-uh. Lay yer lily-whites to the handles of a hillside plow-uh. After a round or two on a rocky slope, you'll be a prayin mann-uhh. Praise the Lord! — or the worst infidel in the county."

The three pastors squirmed.

Then that red-haired preacher swung back to the congregation and set his eyes on Howard. It was no coincidence that Howard and Andy and their friends were seated on the farthest bench from the pulpit. Howard was barely six feet from the door. The preacher stomped down the aisle and dropped to the floor on one knee beside Howard. He laid a hand on Howard's shoulder and shook him — more than gently.

Tall, lean, Howard fastened his big blue eyes on a flickering lamp. He chewed his Teaberry gum while the Reverend applied the mental whip.

"What are ye doin with yore life, young man? Are ye lopin the roads rabble rousin? Are ye grievin yore pore ol' mother? Have ye had a nip or two of the devil's brew? Repent! Repent I say, an' turn from yore wicked ways!" Sweat streamed down the preacher's face as he urged Howard to come forward.

Howard kept his eyes glued to the lamp and cracked his gum like the coolest tom cat in the hills.

This fiery preacher had broken the stubborn will of flinty-eyed boot-leggers and mossy-backed sinners with less effort than he'd spent on this blue-eyed lad. Finally, Reverend Shavers gave up in disgust and rose to his feet. With one loud clap of the hands he dismissed Howard and wagged a finger in his face."Go to Hell then — if. you. be. so. set. on. goin. there!" He wheeled around and stomped back to the pulpit.

Howard had never seen a preacher do so much wheeling and stomping.

The church was hot. Folk fanned their faces with song books, hats, or whatever they could lay a hand on that would stir the air. Mothers cooed to fretting babies. The water pitcher on the table up front was dry."Brother Superintendent, le's open the winders and let the cool mountain air in here," their pastor said. As the windows went up, Howard and Andy and their two friends eased out the door.

The preacher saw them and jumped for joy."Well, brothers and sisters, we've got the devil on the run — I seed 'im hoofin out the door. Praise the Lord!"

Folk commenced shouting all over the congregation. Mandy shivered. She'd never gotten used to the drama. She'd seen church members converge on many a stubborn sinner and pray him to his knees, and they didn't let up till he was saved. Although Mandy had reached the age of accountability, she hunkered down and tried to look small. She knew she needed to be saved, but she didn't want to be singled out as Howard had been. What kind a-preacher was Reverend Shavers anyway, a-callin her brothers the devil?

As Howard and the boys sneaked behind the church to the deacon's window, they could hardly keep from laughing aloud.

"Oh, wouldn't I like to see that preacher's face when these hornets come a-barrelin through the winder," Howard whispered.

The boys retrieved two sticks they'd stashed under the church house. Howard and Andy crept as close to the nest as they dared whilst their friends watched the front entrance. Howard whispered, "Now!" They plunged the sticks in the nest and skedaddled. When they reached a safe distance they stopped, and looked back and listened. The preacher was still going strong.

A piercing scream rent the night air. Andy and their two friends tensed up, ready for flight. Howard raised a staying hand."Hold it, boys, that's just Sister Clark a-cuttin loose." He squinted at the church window."Do ye reckon 'em stupid bees stayed in the nest? I'm shore I gouged the guts out of it."

Suddenly, the double-door at the church entrance rattled and bulged outward, then caved inward with a bang. Brethren lunged over the threshold shouting and slapping their heads and yes, some even cursed."If I git my han's on 'em damned sssoooofffbbbss..."

"Head fer the woods, boys, it's a stampede!" They took off helter-skelter.

The boys tried to keep up with Howard, but he disappeared into the undergrowth. When they thought it safe, Howard ventured forth and gave the boys a lecture."Remember what that preacher said about tattlin tongues, fellers."

Inside the church, the hornets accomplished what the red-haired preacher failed to do—awake the deacon. The old man's peaceful nap came to a painful end. Furious hornets in a digging frenzy speckled his beard as they sought bare flesh. The congregation slapped at the bees whizzing around their heads.

Reverend Shavers stared in amazement. He'd never known his preaching to have such an effect. Then a big hornet crashed on his sweaty brow—scratching for traction. He slapped himself with a loud, thwack! The hornet dropped to the floor—he stomped it."We've got the devil stirred up, brethren. He'd like to run us outta here, but this preacher ain't budgin! Slap them rascals to the floor—grind 'em to powder!"

A black swarm cut a swath through the choir. Songsters fell sideways like a wave of wheat in the teeth of the sickle. Punkun grunted and shoved Mandy."Git offa me."

As Mandy straightened up, she heard an angry buzz from a hornet entangled in her hair. She boxed her own ears. It stabbed her earlobe."Le's git outta here, Punkun!" As they pushed past bony knees they noticed everyone on the move. The brethren proved their manners by ramming their way through the door like brutes with women and children at their heels.

The enraged preacher besought heaven in a loud, shaky, condescending voice."Lord, forgive these weak-kneed people — runnin from a bee! Where are the men like Daniel of old who warn't afraid to walk up an' spit in a lion's eye? Where are the Shadrachs — the Meshachs — the 'bednegoes?"

"Who gives a fig?" That loud retort rang out from the first soprano bench. Mary Ann sprang to her feet and made a dash for the back door — clawing at her blouse — buttons popping. As she cleared the doorway, she flung a black bombardier from her bosom. Her eyes darted left and right, but nobody had seen her shocking exposure. The entire congregation was fighting their own battle with the bees.

Mandy and Punkun barely escaped being trampled. In a matter of minutes the church emptied. The churchyard swarmed with mad yapping people rubbing their stings and looking for somebody to whip.

The tall, handsome red-haired preacher stood in the pulpit and watched the panicked flock almost take the door off its hinges. He heaved a heavy sigh, picked up his jacket and stepped down. He looked around the vacant building — even the amen corner was empty. Overturned ladder-back chairs, scattered hymnbooks and a dozen twitching bombardiers on the floor testified to a battle and a rout. He raised his foot and brought his shiny shoe down on each hornet, grinding it to a smidgen.

Most of the bees had flown out the open windows by this time, but finding their nest in tatters — returned to the light. Near the ceiling, a circling swarm of black bombardiers revved their engines. They aimed their big guns at the preacher's snow-white shirt and dove for the kill. He was last seen going out the backdoor — backwards — swinging his jacket like a wild man.

The next Saturday morning, Howard was shining up his bicycle when he saw the deacon coming up the path. Oh, Lordy, this don't look good, he thought. So he hopped on his bike and pedaled over the hill. He sat on a rock and pondered his situation. He wasn't afraid of that old man, but he didn't want to go to the chain gang. He wondered if the deacon had proof that he bestirred the hornets. Of course he did. Howard's two friends had spilled the beans.

Clarinda was putting a quilt in the frame when the deacon knocked at the door.

She stepped outdoors to greet him on the porch."What brangs you here, Deacon?"

The old man turned his head sideways, cupped a hand behind one ear, and leaned toward her."What's ye say?"

She took a deep breath and shouted, "What brangs you here?"

"Well... I come to talk to ye about yore boys. They're a-stirrin up trouble at the church."

"I don't know what you're talkin 'bout! What kind a-trouble?"

He hooked a knobby finger under his shirt collar and stretched his scrawny neck to the side."Hornets—looky here!" Red welts dotted his neck."Two a-yore boys gouged a hornet's nest under the church winder. I ain't shet my eyes fer three nights straight."

Clarinda knew about the hornets because Mandy came home from church and told her, but she hadn't mentioned that Howard and Andy were responsible for the big sting. Clarinda heard the deacon out before she spoke."Well ... I intend to heer Howard an' Andy's side a-this tale fore I mete out punishment."

The deacon flew into a rage and shook his finger."You better straighten 'em boys out afore somebody does it fer ye. If I 'as younger, I'd tan that Hairrd's hide. He's the rangleader a-that bunch—I jest might git somebody to do it fer me!"

Clarinda slapped his finger out of her face."Why, you ol' lyin, dishonest rascal, I wouldn't trust you fer the truth on yore death bed. If anybody ever lays a hand on one of my younguns they'll answer to me. Now git offa my porch or I'll kick ye off."

The deacon hitched up his overalls and shuffled down the path as fast as he could move. When he was out of sight, Clarinda stepped into the yard and hollered for Howard and Andy. The boys came to the house looking sheepish. She knew they'd done something amiss.

"Well, younguns I've done my best to brang you up right. Since you'uns was babies on my knees I've tried to teach ye right from wrong. If you'uns stirred up them hornets you oughta be ashamed—you broke up a service in the Lord's House."

"Aw, Mama, we didn't mean no harm, we just wanted to wake that ol' deacon up," Howard confessed.

"An' we wanted the preacher to git popped, too," Andy added.

Howard glared at him."Shut up!"

"Well, you said you hoped he got stung smack-dab betwixt the eyes."

Clarinda paced the porch while the anxious boys watched and waited."Now younguns, they ain't no use a-hemmin an' a-hawin about what's already done. The thing ye need to do is pray, an' ast the good Lord to forgive you. He'll forgive ye if yer sorry. Don't either one of you ever commit sech tomfool'ry around the church agin. Do ye heer?"

The boys nodded that they heard.

Howard breathed out with relief, albeit surprised that they'd gotten off so easy.

"Yore Aint Etta has been down on the lift fer several days," Clarinda said, "and you younguns are goin to git her stovewood an' carry her water this week."

Howard groaned. Aunt Etta's spring was a quarter mile from her house. He didn't like chopping wood either."Mama, that new preacher said that choppin wood was women's work."

"That preacher ain't the head a-this house. The quicker ye git started, the sooner you'll be done."

The boys left for Aunt Etta's, arguing over the chores."Andy, you can carry water an' I'll chop wood..."

"No ... I'll chop wood an' you can carry the water."

Twenty-four

October • 1944

The Wayfaring Stranger

I'll soon be free from every trial,
This form will rest beneath the sod;
I'll drop the cross of self-denial,
And enter in my home with God.
I'm going there to see my Saviour,
Who shed for me His precious blood;
I am just going over Jordan,
I am just going over home.

–Traditional Folk Song

Clarinda stooped over, combed the long grass with her fingers, and brought forth an apple. She added it to the half-dozen in her apron. A stiff wind had brought the Rusty Coats to the ground. Wadell sat on a stump nearby enjoying a fresh cud of tobacco.

"Mama, somebody's here to see you," Mary Ann called from the porch.

Clarinda's hand froze in motion at the tremor in Mary Ann's voice. She straightened up and looked toward the house. She swayed in her tracks as her legs went weak. Reaching out, she clutched at a limb to steady herself. One by one the apples fell from her apron and rolled through the trampled grass.

Mary Ann stood on the porch speaking with a soldier. Clarinda took a few steps toward them like a toddler taking its first steps. Mary Ann rushed to her side. Clarinda clung to her with trembling hands."He's here about Olus, ain't he? Olus is dead."

Mary Ann helped her to the porch and settled her in a chair. Clarinda's eyes begged for good news as they searched the soldier's face. Her chin quivered."You're a-bringin bad news, ain't ye?"

The soldier knelt by her chair and gave her the news as gently as possible. Olus had fought and died with courage and honor on a battlefield in France. He had given his life for his country.

Clarinda's heart fell and quivered like a wounded sparrow. She closed her eyes and leaned her head against the porch post. Her mind fled from the dreadful present and sought refuge in the past. She saw Olus climbing the tall blackheart cherry tree in Lonesome Hollow as a little boy."*Look at me, Mama,*" he yelled from the topmost limb.

Mary Ann took her mother's hand."Mama, are you all right? Go lay down fer awhile."

Clarinda opened her eyes and pointed a trembling finger toward the path."Two year ago, I watched him walk away to that war. I knowed I'd never see my boy agin. Oh, God, I knowed it."

Mary Ann tugged at her hand."Come... Mama, come an' lay down."

She withdrew her hand from Mary Ann's."No. I'm all right. I need to know some things."

The officer told her all that he knew. Olus had been killed in battle September 23, 1944. His body had been transported to Luxembourg and buried there. He would be disinterred and brought home when the war was over.

When the officer left, Mary Ann noticed that Wadell still sat on his stump. He made no move to inquire about the soldier or the news he'd brought. Mary Ann hoped he'd offer a spoken word of comfort to her mother, but he didn't.

The children gathered in the settin room and waited for they knew not what, because they'd seen the soldier kneeling by their Mama's chair. Mary Ann stepped inside and joined them."Lee, go git Aint Etta. Tell her Mama's had bad news and needs her." Etta would be a comfort to Clarinda. She'd lost a son in the war too. Mary Ann didn't tell the younger children the bad news, because she knew her mother was in no condition to deal with their grief at that time.

The following day, Clarinda returned to her apple gathering and Mandy helped her. As Clarinda stooped over, big tears splashed on her hand and it wrenched Mandy's heart to see her mother cry."What's a-matter, Mama? Why 're you cryin?"

"Olus is dead." Clarinda told Mandy all that was necessary, but didn't go into details.

Mandy's hand flew to her mouth to stifle a cry. Her eyes welled up. Olus was her handsome hero. He'd always asked about her and her twin brother in his letters home. She and Andy had danced around their mother as she read them."What did he say about us, Mama?"

"He says to tell Pug to study hard in school and to tell Cottontop to be a brave soldier."

But now, Olus was in heaven, and Mandy knew she'd never see him on earth again. She ran behind the chicken house and cried her eyes out.

Clyde was still in Sicily when he received word of his brother's demise. He grieved for Olus, but he couldn't go to France because he was on the front lines too.

Clarinda received a letter from a beautiful Austrian girl. She'd enclosed a photograph of Olus' grave and also included a photo of herself. She wrote that she was tending his grave. She and Clarinda exchanged several letters. Although Edisha wrote in English, her pen had a foreign slant that was difficult to read. Other family members read them and assured Clarinda that Olus' grave was well tended. Clarinda imagined that Olus had a close friendship with Edisha or maybe they were sweethearts. Many a night, she lay awake and wished that she could travel to Luxembourg. It would have been a comfort to visit her son's grave and speak with the girl that he must have known. And every night she asked the Lord to keep Clyde safe. Soon as the war was over, she and Etta would receive their sons in flag-draped coffins. She asked God for strength to endure the homecoming.

During the long winter months Clarinda hooked rag-rugs to clothe her children and made quilts to keep them warm. In early spring she took to the outdoors and chopped trees and brush that she piled and burned so that she could make garden in new ground. She took a scythe and ax and climbed to the very top of Levi's Mountain. While she cleared briars, sprouts, and bushes from Ol' Pied's pasture—Wadell sat on a stump and watched her work.

When she got the garden laid by, she gathered mattock, spade, scythe and hoe and headed for the family cemetery. Olus would be coming home soon and she wanted his burying ground free of every weed and sprout.

Lee brought home an old rusty reel-type push-mower that Claude gave him. Clarinda oiled it and sharpened the blades until it cut grass like new. Then she and the little ones worked on the cemetery. Andy chopped sprouts with a hatchet that Billy Dan made from an old scythe blade. Clarinda grubbed tough locust roots and stubborn vines with a mattock—and Wadell sat on a tombstone, twiddled his thumbs and watched them work. Ain't none a-my blood kin buried under this sod. I ain't strikin a tap, he thought.

Mandy tried to mow with the reel-mower, but it was more than she could handle. She saw Wadell sitting on a tombstone twiddling his thumbs—and she stopped, stuck out her lower lip and puffed back the wisps of hair clinging to her damp forehead."Mr. Wad, how 'bout mowin a little—I'm tard."

Wadell's jaw dropped so fast he almost lost his cud of tobacco. Perhaps something in Mandy's manner reminded him of a daughter or grandchild. Anyway, her request moved him. He stood up and seized the mower."I'll be dad-gummed, now this'ns gonna drive me around."

Mandy sat by her Papa Rufus' headstone and watched Wadell mow.

Suddenly, Wadell picked up speed."I'll show these weaklin's how tuh mow," he muttered. But he passed over Rufus's grave too fast and a clump of grass rose behind him. When he swung the mower around for the next pass, he saw Mandy come to her feet and put her hands on her hips, exactly like her Mother. Glaring at him with her jaw set, she stabbed her forefinger toward the ground."Mr. Wad, you missed a buncha grass on my Papa's grave."

Wadell's frown turned to a scowl as black as a thundercloud. He stopped, took three steps backward, and took off with the reel-mower like a whirlwind. He went round and round and back and forth in his own green tornado. He hadn't moved that fast in forty years. As he passed over Rufus' grave the wind from the mower threw grass on Mandy, but he didn't stop until every green blade in the cemetery lay withering in the sun.

"Dang you, Mr. Wad, you th'oed grass in my hair," Mandy groused. Raking her fingers through her hair, she turned and saw her mother leaning against the fence, fanning herself with her big straw hat and laughing her head off."What's so funny, Mama?"

"Oh, nothin," she replied, and laughed even louder.

Mandy looked at her with a quizzical expression. Sometimes yer a puzzle, Mama, she thought.

A few minutes later, Mandy noticed that the mower had been shoved through the gate and abandoned."Mama, where's Mr. Wad?"

Clarinda straightened up from her work and started laughing again."Well, it 'pears like he's a-burnin shoe leather to'ard home. Maybe he was afeard you'd put the mattick in his hands." Mandy stared at her mother in amazement. How did Mama know I was a-fixin to ast Mr. Wad to use that mattick?

Twenty-five

June • 1947

The Last Goodbye

Unfurl the Stars and Stripes,
Let breezes raise Old Glory high—
His comrades fire a loud salute,
Then low, the bugle's mournful cry.
A soldier journeyed from afar
To find his rightful place of rest—
A mother kneels beside the bier,
A purple heart clutched to her breast.

Mary Ann looked out the settin room window and her hand flew to her heart. An Army officer and six men from the community moved toward the cabin bearing a flag-draped coffin. She turned from the window."Mama, Olus is home."

Olus, killed on a battlefield in France, had lain in a foreign grave for three years. During that time, Clarinda badgered the Veteran's Administration Office to get him home. Doubtless, they grew weary of the dark-haired mountain woman knocking at their door."Have ye got any news about my son? He'd be wantin ye to git his body on home now. His gravesite is ready."

Olus' remains were disinterred from the American Military Cemetery in Luxembourg and transported to the local funeral home. The Veterans Administration and the funeral home notified Clarinda prior to his arrival. The hearse parked by the roadside and the pall bearers carried Olus' casket up a steep woodland path to Clarinda's cabin. In the settin room, Clarinda and her family rose to their feet to receive their loved one.

Clarinda moved toward the door, but her strength failed. Big Avery caught her as she fell. He carried his mother to the sofa. Mary Ann hovered over her, wiping her face with a wet cloth."Don't git up, Mama. I can take keer of this."

"No. Don't try to spare me. I havta do it. Olus would want me to." She regained her feet and with Mary Ann's support, greeted the Army officer at the door.

He stepped inside and took her hand."Ma'am, I'm Lieutenant Colonel Young, I'm sorry…"

Clarinda's mind couldn't take in the army officer's words of comfort. In slow motion she turned and pointed to a section of the room where the bier awaited the coffin. LTC Young opened the door wide and beckoned to the pallbearers. The narrow doorway would not allow the coffin with three pallbearers on each side to pass through."Two to the head, two to the foot and two step away," he instructed. Slow and precise they completed the maneuver. Then the six men settled the coffin in place.

Clarinda had refused the heavy red-velvet drapery provided by the funeral home. She said it made the room too dark. Instead, blue organdy ruffled curtains crisscrossed the open windows which allowed an abundance of sunshine and fresh air inside. Breezes swayed the curtains and played around the corners of Old Glory. LTC Young stepped to the foot of the coffin, brought his heels together with a click and saluted Olus' remains. With perfect precision, he did an about-face, moved aside and stood at ease with solemn dignity.

Near the coffin, on a linen-covered lamp table, a large photograph of Olus in army dress uniform grinned at all who entered the door. This handsome picture and the flag-draped coffin presented a heartrending sight to those who knew and loved him.

Mary Ann stepped forward and shook hands with LTC Young."Mama wants to be alone with Olus fer awhile."

He nodded and stepped outside.

Clarinda moved to the coffin and leaned across it with outstretched arms."My son…my son," she whispered, "my arms ache to hold you… oh, my son…" Her hands moved over the Stars and Stripes, smoothing the wrinkles like the covers of his bed. Then she knelt down and deep groans shook her body to the core. Henry and Mary Ann knelt beside her for a time. After awhile, she was persuaded to go lie down.

Before the morning dew dried on the grass, men folk in the community gathered at the family cemetery to dig Olus' grave. The small grassy knoll surrounded by woodland, held ten graves. In the late 1880's, Clarinda's maternal grandparents were the first lain to rest there. Their children followed.

Clarinda cherished this secluded place. As a child she'd helped her mother decorate the graves after Malinda Rose died. In 1932, Clarinda and Rufus' infant twins died, and two more graves were added. Rufus died five year later and another mound appeared.

Clarinda and her children maintained the cemetery. She and Henry replaced the wooden grave-markers with tombstones they made themselves. Clarinda took measurements from a medium-sized tombstone in a church cemetery. With rough lumber she made the forms 3'x2' with beveled upright corners. They filled the forms with concrete 3" thick. Before the concrete hardened, Clarinda took her awl and etched the name of the deceased on each tombstone, including date of birth and death. With a steady hand she etched a small cross for adornment. The military would provide a white marble tombstone for Olus. It would nestle amidst the rough-hewn ones.

A midsummer breeze stirred the timber around the cemetery as the men folk labored. Now and then, one would comment on his surroundings."Ain't this a peaceful place to rest till Gabriel blows 'is trumpet?"

"Yep…shore is. I hope my ol'bones can find a dwellin place like this when I die."

Lank, the storyteller, shoved his old battered Stetson to the back of his head and paused to look at the horizon."Look at 'em purty white clouds a-peepin over the mountain. Watch the cloud shadders move acrost this ground. Listen to the streams a-tawkin. I tell ye fellers, from the dawn a-time this hilltop 'as meant tuh be a buryin ground fer the faithful."

The clank of shovels ceased. The men looked at Lank in amazement. They'd never heard him speak so eloquent before. Suddenly, with no disrespect intended, the conversation turned lively. Lank wiped his brow on his shirt sleeve and leaned on his shovel."Dayum, this is too much like work tuh suit me."

"This ain't the time, nar the place fer foolishness," one high-strung fellow barked.

Lank, usually a mild-mannered fellow, flushed red with anger."I'll tell ye what's foolish. It's you a-trottin around this hole like a little feist dog a-chasin hit's tail. Git yer bony carcass down here an' dig afore I lay ye out with this here shovel." He pitched his hat toward the barking fellow's abandoned upright shovel and, of course, it twirled around the end of the handle and settled there. Nimble-footed he sprang from the grave, collected his hat, and pulled a pouch of Chattanooga Chew from his hind pocket. He ambled to the outer edge of the cemetery and ruminated till his temper cooled. And thus, the time flew by. Shortly before noon, the grave was ready.

Throughout the day, kinfolk and neighbors arrived at the cabin with food for the wake. Platters of fried chicken, bowls of green beans, creamed corn, wild creasy greens, potato salad, pickled eggs, and plates of biscuits, cornbread, and stacks of fried apple, wild raspberry and strawberry pies filled the table. One fellow brought a red can of ground Luzianne coffee."Ain't no way a feller can set up all night 'thout a cup a-java," he declared.

Clarinda's cabin stood in mountain shadow with its six rooms packed to capacity when Tom arrived from Caldwell County. Tom and Olus were fifteen-months apart in age and as close as twins. Tom stood in the doorway and took in the scene. A hush fell over the room. Clarinda met him and they embraced in sorrow. She laid her head against his broad chest and wept. Tom patted her back and spoke in a husky voice."Don't worry, Mama, Olus is at peace…he's home." He released his mother and moved to the coffin. Kneeling by the bier, he reached out and took Olus' picture from the table. Blinking away tears, he looked at his brother and spoke softly, "Hey, brother, ol' buddy… I've missed ye…some homecoming, eh?" His head dropped. Tears rolled down his nose and fell on the picture glass. With an unsteady hand he set the picture back in place, then rose to his feet and walked out the door.

Clarinda's sister, Etta, rose from her chair."He needs somebody with him."

"No. He wants to be alone." Mary Ann laid a restraining hand on her arm. Etta reluctantly sat down.

When twilight fell, the crowd dispersed. Many went home to do up the night work, and then would return later. By this time, Clarinda's children talked with the Army officer like old friends. They convinced him that it was unnecessary to stay by Olus' coffin all night. So, stuffed with mountain fare, he stated that he'd return before noon the next day, and then he left.

Olus' second burying day dawned fair with fleecy clouds sailing high. Attendees of the all night wake went home at the first rooster's crow. Clarinda and her family needed privacy to prepare for the graveside service scheduled for two o'clock. LTC Young returned at mid-morning. At one o'clock, six soldiers arrived to transport Olus to his final resting place.

For awhile, surrounded by family and friends, Clarinda had livened up a bit. But now, as the soldiers carried Olus' coffin away, her grief returned full force. Leaning on LTC Young and Mary Ann, she trudged to the forks of the road where the hearse and several cars waited. She and Mary Ann were ushered into his car for the trip to the cemetery. The rest of the family walked behind the hearse. Due to the rough road, they almost kept pace with the slow motorcade.

The long black limousine backed up to the cemetery gate. The undertaker emerged from the driver's seat, walked to the back and opened the double doors. The Honor Guard in military mode, assembled at the back of the hearse. Hand to hand, span by span, they reverently brought the flag-draped coffin forth. LTC Young helped Clarinda and Mary Ann from his car and they followed the solemn procession up the hill. At the open grave, the Honor Guard settled the coffin in place and stood at attention. The family gathered. Chairs were provided for Clarinda and several family members. The Honor Guard then moved with measured steps to the graveside and stood at ease.

Olus' pastor read Scripture and spoke words of comfort to the grieving family. He spoke of a day when wars would cease and peace would flow like a river."Dear grievin mother, let not yore heart be troubled, yer son is at peace in heaven. Carry this thought with you. Someday, you'll see him again and yore sorrow will turn to joy. Yes, indeed, you'll see yore son again and there'll be rejoicin. Won't that be a wonderful day when we meet our loved ones in heaven? God will wipe away our tears and we'll dwell with them forever." Then he asked that all heads be bowed for the benediction prayer.

After the last amen, the Honor Guard returned to the coffin and with slow exact movements they folded the flag. LTC Young stepped forward with a salute and received it. Then he turned, knelt by Clarinda's chair and made the formal presentation. He spoke softly with her for some time. She held the flag to her heart. Then he rose to his feet and joined the Honor Guard who stood in formation a short distance from the crowd.

In flawless movement, they raised their rifles to their shoulders and fired three volleys in loud tribute. Through a blue haze of gun-smoke, Olus' naked coffin shined like burnished gold in the evening sun. Tears dimmed the eyes of those who barely knew him. The wails of the grieving rose and fell...rose and fell... amid the crowd. The beautiful, melancholy sound of final Taps increased tenfold as it traveled through Lonesome Hollow and echoed from the mountainside.

Mandy shivered.

Tom sank to his knees with clenched fists and turned his face skyward. From the depth of his broken heart came a loud anguished cry,

"Oh God…oh God!" His chin dropped to his chest and his broad shoulders shook with silent weeping.

"He loved his brother so much," someone whispered."He'll remember this day fer the rest of his life."

Clarinda could barely walk as LTC Young and Mary Ann helped her from the cemetery. Back at the cabin, she found that some thoughtful person had put the settin room furniture back in its place. She appreciated that.

Pale and shaken, Tom and three older brothers arrived from the cemetery an hour later. They all sat around, discussed the funeral and tried to talk through their grief. But it was too soon for Tom, too painful. He went to bed and fell asleep from exhaustion. The following day, he loaded up his family and returned to Caldwell County, sad and depressed.

After Tom left, Clarinda and Mandy gathered wildflowers and returned to the cemetery. They placed bouquets on all the graves in the cemetery. Mandy saw her mother kneel by Olus' grave and heard her pray, "Oh, Lord, I miss him. It's so hard to give 'im up ... so hard."

Mandy turned and ran for the gate with tears streaming down her face. She couldn't stand to hear her mother's heartache a minute longer. She turned her back to the cemetery, leaned against the gate and buried her face in the crook of one arm. Before long, she felt her mother's warm calloused hand on her shoulder."Don't ye think it's time we 'as gitten home? Ol' Daisy 'ill be a-buttin the bars at the milk gap."

Mandy turned and threw her arms around her mother and hugged her hard—and Mama hugged back. Mama ain't so sad now. Oh, I believe she's gonna be okay, she thought. Hand in hand they headed for home.

Olus had given his guitar to Tom before he went overseas. Tom kept the Gibson stored in its case in the closet for a year after the funeral. The day he brought it out, he sat on his porch with tears coursing down his cheeks and shined it with a soft cloth.

His wife tried to console him."Tom, why don't you find somebody to play with, establish your own group?"

"Nah, my heart ain't in it anymore. Besides, I'd never find anybody that could sing tenor like Olus."

Probably not, but your brother Howard can sure sing tenor. I heard him singing with Andy and Mandy the last time we visited your mother."

Tom grew quiet in thought. Then he started tuning Olus' guitar and his wife went about her work and left him alone. Later, she heard him playing the guitar.

The next weekend Tom loaded up his family and drove up the Blue Ridge to Levi's Mountain. What a joy to be home again! He took Olus' guitar from its case and he and his brothers gathered on the front porch for a music session. When they sang "The Crawdad Song," Howard sang tenor.

"Howard, I don't think I've ever heard a better tenor voice than yores," Tom said."If Olus was here today, I know he'd say that you hit 'em high notes better'n he could."

Howard blushed and grinned, a compliment from Tom made him proud, indeed. Tom gave Henry a playful poke in the ribs."Have ye fergot how to play 'The Orange Blossom Special?'"

Henry tucked the fiddle under his chin and smoked the strings. Clarinda couldn't keep her feet still. She tossed her embroidery work on the sofa and did a do-si-do to the kitchen. She hummed as she prepared the boys some refreshment. It did her heart good to hear Tom and his brothers enjoy their music making. She felt richly blest to have children who had a common interest. For certain it kept the household lively and would continue to do so. Life goes on, she thought, though grief and sorrow bow us low for a time, life goes on.

Twenty-six

1948

Mandy flipped through the new Montgomery Ward catalog that had just arrived in the mail. Her eye lit on a pretty pink ruffled blouse in the young girl's section. She pictured herself wearing the blouse with the new skirt Mama had made from two flour sacks. The flowered skirt's tiny pink roses were a perfect match for the blouse. She wanted that blouse and the lovely green sandals in the shoe section as well. Her mother had no money to buy them. She'd have to earn them herself.

She laid the catalog aside and walked out the front door. In the woodshed she found the mattock and two hemp sacks. So, with sacks rolled and tucked under her arm and digging implement in hand, she headed up the mountain—unaware that Howard and one of his pals were five minutes ahead.

Stoneroot, a wild herb with roots shaped like the palm of a hand and hard as a rock, grew on the highest reaches of the mountain. She could get twelve cents a pound for the herb at Hedgeweth's Store. At the edge of the mountain field she found a large patch. She tramped to the center and poured on the elbow grease—as mountain folk called energetic work. The black loamy earth was soft as kitten fur, but fist-sized rocks made for a hard dig. Every swing of the mattock landed with a clink.

An hour passed, then two. Suddenly, she dropped the mattock and looked at her hands. Between her right thumb and forefinger a large blood blister had risen and burst. Raw weeping flesh on her left hand had rolled up around the base of her fingers. She stooped over, placed her hands between her knees and gritted her teeth in pain. Despite the discomfort, she managed to sack-up the roots and tie them securely with twine string. She tugged the heavy bundles to a steep drop-off, and gave them a hard shove."Whoopee!" Down the mountain the sacks tumbled end over end, picking up speed. They struck a boulder with a thud and split in twain. Roots scattered through the undergrowth.

Overcome with self-pity, she plopped down on the ground and looked at her poor blistered hands. She sniffled for a few minutes.

Ain't no dang use of boo-hooin, she thought. Springing to her feet, she threw the mattock down the mountain and cursed like a hillside plowman."Damn the mattock—to hell with the sacks—devil take the roots!"

In the laurels nearby, Howard snickered."Le's skeer the stuffins out of 'er."

His pal took a draw from his Stud tobacco cigarette and blew smoke rings."Yeah…we'll put a stop to that little hissy fit."

Suddenly, Mandy's conscience spoke. 'Young lady, you've shore got some nerve to cuss like that. You're on this mountaintop all alone. Ol' Scratch's mean red eyes are peepin at ye through them laurels right now. ' Mandy turned her head slowly and looked toward the laurels nearby. Fright tickled her scalp and the hair on the nape of her neck stood up. She smelled something burning. Wide-eyed, she watched smoke rings rise from the bushes. Chains rattled—a hellcat snarled—the bushes shook! Panic-stricken she sent up a prayer, "Hep me, Lord. Ol' Scratch is after me!" She took off helter-skelter down the mountain.

Five minutes later, she stood in the cabin yard breathing hard. The soles of her bare feet stung from the scrapes of sharp rocks even though they were tough as shoe leather. She stamped her foot."Dad-gummit, I want that stoneroot!" After pondering the situation, she decided that her imagination had just got the better of her. So she took Andy's sled and climbed the mountain again.

She hummed a jolly tune as she climbed the trail pulling the sled. The sound of her own voice kept her imagination under control. In haste she gathered the roots, but took her time descending the mountain till a crash in the undergrowth put wings on her feet again. She held the sled rope tight as it slid into the yard sideways.

Mandy washed the roots in the wooden barrel at the water spout and spread them to dry on the chicken house roof. As she descended the ladder, Howard and his pal strolled into the yard. Howard carried the mattock she'd left behind. He tossed it toward her, snickering."Here's yer mattick. I saw you slang it in the bushes when you tho'ed that hissy fit."

Mandy gritted her teeth. She'd get even with Howard later, but right now she was too pooped to fight.

Within two weeks the roots were ready for market. She begged Andy to help her sled them to the store. He agreed, but it cost her dearly.

"I havta have a third of the money they brang," he said.

"What? After all the stuff I've done fer you?"

"I don't keer. I havta have a third."

Suddenly Mandy's face lit up."Andy, you ain't stutterin. What's happenin to ye? Do ye reckon it's the money you was thinkin 'bout gitten—you greedy rat."

"Maybe...I don't keer what ye call me. I ain't doin yer haulin fer nothin."

Finally, Andy loaded the roots on his sled and they set out on the long haul. The herbs brought $18. 00. She had to fork over six dollars to Andy as she'd promised. But today, she was going to the store on family business and Andy was calling.

"Hurry up, Mandy! I'm ready to go."

Mandy stood before the mirror and gazed at herself. Then she put on a dab of pink lipstick. The color matched her pretty pink blouse and the tiny pink roses in her flour sack skirt. She slipped on her new green sandals and turned her foot this way and that, admiring the perfect fit. Brushing her shoulder-length hair over her wrist, she created a smooth look that was fashionable amongst girls her age. Octagon laundry soap and a vinegar-water rinse brought out the shine. She did a dipsy-doodle twirl and hoped Clarinda wouldn't notice the lipstick.

"Mandy, are you comin or not? I ain't waitin on ye all day."

Mandy stepped out the door and found Andy with a chicken under his arm and Clarinda holding a black hen. Clarinda shoved the hen under Mandy's arm with instructions."Hold her with a firm hand, but don't squeeze the breath out of 'er. Don't let 'er git away from ye."

Mandy stood stiff as a board with an expression of disgust on her face."Why, I-I ain't gonna carry this dirty ol' chicken," she sputtered."I've got my new clothes on. Besides, I'm ashamed to go in the store with a chicken under my arm."

"You listen to me, young lady, that dirty ol' hen will buy a sack of flour. You like biscuits fer breakfast don't ye?" Before Mandy could reply, Clarinda turned her back and headed for the garden.

"Shewee! I'll stank like chicken manure sure as the world."

"Well, you might as well stank as me," Andy remarked.

It was a three mile walk to Hedgeweth's Store and every now and then Mandy's chicken took a crazy spell and tried to get loose. If I let 'er git away, Mama will never stop scoldin me, she thought."Andy, when we git to the store, will you carry my chicken inside and give it to the store clerk?"

"Heck, no! Carry yore own chicken. You ain't no better'n me to look like a hillbilly."

"Well, le's swap. My hen's plumb foolish."

"No! My hen is purt nigh asleep—look at 'er." Andy's red hen had droopy eyelids. Her eyes looked like two tiny window panes with the shades pulled halfway down.

"I wisht my hen was happy like that. Maybe she knows I hate her guts and thinks I'm headed fer the chop block." She tried to stroke her hen's head, but the grouch pecked her wrist hard."I hope yer hind end gits dumped in somebody's stew pot this Sunday."

Suddenly they heard a car coming—Mandy looked over her shoulder and almost fainted. It was Mary Ann's boyfriend, R.J. and he had his nephew with him. Mandy had seen R.J. 's nephew a couple of times. He was about fifteen-years-old with blonde wavy hair and beautiful blue eyes. She thought him the handsomest boy in the whole world.

"Andy, take this chicken, please!"

"No!"

"You take this damn chicken right now!"

"No! I'm gonna tell Mama you cussed."

Mandy heard the car slow down to an idle as it rolled along beside them.

"Where are you younguns headed with them chickens?" R.J. inquired.

"We're goin to the store," Andy replied.

Mandy kept walking with her eyes focused on the ground. She could feel her face getting red.

R.J. 's nephew hung his head out the car window and snickered."Do you reckon them ol' chickens will buy ye some Coca-Cola and candy?"

R.J. poked him in the ribs and gave him a mean look.

"What business is it of yores?" Andy retorted.

Mandy hated R.J. 's nephew. Why, he's makin fun of us, she thought. She wished the earth would open up and swallow her. Suddenly the black hen squirmed from underneath her arm and took a conniption fit. Squawking and pooping, the hen pummeled Mandy's head with her wings. Feathers flew. Mandy gritted her teeth, grabbed the old biddy by the neck and choked the daylights out of her. The hen slumped over and Mandy tucked her under her arm again. She walked on, but she heard R.J. and his nephew laughing.

"Mandy, are you sure that chicken ain't dead?" R.J. asked.

"Nah, she ain't dead, she's playin possum."

"Hey, do you younguns want a ride?"

"No," Mandy replied tartly, but Andy said, "yes!"

"Well, I'm goin to see Mary Ann so I'll wait at the store till you're ready to go."

"Okay," Andy replied.

Inside the store, Mandy gave the chicken to Myrtle, the store clerk, and brushed the feathers from her hair with her fingers. Myrtle weighed their chickens and dropped them through a trapdoor in the floor. Judging by the racket down there, the poultry business was booming—and prices were good. They had eighty-two cents leftover after supplies.

Mandy looked at the money in her hand and whispered, "Andy, le's git some Coca-Cola—I'd like to know how it tastes. We ain't never had any soda pop in our lives."

"I don't know. We might not have enough money fer two bottles."

"Miss Myrtle, how much is a bottle of Coca-Cola?" Mandy asked.

"A nickel. Do you want some?"

"Yes, Ma'am. We'd like two bottles, please."

Mandy dropped a dime in Myrtle's hand.

"You owe me two cents more, Mandy."

She looked at Myrtle and frowned."You said a nickel a bottle. I gave you a dime fer two bottles."

"I know you did, but I havta charge a penny extra on every bottle to pay the 'lectric bill. That's what keeps the drinks cold."

"Well, I knowed that." Mandy opened her sweaty palm and forked over the two pennies."The next time I'll know the price is 12 cents fer two bottles."

Myrtle wagged her finger."Unless the price goes up... unless the price goes up."

Andy removed the caps from their Colas with the bottle opener located on the big red Coca-Cola cooler. Mandy lifted the cold bottle to her lips and took a sip. The fizz tickled her nose and the first swallow cleared her throat. She'd never tasted anything like it before. It brought to mind the rich scent of autumn woods— ripe hickory nuts, sun-dried wild grapes and berries. It had an earthy taste and she loved it.

Andy tossed the sack of flour on his shoulder and Mandy carried the oil, sugar, baking powder and matches. They found R.J. parked beside the water spout. The rusty water pipe poked out from the road bank and supplied the store and its customers with water. It was muddy where R.J. parked and Mandy slid into a mud hole. She felt her sandal straps snap from both feet. Her temper surged, but she managed to hold her tongue. After much difficulty she got her supplies and herself in the back seat with Andy. She clutched her Coca-Cola tight and settled back for the ride.

A car ride would have been exciting under different circumstances, but today it was just a convenience. It seemed amazing that the black coupe could carry such a load up the steep mountain. Blue smoke boiled behind them as it bounced from one deep rut to another. They didn't mind the rough ride as it was preferable to hiking three miles with a load to carry. Conversation was impossible because of the roar. Mandy was glad because she didn't feel like talking anyway, she just wanted to relax and sip her Coca-Cola.

The blonde handsome lad she'd adored from afar sat beside his uncle R.J. and looked straight ahead. Suddenly she had an urge to reach forward and dump the rest of the Cola over his head, but that was wishful thinking, of course. She was mad at R.J. too. If he hadn't parked beside a mud hole her sandals wouldn't be ruined. But mostly she was mad at the whole world because her family was so poor they had to trade chickens for biscuits. She didn't know of a girl anywhere that had to carry a stinking chicken to the store to buy a sack of flour.

R.J. couldn't get his car all the way to Mandy and Andy's house because the road came to a dead end."Younguns, tell Mary Ann that I want to see her. I would hep y'all carry them groceries to the house, but Mary Ann gits mad when I show up on a week day an' see her in work clothes."

"Okay, thanks fer the ride."

Mandy went clopping up the path, muddy all the way to her skirt hem. In a fit of anger she kicked her sandals into the sweet fern."Ye ain't worth a cuss, ye cain't even stand up to a mud hole."

"Mandy, where did you git into all that mud—and where are yore new sandals?" Clarinda asked.

"I don't wanna talk about it, Mama—Mary Ann, R.J. wants to see you."

"Where is he?"

"He's waitin in his car."

Mary Ann commenced fussing, "I've told him a dozen times not to come here on a week day." She rushed to the looking glass."Lord, have mercy! My head looks like a shock a-oats. Oh, I ain't got a dang thing to wear!"

Mandy grabbed a bar of soap, towel, wash cloth, and clean clothes and headed for the water spout. It took the better part of an hour to scrub the mud from her feet and legs and the chicken odor from her face and hair. If she'd had privacy she would've removed her clothes and jumped into the wooden barrel even if the teeth-chattering water gave her pneumonia.

She fretted over the loss of her pretty green sandals. She decided that she would live in the city when she grew up. She'd walk on concrete sidewalks instead of sliding around in mud holes. She'd have a lovely house and a nice green grassy yard. She'd plant beautiful flowers, and no pooping chickens would be allowed within a mile of her property. Yes indeed, she'd get a good job an' buy groceries with money. She wouldn't have to dig stoneroot or be pestered by her naughty brothers either. She could hardly wait till she was old enough to move to the city.

Twenty-seven

1949

Grand Ole Opry Time

We gathered 'round the radio
And searched the dial from end to end.
When o'er the airways music soared—
Our faces broke into a grin.
A hoedown set our feet a-tap—
"Yee haa!" Oh, how the banjo rang!
A fiddle welcomed all aboard
That Orange Blossom Special train.
Harmonica did hitch a ride
And boogie-woogie with the wheels,
Wha-wha whaaw ... choo-choo clacka choo
Had grandma kicking up her heels;
Then down the track a mile or two,
An empty 'shine jug popped its cork
And joined the rhythm of the spoons,
Plumb into Nashville after dark.

*B*illy Dan helped a neighbor around his farm so that he could get himself a secondhand radio—the Crosley, a table model with burned out tubes and a dead battery played like new when he finished tinkering on it.

"Billy Dan, can I listen to, *Our Gal Sunday*?" asked Mary Ann.

"What's that?"

"It's a soap opera. I listened to it once't on Alena's radio." Alena was Mary Ann's sister-in-law.

"I reckon ye can, but don't run the batt'ry down. I want a-listen to the Grand Ole Opry this Saturday night."

"I'll turn it off soon'es I listen to my program," Mary Ann promised.

The following day was wash day. Mary Ann cranked up the gas-powered wringer washer and had the clothes lines full of laundry before noon. *Our Gal Sunday* came on the radio at twelve-thirty and she wanted to finish the laundry beforehand. Clean white sheets flapped in the breeze as she rinsed her last load of overalls. After sending them through the wringer, she carried them to the clothesline.

She was proud of her snowy-white sheets and her brothers' Sunday shirts. She reached out and touched a blue cotton shirt to see if it was dry and felt something sticky. Ambeer! Wadell had spit ambeer all over the boys' shirts. Mary Ann knew he did it. He was the only tobacco chewer in the household. She gritted her teeth and yanked the shirts from the line."You ain't gitten away with this ol' man. I'll whip yore hind end before the sun goes down." By the time she rewashed and rinsed the shirts and put the laundry bench in order, she was very tired, but she fixed dinner anyway.

Clarinda and the boys came from the mountainside at noon. They'd been cutting wood all morning and were thankful for the hot meal on the table. Clarinda's tired face lit up when she saw a bowl of wild creasy greens on the table."I'm so hungry I could eat my weight in creasies," she declared.

Wadell looked at the flavorful greens with disgust and groused, "I'd druther eat a forkful a-moldy hay as 'em dern thangs."

"You don't deserve a crumb a-nothin," Mary Ann blared out."Why don't you git yore lazy carcass up the mountain an' help Mama and the boys cut wood?"

Wadell dropped his eyes to his plate and didn't say another word. Mary Ann wanted to tell Clarinda about the shirts, but her mother looked so weary that she decided to let it pass for the time being. After dinner, Clarinda and the boys returned to their wood cutting and Wadell disappeared.

Mary Ann rushed to clear the table. It was almost time for *Our Gal Sunday*. She put the dishes in a large pan of hot water to soak and settled herself in a ladder-back chair by the radio. As the theme song came over the airways, she leaned back in her chair and relaxed.

Wadell eased into the settin room with ash bucket in hand and commenced cleaning out the coal-burning stove. He gave the grates a noisy rattle and saw Mary Ann stiffen. He snickered and shook the grates with gusto.

Mary Ann looked over her shoulder and saw his gleeful expression through a fog of ashes."You're a-doin that fer spite, ol' man." Her voice was flat as a board.

Wadell sprang to his feet and headed for the door. As he jumped off the porch, Mary Ann threw the ash bucket."You didn't finish the job, you damn slacker!" It slammed into his rear end, filling his back pockets with ashes and hot cinders. She poked her head out the door and hollered at his fleeing figure, "Snicker now, damn ye, snicker now."

Come Saturday night, all the children gathered around the radio for the Grand Ole Opry. Charlotty and Eddie Jack, and Billy Dan's friends had joined them for this exciting event. Grandma would surely enjoy the program too, as she had been a fine fiddler in her younger days. The settin room was crowded as Clarinda and Wadell seated themselves amid the throng. Billy Dan, as proud owner of this marvelous apparatus had the privilege of tuning it in.

The children's faces lit up as George D. Hay, The Solemn Ol' Judge, opened up the Opry with, "Let 'er go boys," then the Possum Hunters scorched the airways with a red-hot fiddle tune.

"Ah... ha... ," crooned Howard as he imitated playing a fiddle.

"Fool," Wadell muttered under his breath. He hated that radio. Clarinda's brats had purt nigh drove him batty with their fiddlin an' plunkin an' twangin. He'd druther talk horses and racetracks and how he'd groomed champeans in olden days.

Then Roy Acuff's "Wabash Cannonball" filled the room.

Billy Dan tapped his foot."Would you listen to that dobro?"

At times, the music faded into static and everyone except Wadell leaned toward the radio. When the signal cleared, they straightened up and relaxed.

"I want a-hear Bill Monroe. He's the best player and singer of all the Opry stars," Howard said.

Wadell scowled, but no one noticed his displeasure.

Billy Dan turned up the volume."He'll be on in a few minutes."

Bill Monroe was singing, "Blue Moon of Kentucky" when Wadell leaned back in his chair, poked out his chest, and bragged."You ortuh seen that fine filly I groomed in ol' Kaintuck."

Mary Ann swung around and shook her finger in his face."Shut up! Nobody wants to hear yer fartin filly tales."

Clarinda gasped."Mary Ann!"

"Well, I'm tard of—"

"Shhh!" Everybody said. Wadell eased out of his chair and left the room. I'll git shet a-that squawk box and they'll never know what happened to it, he vowed to himself.

The radio brought joy to the household and opened the door to a new world of fun for the children. They sang every song and played every tune they heard on the Opry. They even commenced talking about getting on the radio themselves. Andy and Mandy, along with a niece and two nephews, commenced singing gospel songs in church. Their official title was the Happy Land Quartet. They traveled to churches and Gospel Sings throughout the area. Their home church was very supportive and one of the deacons suggested they go on the radio so he made the arrangements.

Every Saturday morning, Andy and Mandy's brother, Big Avery, loaded the songbooks, instruments and children into his big blue Buick and headed for the radio station in town. The Happy Land Quartet's Program came on the air at twelve-thirty. Big Avery's wife was their manager. Soon, song requests and invitations to churches came pouring in. What a wonderful time they had! They were constantly practicing new songs, and now and then they'd sing an old hymn in a different way to add variety to their program.

Little Avery, Clarinda's first grandson, played rhythm guitar. He had a remarkable low-pitched voice for a twelve-year-old. At their Wednesday night practice session, the quartet sang that wonderful old hymn, "God Put a Rainbow in the Cloud." Little Avery knocked the bottom out of the low notes. It was suggested that he sing the chorus while the rest of the quartet hummed the harmony. This adaptation made the song exceptional because no one else sung it that way. They practiced until they had it down pat, but when they rose to sing in church Little Avery would always say, "Choose another song," and refused to sing it. Finally, they dropped it from practice.

One Saturday night, they gathered around the microphone in a packed church house. Fifteen quartets were scheduled to sing. The director of the program set a limit of two songs per quartet which gave every group an opportunity to perform. Several popular groups in attendance could sing as well as professionals. Their music was piano which established them as traditional, accepted church quartets.

Some churches frowned on stringed instruments in those days. The fiddle, guitar, and mandolin were considered instruments for dancing and worldly frolics. The Happy Land Quartet's music was Andy's acoustical guitar and Little Avery's electrified rhythm bass. Mandy's confidence wavered as her eyes roamed over the congregation. Why, this high falutin crowd don't want a-listen to a buncha little hillbilly squirts like us, she thought. Her twin brother, Andy, stood poised with his Gibson guitar, ready to start playing their selection. He wasn't nervous. In fact, he seemed eager to begin and that made Mandy feel better.

"Which song do y'all wanna sing first?" she whispered.

Little Avery leaned his bass guitar against the lectern and stepped up to the microphone. He was so short he had to stand on tip-toe to reach it. With a firm hand he laid hold of it and tilted it sideways to his mouth."Christian friends, we're gonna try an old hymn that we ain't practiced in a long time, we hope you'll bear with us. The song is titled, "God Put a Rainbow in the Cloud." The Happy Land Quartet took a deep breath and sang,

When God shut Noah in the grand old ark,
He put a rainbow in the cloud;
When the thunders rolled and the sky was dark,
God put a rainbow cloud.
God put a rainbow in the cloud, (yes, in the cloud,)
God put a rainbow in the cloud, (in the cloud,)

The hallelujahs commenced popping. Little Avery sensed that everyone liked their singing so he sang his solo part with gusto. When the notes started dropping, so did little Avery, taking the microphone down with him."When it looked like the sun wouldn't shine any mo ... ooh ... oore. God put a rainbow in the cloou... ouud." He ended up on one knee.

"Amen! Amen!" Hand clapping broke out over the church. In that day and time, applause in church was out of place, and considered as glorifying the flesh. One sour-faced deacon rose to his feet."Brethren, church ain't the place fer competition."

"Aw... brother, a little competition never hurt anybody, it makes everybody sing better," someone said.

That remark brought forth abundant applause. Then another voice called, "Le's heer that song agin!"

The deacon slumped down on the bench like a punctured balloon.

Little Avery knew he had the congregation in his pocket so he gave them all he had. He nailed that last low note to the floor of Noah's Ark then sprang to his feet and danced on it.

The congregation exploded with applause.

The deacon was fit to be tied.

Avery's bashful phase vanished that night. He became the speaker for the Happy Land Quartet on their radio program."God Put a Rainbow in the Cloud" was their most requested song for a long time.

It was almost midnight when the Happy Land Quartet got home. Big Avery thought that Andy and Mandy would be spending the night at his house so he and his wife bundled their smallest children off to bed and retired themselves.

Mandy paused with her hand on the doorknob."Andy, we better git home, Mama will be worried about us."

"I'm stayin all night with Little Avery, but we'll walk you home if yer skeerd."

"Oh, I ain't skeerd, but Mama might give you a whippin because you didn't git permission to stay."

"Aw, she won't keer," Little Avery said."You're just a big fraidy cat."

"I am not. I ain't skeerd a-nothin." Mandy walked out the door in a huff. For five minutes she felt brave enough to tackle anything. She looked up at the sky and saw a trillion stars. Then she thought of Star Springs Branch up the path ahead, and her courage fizzled.

Star Springs is a haunted place. It acquired its name from five springs that come together in one place to form a bold branch. The water goes underground and burbles up in a bog where it crosses the path. Legend has it that something dreadful happened there in yesteryear. Some say an early settler's wagon was ambushed by robbers.

Mandy's vision adjusted to starlight. She had no trouble following the path, but each footstep brought her nearer Star Springs. She paused where the path descended into the abyss. Looking up at the Big Dipper she prayed, "Dear Lord, please hep me git through this Hell hole." She stepped into the dark laurels and the lights of heaven went out.

Her heart raced, thump-ump thump-ump. Well, I ain't turnin back. I'm over halfway home now, she thought. She found her way by holding her arms out and letting her fingers brush against the laurels on each side of the path. Suddenly, straight ahead, she saw a light, but it winked out. She paused, held her breath and listened…The gurgle of Star Springs surrounded her. Maybe I imagined I saw a light, she thought. Cold water filled her shoes—she was sinking—stuck in mud up to her ankles. She struggled in black slimy ooze searching for a foothold. The mud sucked her shoes off and she mired deeper. Abruptly, the gurgling sound of Star Springs changed to a baby's heartrending cry. Three loud pops exploded in the laurels. The bloodcurdling scream of a woman in death-throes split the air and faded up the mountainside. Mandy froze and peed in her bloomers."Lord, hep me, hep me," she whimpered."Guurrhh-uuhh!" — The bushes shook.

She sprang from the mud like a Jack in the Box and took off as fast as feet can travel. She felt her dress rip on ivy stubs. Tree branches slapped her face as she emerged from the horrible place. It was uphill the rest of the way home, but that didn't slow her down. She knew a varmint was in hot pursuit because she heard it panting, "huff-uff huff-uff huff-uff," and its paws hitting the ground behind her, "whop-op whop-op whop-op." Any second a black hairy paw would rake between her shoulder blades and maul her to the ground! At last, the lamplight in the window of home sweet home came in view. She fell prostrate on the porch with not enough breath for a whisper.

Howard whooped and hollered.

Everyone sprang from bed to investigate the ruckus and found Mandy stretched out on the porch, sniveling. Howard thought it funny that he'd scared Mandy stiff. But Clarinda did not. She gave Howard a severe tongue lashing."Howard, you oughta be ashamed to treat yore sister that a-way. What a mean prank! March right back to that branch and git her shoes and clean every speck a-mud off 'em. Do you heer me?"

"Oh, all right, but why's she out so late? Why do I always havta go lookin for 'em, an' where's Andy?"

"That's fer me to find out. Go! Do as I told ye."

Howard obeyed. He knew he'd get a whipping if he refused.

Clarinda had become worried about Andy and Mandy. It wasn't like them to stay out so late. When Wadell's clock struck eleven, she sent fourteen-year-old Howard to bring them home. Howard heard Mandy coming up the path and thought Andy was with her. I'm gitten tard of bein sent out in the dark a-searchin fer 'em, he thought, I'll give 'em a skeer they'll remember fer many a year. He snuffed the lantern light and stepped in the bushes.

Howard had amazing talent. He carried himself with pride and confidence because he knew he had all the attributes a young fellow needed to succeed in life. He excelled in athletics, music, and had a superb singing voice. Further, he'd been blessed with good looks and a winsome personality. He could charm the wool off a sheep's back in the dead of winter. Oftentimes, though, he used his gift for mimicry in a mischievous manner. His ghost stories had the sounds of creaky doors, rickety rocking chairs, and spooky footsteps in woolen socks on a splintery floor. He'd cup his hand around his mouth and bats flapped in the stovepipe. His antics scared Andy and Mandy pop-eyed.

The next day, Mandy confronted Howard about the scare at Star Springs. He swore that he did not imitate the baby's cry. He claimed that it scared him so bad he could hardly keep from running too.

Mandy glared at him."What about them gunshots?"

Howard snickered."Heck, that 'as easy. I found two firecrackers and some matches in my old black coat pocket." He let out a big guffaw."You talk about runnin, a greyhound couldn't a-caught you."

Mandy pounced on him. Andy joined in to help her out.

Clarinda settled the fight with a switch.

Twenty-eight

1951

The days were getting longer and another cold winter was now a memory. Springtime blossomed-up the mountainside. The warm south wind and showers put the old Rebel apple tree into full bud. Clarinda still harvested the apples from her old home place where she and the boys had built their cabin. The children were all married except Mary Ann and Mandy, but their upcoming nuptials were close at hand.

This lovely spring day found Clarinda, Mary Ann, and Mandy digging a new cellar. The old one had collapsed. Mary Ann paused and sighed."This'll be the last hole I dig on Levi's Mountain."

Mandy pitched a shovel full of dirt on the pile."You ain't sorry of it, are ye?"

"Why, heck no. It'll just be different, livin in town an' all."

In a couple of weeks, Mary Ann would be married and living in Florida. Her fiancé was a military man stationed in West Palm Beach. She stepped on her shovel blade and sank it into the ground."Well, I might get homesick, but I'll git over it."

Mary Ann had met her future husband in the Five and Dime. She and Charlotty were gift shopping for their current boyfriends. Whilst browsing through the men's shaving colognes they met a friend. An Air Force Sergeant was with him. After introductions, the girls chatted with the fellows briefly then went their way.

Mary Ann kept her thoughts to herself because she was definitely attracted to the military man. Charlotty commented on the handsome fellow with their friend, but Mary Ann said nothing. Charlotty looked at her curiously."Didn't you think he was good-lookin?"

"Ay…he looked fairly common, I reckon."

Charlotty snorted."Mary Ann, you puzzle me."

The following week, Mary Ann received a letter from the handsome Air Force Sergeant. He wanted to take her to the movies before his furlough expired. She waited a couple of days then replied by mail, accepting his invitation to the movies. Within three months they were engaged.

Clarinda tried to keep her chin up, but she knew that her home would never be the same without Mary Ann. Clarinda felt guilty that Mary Ann had had such a hard life. But she'd had many wonderful times too. There was always frolic and games throughout the community and Mary Ann and Charlotty were involved in every merriment. She would be sorely missed.

Occasionally, even Mary Ann got the blues. Florida seemed like a world away. More than likely I'll git homesick, she thought.

Wadell seemed happy for Mary Ann. In fact, he seemed quite jolly. She'd quarreled and fussed at him for years. When she leaves, I ain't splittin no more wood, he thought. The only work I intend to do is feed the hogs. I like pork too good to let anybody else do that job. Wadell enjoyed scratching their backs with a stick."They ain't no vittles that smells as good as a big pot a-backbones n' ribs a-bilin on the stove," he'd often say.

Mary Ann purchased a cedar chest for storing her trousseau. While packing for her move to Florida, she noticed how pleased Wadell looked."What're you a-grinnin about? You needn't look so happy. I might just change my mind about leavin."

Wadell's smile faded. He cleared his throat and eased out the kitchen door.

Mary Ann's conscience smote her. Fer the love of Pete, you're gitten meaner'n Ol' Scratch. She resolved to bridle her tongue.

As the wedding day drew near, Mandy became all wrapped up in the event."Mary Ann, do you suppose you'll git a farewell serenade from the mountain boys? I heard a little rumor that a few sticks of dynamite would light up the mountainside on yore weddin night. Some girls are plannin to give you a ride in a wash tub, too."

Mary Ann laughed, "I'd like to see 'em try it."

Mandy smiled."I really cain't see it happenin either."

The day of the wedding arrived and Mandy went with Mary Ann and the handsome groom to the preacher's house. This preacher had performed the wedding ceremony for every one of Clarinda's children thus far.

The preacher shook the bride's hand."They's a bunch a-you younguns, ain't they?" Mary Ann nodded."Yeah, I'm number ten—the ol' maid of the family." The groom grinned and squeezed her hand.

The preacher laughed at her bluntness."You shore don't look old to me. By crackies, I mayn't be alive to marry all of you'uns, but I do enjoy hitchin up young folks. If you'll stand before me and jine right hands, we'll put a stop to this old maid stuff."

Mandy giggled. She knew that Mary Ann was very nervous because she had a big rosy spot on each cheek. The preacher performed the marriage ceremony from memory and just held the Bible in his hands. Within two minutes Mary Ann was Mrs. Boyd.

When they reached home, Clarinda gave Mary Ann an envelope. Enclosed was fifty dollars. Mary Ann didn't want to take it, but Clarinda insisted."If ye git dissatisfied that'll buy a bus ticket home."

Mary Ann laughed."Didn't you tell us younguns that if we got burnt in marriage we'd havta set on the blister?"

Clarinda smiled."I've changed my mind about that."

There was so much rushing around there was no time to sniffle until after they left. The empty house drove Clarinda outdoors. She noticed Wadell's joy at Mary Ann's departure and she resented it.

Six months later, Clarinda's children gave her money for Christmas. She used it to have the house wired for electricity. She'd saved every cent of her tobacco crop money for an electric washing machine and iron. She fairly sailed through her laundry chores.

She tried to get Wadell to help buy a refrigerator, but he was too stingy. He would squeeze a buffalo nickel till it bellowed. As Wadell grew older, he became even more tight-fisted. Clarinda wished a million times that she'd never married him. Mary Ann was right all along. Wadell cared for no one but himself. They could have had a good life on his farm, but from the very beginning of their marriage he resented her children and that turned her against him.

Clarinda observed a change in Wadell's behavior after Mary Ann left. She saw him spit on the floor, and she raked him over the coals."Wad, I have put up with yore messes about all I'm goin to. Either you straighten up or I'm sendin for yore folks to come and git you."

Wadell did better for awhile, but he was very old and couldn't hear a thing. Clarinda had always cooked and waited on him, but the burden of his care became too much. Arthritis had taken its toll on her health as well. She sent word to his family that she'd done all she could for him. They took him away and put him in a nursing home. She felt sorry for him, but knew she'd made the right decision.

Later, she heard that he was a patient in the hospital. Billy Dan's wife took her to visit him. Clarinda wept, and so did Wadell. She never saw him again. He lived to be over a hundred-years-old. Clarinda received nothing for the years she waited on Wadell. He'd deeded his big farm to his children and she assumed that his money went toward his care in the nursing home. She certainly had a clear conscience concerning his welfare. She'd repaid him the money, with interest, that he'd loaned her to buy the small farm on Levi's Mountain. She earned the money by growing tobacco crops."The Rock Pile", as Wadell called her farm, had paid for itself. Yes indeed, she didn't rest a peaceful night till she'd paid him every dime of that debt.

August brought hot weather. 'It was ninety in the shade,' as the old saying goes. Clarinda and Mandy rejoiced that the garden beans were canned and in the cellar. Several years had passed. Clarinda's children were all married and she lived alone, but Mandy lived nearby and Clarinda's older grandchildren took turns staying with her from time to time.

A big family reunion was planned for the upcoming weekend and Mary Ann and family were expected from Florida any day. Invitations went out near and far. Kindred from north and south would attend. The local high school lunch room and auditorium had been reserved for the event.

Clarinda's son, Henry, and her oldest grandson, Avery were bringing their bluegrass band down from Ohio. After the reunion dinner, they would perform in the school's auditorium at seven o'clock.

Mary Ann arrived on Wednesday. The next three day's Clarinda's cabin was filled with children's laughter and the aroma of good things a-cookin on the new electric range. Mary Ann did most of the cooking for the big get-together, because arthritis had taken its toll on her mother's health.

Finally, the great day arrived. By ten o'clock they had their dinner packed and Mary Ann's husband took them all to the school house in his car. The reunion was held at the same school Mary Ann and Mandy had attended.

Mandy counted forty-three cars already in the parking lot, and they weren't supposed to eat until one o'clock. By eleven-thirty, all Clarinda's children and their families were there. Her eleven sons took turns staying close to to their mama, attempting to take care of her for a change. Eva Jean, Mary Ann and Mandy served food and chased children, but kept Mama in their line of vision as they worked. The family wasn't complete however. Death had taken Rufus, Joey and Julie, and Olus. Sickness and war had demanded their toll.

Soon the cafeteria was filled with aunts, uncles and kindred from afar. They came mostly from Ohio, West Virginia, Tennessee and a sprinkling from Michigan and Florida.

What a grand spread they had! The tables groaned with food, but they kept piling it on. They all circled the room five rows deep and introduced themselves. Clarinda's children saw several aunts, uncles and cousins for the first time.

When everyone had eaten until they could hold no more, a question-naire was passed around so that each family member could record their name, age and address. Reunions in the future would be more complete with this record in hand.

Someone asked Clarinda how many grandchildren she had. She declared that she didn't know. Mandy stood up and said, "Mama has forty-four grandchildren, ninety-three great- grandchildren, and sixteen great-great-grandchildren. There are three sets of twins amongst the great-grandchildren and one set are identical boys. I have the names writ-ten down if you want to read them." The applause was deafening. Clar-inda's face lit up and the dark shadows around her eyes faded away.

Clarinda looked around the crowded dining room and silently gave thanks. God had truly blessed her beyond anything she had ever dreamed of. She couldn't wish for anything more. They had fellowship and told tales of bygone days till five o'clock. When Clarinda and family left the school house it was almost five-thirty. They would have to hurry home and be back at the school by seven o'clock for the bluegrass concert.

When they reached home, Clarinda settled down in her rocking chair and took Mary Ann's little boy on her lap. She began rocking and hum-ming a lullaby while Mary Ann put the leftover food away and washed up the dishes. When Mary Ann went to check on them she found both asleep. She didn't want to awake them, but her husband told her she had better not let Clarinda miss the concert.

Mary Ann shook Clarinda gently."Mama, it's time to git ready. We don't want to be late for the music makin."

Clarinda awoke with a start."Well, I'll swannie, I must a-drapped off to sleep."

The auditorium was filled to capacity when they arrived and some kind folk gave Clarinda and Mary Ann their seats. When the show be-gan, Henry scorched the fiddle strings with an old time hoedown tune. Then Little Avery sang a duet with Henry. Next, the band demonstrated their talent on several bluegrass instrumentals. The audience came to their feet during a rousing banjo tune. Clarinda had never heard such loud applause in all her life.

"Where's Howard? Why ain't he up there on that stage?" folk kept asking.

Howard, the most talented member of the clan, didn't participate in the concert. He refused to intrude on Henry and Little Avery's band, and no amount of persuasion could get him off his seat in the back row of the auditorium. Although Howard cut his teeth on folk and bluegrass music, he preferred a smooth ballad with his own style of guitar. Lately, he seemed to be leaning toward gospel music. He'd recently played rhythm guitar on a recording made by a professional group.

Little Avery made Clarinda proud, too. He moved around the stage, picking his rhythm guitar and poking fun at his band mates. Those in the audience who remembered his songs of younger days, called for, "God Put a Rainbow in the Cloud". Well, Little Avery showed them that he still had it. When the band reached the chorus, he went down on one knee, taking the microphone with him. He nailed that last low note to the floor and danced a jig too. The audience loved it.

It was midnight when Clarinda and family reached home. Mary Ann put her sleepy children to bed and they all retired for the night. Still hearing the evening's concert in her head, Clarinda stretched out on her fleecy cloud mattress. Within minutes, the boom of the bass and the loud applause faded. As she fell into peaceful sleep, she meandered into a dream. The twang of an old time banjo playing a cherished heartsong rang softly in her ear. Her right hand moved… reaching into the darkness. Rufus' spirit whispered…"*Meet me on the mountaintop.*"

Still dreaming, Clarinda took berry bucket in hand and with her little dog at her heels they headed up Levi's Mountain, both well along in years and their going slow. Trixie still barked at chipmunks and things, but being too feeble for chase, she stayed by Clarinda's side. They waded through lacy fern, picked wild orchids and paused to rest on a mossy log.

The mountain cast a long shadow across the valley when they reached the top. The aroma of fresh strawberries filled the air. Using her walking stick, Clarinda eased herself to her knees. Dipping her hands in the sweetness of nature's bounty she filled her vessel to the brim. Trixie sat on her haunches and watched. Sunset glow flooded the field. Clarinda's spectacles became bothersome. She removed them and saw a white church in a distant valley with perfect vision.

Suddenly, a familiar voice called her name from afar, "*Clarriinnda...*" In the farthest corner of the field a man appeared. He waved and ran toward her calling her name over and over. Youthful strength surged through her body as she rose to her feet. The berry bucket slipped from her fingers. Leaping for joy, she ran toward him calling, "*Ruufuus...Ruufuus...*" She felt buoyant. Her spirit left its house of clay and took wing. Her flowered house dress faded into a long flowing white gown and robe. Her braided hair, as black as a raven's wing, tumbled down over her shoulders. They met with a joyous whoop. Rufus, young and handsome as ever, swept her up in his strong arms. The past slipped away and the two stood together with no boundaries of time.

"*Are ye ready to dance?*" he asks with a fetching grin.

She nods that she is.

"*Are ye ready to go?*"

She nods again. With Trixie leaping at their heels, they go high-stepping along the last golden ray of sunset and disappear behind the mountain.

Twenty-nine

Levi's Mountain • 1985

Mandy clutched the dashboard of her brother's Ford Ranger as it lurched to a halt. Billy Dan reached for the ignition key, turned it off and looked at Mandy with a lop-sided grin."Well, Sis, I hope you're ready fer a hike. We'll havta hoof it the rest of the way. They ain't no use a-knockin the muffler off on a rock."

Mandy opened the truck door, pushing aside slender branches of birch."I hiked this ol' trail fer many a year. Surely I can make it one more time." She stepped out, broke off a twig and popped it into her mouth. She'd always liked the refreshing taste of a birch-twig toothbrush.

Billy Dan set the parking brake and joined her. With Billy Dan in the lead, they left the rough road, veered to the right and headed up the mountainside toward their old home place. The forest had reclaimed the well-worn path of half a century ago, but they could have found their way in pitch darkness. Mandy stopped and raised a staying hand."Lissen… ol' Levi's a-roarin. It'll weather tonight."

Billy Dan chuckled."You sound just like Mama. She'd say, 'Younguns, do ye heer that ol' mountain a-roarin? A storm's a-comin. Le's make shore the woodshed's full. The snow's apt to be knee deep by mornin.'"

Mandy laughed."Nine times outta ten she 'as right, too."

They resumed their climb, each step taking them farther into yester-year. Abruptly, Billy Dan paused and looked at his surroundings."We're standin in the crook of Levi's elbow."

"Yep, we're almost home." Mandy took the lead and moved ahead.

They huffed and puffed up Levi's steep rocky arm and sank down on his shoulder."Ye know, Sis, I didn't find the mountain this steep in my younger days."

She grinned, too breathless to speak. After resting a spell, they rose to their feet and strolled through rich autumn woods. The pleasant aroma of possum grapes, hickory nuts, chinquapins and wintergreen berries floated on every breeze. Billy Dan stopped and pointed toward the top of a sourwood tree. Mandy paused and looked up through the fluttering leaves. They noticed a hole where the tree had lost a limb. Honeybees flew in and out. Billy Dan sighed."If I 'as younger I'd rob them bees. Guess I'll leave it fer the bears an' coons, though."

"Yeah, a few quarts a-honey ain't worth riskin yer neck for."

A bit further on, the forest floor sloped downward. The sound of a gurgling stream grew louder as they approached it. Billy Dan stopped and pulled a faded deed from his hind pocket. Squinting at the faded typing he read, "Beginning on a rock in the branch and runs South 30 West 40 poles to a chestnut stump; thence South 75 East 28 poles to a sourwood tree." He folded the deed."It's little wonder the surveyor lost the damn property line. The chestnuts have been dead an' gone fer over fifty year."

Mandy's brow wrinkled with concern."What can ye do if the old landmarks are gone?"

"I'll search fer a steel stake by a black gum tree and see if it points me in this direction. You go ahead and look around the home place I'll be back in a bit."

"Okay."

Billy Dan headed off around the mountainside.

Mandy picked her way across the stream, stepping from rock to rock. She climbed the bank, grabbing at clumps of Lady Fern to keep her balance. Ten yards beyond, she emerged into a clearing. She was home. For a full minute she stood still and enjoyed the fragrance of spearmint. Could that be shouts of children from the mountainside or a noisy jay? She looked around. Their old cabin sat on its haunches, its glassless windows turned heavenward.

Lest she step on a copperhead, she picked up a stick and poked at the overgrown path before her. Her foot struck the stepping stone at the kitchen door. Her eyes widened in amazement as she shoved the long tangled grass off its smooth granite surface with her stick. How in the world had Mama moved such a stone from the mountain under her own power? Yet, she had. Mandy remembered watching her maneuver it in place with a stout pronged pole. After supper every evening her mother took broom in hand and swept it clean. Mandy shook her head and muttered, "Mama, you shore had determination."

The kitchen door stood ajar and wouldn't budge. Mandy ambled along the outside wall till she found the kitchen window. She leaned through it, observing the shattered glass and rotted frame. A decayed wooden bench stood against the inside wall. She reached down and touched it. How many meals had she enjoyed whilst sitting here as a child, laughing at her brothers' jokes and listening to the chatter of her large family around the table?

Suddenly, her face took on a pensive expression. She stood at the window, five-year-old with nose pressed against the pane as she watched her Mama circle the yard with her apron full of baby chicks. The rain fell in sheets. Mandy screamed, "Mama's gonna git drownded!"

Her older sister, Mary Ann, flung the door wide and yelled, "Mama!"

Mandy saw her sister's lips move, but the sound of her voice was lost in the deafening clap of a lightening strike. The old Rebel apple tree in the yard took a direct hit. The bolt wrenched a large limb from its socket and hurled it against the ground. Blue smoke drifted across the yard.

Leaning forward to shelter her precious cargo, her mother ran for the cabin door as another bolt forked down. Soaked to the skin, she lunged over the threshold and dropped to her knees. She emptied her dripping apron on the kitchen floor."I couldn't find the mother hen, a fox must a-nabbed 'er." With outstretched arms she encircled the bedraggled chicks and pulled them toward her like a mother hen gathering her brood."Mary Ann, hand me that basket a-hangin on the wall."

"It brings back memories, don't it, Sis?"

Mandy lifted her head and saw Billy Dan picking his way through the briars and thistles."Yeah...it sure does. Did ye find the stake?"

"Yep... but the black gum tree had knocked it down when it fell. I'll havta git the surveyor to come back and rerun part of the line."

Mandy broke off a piece of decayed window sill, crumbled it in her hand and let it fall through her fingers."You know...when we lived here as children, I never thought I'd be startin over at forty-seven. We never know how our lives will turn out, do we?"

"You got yer divorce?"

Mandy nodded."Last Thursday at three o'clock I walked out of that courthouse a free woman. I expected to be joyful, but I just felt sad—like a big chunk of my life had been wasted on a hopeless marriage. Thirty year of unhappiness took its toll on me."

"You should a-left him years ago."

"I know...but I stayed with him fer several reasons. Anyway, I had no vehicle and no babysitter."

"Mama would a-helped ye with the babysittin."

Mandy gave Billy Dan a long solemn look."You surely don't think I would ast Mama to baby sit after she'd cradle-rocked seventeen youn-guns. Do ye?"

Billy Dan shrugged.

"Besides, she warned me about marryin him. She saw somethin in his nature that I didn't. I regret that I didn't listen to her."

"Well, it's over an' yer better off without 'im. You can live in peace, now."

"Yeah, I know, but I don't know if I'm strong enough to forge ahead. I had no say-so about anything important. I don't have any experience makin decisions."

Billy Dan took Mandy by the shoulders and gave her a gentle shake."Lissen, Sis, you took him to court an' got a good settlement as far as I can see. You've got a good home an' enough land to grow anything ye want."

Mandy smiled."Yeah…I finely got some grit in my craw when he disappeared from the mountains with that…that strumpet he took up with."

Billy Dan looked at Mandy with concern. Her eyes had lost their sparkle. What had happened to his feisty little sister? He feared that her spirit was broken."Sis, have you talked to anybody about what you've been through?"

"Yeah…I talk to God every day. Mama taught me how to pray. Right here in this ol' cabin, I'd wake in the middle of the night and she'd be on her knees by the bedside prayin."

"Well, you can talk to me too, anytime, day or night."

Mandy plucked a sprig of burning bush and played with it absently."You know, Billy Dan, my marriage was doomed from the very beginnin."

"Really?"

"Yeah…on my weddin day the handsome groom's mother said, "You belong tuh my son now, and you'll do perzactly what he tells ye tuh do, little Missy!"

Billy Dan snorted."Did ye set her straight?"

"No. I was afraid of 'er. Everybody called her Granny an' laughed at her shenanigans. She'd explode in fits of temper for no reason that I could see." With hands on hips Mandy snapped her head imitating her mother-in-law."'I'm a-goin tuh visit my daughter fer a spell. You'uns can stay at my place. '"

"Granny pointed her finger toward the garden an' spoke her piece, 'Missy, do ye see that patch a-late beans out yander? I expect tuh see 'em in the can and in the cellar when I git back. '"

Billy Dan folded his arms and listened as Mandy poured out her pent-up resentment."I spent my honeymoon in the dern bean patch. I picked and canned twenty-eight quarts a-green beans."

Billy Dan's jaw dropped.

Mandy laughed with self-contempt."I cain't believe I 'as goofy enough to do that."

"Why did ye do it?"

"Romeo thought I should at least try to can 'em since his mother had been so obligin by leavin us alone."

"Did she thank ye for all yer hard work when she got back?"

"Heck, no. She pecked the jar lids with a fork and said, 'my son won't eat no sech vittles as this. They look sp'ilt tuh me. '"

"'I know how to can beans,'" says I, "'every can sealed—I heard 'em ping. '"

"Granny whirled around and glared at me with her birch-twig toothbrush a-wigglin. 'I'll feed some tuh the chickens. If they don't drap dead, I might try a bite er two. '"

Billy Dan shook his head, trying to keep a straight face."I don't mean to be heartless, Sis, but that's—"

"Ain't it though?" Mandy tilted her head back and laughed out loud."And do ye know where the groom spent most of his honeymoon?"

"In the woods squirrel huntin?"

"That's right. I had to make squirrel gravy and dumplins fer dinner ever day. Next, he walked through the door with a full-grown groundhog squatted on his shoulder. It turned out to be a family pet with full range of the house. That was the most wretched two weeks of my life."

Billy Dan didn't know whether to laugh, cry or spit so he poked the ground with his stick and muttered, "That shore wasn't no ordinary honeymoon."

"He wasn't no ordinary man, either. He worked from daylight till dark—thrifty as they come. We grew corn and tobacco—raised two big hogs every year. He shore knowed how to cure hams. I milked the cows and took care of the younguns and the house. It's a pity he inherited his mother's temper and cruel nature."

"Did he ever strike ye?"

Mandy turned her eyes toward the mountaintop."The sun's a-goin down. We'd better head home."

Billy Dan's face turned red with anger."I figured him fer that kind a-man. I don't keer how thrifty an' hard workin he was. It takes a mighty sorry man to strike a woman."

"Oh, well, better days are comin, Billy Dan."

"You're like Mama…you have her strength."

"No…I ain't never seen nobody with Mama's strength an' courage."

"Well...she had to be strong otherwise we might a-perished. After Papa died, us boys thought we'd run wild an' footloose. She knowed we'd git hungry an' come sneakin in at night. At the crack a-daylight she'd throw our kivers back an' lay on the lash." Billy Dan laughed."We'd roll off the straw tick an' stack up aginst the wall like cord wood. The one that couldn't git under the bed fast enough got the worst of it."

Mandy laughed."I got my share of switchin's too. She even made me go git the switch fer my own whippin. Of course, I always got the puniest thing a-growin."

"You 'as lucky."

"Maybe. But I learnt to bridle my tongue. Mama couldn't stand a sassy youngun."

Billy Dan pointed to the dilapidated building."Olus an' Tom an' Mama built that cabin. The boys was just teenagers. Their only experience with wood was sawin an' choppin it. Like most mountain boys, they 'as experts at makin whimmydiddles, sourwood whistles an' slingshots, but when Mama lit into 'em they learnt how to build a house, too."

Mandy laughed."Mama, put 'em to work—didn't she?"

"She did fer certain. They put a roof over our heads when we didn't have one. The cabin's down now, but it stood as long as we had need of it. Mama tackled any job that needed doin."

Billy Dan pointed his walking stick toward the cemetery located a mile away."Le's go to the cemetery next Tuesday and check on them tombstones she made fifty year ago."

"That we'll do, but I guarantee her tombstones are still standin tall a-facin the sunrise. Mandy's eyes misted up."You know… last Sunday after church, a deacon spoke of Mama to me. He said he hired her at harvest time an' had never had a better worker. He said she always ast for her wages in corn. She used that corn fer our bread. She sacrificed so much fer us, Billy Dan."

"Yeah… I know she did." Billy Dan pulled a handkerchief from his pocket and turned away.

Mandy pointed to an ancient gnarled apple tree in the yard."Look at that ol' Rebel apple tree. It's loaded with apples. Mama loved it. She said it was the best apple the sun ever shined on fer makin stack cakes an' apple butter. They're almost ready to pick. We'll havta come back in a couple a-weeks an' gather 'em."

Billy Dan ambled over and inspected a large scar running down its trunk."This tree an' Mama had a lot in common. Life dealt 'em many a blow but they kept standin. They 'as two of a kind. If I could write worth a dern I'd put it down on paper."

Mandy followed him. Reaching up, she picked a big red-striped apple and took a bite. Who knows...somebody will try it one a-these days, she thought. When somebody opens her heart an' soul and puts pen to paper.

FRANKLIN COUNTY LIBRARY
906 NORTH MAIN STREET
LOUISBURG, NC 27549
BRANCHES IN BUNN.
FRANKLINTON, & YOUNGSVILLE

Acknowledgements

I would like to thank all the people who encouraged me to write *Autumn Bends the Rebel Tree*. Louise Greene, a friend for many years; Sandy Horton and Chloe Coleman whose encouragement and suggestions kept me on the path to my goal. The Fellowship of the Rose, our small writing group whose contributions were invaluable in my journey back in time.

Permission granted from Duke University Press for one time use of the following described copyrighted material: Frank C. Brown, "Excerpted song lyrics from the song 'Sindy' (aka. Cindy)," in *The Frank C. Brown Collection of Folklore: Folk Songs*, pp. 482-483. Copyright, 1952, Duke University Press.

License granted by R. E. Winsett Music Company for one time use of "God Put a Rainbow in the Cloud."

Permission granted by LifeWay Worship for use of "Standing on the Promises."

Hymns: "Wayfaring Stranger — Rock of Ages — Leaning on the Everlasting Arms " are in the public domain.

Traditional folk songs: "Crawdad Song — Groundhog — Rabbit in a Log — Froggie Went a Courting" are traditional folk songs in the public domain.

About the Author

Carolyn Guy was born in the high country of western North Carolina. She was the 16th child, and her twin, the 17th in the family.

She wrote this book because the characters that inhabit its pages are an inspiration to her. Clarinda, the main character, fills the niche of the early Appalachian woman in dramatic fashion. Clarinda's sacrifices were praiseworthy and Guy felt her story must be told.

Carolyn Guy is a retired hospital Dietary Manager, the mother of two children, five grandchildren and four great grandchildren. She is a member of the High Country Writers in Boone, North Carolina, an active member of a small writing critique group, and a member of Appalachian Voices. Her poetry has been published in Ideal Magazines and Guidepost books. She resides in her beloved Western North Carolina Mountains where she maintains a large vegetable garden and a blueberry patch.